FROM THE FIERY CRUCIBLE OF THE HEART
CAME THEIR SWORD OF VENGEANCE . . .
AND OF LOVE.

NEKO—Proud and powerful, his true identity remained hidden until his daring return to Egypt . . . to slay his dreaded enemy, the childseller Hakoris, to find the woman he loved . . . and to kill the king.

TETI—Singularly beautiful, her place in destiny was assured by the birthmark she bore and the secret formula she found to make a special sword . . . and forge a new alliance of pride and passionate courage.

RIKI—Defiantly fierce, his valor in battle would win this former street-urchin the admiration of a pharoah and carry him closer to solving the stunning mystery of his birth.

ASET—Innocent and brave, her selfless love for a hero would show her mettle as a woman even as it broke her heart, but her strange fate lay with a man who bore the mark of the Lion.

JOSEPH—Vizier to the cruel tyrant Apophis, his fortunes and that of the brothers who sold him into bondage depended on a ruler he despised . . . and his troubled dreams foretold of a revolt he both longed for and feared.

Volume VII

THE PROPHECY

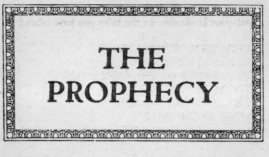

PETER DANIELSON

Created by the producers of
Wagons West, White Indian,
America 2040, and The Kent
Family Chronicles.

Chairman of the Board: Lyle Kenyon Engel

BANTAM BOOKS
TORONTO · NEW YORK · LONDON · SYDNEY · AUCKLAND

THE PROPHECY

*A Bantam Book / published by arrangement with
Book Creations, Inc.*

Bantam edition / February 1987

*Produced by Book Creations, Inc.
Chairman of the Board: Lyle Kenyon Engel*

ISBN 0-553-26325-0

Published simultaneously in the United States and Canada

*Bantam Books are published by Bantam Books, Inc. Its trade-
mark, consisting of the words "Bantam Books" and the portrayal
of a rooster, is Registered in U.S. Patent and Trademark Office
and in other countries. Marca Registrada. Bantam Books, Inc.,
666 Fifth Avenue, New York, New York 10103.*

PRINTED IN THE UNITED STATES OF AMERICA

KR   0 9 8 7 6 5 4 3 2 1

Cast of Characters
CHILDREN OF THE LION, Volume Seven
THE PROPHECY

Lower Egypt, the Black Lands

Avaris—Capital city

Apophis—Hai ruler, once known as Aram

Joseph—Canaanite vizier and seer for King Apophis

Neferhotep—Power-hungry magus, adviser to the king

Hakoris—Evil supervisor of the Children's Refuge, adviser to the king

Kamose—Apophis's natural son, the Prophecy's deliverer of the oppressed Egyptians, who is expected to murder his father and drive the Hai from Egypt forever

Mara—Once Hakoris's slave, now an important member of a conspiracy to overthrow Apophis

Upper Egypt, the Red Lands

Thebes—The last stronghold of the native Egyptians against the Hai oppressors

Sekenenre—Egypt's pharaoh

Baliniri—The commander of the Upper Egyptian army, then vizier to Sekenenre

Baba of El-Kab—Military commander of Lisht

Riki—Brilliant young military officer; Baliniri's protégé

Children of the Lion—Descendents of Cain, this family's destiny is to be armorers to the world; their birthmark, a wine-colored lion's paw print, identifies them

Teti—Woman armorer, Child of the Lion, her skills are Baliniri's secret weapon

Ketan—Teti's fraternal twin brother

Seth—Cousin to Teti and Ketan, his brilliant mind can shed light on any problem

Tuya—Seth's mother

CANAAN

DAMIETTA

SAÏS AVARIS

BUBASTIS

LOWER
EGYPT
(THE BLACK   LANDS)

THE
FAYUM

MEMPHIS

LISHT

THE
GREAT
DESERT

0   75   150
MILES

N

NILE

UPPER   EGYPT

(THE RED   LANDS)

THEBES
DEIR EL-BAHARI

EL-KAB

EDFU

FIRST CATARACT
ELEPHANTINE

NUBIA

EGYPT IS A DIVIDED LAND.
THE HAI CONQUERORS
CONTROL LOWER EGYPT,
WITH THE CAPITAL AT
AVARIS. THEIR KING IS
APOPHIS; THEIR VIZIER
THE SEER JOSEPH. UPPER
EGYPT, WITH ITS PEOPLE
UNDER THE PROTECTION OF
THE GARRISON AT THEBES,
IS RULED BY THE YOUNG
PHARAOH SEKENENRE.
HIS VIZIER IS BAKA,
THEN BALINIRI.

© BOOK CREATIONS 1986 · R. TOELKE '86

A LETTER TO THE READER:

The final pages of *Vengeance of the Lion*, Volume III of the Children of the Lion Series, carried a letter to you from me. In the years since then, your response has been truly amazing, your comments warm, gratifying, and informative.

Even more astonishing than the volume of mail has been the diversity of the correspondents: lay people and ordained ministers, many of whom are using the series in study groups; college professors, fellow writers, scholars in ancient history, even a Metropolitan Opera singer.

I've carefully read all your letters and given you a hand in the assembling of this enormous mosaic—along with myself, book producer Lyle Engel, and Lyle's fine staff of ace editors and researchers. But what is it that we've been creating? On the surface it appears to be a vast continuous novel, well over a million words already. At a deeper level, we are building a legend of ancient times that has great bearing on our own time.

The Children of the Lion Series concerns itself with human nature and the desperate and lonely journey each person makes through life. It deals with people who think they're small and insignificant, but discover they're large and important; with people who think they're abandoned and alone, only to learn there's enough love in the world to embrace them as well. Together we have learned that there are no ordinary, common people, for each life touches so many others. Your letters have proved that.

The more letters I receive from you, the better I like it. Please continue to write to me in care of Bantam Books, 666 Fifth Avenue, New York, New York 10103. I will continue to listen closely to what you have to say. And ask your bookseller to stock the entire Children of the Lion Series.

Thank you!

With warmest good wishes,
PETER DANIELSON

Prologue

The sun had only moments before fallen below the western horizon, and its fleeting afterglow hung briefly over the little gathering around the campfire beside the oasis. Still visible in the half light were gigantic clouds, which had blown down from the north only an hour before: towering rain clouds, dark and brooding, which spoke of a coming storm.

The air, usually dry and clear, had about it an uncharacteristically moist quality, a freshness, which none of the gathering could mistake. Rain was coming at last to the parched lands, perhaps before morning. A dank and chill wind stirred the flames, then suddenly was gone. There was a great silence on its passing, until the sigh of the dying zephyr gave way to the sigh of human throats. For now, from behind the screen of towering palms, a tall and spare figure in tattered robes stepped into view, his gaunt face immobile at first. Then his burning, hypnotic eyes moved from face to *face as his measured steps—those of an old man—brought him to within a body's length of the dancing flames.*

The Teller of Tales!

He looked up at the far-off thunderhead just once, when the last sunlight faded, and his lean old face, white-bearded, became visible for the first time by the light of the fire, whose leaping flames gleamed in his dark eyes. He spoke, and in the expectant hush that hung over them all, his words carried easily to the family on the outermost fringes of the half-circle of faces.

"In the name of God, the merciful, the compassionate . . ."

As always, his first words were uttered in a ringing, incantatory singsong, and his spare old body seemed to sway gently to their rhythm.

"Hear now," he said, "the tales of the Children of the Lion, the men and women of no people, and of their eternal wanderings among the nations of the world. . . ."

The grizzled old head went back, and he stood, seeming to challenge the oncoming cloudburst.

"You have heard," he continued, "how drought beggared all the lands beside the Great Sea except those straddling the Nile, so all peoples were forced to pay costly tribute to Egypt for food, and many, because of this, became slaves of the ruling Hai. Of all those who migrated to Egypt, only the family of Jacob, father of Egypt's vizier, prospered.

"You have heard how Aram, son of a Hai warlord, rose against the mad king Salitis and took his throne, defying The Prophecy that someday his own son would kill him and drive the Hai from the Egyptian lands they had stolen. Aram could not know that the child of The Prophecy—his own natural son—was a nameless slave, held captive in the worst prison in the Nile delta.

"You have also heard how the armies of the exiled Egyptian pharaoh Dedmose turned back hordes of Nubian invaders, then with growing apprehension were made to face the hostile Hai borders as Aram, who now called himself Apophis, armed for the final onslaught against the remnants of the once-mighty native Egyptian resistance.

"You have heard, in all this, of the lonely death of Ben-Hadad, Child of the Lion, at the hands of the renegade

Hakoris; of the maturing of Shobai's twin children, Kotan and Teti; and of the strange fate that led Teti, the first female to bear the mark of the Lion, to take up the armsman's profession and, in self-imposed exile, learn the secret of the smelting of iron, the black metal before which no bronze weapon could stand.

"Now," he said, his words punctuated by a distant rumble of thunder, "hear of how drought was replaced by storm. Hear of how revolt grew in the heart of the land, and of how a new king came to Egypt in secret and in silence, bringing new spirit to the struggle against the Hai. Hear of how darkness came to the lands of Egypt, just before the first healing rays of dawn.

"Hear," he said in a voice that was hardly more than a hoarse whisper, hardly audible above the far-off thunder, "hear of the final conflict between Egypt and the Hai, of the search for the fateful sword that would win it in the end, and the ultimate fulfillment of The Prophecy. . . ."

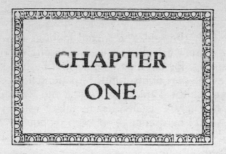

CHAPTER ONE

Along the North Coast of Egypt

I

The Thracian died sometime after noon. He had never regained consciousness after falling from atop the yard while trying to help shorten sail during the gray hour before dawn. The other man, now the lone survivor, shipped the steering oar for a moment and checked his comrade's condition. He had found the brown eyes open and staring, the tanned face rigid, the lean body already starting to turn cold.

With hardly a second thought, he stooped, got both hands under the man's inert body, and hefted it with a sudden, powerful jerk, the big muscles of his upper arms bulging with the strain. He wondered for a moment, standing there with the body in his arms, whether Thracians had any death rituals; but he knew of none, and there was no time for improvising one for sentimentality's sake—the wind was starting up again, and the clouds to the west were black and menacing. He heaved mightily, and the body fell into the Great Sea with a dull splash.

"Farewell," he said, the mixed feelings churning in his heart. The Thracian had been a good enough comrade, reliable and strong, for the month or so that he had known him. But there was a part of his mind, impatient, high-strung, that wanted to curse the Thracian for dying and leaving him alone to manage this ugly, ungainly, beamy tub of a stolen Phoenician trader—a vessel hard enough to keep on course with a crew of six, and a treacherous, hateful man-killer of a boat for a single person.

Particularly in a squall. And here was another one coming up, and him without a second pair of strong hands to help keep the unwieldy, top-heavy boat on some kind of course. He gave her a trifling bit of sail just to keep her from floundering outright, then tried to steer with a single oar on one side, but the boat, with twin steering oars, was meant to be manned by two, one man on the port side, one on the starboard. Oar and sail fought him like caged animals, and he cursed the dead Thracian and the three men who had died before him, then spat into the sea about him.

As he stood thinking about it, wild-haired, sunburnt, mother-naked—the wind had torn the last of his clothing from him in the last blow—the gusts began once more, caught the shortened sail, and tugged hard at the yard. Rudderless, the boat spun and almost knocked him off his feet. And now the rain began: cold, stinging drops that chilled him to the bone, that washed the dried salt water out of his hair and into his smarting eyes. He cursed the rain, and the wind, and the sea, and leaped for the steering oar, hoping against hope to be able to control things this time.

But the wind roared down upon him, billowing out the long sail and pulling the twin braces taut. The boat pulled hard against the oar and nearly tore it from his hands. He let out a string of curses in four languages, the vilest imprecations that came to mind.

He would have to shorten sail further, whether he liked it or not. There was too much wind even for the sliver of sail that showed below the high yard. At this rate he would capsize the moment the main thrust of the squall hit. No doubt more, and worse, was to come. Visibility was virtually nil to the west, and the waves were getting higher every moment.

He shipped the oar again, not without difficulty, and worked his way on feet grown unsteady on the shifting deck to the seven brails that controlled the yard. He freed one rope and yanked hard. The wind fought him, but he managed to pull the heavy sail up nine inches or more. Then he did the same with the next brail, and the next.

But before the operation was complete, the wind suddenly was upon him, shrieking with insane fury. The still-unshortened sail billowed; his loose knots, the work of hands numbed by the cold, gave in, the sail came loose, full of a wind it was never constructed to hold. With a deafening crack the mast snapped, broken through by the wind. The vessel heeled over hard, and he was thrown violently to the deck.

The lines above his head whipped wildly in the wind. The wind howled, and the rain pummeled his face. He could hardly catch his breath now; with every gulp of air came a mouthful, a noseful, of stinging salt water. He tried to get to his feet, but the boat, totally out of control, was lurching back and forth. He fell to his knees, the freed lines lashing him like whips manned by a crazed slavemaster.

A towering wave crashed over the bow and filled the starboard deck with freezing water up to his thighs. He got both hands on the rail and staggered to his feet, just in time to take another great wave in the face. The boat was spinning, spinning. He tried to fight his way to his old post midway between the two steering oars, hoping to be able to bring the boat once more under some control, but he knew it was no use.

Not even a seasoned sailor could save this thing, he thought. And he? He was no sailor. He had been a galley slave, yanking dumbly on an oar to the beat of a drum, and he had been a mercenary, a seaborne fighter, and a pirate. For him, his years at sea had had only one purpose: to bring him back to Egypt, and . . .

He gulped, steadied himself against another great lurch of the fat-bellied, ungainly vessel, and cast a single desperate glance at the wavering horizon off the starboard rail. Where was he? He had not the faintest idea, except that six days ago the land off that lee rail had been Libya. Then he had passed the Rosetta mouth of the Nile, he knew; but since then everything had become unclear. They had all caught the fever, and three men had died of it, puking their guts out on the pitch-smeared boards of the black deck. He and the Thracian had barely recovered when the wind, which had been in their teeth for the whole bitter, stomach-turning siege, had changed, and the squall had struck up.

That was the sea for you—a thing over which no man had any control. The Phoenician ships were among the most efficient, if least lovable, vessels in the world, but no Phoenician tub could sail to windward, and when the wind was in your teeth, only the most complex tacking that a full crew could manage could move the boat forward. And when you were not becalmed and forced to row the too-large boat, you were fighting a damned gale like the present one, with a vicious sea that would not let you stand erect, much less get your bearings.

The thought had hardly formed in his mind when a combination of wind and wave caught the ship broadside and heaved her on her side, hurling him into the water. After the first shock of the icy water he struggled to the surface, gasping for air, only to see the great bulk of the foundering vessel come thundering down toward him. In a panic he dived, not a moment too soon. The rail cleaved the water, catching him across one leg with a numbing blow. He swam furiously, blindly; when he came to the surface he was being carried up the side of a tall wave beyond the slowly sinking boat. As he reached the crest, the splintered end of the broken spar came into view; he struggled to get one arm over its top before being plunged once again into the trench. Here the yard was torn from his grasp, but he managed to get hold of it once more, this time hanging on for dear life as the rain battered down on him and the maddened seas tossed him wildly about.

Overhead there was a horrid flash, and a moment later the deafening crash of thunder. Above the roiling sea, fool's fire flickered and died. He rose to the top of the waves again and again, always hanging onto the spar like a barnacle. By

now the iron grip he had on the broken yard was a thing that
functioned of itself, independently of any thought he might
give the matter, if indeed his mind had been capable by now
of anything resembling thought.

Again the flash of light, closer this time; again the thunder, sounding as if it were right on top of him. His legs were
numb beneath him, but the rigid arms held onto the splintered yard. His glassy eyes stared half-blinded into the storm,
into the driving, pounding rain, into the gray nothingness
that the world had become, broken only by the fierce and
frightening flashes of lightning and the vague, threatening
outlines of the towering waves dozens of feet above his
head. . . .

The storm had been the worst one Aset had ever seen in
all the years she and her brother, Isesi, had come here to
spend their holidays beside the sea. All day it had pounded
away at the packed-earth walls of their little house, the winds
above ripping the palm fronds from the trees and sending
them crashing down on the rooftop, the rain roaring down.
After supper she had sat by the fire, mending old clothing,
shuddering every time the roar of thunder, far out to sea,
broke into her haunted reveries. From time to time Isesi,
knowing her long-standing fears, would look up and attempt
to reassure her; but then he would go back to his writing and
leave her to her growing terror.

Only in the small hours of the night did the storm at last
abate. Then, to her delighted surprise, the morning broke
clear and pink and fresh all over again, and as she stood by
the window in her shift looking out, a great feeling of relief
came over her. "Oh, look, Isesi," she said as her brother
struggled to his feet, blinking. "It's clear. It's going to be a
beautiful day."

"That's nice," Isesi responded, yawning.

"It's going to be wonderful," she said fervently. "And
you know what? I think we're going to have nice weather for
the rest of our holiday."

"That's good," he said. He scratched his head and peered
down at the papyrus he had labored over the previous night.

"Where did I put my brush? There's a mistake. You'd think I'd have caught it last night, as many times as I read and reread that. I feel like an idiot."

"Spoken like a true scribe," she said in exasperated affection. "Look, it's going to be a beautiful day, Isesi. Can't you forget about your papyrus just once and take advantage of a beautiful morning?"

"Now, Aset," her brother said, "this is an important proclamation. It has to be done just right. And I have to make sure no one can recognize my handwriting or connect this thing with me. That's why we came this far from Avaris, so that I could work on it in secret."

She smiled at him, shaking her head slowly. "That may have been why *you* came to the seashore, dear brother," she said. "But it's not why *I* came here. I came to get away from the city noise and congestion and the bad-tempered people yelling at each other. I'm going to go have myself a nice swim while there's still a pretty pink glow on the water. You can join me if you like." She paused to look at him, but it was obvious that his mind was on the scroll spread across the tabletop before him.

"All right," she said. "Be that way. I'll see you in an hour or so." Passing him on the way to the door, she gave him an affectionate pat on the back. He grunted unintelligibly, not looking up.

Outside, the morning air was fresh and clean. She deeply inhaled the tangy salt fragrance and listened to the sharp cries of seabirds down by the shore. She climbed the tall dune, her bare toes digging into the sand, and looked down.

The storm had left behind the usual flotsam on the beach. Perhaps a ship had gone down somewhere far out to sea; she could see broken planks and a splintered spar far up on the beach, left there when the tide had gone out. Kelp dotted the shore, and there was other debris in the shallows, far down the beach, that she could not identify.

The water looked simply beautiful! She glanced this way and that and impulsively threw aside her shift and ran lightly down the dune. The air felt splendid on her suddenly naked body, and there was in her impulsiveness the added fillip of adventure: She had left her shift far behind her, where she could not get to it if she were to meet a stranger on the beach. . . .

But of course there would be nobody there. That was the wonder of this little house their parents had left them: It had been the last relic of a town that had once flourished but then died and had been looted during the great famine. That all had occurred before she was born, and one never saw a soul near here now, so there was really no risk in her going naked, even if she were to leave her clothes back at the cabin. But for the touch of adventure she could always pretend. . . .

The pretense gave her little dash along the beach a special flavor and made her skin tingle all the more in the cool morning air. She shivered with delight and forced herself to run down to the water and dive in and, once chilled by the water, to swim far out into the surf before turning around to look back at the shore.

Where was her shift, now? Good heavens, she could not have come that far, could she? What if somebody did come? She gave herself over gleefully to the let's-pretend game and swam hurriedly back to shore, where she stood shivering in the cool of morning, her skin gooseflesh all over, peering up and down the beach for signs of life.

But there were none. The beach was long and deserted, and since she needed the thin rays of the morning sun to dry her off before dressing once again, she meandered slowly, thoughtfully, down the long white strand, ankle-deep in the low-tide surf, pausing here and there to pick up a seashell or a rock.

She stopped.

What was that up ahead?

Timidly she edged forward, one cautious step at a time, ready to bolt and run if it moved.

For a moment the young man's naked body looked as though it were partly clothed in tatters of dark green. Now she saw it was kelp, thrown by the storm that had beached him the night before. Other than this the body —thickly muscled, broad-chested, burned dark by the sun—was as naked as her own. He lay in the shallows, the gentle waters lapping at his ankles. *Oh, the poor man*, she thought. *Drowned in the—*

She froze again, this time in terror, as one of the brown hands moved, flexed, and clawed convulsively at the sand.

Alive! He was alive!

II

For a moment she thought he might awaken. But the hand stopped moving, and the head did not rise. Timidly she approached, and only by bending low over the body could she detect the slow up-and-down movement of the broad chest. She stood, looked down, and tried to decide what to do.

Then, once more, reflex action in the man's hands made up her mind for her. The fingers cupped and clawed. She gave a little yip of fear and danced back out of the shallows, protective hands masking breasts and crotch.

This was something for which she had better get help. Isesi would know what to do. He was grown; he had been out in the world. Even his scribe's life had been more adventurous than her own: She had stayed home and looked after their mother until her death. Aset gave the body a last glance—did the eyes blink once, or was it her imagination? —and turned tail to run back up the beach like a frightened deer to where she had left her shift.

Dressed again, she ran through the open door of the little house. "Isesi!" she gasped, breathless. "There's a man and he's washed up on the beach, and . . . and he's alive, I think. Come quickly! Come now, Isesi!"

Isesi looked up from his scroll. "A man? Here? What did you say?"

She told him, this time a bit more coherently. "We've got to go help. I think there was a shipwreck. He must have swum to shore and passed out."

He heard her out, frowning. Then he carefully put the scroll away and reached up to the place on the wall where he had hung their father's old short sword. "Bring your bow and the quiver," he said. "No use taking any chances. We're out here by ourselves. If he's a friend, we help him. If he's foe—"

"Oh, Isesi! Come on, now! He's hurt! He may be dying!" But when the two of them hurried out the door, she had bow and arrows close by her side, as he had suggested. He was right. There was no sense in taking chances.

When they approached the man, they saw that the kelp still clung to his body, giving him a curious piebald look.

"Are you awake?" Isesi asked, looking into the bleary, open eyes that regarded him. "Do you speak our language? Who are you?"

The man, with a supreme effort, managed to rise to one elbow. He blinked at the two of them and rasped in a barely audible voice, "This is Egypt, then. I'm home." He got the words out, intelligibly, unaccented; then, exhausted, he sank back to the sand and lay like a dead man, his eyes staring up into the gentle blue of the morning sky.

He was heavier than he looked, and the muscled body under the chilled skin was hard and compact. It was all they could do to get him back to the cabin. His legs could hardly bear his weight, and only by leaning on both of them at the same time could he make it. As it was, they virtually had to carry him across the dune. And when they managed to get him into the spare bed, he immediately fell into a deep sleep and did not awaken for a day.

From time to time Aset would look in on him. He was bearded after the foreign fashion, but the face under all the whiskers was a young one—not much more than twenty, she was sure.

And it was a good face. A strong face, with strong features that seemed gentle in the repose of deep sleep. One of the broad, capable-looking hands hung off the bed. Aset took note of the simultaneous impression of power and gracefulness that it gave. She knew from the hard calluses on the palm that these were the hands of a man who had had to work hard all his life. There was a certain rough beauty in the hand, and it was all she could do not to reach out and touch it.

She came back from the little room into the outer one. "Isesi," she said, "who do you suppose he is?"

"I have no idea," her brother answered. "We'll know soon enough. I still think it's a good idea to keep the weapons handy to our reach and not to his. Here, stick this knife in your belt, will you? I'll feel better for it."

She sat down across the table from him and regarded him with large, serious eyes. "Oh, Isesi. You're always so fearful and cautious."

Now it was his turn to look at her. "Well, what do you expect?" he asked with astonishment and something rather like anger. "We're up to something very, very dangerous. If we fail—if we're caught—you have no idea how bad things can get for us."

"Well, it isn't too late to change your mind," she reminded him. "I never wanted you to get involved in the first place. You've been a different person ever since you first got the idea. This isn't only dangerous in terms of things like getting caught; it's dangerous for your state of mind. You've always been such a—" She paused. How could she say he had always been a goody-goody without hurting his feelings? And here he was, plotting with a bunch of young conspirators to create a diversion in the street so some of them could sneak in and . . .

"I've been a coward," he finished for her. "I don't much like saying it, Aset, but it's the truth and must be faced. I've always sat back and taken the safe way out, ignoring injustice and telling myself it was none of my business. But Aset, injustice *is* my business, as it's yours. It's the proper business of everybody in the world who has a conscience. And to see that . . . that swine getting away with—"

"I know!" she said. "I know. It horrifies me even to think of it. Don't forget, I went to the same meeting. I heard the children tell of their experiences. I still have bad dreams about what they told us. To think that people could be so brutal, so evil! But—"

"But nothing," Isesi interrupted, standing and pounding his skinny fist onto the tabletop for emphasis. "It's time to act, Asct. It's the first time in the past year when we could even *consider* acting. The army is mustering up near the border, the local constabulary is understaffed, and there's nowhere near enough guards in Avaris just now to handle even the normal number of disturbances, let alone the new ones we'll create to distract from our affairs. And once they're all tied up answering alarms here and there, we can hit the place in force and break it wide open. With any luck at all we'll get all the children out of that terrible prison."

She sat staring numbly at him. She always hated it when he got upset like this, raising his voice, getting angry— especially since he was usually a quiet, scholarly little man who had never struck a violent blow in his whole life.

But these were violent times, and everybody talked like that now. Perhaps it was the alignment of stars, or something in the air. The very reason Isesi and his friends were able to contemplate such a move—a lightning raid on the horrible Children's Refuge, under cover of a riot staged to draw the guardsmen away from the quarter—was one connected with violence. It was no secret, even in the shabbier neighbor- hoods where they lived, that Apophis, the king of Lower Egypt, was planning a great military offensive against Upper Egypt, one aimed at crushing the last resistance to the rule of the foreign Hai kings in Egypt and consolidating all of the great land of Egypt north of the Nubian border under one rule once and for all.

To this end Apophis's brutal crimps had been combing the streets of the Lower Egyptian cities, looking for young men and immediately impressing them into the army if they could not prove they were employed in work necessary to the orderly running of things. Even Isesi—gentle, weak-armed little Isesi—had been approached by them, and if he had not been a member of the caste of scribes, with a minor but important job of keeping records on the king's livestock, he would have been taken away with no more fuss than that.

All the more reason for him to keep as quiet as a mouse now and not get involved in desperate attempts to right civic wrongs—attempts that could end in disaster for all of them if only the smallest thing were to go wrong.

Isesi . . . he had always been such a *good* boy. And now

that he was a young man, he had not changed a whit. He had the same overdeveloped conscience that had led him to protest injustice all through his childhood, even when it had almost got him thrown out of the school for scribes.

No doubt about it, the thing they proposed to strike out against was horrible. The Children's Refuge had been started years ago by a rich freedwoman who had been left a fortune by her former master, a retired general of the Hai army. She had intended for it to become a place for the children of the poor, where they could find free shelter and food and be given a chance to earn money of their own at simple tasks while learning adult trades. It had been a wonderful idea.

But the rich benefactress had left Lower Egypt after setting up a trust, and unscrupulous men had taken control of the money and diverted it to other ends. And after a time the power that had been shared by several irresponsible men became concentrated in the hands of one man who was worse, harder, crueler than any of the others. His name was Hakoris.

In the years since then, Hakoris—a hard-eyed, cold-hearted foreigner, whose accent and desert headdress stamped him as a man from one of the northern countries but whose true background no man knew—had made the Children's Refuge into a nightmare. Hakoris had made the gentle refuge an instrument of oppression. The children entered the place free, only to become slaves. They were overworked, beaten, starved, rented out as prostitutes, catamites, and sexual slaves to wealthy perverts. Avaris, the capital of the Hai empire, was riddled with vice, and there was ample custom for Hakoris's pandering. If a child thus abused happened to disappear now and then—and if Hakoris's coffers were simultaneously enriched by a generous gift of money or influence—who was to be the wiser?

Worse, the number of children in the refuge was constantly being increased by outright kidnapping, and Hakoris's brutal minions roamed the streets of Avaris looking for unattached children who, once spotted, never were heard from again, having disappeared forever into the dark walls of the refuge.

The total disregard for the welfare of Lower Egypt's

children had begun with King Apophis's predecessor, Salitis, whose brilliant vizier, Joseph, had prophesied that somewhere in Egypt was the child who, when he grew up, would become the promised deliverer of the Egyptian people and would drive the Hai invaders out of the country forever and permanently reestablish Egyptian rule. To guard against such an occurrence, Salitis had authorized his soldiers to kidnap and kill every male child ten years of age in the whole Egyptian delta.

Now Apophis, Salitis's replacement, was himself growing impatient, and even a little desperate. There had, after all, been a second prophecy made, which spoke of a son of Apophis's own blood arising to overthrow him and his throne. It was common knowledge that the king regarded this as an extension of the first prophecy. It was clear Apophis believed in this phantom deliverer and feared him. Who he could be, none could say. Apophis was said to have a natural son by a woman long dead, but whether this was fact or wishful thinking, no one could say. But in the fearful climate surrounding the palace now, it was easy for Hakoris's kidnappers to continue their deadly work with impunity and with the usual sordid and brutal results.

And now a little band of citizens—most young, none affluent or powerful—planned to stage a raid on the refuge and free the seventy or so miserable, abused children there and channel them along a prearranged network of households whose heads had agreed secretly to provide shelter for them. Heaven knew it was a worthy cause. But so dangerous!

She must have spoken these last words aloud. "Dangerous?" Isesi said angrily, looking at her hot-eyed. "Of course it's dangerous. But it's a thing long overdue. And the longer we allow this to go on, the less claim we have to call ourselves better than the Hai."

"But what if Hakoris catches you? And you have to fight? Could you . . . could you kill him? With your own hands? You, Isesi?"

The question caught him off balance. He stood looking at her openmouthed, poised between the two poles of self-defense and his own nonviolent nature.

He was still standing there when the stranger suddenly

appeared in the open doorway and stood swaying, weak and haggard looking, his dark eyes going from Aset to Isesi. His voice was still hoarse when he spoke, but there was a bite to it.

"Hakoris?" he echoed, almost spitting the hateful word out. "Did I hear someone speak of Hakoris?"

III

Aset and Isesi exchanged a sudden fearful glance. How much had the stranger heard? If he were a spy for the government—

Both looked at the figure in the doorway. His knees were buckling, and he was on the verge of fainting dead away. Aset rushed to his side and managed to support his weight long enough for Isesi to come and help him move back to the bed.

When they had him laid out once more, Isesi spoke, false heartiness in his voice. "Here, now, my friend. You don't want to be getting up quite yet. You're still pretty weak."

The stranger sank back on the pillow, looking up with tired eyes at the two of them. "You're right," he admitted in a dull voice, barely audible. "I overestimated my strength. But when I heard you say—"

"You must be hungry," Aset broke in, suddenly changing the subject. "I'll heat some broth. You won't be able to hold anything more than that in your stomach."

The stranger would perhaps have continued in the same vein, but Isesi, watching Aset's retreat into the other room, quickly steered the conversation into safer waters. "I take it your boat went down?"

The stranger's eyes went out of focus and stared at the ceiling. "Yes. There was a fever on the ship. We were all ill. I thought the Thracian was going to survive, but he died on

me, just like all the rest. I was the only one who lived
through the fever, and I couldn't manage the boat alone."

Isesi sat beside his bed. "You were a sailor?"

"No, no," the man responded a little impatiently. "We
were impressed into service, back in Crete. We mutinied—
took the ship over ourselves. But we couldn't run it. There
was a spell on it, the Thracian said. I didn't care. All I wanted
to do was get back to Egypt." There was a sudden new edge
on his voice now as he added, "I have *business* here." The
word came out acid and angry.

"There, there," Isesi said soothingly. "Take it easy, now.
My sister is making some broth. If you had the fever, you
won't have eaten much in some time, I suspect."

"Days. Days and days. It doesn't matter." One of the
large, competent-looking hands came up before his face, as if
wiping the idea away. "Where am I, exactly?"

"You're on the outer banks, past Lake Manzala, about
fifteen leagues east of Damietta. There used to be a town
here. Our father left my sister and me this little house. We
come here whenever I get a holiday and can't stand things in
Avaris anymore. My name is—"

He did not get to finish. Again the head turned his way,
the dark eyes drilled into him. "Avaris? You're from Avaris?
Then I probably did hear right. You said the name—Hakoris.
Is Hakoris still alive, then? No one has beaten me to him?"

He rose to one elbow as he said this, and there was such
a supercharged tone of hatred in his voice that Isesi blinked
and sat back in his chair. When he looked up, Aset stood in
the doorway, holding a tray with a bowl of steaming broth
atop it.

Aset looked at her brother. "Well, he's no friend of
Hakoris's," she said. "That's something." She smiled. "Isesi,
prop the pillow up behind him. I'll try to feed him some
soup."

"Friend of—?" the stranger hissed. He let Isesi help him
sit, and moment by moment they watched him get his anger
under control. At last he smiled bitterly and relaxed a little.
"Here, I'll take that. Thank you." He sat up and put the tray
in his lap. "If you hate Hakoris—and I gather you do—then
I'm among friends. He's one of the reasons I came back to

Egypt." He brought the bowl of broth to his lips and blew on it before sipping it. "Ah, that's good. Thank you."

Aset sat down on the chair opposite her brother, on the far side of the bed. "I'm Aset," she said. "This is my brother, Isesi. He's a scribe. If you know about Hakoris, you probably know why we don't like him."

"Aset, you shouldn't just tell . . ."

"Hush, Isesi. You can see from his face that he hates Hakoris as much as we do." She spoke to the stranger again when it became apparent that he was not going to give his name. "We're part of a little conspiracy, you see. We're going to attack the Children's Refuge, let the children out, and take them to somewhere they'll be safe."

Isesi rolled his eyes heavenward at her confession, but Aset ignored him. She sat looking at the stranger, broth poised at the edge of his mouth. Now he put the bowl down.

"May the gods bless you," he said fervently. "Both of you. And, yes, your secret is safe with me. On two conditions."

"What?" Isesi asked, looking a bit worried.

"That you let me join you," the stranger answered. "And if Hakoris is there when you raid the place, you don't interfere while I kill him."

"Kill—?" Isesi echoed, blinking. "Well, we had originally wanted to keep the violence at a minimum. I mean, the idea was to tie him up and leave him for the guards to discover."

"And tell them your names," the stranger pointed out in a flat voice. "And turn you over to—" He stopped. "I take it my— I take it Apophis is still king here? He's still on top of the dunghill, sharing power with that damned charlatan Neferhotep and that priest . . . what's the name, now?"

"Petephres. Yes. And Joseph, the Canaanite, the one who prophesies, is still nominally vizier of Egypt, but he's essentially powerless. He holds the job on sufferance, because he's Petephres's son-in-law. But he moved his father and family and all their chattels, slaves, wives, children, and possessions here some years ago. When Petephres took ill a while back, Apophis seized their goods. 'For the good of the state.' You know how that goes. At least, I presume you do, uh . . . excuse me. I didn't get the name."

The stranger ignored the inquiry. "Petephres is ill? That's bad. He's been a necessary brake on Apophis's activities for quite a long while. Since before I left Egypt, as a matter of fact. How ill is he? Is it serious?"

"Apparently," Isesi said. "Apophis is planning a major military venture, one that Petephres would have vetoed if he were feeling better. I think he's going to die. A friend of mine who works for Neferhotep thinks that if Petephres doesn't die of natural causes, it's more than likely he'll be poisoned by Neferhotep. It'd be easy. All the magus would have to do is slip the poison into the medicine."

The stranger stared at him. The broth lay neglected in its bowl on the tray in his lap. "The situation is well advanced. I returned at the right time."

"Excuse me," Isesi said at last, unable to restrain his curiosity any longer. "We've made ourselves very vulnerable, talking like this. Revealing the things we've said to someone we don't know anything about . . ."

The stranger's face was expressionless; his voice was matter-of-fact. "Oh, you want my name, and something of my background, and my purpose in returning to Egypt. Is that it?"

"Yes," Aset said. "I don't think it's too much to ask, really."

The stranger almost smiled. The chuckle that rose from his throat was a singularly humorless one, however. "You're quite right. Who am I? Well, I'm . . . how do I say it? If I hadn't escaped about five years ago and run away to sea, I'd have been one of those children like those you're planning to free, back in Avaris at the Children's Refuge. Or perhaps I'd have been dead by now. Who knows? I was lucky. Or perhaps some god, some lucky star, was looking out for me."

"You were there?"

"Yes. So you see why I look on Hakoris as I do. There's more, though. My mother was murdered by Apophis, back when he still called himself Aram, before he'd arranged the coup and stolen Salitis's filthy crown. He would have murdered me, too, but I got away and jumped in the river. The only reason I'm alive is that when Hakoris's crimps captured

me and led me off to the refuge, I had the presence of mind
to give a false name."

"Ah," Isesi said sympathetically. "But the real one?"

The stranger's eyes narrowed. "Forgive me," he said. "I
don't mean to sound secretive. It's just that I haven't used my
real name for many years. And merely the fact of you knowing it, just now, might well put both of you in an even greater
danger than your little conspiracy has already. For the time
being, just call me Neko. That's what they called me on the
ships. It was a name given me by a Libyan shipmate."

Isesi mulled this over for a moment, clearly not satisfied.
"All right, Neko it is," he said at last. "But only if you'll tell
us your real name after the raid. By then we'll all be in this so
deep that there'll be no place for secrets between us."

"Meanwhile, Neko," Aset said with a smile, "drink your
broth. It's getting cold."

When the brother and sister were alone and the newcomer had slipped into a fitful sleep, Isesi and Aset strolled
out and climbed one of the dunes to chat privately. "Well,
Aset," Isesi said, "what do you think?"

She hesitated. The first thing that came to mind was the
memory of Neko standing there in the doorway for the first
time, his muscular body bulging out of Isesi's too small robe.
He's beautiful, she thought . . . but, of course, that was not
the response Isesi wanted just now. "I think he can be
trusted," she said. "I think he's a good person. I don't know
why I think that. It's just a feeling I have."

Isesi's thin features screwed themselves into a fretful
frown. "I confess I'm of a divided mind. On the one hand,
the hatred he feels for Hakoris—and Apophis as well—seems
quite genuine. I'm sure that if we let him go along on the
raid, he'll be an asset. He looks like a man who can take care
of himself, but—"

He hesitated for a long interval. When he did speak, it
was with difficulty. "Why is it," he said, "that I don't want to
trust a man who won't give me his real name, even though he
is willing to put his neck on the block with us?"

Aset put one small hand on her brother's thin arm.

"There's another way to look at it," she suggested. "At least he's honest about his reluctance to talk. If he were an untrustworthy person, I think he'd have lied about his name. He'd have said 'My name is Neko' and let it go at that. Wouldn't he?"

Isesi looked out over the now calm sea, at the faraway clouds, which marked where the storm had gone. "I want to agree with you," he said slowly and thoughtfully. "And . . . like you, I think I rather like him, too." He smiled at her and gave her hand an affectionate squeeze. "There's more to it than that, isn't there, dear? He is, after all, a fine figure of a man. I watched your eyes when we were talking to him. You're already a bit taken with him, aren't you? No, be honest with me, now. Eh?" His tone softened. "Poor Aset. These have been terrible times for a girl with no marriage portion to bring to a match, haven't they? If only I made more money, or if there'd been anything left of our inheritance after the tax gatherers were done . . ."

Aset slipped a thin arm around her brother's waist and gave him a hug. "There, now," she soothed. "Don't think that way. I lead a very good life. I'm not unhappy. I forbid you to give yourself a bad time over things neither of us can control. Nobody's lived a normal life here since the Hai came."

Isesi held her to his breast, grateful for the absolution. "Aset, what if the Hai were to be driven out of Egypt forever? What if there were something *to* that prophecy of Joseph's, the one about the Egyptian people finding a savior who would organize them to fight and defeat the Hai Army and drive them into the desert to die?"

The same thought occurred to both of them at the same moment. They backed away to stand at arm's length and stared each other in the eye.

Aset finished his sentence for him, and his thought. "And kill Apophis, and take his crown, and give Egypt back to the Egyptians?" she said in a soft, awed whisper. "Surely you remember the rest of The Prophecy? The part about who the deliverer will turn out to be? The man who'll slay the king will be—"

Isesi stood openmouthed, looking her in the eye but not seeing her at all. "His son," he finished. "A son of his own blood."

IV

As the stranger who had called himself Neko slept fitfully, Aset, looking in on him from time to time, pondered the thought Isesi had put in her head. Could the stranger be Apophis's son? Watching Neko's strong, darkly handsome features in repose, she searched for some sign either to confirm or refute the strange and terrible idea.

She knew, of course, what Apophis looked like; everyone who lived in Avaris did, she fancied. The Hai usurper—he had been born Aram, son and grandson of Shepherd princes—had, in an attempt to gain popular support for his regime, initiated a vigorous campaign of public appearances in the ten years of his reign, and his features were unquestionably those of the invaders: dark hair, black eyes, strong nose. The racial elements in Neko's features were more difficult to identify as specifically Hai, despite the strong nose and dark eyes. *What was his mother?* Aset wondered. *Hai . . . or Egyptian?*

Oddly enough, Isesi seemed to have dismissed or lost interest in the idea only moments after verbalizing it and went back to drafting the proclamation he and his friends had voted to leave at the Children's Refuge once their raid had been carried out.

Aset was left with her thoughts, which were puzzling and contradictory, full of ambivalence and ill-defined disquiet. As the evening wore on, she found the vague unease that accompanied all thoughts about the newcomer translating itself into physical unrest and discomfort. Her flesh was atingle with a strange and unfamiliar sensation.

When Isesi finally said good-night and went to sleep, she sat up for a time, casting nervous glances at the half-open door to the room where they had put the stranger. She knew she would never be able to sleep now, so persistent was this feeling of unease.

On a sudden impulse she rose and stepped out into the night. The moon above was full and bright, a cool white orb, which gave off a malignant and baleful aura. A gentle, balmy breeze was blowing, the night air felt lovely against her skin, and the cool sand caressed the soles of her bare feet with a delicate touch. The soft murmur of the waves, the scent of ocean air, the salt breeze—all usually had a soothing effect. She could walk, and feel, and not think at all. . . .

Her body was still aflame with the strange new feeling, one she could not put a name to—but it had something to do with the stranger and when, naked on this stretch of beach, she had for a moment stood almost within arm's length of his own bare body, looking down on it. . . .

Almost before she knew it, she lifted her shift over her head. This time she did not throw it down; she would never be able to find it again if she did. Instead she threw it over one arm and began to walk slowly along the shore, glorying in the delicious touch of the breeze on every part of her body.

Alone. She was alone. Those times Aset spent alone with her thoughts and feelings were usually her happiest ones, but she now found herself wanting companionship.

If Neko would come to her now, she would— what would she do?

She stopped and looked down at her slim nudity, then felt like a silly little fool. What if someone *should* come? Someone who could not be trusted?

But what if Neko himself should come? What would she do? What would she say? If he were to . . . well, want her, as a man desired a woman? Would she be able to turn him away? Would she *want* to turn him away?

Or would she embrace him without shame, beg him to take her right there on the sands, beneath the moon and stars? Was there inside her a person capable of that?

She shook her head, embarrassed. These fantasies were merely untutored imaginings of a silly little virgin. She quickly pulled the shift over her head to cover herself, feeling ashamed.

Aset shuddered at her folly, then looked up at the top of

the dune and with a shock saw him standing there, arms crossed over his chest, looking down at her!

She thought her heart would stop. Her mouth hung open; her eyes stared unblinkingly.

"N-neko!" she gasped. "You gave me such a start!"

He walked slowly and unevenly down the dune and stood awaiting her. "I'm sorry," he said. "I couldn't sleep any longer. I didn't mean to startle you. I didn't know you were here."

She moved toward him shyly. "How long have you been here?"

She could see the white gleam of his teeth in the moonlight, a kind and indulgent smile. "Long enough. Don't worry, I won't tell anyone." A driftwood log had washed up on the beach nearby; he sat down on it and beckoned to her. "Come talk to me."

She hesitated, but the reassuring tone in his voice gave her courage. She sat down on the far end of the log. "You seem to be getting your strength back."

"Yes," he said. "The storm was an ordeal, but ordinarily I could have handled the boat. The fever weakened me. I'll be all right now. Thanks," he said with gratitude in his voice, "to your own efforts."

"Well," she said, embarrassed, "we wouldn't have turned you away. Particularly not when we learned you had been . . . there."

"Well, rest assured that you've made a friend for life, you and your brother. There's just the two of you?"

"Yes. Our parents are dead. Isesi's a scribe."

"And his education used up what might have been your marriage portion?"

"Well—"

"Don't worry about it. Nobody has much of a dowry, thanks to our invader friends. You'll find a man who won't care, who'll kiss your feet and treat you like a princess. You're an enchanting child."

"I'm not a child!"

"Yes, you are," he said, all too seriously. "You *and* Isesi. Thinking that you can just break into Hakoris's place and rob him of his property"—his voice tightened as he said the ironic word "and just walk away from it. And all without violence. Don't get me wrong. I applaud your motives and thank the gods there are still people like you around. And what wouldn't I have given for something like this ten years ago." He broke off a moment, unable to speak. Then he mastered himself. "I'm not going to let you get hurt doing this."

She turned to look at him.

He went on, almost as if speaking to himself. "No, I'm going to help organize this. I'm going to fix it up so that no one gets killed."

"We're not afraid," she protested.

"I know. You haven't the sense or experience to know how frightened you ought to be. I *know* Hakoris. When I was thirteen he killed my best friend right before my eyes. I spent years in that hellhole of his, and sometimes I think I'll never be clean again for it."

She could not resist. "Neko," she said suddenly in a quiet voice. "Apophis—the king—is he your father?"

She was prepared for any answer. But he gave her no answer at all. The silence was broken only by the murmur of the distant waves.

Neko stared far out to sea, and his face was motionless, carved in stone. Finally he spoke. "I sometimes think that it would be easier just to kill him outright than it has been to talk about it. In the years since I escaped from the refuge I've not spoken of it at all. I've taken sanctuary in a succession of false identities, in a web of lies about who I am and where I come from."

He turned toward her, and while the moon was behind him and his face was in shadow, she could feel his dark eyes on her. "I find myself unable to lie to you, little Aset," he said with a sigh. "Maybe I can sense your honesty and decency—qualities that have been largely absent from my life. If I mislead you further, it would be a kind of betrayal—as much of myself as of you and your foolish, brave young brother. There is much good in the two of you, and it calls forth whatever good there is left in me. There isn't much, I'm afraid, after a lifetime spent first being soiled by a savage like Hakoris, then continuing the job by soiling myself."

"Oh, no," she said, deeply moved. "You're not bad, Neko! You're a good man. I can tell. A bad man would have taken advantage of us by now. Don't speak ill of yourself. I won't let you."

"Thank you for your vote of confidence," he said with sincere affection. "You can't possibly begin to know what it means to me. But I can't lie to myself about this, not even to make you feel better. The only thing I can say in my defense is that the evil I've seen in the world, and the terrible things I've had to do to protect myself, may at last be put to good use in the times to come."

"I don't understand," she said.

"You couldn't," the man who called himself Neko said. "You've guessed my identity. May I ask you, as a special favor, to promise me that you won't reveal the fact, or anything else I'm about to tell you, until I tell you it's all right." He leaned forward, his voice low and urgent. "Not even to Isesi. The fewer people who know, the better."

Aset gulped. There was something very moving and exciting about being singled out for such confidence. "I promise," she breathed. "I won't tell, Neko."

He looked at her for a moment, then picked up a twig that had broken off from the trunk and stirred the sand with it. "It's very strange," he said in a slow, thoughtful voice. "Whenever I have envisioned myself talking about this, i was in a voice of great resolve, like a leader of men. Men have a voice they use with each other that's different from the one they use with women."

"Men usually don't speak of things like this to women at all," she said. "Of course, Isesi's different. He tells me almost everything."

"Yes, I can understand why he would," he confessed. "I'd never imagined that the person I'd talk to about it would be a girl like you. But I feel I can trust you, so here I am." She could see the gently ironic smile on his face as he shook his head. "Another demonstration of the unavoidable fact that a man doesn't know his own mind."

She was about to speak; but something told her that her listener's rapt silence was more appropriate now. "To answer your question," he said, "yes, I'm Aram's bastard. He neve

acknowledged me. When he heard The Prophecy about a
ten-year-old boy who would kill him and drive the Hai out of
Egypt forever, he tried to kill me, as he'd just killed Mother.
I had a brave young friend who saved me, a fellow named
Riki of Thebes. I'll never forget him. . . ."

"Riki?" she echoed. "Where have I heard that name?
But no matter. Go on, please."

"I'm sure that if Aram—if Apophis, as he calls himself—
knew I was alive, he'd shake in his boots and make any man
rich who turned me over to him for execution."

"Your secret's safe with me," she promised.

"I know." She could see his smile at last, and it was
broad and benign. "And thank you. But hear the rest. I'm
cast up on this shore naked and without a friend in the world.
I have come back to Egypt for a purpose, and nothing can
stop me. Not Apophis or his army. Not even death itself."

"I believe you, Neko."

"Thank you. Hear my purpose now. My mother was of
pure Egyptian blood, and this is a matrilineal society. I've
come home to rid the lands of the Nile of the Hai, just as
Joseph the Canaanite prophesied. I've come home to rally
the armies of my nation against the enemy, to drive my father
and his people into the desert, never to return. And to claim
the kingdom of Egypt once and for all and reign over Black
Land and Red Land alike, as no king has reigned for three
hundred years in this troubled land."

His voice trembled with emotion, and the sound of it
thrilled Aset. "I believe you!" she said fervently. "I do!"

CHAPTER TWO

Avaris

I

The drums awakened Joseph around dawn, as they had done every day for the past two months. Drums—savage, insistent, martial. He sat up, the first hot flash of anger slicing through him, his hands already clenched, tense. He looked over at the tranquilly sleeping body of his wife, Asenath, and saw that the sound had not disturbed her slumber. He sighed, rolled over, and put his feet down on the cold floor.

Why had the sound awakened him and not her? He thought about it, rubbing his eyes with the heels of his hands. Well, it was his fight and not hers. Asenath tended to ignore political issues until they began to impinge directly upon her life. So long as he, her husband, and their sons were not to be directly involved with the army, she would ignore the constant threat posed by the accelerating military buildup in the Nile delta. And she would think him ill-tempered and foolish for continuing to oppose the will of King Apophis in this matter.

30

He yawned, grimaced as the drums shifted to a new beat, and stood up. Naked in the soft light, he was still lean and hard and looked a dozen years younger than his age. For this and other reasons, his peers at the royal court—Neferhotep, in particular, and his deadly cohort Hakoris—tended to treat Joseph as a man younger than they, although they and Apophis were all of an age.

It made it easier for them, he supposed, to deal with him . . . and to rob him of his influence, as they were doing, more and more with each passing day. His father-in-law, Petephres, was his only source of power at court. But Petephres was ailing and growing weaker daily, so Joseph could see his own days were numbered, and his twenty-odd years of command at the Egyptian court, one step below the pharaoh himself, drawing to an end.

He shook his head and, frowning, wrapped his loincloth about his waist. What folly it had been for him, a decade before, to decide to bring his father, Jacob, and the rest of his family here from Canaan on the theory that he would be able to take better care of them in a land of plenty!

He padded into the outer room, combing his hair back with his fingers. *Folly,* he thought, *sheer folly.* Yet it had seemed so logical at the time. Because of the famine, Jacob had not been able to take care of his sons and their families, much less the many others not related to him, who depended upon him. Jacob, very old and tired but still able to think clearly, refused to pass his prerogatives as head of the tribe to any of his sons. Joseph's solution had seemed so perfect: bring his father, his brother, Benjamin, and his half brothers, and all their wives and progeny to Egypt, where they could live in luxury on his, Joseph's, bounty. After all, Egypt was the only land in the known world that had not been devastated by the great drought.

But as soon as the family had relocated from Canaan, the palace revolution had taken place. Aram and his coconspirators had seized all power. Aram—now King Apophis—depended upon the magus Neferhotep, who wanted Joseph deposed as vizier, perhaps killed.

Joseph had been saved by Asenath's father, the high priest Petephres, who had played an important role in the success of the new government. Petephres had been a member of Aram's conspiracy from the first. As high priest of the state's official religion, Petephres had the power to make or break the new regime. Thus Aram—Apophis—had been forced to make Petephres an equal partner in the enterprise in exchange for the invaluable support and approval of the temples of Amon.

Petephres had demanded that royal protection extend to Joseph—and to all whom Joseph cared to shelter. For almost ten years the patriarch Jacob and his sons had lived as men of means and influence in Apophis's Egypt, owners of property and chattels, above the routine ups and downs of the shaky delta economy.

But when Petephres had fallen ill, all this had changed. When Apophis had needed land on which to train his burgeoning army and funds with which to feed them, he had seized the properties of various nobles who had no powerful protector at court, and among these had been Jacob and his sons. The Canaanites were now reduced to a fraction of their former affluence and stood to lose even more if Petephres were to die, for then Joseph would lose the struggle for power in the delta.

So far Joseph had been able to keep his brothers' sons from being impressed into military service, but he no longer had any idea how long he could keep this up. Apophis was hell-bent on assembling, as quickly as possible, an army capable of attacking and crushing the already numerically inferior forces of Upper Egypt. As a result, he had embarked on a program to fatten the military ranks by whatever means possible.

Take these drums now: The new unit Apophis had quartered on the lands next to Joseph's country estate were Maaziou Bedouins, mercenaries drawn over into the delta from their native Libya by the promise of high wages and even better booty. Ordinarily the Maaziou were the delta people's deadliest enemies. For centuries these fierce, savage fighters had raided delta farms, raping, killing, and carrying off Egyptian children and women into slavery. Yet here they were on Egyptian soil by the king's own invitation. Already there had been trouble, with Bedouin mercenaries raping local girls and then getting in vicious knife fights with local youths who rose against them in revenge.

Nor would these barbarian units abide by the usual laws Egypt had enforced on its own soldiers. By custom, only officers and underofficers were allowed to carry their weapons with them while off duty, and training exercises were usually conducted with mock weapons. The Maaziou, however, insisted on going armed everywhere they went. This had led to allowing the Egyptian army, too, to go armed, for they had refused to abide by laws foreigners were not required to obey.

As the foreigners in their midst grew in numbers, there was the threat that they would soon grow more numerous than the native-born Egyptians or their Hai oppressors. This clearly could not be allowed, so the levy on Egyptian youth had increased in proportion. For the first time, the condition of military service was now being insisted upon, and the size and complexity of the army grew daily. Daily, the sons of rich and poor alike had to show up at a given time and be weeded out by the inspecting officers, and a high percentage of those able to bear arms were taken away to the training camps for processing.

Joseph had presided over several of these tribunals and soon had balked at accepting further responsibility for the impressment of boys into the army. It was well known that he opposed both the buildup and the offensive that would follow it.

Now, as he dressed for the day and prepared to go to court, he shook his head sadly at Apophis's objective: to muster an offensive that could crush the defenses of the Upper Egyptians once and for all. But the Hai armies had failed again and again over the last twenty years to break through the lines established by the great Upper Egyptian commander Baka.

Apophis would argue now that Baka was getting old and the Upper Egyptian army was not what it was. If the Hai's delta troops from Lower Egypt, doubled in size and augmented by mercenaries from all the lands beside the Great Sea, were to strike simultaneously all along the entire front, attacking in waves, Baka's men would be battered to their knees.

Joseph sighed. While it was true that Baka was getting old, he had a commander, Baliniri the Babylonian, who could ably replace him. Baliniri, with his old friend Mekim at his side, had rebuilt and trained the small Upper Egyptian army until, man for man, it was the glorious equal of anything the Egyptian countryside had ever seen.

Joseph also knew Baliniri's worth; the Babylonian had once been a valuable officer in the Lower Egyptian army. But then he had been ordered to implement the mass slaying of all ten-year-old boys, after Joseph's prophecy regarding the young boy who would grow up to become the promised deliverer of Egypt from Hai rule. Baliniri had changed over to the Upper Egyptian side.

Now the Hai could see what they had let slip through their fingers: Egyptian morale was high; discipline was admirable; the turnout and training of the soldiers of Upper Egypt's Red Lands was impeccable. Compared to them, Apophis's hastily assembled army had only its greater numbers to offer— and no leader of the stature of either Baliniri or Mekim.

Worse, the armies of Lower Egypt's Black Lands, idled while Apophis established and consolidated his power in the delta, were for the most part untried striplings who had never seen real battle, while Baliniri's veterans had seen service in the war against the Nubians ten years before.

Now there had been peace for ten years between Upper Egypt and Nubia's young king Nehsi and his mother, Ebana. But Baliniri had not been content with keeping his army idle and had loaned out military units to Nehsi to help the Nubian king put down rebellion in his southern domains. The experience had been invaluable; Baliniri's men were tough, trained, and blooded.

Joseph had confirmed this many times, for he had had spies located in Upper Egypt, reporting back to him. They had also spoken of an elite corps of women-warriors deep in the desert south of the Fayum, guarding trade routes from foreign invasion and levying taxes on caravans that came through. But in recent months Baliniri had tightened security to such a point that Joseph's spies had gone mute; he suspected the bulk of them had been captured, tortured to reveal their own secrets, and executed.

As Joseph strode out the front door and hailed his chariot driver, he shook his head in disapproval. Apophis's hastily and ill-conceived offensive could only founder. And when it did, whom would Apophis blame as he cast about for a scapegoat? What innocents would suffer?

Clearly the situation was ominous. And his own position grew more precarious every day. Suddenly he found himself wondering what his father-in-law thought of all this, and what advice he might give from his long knowledge of Apophis and his ways. Yes, he would visit Petephres today. Surely there was something he could do to stop this business before it got totally out of hand. . . .

II

As Joseph prepared to mount, signs of a commotion at the gate drew his attention and he motioned his driver to hold. He strode over to the half-open doorway and saw his brother Reuben, gray and grizzled but still vigorous and excitable, arguing with his gate guards.

"Here now!" Joseph said. "Let him in. Haven't I told you that my brothers are always to be allowed to enter?"

He would have taken the matter further, but the source of the problem was immediately apparent. The two young guards were new. "My apologies, sir," the younger began. "He refused to show identification and—"

Reuben would have broken in angrily, but Joseph held up one hand. "It's all right," he said. "Just don't make the same mistake again." He dismissed the guards and stood facing his brother. There had never been much love between them, and now a cool cordiality ruled. "What can I do for you, Reuben?" Joseph asked.

Reuben's rugged face worked in anguish, but he held back the harsh words. "I was going to ask you to have our property restored to us," he admitted, "but I realize that sort of thing is no longer under your control."

"And neither is the matter of letting you return to Canaan," Joseph said sadly. "If I had known how things would work out, I'd never have brought any of you here. What can I say?" He paused for a reply but got none. "How's Father?"

"Not well. I don't think he'll be with us much longer," Reuben answered. Jacob had been almost totally blind for a year now, and only some of the time did he recognize his sons accurately by their voices. "He told me to assemble all of us for his blessing. I think it's mainly a matter of saying good-bye."

Joseph sighed. "I was afraid of that. I'll have Asenath get the boys together. He'll want them too."

"I'd hoped he'd die on his own lands, up north," Reuben said. "He says again and again that God has told him His people would never prosper on foreign soil, away from the Land of Promise."

"A few years ago," Joseph said resignedly, "I'd have disputed that. I prospered in a foreign land. But my fortune is not what it was." He looked around, pain showing on his face. "I know that sounds like hypocrisy. I live well enough, particularly by normal standards. But I used to own vast lands and properties."

"I understand your power isn't what it was," Reuben responded, not without sympathy. "Speaking of these matters, how is our illustrious benefactor, the heathen priest?"

"Petephres?" Joseph asked. "I was just going to visit him. But if you think the business with Father is more critical . . ."

"Who knows?" Reuben said with frustration. "He may already have died as we stand here; he may live another year. Father wants us all together with him two days from now, in the morning. Go to your appointments; the heathen's health affects us all. Keep us posted, will you?"

Reuben turned to go; then he turned back, a strange expression on his rugged features. "Oh, by the way," he said, "Judah thinks he saw . . . but no matter. It's probably just his imagination."

"Judah doesn't *have* any imagination," Joseph said. "You know that. Whom did he see?"

Reuben's brow creased. "Well, it could just be a trick of the light, but the other day, across the square in the bazaar, by fading light, he saw a face. He wasn't sure he recognized it—but he's quite sure the person recognized *him*. Their eyes caught and held."

"Who?" Joseph asked impatiently.

"Well, the man was wearing a Bedouin headdress, from one of the Ishmaelite tribes Judah didn't recognize, but there was something familiar about the planes of the man's face, and his eyes. Judah said, 'I'd recognize those eyes anywhere.'"

Joseph's patience was wearing thin now. "Surely this Bedouin transient has a name," he said.

"He wasn't dressed as a transient. He was dressed as an Egyptian, and one of some wealth. Judah could have been mistaken, but he says the man is Shamir ben-Hashum. You know, the one who used to bedevil your friend Ben-Hadad when we were young?"

"Yes," Joseph said, looking sharply at him, "I remember Shamir. One does not easily forget a man as wicked as Shamir."

"There was another thing: His headdress was pulled very low, down to . . . just here." Reuben marked a spot on his own brow, just above the eyebrows. "After you left, on Father's orders, we branded Shamir as a felon." He shuddered in spite of himself. "I held the iron myself. I'll never forget his eyes, so filled with hate, when the hot iron touched his forehead."

Joseph had shot him a sharp look at the word "left," but decided to let it pass. "You know, I *thought* there was something about . . ." He made a face. "But then I dismissed it. Of course, I knew nothing of the branding. And, seeing the headdress, I took him for what he seemed to be."

"You *know* him?" Reuben asked. "But of course if you *had* recognized him during the time you still had power here, you'd have done something."

Joseph's forehead creased. "I wish I had. If he's the man I'm thinking about, he's just what you'd imagine Shamir would turn into when he was grown—the worst man in the delta."

"I take it he's powerful as well as rich." Reuben spat viciously onto the ground before them. "He *would* be."

"Powerful," Joseph confirmed, "beyond what a villain like him deserves. Oh, Reuben, I hope we're wrong, because the man I'm thinking of is one of the conspirators whose chicanery swept Apophis into office. After the magus Neferhotep, no one stands closer to the king than he does."

Reuben was horrified. "Shamir? Third in command in the whole kingdom?"

"Yes," Joseph said. "His name now is Hakoris."

Reuben swallowed. "Joseph! How have you lived this long with Shamir in power? How have all our family? Surely he must know us and must crave revenge for his branding and exile from Canaan."

"If we're right, of course he does. But so far Petephres, my father-in-law—the man," he said with heavy irony, "whom you keep calling 'the heathen'—stands between us and death. That's if he is alive and of sound mind. If they offend him, he pulls the power of the priesthood of Amon out of the coalition, and Apophis's government collapses within a week. If he dies or is incapacitated, his assistant will come to power and strike his own deal with Apophis, which probably won't include me."

Reuben whistled softly through his teeth. "And without that protection we're all goners."

The two pairs of eyes locked. Neither man said anything. Behind him, Joseph could hear the impatient snorting of his magnificent pair of matched Arabian stallions and hear the faint rattle of their harness.

As Joseph approached the palatial home of his father-in-law, it was unsettling to see the tall and commanding form of the magus Neferhotep leaving at the head of a group of armed retainers. Joseph let the magus's party pass, fearful that they would take notice of him, but Neferhotep was busy unrolling a papyrus and trying to read it as the jouncing chariot carried him past.

The priesthood of Amon had its own physicians, and Joseph was met at Petephres's door by such a physician,

named Hesi. Joseph jerked his head backward toward the
departing party of the court doctor. "What was *he* doing
here?" Joseph demanded. "I gave orders that my father-in-
law wasn't to see anyone without my permission."

"You did, sir," said Hesi. "But . . . to tell the truth, sir,
in the first place I'm only a *sunu* and he's a *semsu*, far above
my own rank in the College of Physicians. And he has other,
more potent claims upon my attention . . . if you get my
meaning, sir."

"I know. Eight armed bodyguards. Well, I'm sure I can
trust you not to let him administer medication. There is, I
believe, a rule saying that a *semsu* may not pull rank on you
with a patient without your permission?"

"Yes, sir, but . . ."

Joseph looked the man up and down: fat, weak, irreso-
lute. *This will never do,* he thought. *I'll have to frighten the
fellow into standing up to them.* "Can I trust you with a
matter of importance? Something rather delicate, which must
come to the ears of no one else?"

"Oh, yes, sir," Hesi said.

"Very well. But your promise: talk to no one about this."
Another enthusiastic nod. "All right. I have reason to believe
Petephres is in danger of being poisoned by the magus
Neferhotep."

"Oh, no, sir! Surely—"

"Hear me. I know what I'm talking about. The two have
been political enemies for years."

"But the *semsu* speaks of him with such—"

"Trust me. Did the magus give Petephres any medication?"

"My lord was asleep. But the *semsu* left this for him."
He held up a vial.

"Ah, good," Joseph said, taking the container. "I'll have
an analysis done by my own people. Make sure you intercept
anything he gives Petephres to take, and that you bring it
straight to me."

The *sunu*'s eyes were wide. "Are you quite sure, sir?"

"That this is poison?" Joseph asked. "No. That the plot's
a real one? Yes. I have my own network of spies. I can tell
you what you ate for dinner two weeks ago—" This last was
pure bluff, but the physician believed it; he blanched.

"Very well," Joseph said with a smile. "I know a thing or two *else* about you." This was a bluff also, but it brought a quick glance of fear. "Don't worry. As long as you do what I tell you, you won't be in any trouble. But fail me even once—"

"No, sir!" Hesi promised.

When Joseph entered the room, Petephres was awake and sitting up, looking old and weak. "Joseph," he said.

"Father." Joseph saluted him, using the courtesy title. "How are you?"

"Weak and dizzy," the priest said. "But I've got my wits about me. Enough, anyway, to feign sleep while that old charlatan Neferhotep was here."

"Good. Don't take any medicine he gives you. I mean that. I confiscated this from Hesi." He held up the vial. "I'll have it looked at for poison."

Petephres showed no sign of surprise. "Good. The last time, he gave me a piece of honeycomb with something buried inside it. I waited until he was gone and spat it out."

"I should have known you'd not be fooled," Joseph said, respect and affection in his voice. He had come to rely more and more on his wife's father in recent years. "I wanted to tell you—my brothers think they've found out who Hakoris is."

The older man's eyes narrowed. "Ah! Who?"

"A thief and criminal from my own land named Shamir."

Petephres's voice was weak but firm. "Do you have anything on him that our own laws could be brought to bear on?"

"Not enough to bring down a man that close to Apophis."

"That means we'll have to create something. Or . . ." The men exchanged knowing looks.

"So far I've survived court without killing anyone. I'd like to keep that record intact if I can," Joseph said.

"Would your scruples prevent the engineering of a situation in which Hakoris would be eliminated by someone else?" He looked into Joseph's eyes. "I don't mean hiring a killer, Joseph. I mean something like forging evidence against him that would amount to a death sentence. Or getting someone angry enough at Hakoris to wish him dead."

Joseph searched his conscience. "I . . . I'm not sure," he said.

III

As the bearers rounded the corner and approached the entrance of the great palace of the Hai kings, Neferhotep looked down and saw a familiar face. "Hold!" he called out. "I'll dismount here."

The four bearers came to an instant halt and obediently brought their burden down, responding to crisp orders from the lead bearer. Neferhotep stepped briskly down. He turned to the chief guardsmen. "See to their dismissal," he said in a tone used to command. "I'll make my way inside later."

"But *semsu*," the captain said, "I'm under strict orders not to let you out of my sight."

"Then I countermand them," Neferhotep said, drawing himself up to his impressive full height and transfixing the man with one of his practiced glares. His bushy brows framed steely eyes, and his hawk's nose was set high in a haughty and imperious expression. "Go."

Only then did he turn to Hakoris, to the cold face under the Bedouin headdress. Fleetingly, and for perhaps the thousandth time, he wondered why Hakoris, whose manners and speech were by now convincingly Egyptian, continued to maintain a single foreign custom of dress like the headdress. "Greetings," he said. "What can I do for you, my friend?"

"Come," Hakoris said, motioning him up the street. "We can talk more privately in the inn than here." The two walked briskly through the thinning crowds to a staircase at the end of the street. They had used this particular inn many times for covert conversations and had learned to trust the security of the private room in which they customarily met.

Ushered into the back by a burly man, they shut the door behind them and sat down.

"Petephres is fading," Neferhotep began. "He won't last the month. Now that I'm handling his medication, we may be even closer to our goal."

"If he had died yesterday," Hakoris said, "it wouldn't have come too soon. There's trouble with that Canaanite lot Joseph brought down." He started to say more but feared trusting Neferhotep with the truth.

"Eh? There's more. I can tell. Get it out, my friend," the magus said. "Have no fear. You know enough about me and I have enough on you for both of us to be impaled a dozen times over. If we can't trust each other by now . . ."

Hakoris plainly did not like the idea. But after a moment's hesitation he cursed beneath his breath and spoke with a snarl on his face. "Those damned brothers of Joseph's. They're as thick as thieves. They can't abide one another, really—but let anyone offend one of them, and the rest are up in arms."

Neferhotep leaned forward, interested. "You've a problem with one of them?"

Hakoris shot him an angry glance, unwilling to tell more but unable to think of an alternative. "I . . . in my youth," he said, "I—knew them, but not very well. We weren't the kind to get along. They were always taking up for . . . someone I despised."

Neferhotep's face suddenly turned bland. "I suppose you're referring to your stepbrother, Ben-Hadad," he said innocently. "The one you killed some years ago."

The statement rocked Hakoris. "How did you know about that?" he demanded in a strangled voice.

The magus smiled. "You thought no one knew. And so it was. Of the spies who dug the information out for me, all but one have been killed. The one remaining was blinded; for good measure, his hands were removed along with his tongue. While your paths and mine remain locked in parallel lines, my dear friend, I will never tell."

For a split second Neferhotep could see Hakoris weighing the cost of killing him, along with Joseph and his brothers. He smiled easily, sure of himself now. "And I?" he said.

"I have committed the whole matter to writing, to be sure, but the papyri are in a safe place and will be shared with no one . . . unless I meet with violence, whereupon—"

But Hakoris was under control and waved the thought away. "Bah!" he said. "What are close associates like us doing exchanging threats? Rest easy, my friend. I mean you no ill. But how much do you know?"

"I know your name—Shamir ben-Hashum. I know your history up to a certain point. I know the source of your enmity for Joseph. Then you disappear altogether and turn up here many years later."

Hakoris almost smiled and, to reassure himself, patted the front of his headdress. "Very well," he said, his tone more normal now. "To continue, one of these tribesmen, Joseph's brother Judah, recognized me. If he denounces me to Joseph . . . well, suffice it to say that it'd be best for none of the story to reach our esteemed king." There was a frosty edge of irony over the courtesy title given to the absent Apophis.

"Rest your mind," Neferhotep assured him. "Come, let me order wine and olives, my friend. As Petephres's life dwindles away, so does Joseph's only source of protection and power in the court. You already know what Aram—I mean Apophis—thinks of him."

"I'm not so sure," Hakoris said. "He still thinks Joseph a very potent seer, even if Joseph hasn't had any visions lately."

"Undermining Joseph's image," Neferhotep said, "has been one of my highest priorities for quite some time. By the time Petephres has finally gone to his reward in the Netherworld, his son-in-law will have less prestige than the threadbare conjurers who work the bazaars and pull scarves from their mouths."

"It had better come soon," Hakoris said. "I don't like having anyone around who—" He stopped, reluctant to reveal more, and Neferhotep suddenly wished he had not told the man in the Bedouin headdress how little he knew about him. What *had* happened in that in-between period? Did it have anything to do with his refusal to give up the Bedouin headgear after these many years in Egypt? What did the Canaanites have on him?

The idea came to him: What if he, Neferhotep, were to approach Joseph's brother Judah and pry out of him some of the missing information? It would give him good leverage when his final confrontation with Hakoris inevitably took place.

But now he realized Hakoris was awaiting a reply. "Never mind," Neferhotep said hastily. "Joseph's days are numbered. The poison is working its way through Petephres's system even as we speak, and the moment Joseph loses the support of the priesthood of Amon, he's a dead man. I guarantee it."

"Well, don't let it drag on," Hakoris said menacingly. "If I think you're moving too slowly, I'll take things into my own hands, I promise you."

After the magus had left, Hakoris lingered a moment over his still-untasted wine, reflecting.

So Neferhotep knows who I am! he thought, still shocked. It was plain, however, that the magus did not know about the real source of his breach with Jacob's people, or about the circumstances that had led to his branding.

He reached up and touched the headdress again. The branding . . . it was still a source of anger and hatred in him, and he had vowed years ago to revenge himself upon Jacob and his sons, for it had ruined his life, leading to the horrible jail sentence he had served in the hellish mines of Timna, in sun-blazed Arabah. Yes. He had even had to kill, more than once, to keep the secret of it.

Most serious had been the time when that doctor, Sesetsu, had tried to remove the scar, but failed. In a rage Hakoris had killed the doctor. And when the physician's daughter Mara, had been sold as a slave to cover her father's debts, Hakoris had bought her and made her pay again and again—with humiliation and abuse as the currency—for her father's incompetence. —

Another memory possessed his mind, bringing with it another hot flash of anger. His fingers gingerly touched the side of his head now, where there was still a sensitive place. Mara had hit him with something hard the day she had escaped ten years ago in the company of that damned street

urchin Niki. She would pay for that too, and soon! He had
heard from reliable informants that she had returned to the
delta after some years spent across the border in Egyptian-
controlled territory. And the moment the rumor had reached
him, he had put the word out on the underground circuit of
kidnappers who supplied his Children's Refuge with inmates:
Find Mara! Bring her to Hakoris—alive!

He frowned. All these years he had managed to prosper
here in Hai-controlled Lower Egypt mainly because he had
maintained the same unbroken wall of secrecy. Now, not
one, but quite a number of people knew about him. He did
not like it. Something had to be done about it immediately!

"You're sure?" Joseph asked.

Judah paced in the center of the great room. "No doubt
about it. And he recognized me."

"Do you know what, Judah?" Joseph said. "I'll bet Ben-
Hadad recognized him too. I'll bet he called Hakoris out and
was killed for it." He shook his head slowly. "Well, something has to be done. My father-in-law thinks I ought to have
him assassinated. Well, you *know* I can't do that. It's against
all the laws of God and our people. But I can't just let things
be. All of us brothers, our wives and children, are in danger
while that man is alive."

"There are those among us," Judah said, "who would
agree with Petephres. But you know how that would sit with
Father." He stopped pacing and looked at his younger brother.
"I wish he'd been awake when you came. Perhaps he could
have given us advice."

"I'm not sure I should tell him about it. It doesn't pay to
upset him. He took it very hard when he heard what happened to Ben-Hadad. He had a soft spot for the boy. He had
been almost a second father to Ben-Hadad, back before
Danataya married Hashum and Shamir started tormenting
him."

To his surprise Joseph found the names tugged at his
own heart as well. He and Ben-Hadad had been born on the
same day, and their destinies had been linked from that
moment, although Danataya's bad marriage to Hashum had

separated them through most of their youth. Ben-Hadad's
return to Jacob's lands had been as the despised stepson of a
man with a mean, bullying son of his own and no one to
protect him against Shamir's brutal taunts. Jacob, seeing the
boy's predicament, had stepped in and taken over Ben-Hadad's
care. And from that moment Joseph and Ben-Hadad, reunited at last, had been like blood brothers, inseparable and
totally in sympathy.

But then had come the incident in which Joseph's brothers set in motion the chain of events that had led to Joseph's
being sold into bondage in Egypt, and the two boys had been
separated for years.

When the two met again, Ben-Hadad had been a drunk-
ard and wastrel. And Joseph, having risen from slave to vizier
of the Hai empire, had had his own problems, coping daily
with the growing insanity of the Hai king, Salitis. And he had
not been as sensitive to Ben-Hadad's plight as he could have
been. . . .

One morning Ben-Hadad's body had been found down
by the river, stabbed to death, and nobody had come forth
with any explanation . . . until now, when a single, quite
logical, explanation had forced itself into Joseph's mind: Ben-
Hadad had met and recognized Hakoris.

He looked up now and saw in Judah's frightened eyes
the mirror of his own concern. Neither man spoke for a long
moment. Then Judah spoke, hoarsely, almost angrily. "God
used to speak to Father in times of danger. You've inherited
his gift. Does God never speak to you anymore? And if not,
why not?"

Joseph's stricken eyes did nothing to hide his pain. The
answer to Judah's first question was written all too clearly on
his face. But for the second question he had no answer at all.

IV

The magus, wrapped in highly theatrical dignity, strode down the long colonnade of the great central hall of the king's palace. The effects of the military buildup that had begun showed ever more clearly. Instead of the usual glut of petitioners waiting for the king's late-morning divan, a colorful profusion of soldiers filled the great hall. Neferhotep recognized the unit dress of virtually every regional division in the entire network of Lower Egyptian nomes, and the often bizarre regalia of a dozen different countries.

For not the first time he wondered if he and his fellow conspirators had made the right choice in picking Aram—Apophis—for the throne, which their assassination of King Salitis had left vacant. Apophis had proved an erratic, ill-tempered king, one whose rages and bad manners had only been made tolerable by comparing them with the memory of mad Salitis, who had thought nothing of beating a slave to death for the most trivial offense.

What choice had they? The Hai would never have stood for the accession of an Egyptian, or for any other maneuver that would have weakened their control over the delta lands. Aram was of noble Hai stock. Nor could the conspirators have placed on the throne a man not acceptable to the priesthood of Amon, particularly in the first days of the revolution, when Petephres had exercised great power over the army. They had, in a word, been stuck with Aram, whatever his faults.

But now? He wondered what could be done to force Aram into concessions. His mad idea of throwing the full resources of Lower Egypt behind an all-out military attack on Baka's Upper Egyptian-prepared positions just north of Lisht had the look of criminal folly. All the more so now that Aram had declared that he was prepared to spend ten thousand troops and the wealth of the entire region, if necessary, on crushing Baka.

To be sure, he had the troops to do it. But did he have the leaders? No new leader of stature had arisen in past years, and Hai tradition allowed no promising commanders from among the foreign mercenary troops to rise higher than tactical commands.

And meanwhile, Baka, serving as vizier under the native Egyptian pharaoh Sekenenre, had found strikingly able leaders to replace him as head of the Upper Egyptian army: Baliniri, from the Land of Two Rivers, had ably served King Hammurabi and had rebuilt the army, making of it a formidably efficient fighting unit that had repelled every Hai attack and held the border firm.

And Aram proposed to attack this? What a fool!

The thought came so suddenly to Neferhotep's mind that he faltered in midstep and almost fell.

If Aram were to fail in a way that would permanently damage public confidence in him—particularly among such powerful groups as the army and the priesthood of Amon—but that would not allow Baka to counterattack and retake the delta for the Egyptians . . .

There would be a chance for a second revolution, one that could place on the throne a king more acceptable to his own tastes, one more amenable to suggestions from his old friends. . . .

But who? It would have to be one of the Hai and, most likely, a man descended from noble blood. But where was such a man, particularly one whose warrior blood had been so attenuated by two generations of easy living that he could be manipulated by Neferhotep, to be found?

He would simply have to find someone answering this description and groom him for the job. . . . And somehow get something on him, something so damaging that his loyalty could be permanently assured.

"Sir? I don't mean to intrude, but—"

Neferhotep wheeled, hearing the diffident voice at his elbow. Mehu, Aram's aging retainer, bowed obsequiously, palms pressed together, his bald head gleaming in the sunlight that streamed through the opening in the roof above. "Yes?" he asked. "What is it?"

"Pardon, sir. The king has been looking for you since dawn. It's quite urgent."

"Very well," Neferhotep said, assuming his most pompous attitude and looking down, hawk-eyed, at the little stew ard from beneath beetling brows. "Take me to him. You can tell me what's wrong as we go."

They set off at a brisk clip, Mehu taking two steps to the tall magus's one. "It's his favorite son, Yahi. The boy had another attack of the falling sickness. It was horrible. He fell to the ground, and his eyes rolled back in his head. Everyone in the nursery thought he was dying." The story came out in breathless bursts, as the little retainer struggled to keep pace.

"They're in the nursery?" Neferhotep asked.

"No, no," Mehu said. "He's been waiting for you in his office."

"Confound it!" Neferhotep said. "The one day I decide to go visit Petephres and try to, uh, cure his ailment, and this has to happen. How angry is Ar—I mean Apophis?"

"Very, sir—at first, anyway. Now I think you'd say he was more concerned. The boy seems all right. But that's the way the falling sickness is." He was puffing now, and the words were coming out two or three at a time, with gasps in between. "I think if you're there, you can calm him down. The king, I mean."

"Certainly." As they passed the standing guard and entered the wing that contained the king's private rooms, Neferhotep went silent, organizing his thoughts. His first reaction was one of annoyance. Virtually any ailment other than the falling sickness would have been more welcome just now. As he well knew, there was no cure for the ailment, and it had a way of getting worse as one grew older. Physicians and fellow magi knew this; autocrats like Aram tended not to understand. If you were a wonder-worker by trade, you were supposed to be able to come up with a palliative for virtually any ailment known to man. And if you could not . . .

Damn the luck! And it would, after all, have to be Aram's favorite brat, the son of Aram's favorite little tumble in the bushes, the little sloe-eyed one with the softly rounded little—

Now, though, for some reason his mind went back a few years and reminded him of something. This boy, Yahi, had already, at nine, been formally recognized by Aram as his eventual heir. But . . . was there not an elder son—even though Aram had never married the mother or legitimatized the boy? Neferhotep could not recall the boy's name, but he could remember how frightened Aram was because of The Prophecy about a ten-year-old who would one day drive the Hai out of Egypt and kill the king.

For all practical purposes that child could be assumed to be alive! He would be about nineteen or twenty years old now. Perhaps he was out there somewhere, just biding his time, waiting his chance.

The magus and the servant turned a corner, passed another guardsman, returned his salute, and headed up the long, shallow flight of stairs to Aram's suite of apartments.

An unbidden idea suddenly flashed through his mind: What if he could somehow find this son of Aram's and befriend him, then help him infiltrate Aram's defenses and carry off the bold coup?

Surely, if the lad were alive, he must certainly have dreamed of seizing the throne for himself all these years? He would have had plenty of time to work up a real and enduring hatred for his natural father, considering Aram had murdered his mother and tried to kill him. Enough hatred, perhaps, to allow someone like Neferhotep, who shared his disdain for Aram, to worm his way into the boy's confidence and plot with him.

But now Neferhotep and Mehu were nearing Aram's rooms, their footfalls echoing down the hall. Aram burst into the hallway, a distraught look on his face, his hair and beard in disarray. "There you are, damn you!" he bellowed. "Where have you been? I've had people out searching for you all morning. By all the gods, if you ever disappear like this again, I'll have you gutted and left sitting on a spike before the day's out! Get in here, curse you!"

Neferhotep's face stiffened. "I came as soon as I heard," he said icily. "I was visiting Petephres." He raised his voice a trifle as he pointedly added, "On business that, I'll remind you, you suggested yourself."

He waited a heartbeat or two for this to sink in, raising one eyebrow dramatically and significantly.

Aram's face changed. "And—with what results?"

"He continues to deteriorate. He can't last out the month.

Perhaps not the week. The medication I gave him saw to that." He had no sooner said this than the thought struck him: Mehu was still standing there, listening! He shot the little retainer a hot glance, but Mehu had by now learned all the arts of the courtier, and busying himself with a tray of dates and figs to take in to Aram's son, Mehu's face betrayed no sign of having listened in.

Neferhotep waited until Mehu was in the other room and motioned the king aside, this time keeping his voice low. "Never fear," he said. "It'll go as I said. How's the boy?"

"A bit better. But the very idea of his having these attacks at all . . . It totally unmans me. Here I am, absolute ruler of the world's greatest empire, and yet when my son has one of these seizures, I can't do a thing about it—"

Neferhotep looked closely at the king. Aram's concern, his understanding, were genuine. Neferhotep debated for a moment the notion of telling Aram the truth: *Look, nobody can do anything about this. The boy will have these attacks as long as he's alive. Some things in the world you simply have to learn to live with. And this is one of them. . . .*

But he had to admit that the time for such honesty had not yet arrived. Perhaps later, when Aram was calmer. "I'll go to him and see what I can do," he said.

And while he looked the boy over, a jumble of conflicting thoughts cluttered his mind and upset him. *If I admit defeat in this,* he realized, *what's to stop some other magus— someone less candid about the matter—from muscling me out of the way? Or what is to stop some ambitious young priest of Amon, who covets Petephres's post, from coming in and dosing the lad up with some nostrum and, in the wake of temporary and illusory recovery, seizing from me the power he had intended to grab from Petephres?*

And—the thought came as a sudden, horrid shock—what if Joseph were to regain his power to foresee the future? What if the exotic, rustic god of Joseph were to give him the power to work some miracle cure?

Neferhotep thought of a Joseph restored to power in the new kingdom and shuddered. It could happen! Hakoris was right; Joseph had to die. And soon! And his family with him!

But not before he, Neferhotep, had reached them and learned the secret about Hakoris's past.

He looked at Aram. The king was staring at him anxiously. Neferhotep cleared his throat and spoke in his deep magus's voice. "There's a potion," he said, "that has been known to work wonders with this ailment. I think I have the ingredients to make it. But the spell that accompanies it . . . I learned it in my youth, but forgot it. The spell is from the Hittite country and very rare. My teacher himself had never seen a copy but had learned it by rote, as did I. I would like the services of the chief scribe and two of his assistants, for a day or so. There's a chance the royal library may have a copy of the scroll."

Aram's face contorted with anguish. "Requisition whatever and whoever you need. Just cure my son! Quickly!"

V

From cover, behind a long line of tall palms flanked by low undergrowth, the three—Aset, Isesi, and the stranger called Neko—watched the soldiers at their drills. Isesi shook his head. "Really," he said incredulously, "I've never seen anything even remotely like them, even though we've had mercenaries here from Padan-aram, from Assyria, from Shinar and Elam, and even from the lands of the Hittites."

Aset did not comment; she was trying not to look at certain parts of the soldiers' anatomy. Although these soldiers wore bronze armor that covered their chests, bellies, and shins, and tall, tufted helmets that covered the sides and back of their heads, they wore nothing to protect their arms or loins. It was a strange custom; did they not care if a spear or a sword hit them *there*? She blushed again. Did this mode of dress not embarrass them, as it did her?

Apparently not! As a matter of fact, when the unit broke ranks to reform now, the men—who were boy-lovers to the last man, apparently—patted and caressed one another as if they had been in the baths. *Disgusting!* she thought. *Totally shameless!* And yet . . . she could not keep her eyes away. How shocking!

"Who are they?" Isesi asked now. "They're uncommonly fair-skinned for this part of the world."

"They're not from this part of the world," Neko explained. "They're from the Hellenic mainland. Their ancestors seem to have drifted into the area a century or more ago. As soldiers they speak of themselves as *hoplites*. The basic unit is a *lochos*—a hundred men. That's about the largest unit one of their officers can control, given their basically insubordinate nature. It's divided into two *pentekostyes*—each fifty men strong—which break down in turn into two *enomotiai*. The fighting troops in each *enomotia* line up in groups of eight for battle; there's an officer in front to lead them and another at the rear to keep anyone from turning tail. And yes, I know it doesn't add up properly. They're stronger on fighting than on arithmetic." His quick grin was a kind of half-approving comment in itself.

"How do you know so much about them?" Aset asked.

"I was captured by a group of them once up in Bithynia," Neko said. "They debated whether or not to kill me, then put me to work dog-robbing for their *lochagos*—that's the officer in charge of the whole hundred." He chuckled sourly. "I'm pretty good at stealing food; I learned that in the refuge." The hated word came out full of bile. "I did all right with them."

"What are they doing here?" she asked. "Surely they don't mix well with our own troops. You know what the Hai think of . . . well, boy-lovers." She broke off, embarrassed.

"These?" Now Neko laughed out loud, and Isesi nervously looked about, but no one in the field seemed to have heard. "Don't take their antics too seriously. After a battle they'll mount anyone or anything, male or female. They're animals. Oh, I had to do a bit of fighting to keep my own body inviolate. But I was good at *that*, too, after years in the refuge. The difference here is that they don't really mean it. Let them know you really aren't interested, and they'll leave you alone. You could never say that of the guards at the refuge."

"Oh." It seemed to Aset that every topic of conversation conjured some terrible memory for him. Why couldn't she learn to keep her mouth shut?

Neko saw her face, hurt and withdrawn, and reached out to pat her cheek with a hard-callused hand whose touch was, strangely, as soft as a feather. "Don't feel bad," he said, instantly understanding her discomfiture. "Until we've destroyed the refuge—and perhaps Hakoris with it if we're lucky—I'm too sensitive, like an open wound. I'd be a fool to take offense at anything you say in innocence." He did not remove his hand until he had coaxed a smile from her. Then he turned to Isesi. "I don't remember this countryside as well as I thought I would. Where is Avaris from here?"

"Not far," Isesi replied. "This road is new. It was made for the moving of produce from the farms Apophis seized. If it helps you get your bearings, the river forks just ahead. There's an island with an old abandoned estate on it in the middle of the channel. I thought we'd hide you there while we went into town, just in case the troops are out again looking for people to impress into the army."

Neko nodded his consent. "Time enough for me to make my triumphal return to Avaris"—this was said with a heavy satirical emphasis—"when we're ready to move."

"Isesi!" Aset said suddenly. "That meeting we were going to call for the people joining us in the liberation of the refuge—you said it was too dangerous to do it in the city. Could we hold it on the island?"

Isesi's eyes widened with pleasure. "A splendid idea!" he acknowledged. "That'll be perfectly secure. We can meet in Baliniri's old house, post sentries outside, and—"

He stopped dead when he saw the expression on Neko's face. "What's the matter?" he asked, shocked. "Did I say something wrong? The color has drained from your face."

"It's nothing," Neko said after a brief, tense pause. "I know Baliniri's house. Ar—Apophis murdered my mother there, on the grounds down by the river, just outside the gate."

"Oh, I'm so sorry!" Isesi said. "We'll hold the meeting elsewhere."

"Rest easy," Neko said, looking quite pale. "I mean it. Your idea's a good one—with one important stipulation."

"What's that?" Isesi asked.

"The people you bring over to the island—make quite sure each one can be trusted with your life." His eyes were quite serious. "Because that's what all of us are doing: betting our lives on every associate we have."

Aset and Isesi exchanged glances. This was a dangerous and desperate thing they were about to do, one that, bungled or foiled, would surely result in their deaths.

Aset blinked, swallowed . . . and turned to Neko with a brave smile. Her voice was serious. "We understand," she assured him. "We'll take the greatest precautions, Neko. Really we will. Nobody attends our meetings who isn't perfectly safe."

Isesi still looked a little miffed. "We're not such fools as we look, Neko. Every one of our party has been checked out by our most dedicated member. She knows Hakoris and his treacherous ways as well as anyone—even as well as you, I daresay. And she hates him perhaps more than you do."

"Nobody could do that," Neko said. His face was carved stone. "Nobody."

"Mara could," Isesi insisted stubbornly. "If anybody—"

"Isesi!" Aset said sharply. "You weren't supposed to mention her name! After all, there's a price on her head already, offered by Hakoris himself."

Isesi's face fell. "I'm sorry. It won't happen again. Some conspirator I am!"

Neko's brows knit in thought. "Mara," he said. "I know that name."

"Forget it," Isesi said. "Come, we'll have our meeting elsewhere. There's no sense causing you needless sorrow."

Not until the sun had fallen below the city walls and darkness covered half the sky did Mara venture forth, hair and face veiled by the heavy hood she wore over her long robe. Warily searching the darkening doorways right and left, she hurried down the street in heavy shadow, her hands, deep inside the robe's folds, clutching the long knife she carried with her everywhere.

She knew never to take chances in daylight, not since Hakoris had learned that she was alive and back in the delta. He had put out word that her capture would bring a substantial reward. And at night, in a city made daily more dangerous by the growing threat of war, no woman was safe alone and unarmed in the dark streets. The streets were full of strangers, men of violence with no roots in Egyptian customs and ways, men who would think nothing of raping a young woman. Foreigners, mercenaries, the rabble and scum of the earth whom Apophis had brought here to flesh out the great army he hoped to use to subdue the Egyptians once and for all.

Whenever the name "Hakoris" came into her mind, of course, her first reaction was a white-hot stab of hatred. Her second reaction was fear. And now, as the shadows deepened, that dark terror was upon her once again as she thought of falling into that monster's hands.

It had taken a long time to discover why Hakoris had hated and humiliated her so, had worked her, miserable and naked in all weather, like a beast of burden. Only after the boy Riki had come into her life had the dark facts become gradually clear: Her father, a physician, had failed to remove the terrible scar on Hakoris's forehead—the scar of a branding he had received somewhere far to the north for some felony he had committed. Hakoris had murdered Mara's father, as much for knowing about the scar as for having failed to remove it.

Not content with this, he had bought her as a slave when she was auctioned off to cover her father's debts, and he had made her life miserable for years. Then Riki had come along. . . .

Dear Riki! She felt a rush of regret. The naked, skinny little street-urchin had befriended her and had taken her away after they had attacked Hakoris and left him for dead. She had gone with Riki to the south, into Egyptian territory, and found safety at last. She owed him so very much. Why then had nothing ever developed sexually between them? As he had grown to manhood and she had matured into a lushly beautiful woman, they'd merely remained friends, even though he had been strongly attracted to her as a boy.

Now he had grown into a strong, virile, thoroughly admirable young man of great physical beauty and courage. Mara sighed. Was something wrong with her that she'd never felt any deep attraction for him? Was it because she had first known him as a friend, a brother? Or was it due to the obsession with revenge that ate at her, so that no other emotion could successfully compete with it?

She had loved her father so! When she had learned how he had come to die, nothing but vengeance ever seemed important.

She stopped at the corner and looked both ways before venturing into the street. Satisfied, she turned right and scurried down the dark lane, silent in her soft sandals.

The war! She felt once again the sudden stab of fear—this time for Riki himself. He had gone into the army to apprentice himself to his wonderful friend Baliniri, hero of the siege of Mari, to learn the arts of killing, as happy with his decision as a man who had suddenly fallen in love. And, relieved of the necessity of worrying about their relationship, she had kissed him good-bye and let him go to his own destiny.

She stopped, her heart beating fast. Up ahead there was a beam of light thrown abruptly across her path. A door stood ajar. She shrank back, but a dark figure stepped out of the open doorway and beckoned her inside.

"Mara!"

"Is that you, Mei?" she whispered.

"Yes! Inside, quickly!"

The voice was the key. Old Mei's voice, raspy and high-pitched, was like no one else's. She hurried inside, and he shut the door behind her.

"It's good to see you," he said. "I've got news. I had a letter from Aset. She and Isesi will be in the city tomorrow."

"Oh, splendid!" Mara responded. "Not a moment too soon! From all I hear, Apophis is massing troops on the border; the Maaziou Bedouin units were ordered up today, and the Hellenes will be moved up tomorrow. Other units will follow within the week. Now's the only time we'll ever be able to do it." She took her hood down and saw the look of subdued lust in old Mei's single eye as she shook out her dark hair in all its rich splendor.

"There's more," Mei said, hobbling around to the far side of the table to take a fresh scroll down off the wall. "They're bringing someone with them . . . someone special, Aset says, who'll give a good account of himself when the big day comes."

"Someone new?" she said, instantly alert. "I don't like the sound of that. How do we know we can—"

"Aset vouches for him absolutely. She says they'll arrange a meeting with him as soon as they're within an hour's march from the city. Here, read for yourself." The old man handed over the scroll; she unrolled it and scanned it quickly.

"Hmmm," she said, letting it roll back into a tight cylinder. "She sounds quite taken with this Neko. Well, Aset is young and impressionable. But the endorsement from Isesi is something else. Perhaps he'll turn out to be useful, after all."

"I hope so," Mei said warily. "We'll need all the help we can get. Mara, if we fail—"

"Don't say that!" she interrupted hotly. "Don't even *think* it. We'll succeed. We've got to!"

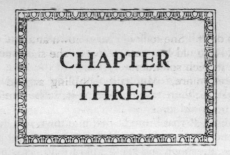

CHAPTER THREE

Thebes

I

Second in command of the Thebes garrison in spite of his youth, Riki would ordinarily lead a long line of aides and underofficers wherever he went, particularly when coming in from the field to confer with Baliniri. Riki's only superior in the garrison, Baliniri was a soldier's soldier, who had been Riki's mentor and model from his first days with the Egyptian army.

Now, alone, in weathered battle dress still dusty from maneuvers in the field, he strode through the streets of the old imperial city and headed for the palace. Chance soldiers and guardsmen passed in the street stiffened to attention and snapped off smart salutes, which were returned with an economy that bordered on sloppiness. Baliniri had not stood on ceremony, and Riki saw no reason to do so either.

He saw the banner above the palace that meant the king, Sekenenre, was in residence. Riki frowned. Had the monarch still been at his country villa, Riki would have had more time to chat with Baliniri without fear of interruption. But with Baka and Mekim away at the front on an inspection trip, Baliniri was acting as temporary vizier to the king. The king would probably keep Baliniri too busy for any lengthy conversation. Well, there was no helping it, so he would have to take what he could get.

The business that brought Riki into town was not terribly urgent in the first place, more like an excuse to get away from camp for an afternoon and see his old friend. Passing the pair of guards at the foot of the palace steps and accepting their salute with the most perfunctory of returns, he skipped up the shallow staircase two steps at a time, ignoring the trickle of petitioners who were making their way back down the stairs after the king's morning divan.

At the top he ran into a soldier he knew slightly. What was the fellow's name? Well, no matter. "Greetings," he said, keeping it neutral. "Is Baliniri in today?"

The soldier stiffened, saluted, relaxed. "Yes, sir. He's been with the king. Should be through any moment now. Sir . . . is there any truth to the rumor that some of us are going to the front next week?"

"How should I know?" Riki said with a grin. "I'm just a field trooper these days. Ask a garrison man. One of those painted staff officers in their dustproof finery." He clapped the soldier on the arm familiarly, grinned again, and moved away down the hall toward Baka's offices, where Baliniri had been temporarily installed.

He was just trying to make up his mind which of the three great doors to knock upon when the middle one opened and two prosperous-looking civilians came out, followed by Baliniri, looking downright regal himself in his garrison finery and his gray-streaked hair. As Riki neared, Baliniri said goodbye to his visitors and greeted his young protégé.

"Well," Baliniri said with a chuckle, "no need to ask where you've just come from. I can smell the horse manure."

"It takes an old captain of cavalry to recognize the aroma," Riki said in the same mood. "Can we talk somewhere?"

Without another word Baliniri ushered him into the office and followed him, closing the door. "What brings you here? I expected to be free of you." There was amused affection in his tone.

"I can take only just so much horse manure," Riki answered, sitting down on the far side of Baka's long conference table.

"So you came to town to reacquaint yourself with the variety of manure they dispense in the capital," his superior said, taking a seat himself. "Well, I can understand that. I spent half my life in the field wishing I were sleeping in a nice warm garrison bed, and the other half in a garrison wishing I were back in the field. As a matter of fact, I've spent the morning wishing just that." He made a face. "Hereditary princelings. War profiteers. Venal chiefs of the upper nomes."

"Ah, yes." Riki's brow went up comically. "Let's see. The official business . . . hmmm. Two sheiks came in to complain once more about having their caravans raided out along the desert paths from oasis to oasis. The old warrior-women story. I've heard it a million times. I'm getting to where I almost believe it myself, Baliniri. Am I losing my grip?"

Baliniri's smile was indulgent. "I keep trying to tell you, Riki, it's all true. Every word of it." Now the smile gave way to a chuckle. "Warrior princesses."

Riki's eyes flashed. "You've pulled that old joke on me once too often. Leading me to believe it was true, then letting me take that crazy story back to camp to make a fool of myself when I tried to tell it to the army."

"Oh? They didn't believe you?" The amusement had reached Baliniri's eyes, and he no longer even bothered to try to keep a straight face. "A good story like that one? Warrior princesses? Stark-naked warrior princesses, armed with spears and swords? Sticking people up on caravans and making them pay tribute?"

"You know damned good and well how they took it. They laughed about it in the mess for days."

"You should have ordered them not to laugh." Baliniri forced the merry smile off his face, but it kept coming back. "Besides," he said in a voice dripping with mock sincerity, "it's all perfectly true. All of it. The bare behinds and all."

"Stop the jokes!" Riki said, getting really angry. "The

point is, someone's holding up shipments along the caravan
routes through the eastern desert, and—"

"Are they, now?" Baliniri said. "Or is it perhaps a case
where some sheik has found a good opportunity for skimming
a bit of cargo off the top for himself when nobody's looking,
and blaming it on the, uh, warrior princesses?"

Riki's eyes went wide. "Damn! I'd never thought it out
that way. It sounds plausible. I'll have it looked into."

"Do," Baliniri said. "However, don't give up on the
naked warrior-girls. They're real."

"Yes," Riki retorted sourly. "They, and the creatures
from the Netherworld who creep out of the graves to carry
away bad children who won't eat their dinners. Let's change
the subject."

"All right," Baliniri said seriously. "I've intercepted a
runner from downriver. Apophis is arming heavily and steadily. He's been hiring mercenary soldiers from everywhere
under the sun and pressing into military service anyone who
can walk and lift a spear."

Riki sat up straight. "How reliable is the runner?"

"Very, I'd say," Baliniri answered. "We've heard the
same information from three separate sources so far. Apophis
is hauling in troops from everywhere."

"This looks like the big push, then?" Baliniri nodded;
Riki went on. "Do Baka and Mekim know it?"

"They must. I can't imagine Baka not having spies across
the border, can you?" But he shrugged, not altogether with
equanimity. "On the other hand, Baka isn't the man he was.
He hasn't been the same since his wife Mereet died, a
decade ago."

"And to my eyes he's always seemed so—well, formida-
ble," the younger man said.

"And well he is, still. But you would have to have known
the Baka of the earlier years. He's a shadow of that self,
believe me. A shadow. 'Everything I ever did as soldier or
administrator,' he told me once, 'I did for her. Everything
was done for her eyes to see, for her ears to hear.' "

"Can a woman do that for you?" Riki asked mildly.

Baliniri looked the young man up and down. Riki was
well below his own towering height but was well-built and

clear-eyed, a fine young figure of a man. *Good blood there*, thought Baliniri, wondering who the boy's father might have been. Word had it that Riki had been born twenty years ago right here in Thebes, the natural son of an important man. The boy's mother took him downriver to raise, probably so he would not be an embarrassment to his well-to-do father. Then Riki's mother had died, and Riki had had to make his own way in the streets of Avaris for years. When the savage order had come down to kill all the ten-year-old boys in Lower Egypt, Riki, always self-possessed and competent, had gathered up his little friend Mara and made the epic journey upcountry to freedom. He suddenly wondered what had happened to little Mara. He had always expected something to develop between Riki and the girl.

"Whatever happened to Mara?" Baliniri asked.

"Someone told me she went back to Avaris," Riki said. "She had this obsession about assassinating Hakoris. I told her to leave well enough alone, but she wouldn't listen. Why do you ask?"

"Just wondered. You've never been in love, then?"

Riki laughed. "Love? I'm a soldier of the Thebes command. You know what soldiers think about love."

Baliniri looked at him knowingly. "You'll learn. Just when you least expect it. A flash of skirt will go by, and you'll drop whatever you're doing and make a damned fool out of yourself, just as the rest of us always have. And she'll break your heart, my friend. It's the thick-shelled people like you who fall the hardest when the time comes."

Riki laughed and shook his head. "Not I," he said. "Bachelor for life. Married to the army." He waved away Baliniri's protestations and deftly steered the conversation right back where he wanted it. "So Apophis is massing troops on the border, then? This looks like the big push at last?"

"Yes. I just hope they wait until we've had a chance to reorganize the defenses. I'd like to take a hand in that myself. Mekim—"

He stopped, puzzled. How to say it? Mekim was his oldest friend in the world. They had been through hell together, soldiers under Hammurabi when he was remaking the whole way of life of the Land of the Two Rivers. Mekim

the perfect underofficer, and look what they had done to him!
They had made a general of him! They had taken him out of
his natural element, in which he was the best man in the
world, and put him into one in which he was grossly
underqualified. General? In charge of the Lisht front? Facing
the enemy directly? While the Hai armed, doubling their
numbers by hiring mercenaries and preparing for a great
offensive to crush the Egyptian armies, Mekim had been put
in charge of defense. This was the stuff of which tragedy was
made. If only the Hai would wait, wait until he, Baliniri,
could get up there and reorganize the Egyptian defenses!

II

At the sound of her name, Tuya turned, looked out
across the sea of faces in the crowded bazaar below her, and
saw her servant Cheta hurrying toward her.

"Ma'am," Cheta said, drawing near at the foot of the
stairs and standing one step down from her mistress, "a lady
came by the house and wanted to see you. She said it was
important. She'll be back this afternoon."

"I may not be home by then," Tuya said. "She didn't
give her name?"

"No, ma'am. And—ma'am, I have a feeling she's some
kind of trouble. She had a young boy with her, about ten. I
didn't like her. I didn't like her face."

"All right. I'll watch my step. Don't let her in when I'm
not there. Was there something else?"

"Yes, ma'am." The servant brushed her graying hair
back with one hand. When she joined Tuya on the same step
she towered over her mistress. Embarrassed, she went back
to the lower step, and the two pairs of eyes met on a level.
"Master Ketan called. He said he'd try to find you here in the
bazaar."

Tuya looked around quickly. "I haven't seen him. Has
Nebet's time come yet?" Her cousin-by-marriage, Ketan, and

his wife, Nebet, a tiny, small-boned ex-dancer, were expecting a child any day now. After three stillbirths, Ketan was a nervous wreck.

"Not yet, ma'am. And, ma'am, somebody came by looking for Master Seth."

"Ah, now." Tuya repressed an indulgent smile. She had not seen her son for several days, and his odd ways had all but exhausted her capacity for surprise. Everyone seemed to be acquainted with him, really. "Somebody in rags? Or somebody looking like the master of the world?"

Cheta grinned. She was very fond of Master Seth. "About halfway between, ma'am, and leaning more like the second way. He described himself as a doctor. He had a funny accent."

Tuya snorted. "At least it's not someone wanting a formula for transmuting metals again. Although even if it were, Seth would probably be more patient with him than I would. Well, a doctor . . . maybe this one can pay for the consultation for a change."

"Yes, ma'am, he looked that well-off. But you know Master Seth. He'll probably forget to charge him."

Tuya sighed in agreement. Whoever this doctor fellow was, he would get an answer out of Seth that he could profit from, and he would probably get it for free. All from a tall, skinny, appallingly absentminded young genius who wore tatters because he forgot to change clothes, whom the street-urchins had to remind to eat at regular intervals, who slept when and where he happened to grow tired, be it day or night . . .

She chuckled and shook her head, thinking of her strange, brilliant, comical, lovable son. What an odd, endearing figure he was! The last time she had seen him—she had brought him an expensive robe, only to see him give it away to a drunk in the street as he talked to her—she had suddenly looked down and saw that he had one foot sandaled, the other foot bare. He had had not the slightest idea where and when he had lost the other shoe. And as he had puzzled over the matter, a young engineer had introduced himself to Seth and asked a question about the construction of siege machinery that had baffled designers and engineers ever since the Twelfth Dynasty. Seth had solved the problem with a single sentence and had days later waved away with complete disinterest the news that the engineer's "invention" had won him handsome rewards at court. Seth could not be bothered about such matters. Once the problem was solved, it was no longer of any interest to him.

Thank God we're rich, she thought. His improvident ways need never cause him to starve. All he had to do was come home to eat and dress well and sleep in a soft bed, and be waited on hand and foot by Cheta and—yes—herself. But he rarely took advantage of that, for he had a total disregard of all creature comforts. Houses, possessions, slaves—they were nothing to him. Beggar and millionaire alike lined up with their problems and were in turn treated exactly alike, with a half-distracted air easily mistaken for indifference.

"Was that all?" Tuya asked now.

"Yes, ma'am," Cheta said.

"You may run along, then. I still have an errand or two. I'll be home in time for dinner. Don't forget Kedar, Seth's old tutor, is due to come by the house this evening."

She watched the woman move away through the crowd. Her eyes lighted on the tall, unmistakable Baliniri, the king's general. He stood there for no more than a heartbeat or two, his eyes idly scanning the crowd, and then he moved away, out of sight. He gave no evidence of having seen her, much less of having recognized her.

She turned away and hurried up the stairs to the top of the street. To her intense chagrin, she found that she was shaking. She gripped the stair rail, angry with herself. *Surely the sight of him can't do this to me now*, she thought. *Not after this many years.*

But there you were. You had no control over these things. She had thought the whole thing dead: her feelings as well as his. Baliniri and she had had that brief, bittersweet affair almost two decades before, at a time when her now-deceased husband, Ben-Hadad, lost in his own emotional turmoil, had been neglecting her shamefully. She had been so lonely, heartbreakingly lonely; but guilt-stricken, she had given up Baliniri and gone back to her husband, only to regret it immediately.

Years later, after Ben-Hadad's death, she and Baliniri had reunited for a single night, trying to rekindle the old feeling. It had been a disaster. And since then, the two of them had done all they could to avoid meeting, and she had lived a celibate life. For all she knew, he had done the same. By now he had the reputation of a man wedded to work and position only.

Now with Seth grown and rarely at home, she had found her loneliness almost too much to bear. If men of a proper age and station had been available here in Thebes . . . But the men here were striplings or too old or only interested in the fortune Ben-Hadad had left her.

Not for the first time she found her thoughts turning toward Kedar, the gentle, good-hearted, sensitive foreigner from the distant north who had been the first to understand fully Seth's amazing mind. Before Kedar had finally succeeded in making contact with the uncommunicative child, most people had thought Seth to be of subnormal intelligence.

It had been different with Kedar from the first day. The tutor said that Seth's intelligence was beyond the average adult's ability to fathom and that the reason the boy had been uncommunicative was that children his own age bored him; indeed, most adults would bore him for the same reasons. So she had eventually moved Kedar into a wing of the house near the boy and allowed him to live there for some years. He had been unassuming and unobtrusive and had insisted on eating with the servants except on such occasions as festival days, when Seth had insisted on his presence with rare firmness.

There had, however, come a time when Kedar had told her that the boy knew everything he knew, and that it was time for Seth to measure himself against the strongest adult minds in Thebes or Lisht. She had reluctantly packed Seth off, with an older boy for company, to a higher school in Lisht. He had lasted no more than six months there before writing her one of his infrequent letters saying that he had exhausted the finest minds there and wanted to come home. But by then Kedar had insisted on finding newer, more modest quarters of his own once again.

She had missed him. How often she had sought him out

over the years, to discuss this and that, not always about
Seth. His answers had always been couched in different
terms than Ben-Hadad's, and if Kedar's judgments about
people were incorrect, he erred on the side of charity. Her
thoughts turned toward him more often, and his good points
had worked their way into her mind and heart. When she
had run into him in the street a week before, she had impulsively invited him to the house tonight. She smiled a secret
smile. She had inquired about him. He had been married
once, and his wife had died. Good: She would have had no
interest in a man who could have remained a bachelor at his
age. It had explained why she had always felt comfortable
around him.

Comfortable. The word, at her stage in life, had a welcome quality all its own, one it would not have had earlier
on, when the juices had still run hot in her veins and she had
still been capable of passion. But passion had been burned
out of her first by Ben-Hadad, then by Baliniri. Now she
wanted a quiet, settled life with a man who would not be
shaking her up all the time. No surprises.

"Tuya!"

The single word broke her reverie, and she looked up to
see her cousin, Ketan, approaching, tall, beautifully dressed,
and distinguished looking.

"Well," she said, smiling fondly, "how's the prospective
father?"

"I'm going crazy," he confessed. "False alarms, one after
the other. Tuya, after three births that ended in—"

"Hush!" she cut in. "It's bad luck. Trust the gods. How
is Nebet doing?"

"Better than I am. Look at me! I'm a mess. I had to close
up the shop until all this was over."

She looked at his elegant turnout and made a face.
"Shop? Then you've definitively made the transition? You're
no longer making weapons?"

"Oh, no," he said. "I make jewelry, expensive jewelry. I
was never very good as an armsmaker, Tuya. I take after my
grandfather Hadad. As a matter of fact, I met a man from
Carchemish who said my designs reminded him of Hadad's.
What a pleasure it was to see the surprise in his eyes when

I told him I was Hadad's grandson. By the way, one of my customers wanted to find Seth." He looked around him. "He used to wander around here, didn't he?"

"That was a long time ago. He set up a new shop in the Market of the Four Winds."

"There?" he said, incredulous. "But that's so . . . so *common!*" He gave the word the emphasis one might give a disease.

"Exactly why he likes it. Among the poor, he says, no questions or concerns are ever trivial, as they are here." She nodded thoughtfully. "From my own childhood I can confirm the truth of that one."

Ketan, who had come from a family never wanting for money, looked confused. "Uh . . . I'll send him there. Wish Nebet and me luck, Tuya. We can use all we can get just now." He gulped. "If anything were to happen—I mean to Nebet . . ."

She squeezed his hand and smiled, silently thanking her lucky stars that her own years of passion and childbearing were done.

III

As Ketan moved down the street, he suddenly felt a stabbing pain in his thigh, so sharp and excruciating that he cried out and bent over to clutch at it, thinking he had been stabbed in some bizarre accident. But he could find no visible reason for the pain: no blood, no contusion, no mark.

The pain forced him to limp out of the street traffic, seeking an unoccupied bench upon which to sit down. He gritted his teeth and pressed his hands on the offending spot, and after a few minutes of acute pain, the sensation began slowly to fade. Several passersby, having noticed his distress, stopped to ask what was wrong, and he motioned them away a little peevishly.

He knew what had happened, of course. It had happened to him fairly frequently all his life, and there was not a thing in the world that he could do about it when it happened.

Teti! he thought. *What sort of trouble has she got herself into now?* And, for easily the thousandth time, he cursed the trick of fate that had created the strange, irrational link between him and his twin sister. Ever since their birth he had been able to feel her pain, and she his. If one had been hurt in a fall, the other cried, regardless of how far apart they happened to be at the time.

But this far apart? he thought. This was really unusual. She had to be many days' march away. He shook his head. The pain was ebbing. It would remain a dull ache for some time, though, and feel quite stiff.

And the irony is we have not been terribly close for some years.

Not since Teti had gone to Nubia as armorer for the army, fallen in love with a brave young soldier, and lost him in the war—while Ketan himself had had that disastrous, violent affair with Taruru the dancer, only to be pulled back from the brink of death by the staunch loyalty and devotion of dear little Nebet, whom he had married soon afterward. For a time he had hoped that, as his and Teti's dependence upon each other lessened, the strange bond that made them feel each other's pain would go away as well. But no such luck!

He massaged the leg and cursed as the pains suddenly came back. Then he shook his head in disgust at the odd twist of fate that had made them, fraternal twins, so different in such important ways. He had been as little like a traditional Child of the Lion as it was possible to be—scion of a long and legendary family of armsmakers, he had little interest in the warlike uses of metal, and the moment he had trained his assistants to take over for him, he had dedicated himself to the more peaceful—and artistic and lucrative—creations of jewelry and small sculptures. A fine Child of the Lion he was! If he had not borne the distinctive birthmark on his back (a port-wine stain shaped like the print of a lion's paw), he would doubt his own bloodlines.

As a Child of the Lion he had proved to be a failure, as had Seth, his kinsman. The only surviving Child of the Lion who successfully carried forward the traditions of the family was Teti. A girl! Yet she unquestionably had the gift, and had from the first. In the earliest days of their apprenticeship, she had had the better fist at making weapons, whereas his own skills leaned toward the artistic, the refined.

Furthermore, Teti was the first, and so far the only, female of their line ever to bear the family birthmark, the legendary Mark of Cain, which, rumor had it, had been put on their remotest ancestor, the rebellious son of First Man and First Woman, after he had killed his brother in a fit of anger.

Well, no matter. As long as she took care of the armorer chores for the family, it freed him to follow his own inclinations. By and large, he could forget about wars . . . that is, until something happened to Teti and he was forced to feel her pain.

Damn you, Teti! he thought. *Why can't you stay out of trouble!*

"You, boy," the distinguished visitor to the Bazaar of the Four Winds said. "I'll give you an *outnou* if you can find for me the savant Seth."

"An *outnou*?" the young man asked, a puzzled and distracted look on his face. He ran his fingers through his already badly mussed hair. "That's far too much for so simple a service. A copper ring, perhaps. No more." He was about to turn away when a thought struck him. "*Hmmm*. I wonder how long copper will stay the medium of exchange. Since the blockade, it's worth almost as much as gold." He looked at the visitor, not as a separate entity but as a soundingboard for the odd thought that had just invaded his mind. "We'll probably use a different standard for money one of these days. Seems very likely. The values have to even out sometime. . . ."

"What are you talking about, boy?" the visitor demanded haughtily. "I asked for directions, not inane irrelevances." He heard loud giggling behind him, high-pitched and disrespectful, and wheeled to find two street-urchins laughing at him. "Get away, you little rabble!" he hissed. "Be off with you!"

They looked at the young man, who was still muttering

to himself. He blinked and nodded at them, and his hand vaguely motioned it all away: the two urchins, the visitor, perhaps even the bazaar itself. "Go along, boys. But—wait. I know you two. Is your mother still ill?"

"Yes. The miller's wife came in this morning to help. But Mother can't get up."

"*Hmmm.*" His brow knitted. "Then you haven't eaten. Go to the baker's. Tell him I sent you. But don't steal any rolls. Do you hear me? We don't steal around here. And . . . uh . . . send the miller's wife to see me. Maybe I can give her something."

"Confound it!" the visitor said, drawing himself up to a not-terribly-impressive height. "Isn't anyone going to pay me any attention around here? I'm looking for—"

"Oh, no," the young man said, looking down at his ragged tunic. He had torn a hole in it. He ripped off the hanging shred and tossed it aside. "I wonder how that happened. I don't think it was that way yesterday. Or was it the day before? I've got to get organized one of these days."

"Maybe you didn't hear me," the exasperated visitor said. "I offered you good money to find me—"

"Oh," the young man said. "That." He shrugged. "You ought to consider whether those directions you need are worth a whole *outnou.* You know what they say about a fool and his money being easily parted."

His tone was annoyingly avuncular, and his visitor stood aghast, looking at him, mouth open, eyes wide and startled. He looked the young man up and down: tousled hair, a vague expression, the single tattered garment, sandals of straw and not leather, a general impression of poverty and neglect.

"Well!" the man said, disgusted. "That's what I get for coming into a bad neighborhood in the first place—insolence from strangers, lectures about how to conserve my money from a ragamuffin who can't even afford proper clothing, and—"

"Please calm yourself, sir," the young man said. "Someone's going to find you crumpled up somewhere, clutching your chest. Tell me: How long has your heart been beating too fast? Do you experience shortness of breath? Do you—"

"What the devil are you talking about?" the visitor demanded, his voice rising. "Do you have any idea whom you are talking to? I'm Mil-kili, personal physician to—"

"I know who you are," the ragamuffin said patiently. All of a sudden he seemed coherent, focused. "But that fancy job won't save you if you disregard your own advice, the advice you charge rich people so much money for. I'm sure you own a good bronze mirror. Well, look at yourself, then. The puffiness in your face, at the red eyes—"

"You have some nerve!" said the visitor, confused by the young man's accurate estimation of his health. "What makes you think . . ."

The younger man gently went on: "Also, sir, you must give up the palm wine. It's going to kill you. If you'd take care of yourself, you may have ten or twelve productive years left." He clapped the visitor on the arm familiarly and was about to turn away, his mind already elsewhere. "Wheat," he said. "The price of wheat. But no. That's even higher than copper, since the crops failed in the Fayum this year. No, no, it has to be something that doesn't fluctuate. . . ."

The visitor stared, stunned. "You?" he asked incredulously. "*You're* Seth?"

"Actually, wood has some advantages, being relatively scarce around here. Trees don't grow south of the line, not until the marsh country near the Sudd. Wooden coins? But no. They wouldn't bear the heavy usage, not the way copper does." He blinked and looked at his visitor, not seeing him at all. "And they'd be no good at all for trade—not in countries with different weather patterns."

"*You're* Seth?" the visitor asked.

"Pardon?" The young man's eyes came back into focus. "Oh, yes. Stop drinking. Today. Now if you'll excuse me . . ."

"Confound it!" the visitor sputtered. "And here I'd hoped to get some help. I'll know better than to ask advice from—"

"I've heard about your problem," Seth said. "You need something to keep a wound from getting infected in the early stages."

"Wh-why, that's right," the visitor said. "Although how you'd know *that*—"

"Are you married?" the young man asked.

"Uh . . . my wife died a year ago, but I don't see what—"

"Any women around your house, young and of marriageable age?"

"I have two daughters."

"Good. Then you'll have an excellent remedy right around the house. What patients are you experimenting upon now?"

"Soldiers from the front. More often, sailors who get into knife fights in the taverns."

"Forget the soldiers. By the time you get them, the wound'll already be infected. Try this on the sailors, the moment they bring them in, while the blood's still flowing."

"Try what? You haven't said—"

"Green eye shadow," the young man said. "Take a vial from your daughters, but make sure they haven't used it yet. They go paddling about in the stuff with dirty fingers, stained with kohl. It's a wonder they don't put their eyes out."

"*Green eye shadow?*"

"Why, yes," the young man said, his interest already beginning to fade. He had prescribed the remedy and had little interest in explaining his reasons. "Clean the wound off with the green eye shadow, then smear on honey, plain honey, right out of the comb. Never mind the aromatic resins you usually add."

"But—"

"It's the copper salts in the eye shadow," the young man said, his tone matter-of-fact. "They're good for cleaning out things. The honey's to keep infection from taking hold." He looked at the visitor in the eye, winked, and smiled. "I'll bet you thought it was the resins that did it. No. It's the honey. Take it from me: Whatever it is that causes the infection, it can't live in honey."

He turned away, his mind already fading away into some strange and different world of his own. And the astonished doctor noted, as the young man turned to go, that his garment was torn in the back as well, showing a generous expanse of bare buttock as he moved away into the sparse crowd, muttering distractedly to himself, his hands gesturing to an imaginary audience visible to no eye but his own.

IV

Coming around a corner, Riki came within a hair of plowing into Seth, who had left the bazaar and was moving willy-nilly down the dusty street, eyes cast down, mouth moving silently, the fingers of one hand ticking off a list on the outstretched fingers of the other. Riki stepped back nimbly and let the young man pass—and, looking beyond, saw Seth's kinsman Ketan standing in a doorway, looking on. The two men's eyes met and locked, and Ketan, indicating Seth with a curt nod of the head, completed Riki's thought with a shrug, as much as to say *Well, that's the way he is, isn't it?*

Riki spoke after Seth was out of earshot. "Someone ought to put a bell on him. Then people would know to step out of the way."

Ketan smiled wryly. "It would make more sense than trying to get him to show some awareness of his surroundings." He changed the subject. "How are you, Riki? I thought you were in the field with the army."

"I was," Riki said. "I came in to talk to Baliniri. And you? I heard you'd left the army."

"Yes," Ketan said, a tinge of defiance in his answer. "I wasn't really cut out for the work."

Riki snorted. "Ah, yes. I heard. Jewelry? A Child of the Lion, making jewelry?" There was something about Ketan that Riki, dyed-in-the-wool soldier that he was, did not like.

"Why not? I hope you don't think ill of my new trade. After all, it was the central concern of my uncle, Hadad of Haran." He sniffed a little haughtily. "And no one thought less of him for it."

Riki almost added: *But Hadad was a cripple and had a cripple's excuse.* . . . "Well, as long as you understand that in time of emergency you'd be pressed into service."

"This far upriver?" Ketan asked in disbelief. "Now Riki, that's hardly likely."

"It could happen," Riki retorted. "There's word that Apophis is arming for a big push. Bringing in mercenaries from everywhere under the sun. I expect an attack in force any day now."

He was about to continue when something in his mind told him not to. His disgust with Ketan made him blurt out more than he had intended. "But keep that to yourself. I shouldn't be talking about it in the street."

Ketan shrugged and started to walk away. "Good fortune to you." What was it about Ketan, Riki asked himself, that so irritated him? Maybe it was that he had chosen to leave the army. People said that all the guts in the family went into the fellow's twin sister, Teti, wherever she was. He had heard that learning the secret of making iron was an obsession with her.

Yes. He remembered it all now: After her lover was killed in battle, she had gone off with an old man, Karkara of Sado, to learn the secret of forging iron from him. She had abandoned all traditional feminine pursuits and, subsidized by the fortune Shobai had left behind, had taken on a boy's tunic, a boy's trade, a boy's rough-and-ready speech.

Well, Baliniri said she had, anyway. He himself had never met her. But apparently Baliniri had at one time become friends with the tall armorer with the close-cropped hair.

Riki frowned. He suddenly wondered if anything had happened between Baliniri and the girl. But no. There would have been too great an age discrepancy. Baliniri was nearing sixty, and Teti was half his age or less. Surely there would be no connection of that kind between the two of them!

But there was also the fact that Baliniri, a man in whom the juices of life still flowed strongly, had had nothing to do with women since he had returned to Thebes.

Riki's curiosity was aroused now, and he thought again about Teti. People always spoke of her as a towering, statu-esque goddess of a woman, a lover fit for a legendary war hero, a consort fit for a warrior king. Where was she now? Surely such a person could not just pass from the world's sight like that. He would have to inquire.

One thing was sure, Baliniri would not tell him. No matter. He would find out somehow. He would find out who she was, and where, if it killed him.

He wondered if Teti had ever learned how to make iron. *Be a good thing for Egypt if she did*, he thought. He had had his hands on a real iron sword once, practiced fencing drills with it, and had begun to get used to it. It had been quite an experience. It was heavy, of course—very heavy. Just learning to fence with it required new and strenuous exercises to develop the muscles of the forearm. And you could not whip the thing about and cut with it quite the same way as a copper weapon. But when you did hit with it—ah, that was another matter! Two strokes with it, forte to forte, on a copper blade, and the other man's sword would be ruined. And the shock of a parried swing could knock the weapon out of the hand of a man armed with a copper sword!

How he wished he owned one! But the only way he would ever get one would be to kill a man who was attacking him with one, and that was not likely.

Unless . . .

He began to walk down toward the river. This big push of Apophis's . . . what if the old rascal had hired some Hittite mercenaries? The Hittites were armed with iron weapons. If he could survive an encounter with the likes of these—

"Psst!" A voice hissed from the opening of an alley just to his left. "Captain!" He wheeled, looked around. A beggar beckoned from the deep shade of the side street. "This way, Captain. Begging your pardon."

"You want me?" Riki asked.

"Yes, sir," the beggar said, his eyes darting to right and left. "This way, Captain. I've got somethin' for you. . . ."

Riki's hand went to his sword, just in case, as he approached cautiously. But as he followed the beggar back into the alley, it was evident the man was alone, incapable of doing serious harm to an armed and fit soldier. "What can I do for you, my friend?"

"It's not what you can do for me, sir. It's what a friend o' mine can perhaps do for you."

"A friend of yours? What are you talking about?"

The beggar turned his gaunt, scarred face toward him. "You put the word out in the bazaars, Captain," the beggar said. "You wanted information about a certain woman of Thebes, who used to live here twenty-odd years ago."

Riki's eyes narrowed. "I did ask around. I offered a reward, too. I suppose that's what you have in mind—"

"Only if the information's good, sir. Only if it all checks out to your satisfaction, Captain. But if we were to earn our reward, sir—"

"Never fear. I'm serious about paying for valuable information. The woman's name was Net. She was my mother. Anything I can learn about her life here in Thebes will be paid for."

"Good sir. I'm sure you'll be more than generous. My friend . . . he can't come to you. There was a judgment against him in the courts here, sir, and he can't cross the river. You'll have to talk to him in Deir el-Bahari. But he promises to give you information you don't have."

"Very well," Riki said. "Let's go there now."

"He won't be available until tonight, sir. He says he'll meet you in front of the fruit stand, over in the artisans' town. At sundown."

"All right," Riki said. "Of course if you've been stringing me along, or if someone thinks he can trick me—"

"Oh, no, sir!"

Riki stood, fists on hips, looking at him. Then, after a moment's thought, he dug into his purse, drew out a coin, and tossed it to the beggar, who caught it with a practiced hand. "There's more where that came from if your friend's information is good."

"Thank you, sir!"

The beggar scurried away down the alley and disappeared at the end of it. Riki frowned.

He'll probably be just another fake, with manufactured evidence. . . . How many of them had there been in the ten years since his return to Thebes and subsequent inquiries into his origins? A dozen at least. And despite all his inquiries, it was as if his mother had never existed, had never borne him.

How could a free woman have been so completely forgotten in a town this small? Or was something else at work here? Had his mother lied to him about his having been born here? About his father having been of high station? Might it have been nothing more than a reassurance to her bastard son that he was not just a faceless nobody born to a girl of the streets, a nobody whose father she could not produce because she did not know his name?

No! he thought. *I'm somebody! My father, whoever he was, had to have been someone of good blood, of stature, of accomplishment! Otherwise . . .*

With the "otherwise" there was a downward tug at his heart.

Damn the otherwise! he thought defiantly. *I'm what I make of myself, and that's a lot! Look at Baliniri, now. He was a self-made man, and he has risen very high in the world. If Baka died, Baliniri would be second in command in the kingdom. And did he need parents, a family, a pedigree to get him there, to make a somebody out of him?*

Gods of the firmament, he thought unhappily, *I'm not like Baliniri. I need to know who I am. I want to know where I came from. Who my father was. And why I have had this feeling all my life, that I'm destined for great things. Maybe if I knew where I have come from, it'd be easier to figure out where I'm going!*

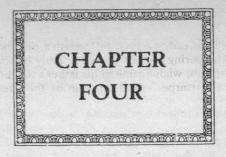

CHAPTER FOUR

Avaris

I

"I still don't feel right about this," Joseph said. He sat with Asenath watching their two sons toss a ball back and forth in the garden of the house Jacob had bought when he had been moved to Egypt from Canaan. "My brothers are sure to take it wrong."

"Let them," his wife said. "Your father's blessing is too important a tradition among your people to be ignored. Look at what his father's blessing meant to him, now."

Joseph did not answer but sat looking at her, seemingly with a stranger's eye. *She's really quite a handsome woman,* he thought, *with those flecks of gray in her hair. Quite regal. The patrician blood of Petephres's line breeds true. All the better for our sons, coming from such stock.*

And now he was planning to take those sons, Ephraim and Manasseh, to see their paternal grandfather, Jacob, and seek the old man's blessing, behind his brothers' backs and without their knowledge. This was surely asking for trouble!

And yet he had readily agreed to Asenath's plan, without his conscience bothering him for doing so. Truly he was a son of his father—Jacob, whose name in his father's tongue could be translated as "usurper"—and an heir to the great line of Abraham!

"Oh, by the way," Asenath said, "how did the magus do, Joseph? I understood he had hopes of curing Apophis's son Yahi. How did that come out?"

"Not well. The boy had a seizure right after Neferhotep gave him the treatment. Apophis flew into a rage, accusing him of casting the wrong spell and making the boy worse."

Asenath smiled with some satisfaction. "Anything that drives a wedge between those two can't be all bad. They've been as thick as thieves for far too long."

"Yes." Joseph sighed. "But let's not be too quick to exult over others' failures. There's always the chance that Apophis will command me to come forth and do my best. I confess I'm nervous about that. God has not spoken to me in a very long time. If I fail the way Neferhotep seems to be—"

"But Joseph, you've never claimed to be a healer. When God's spoken through you, it's always been as a seer, not as a healer. Why should Apophis—"

He threw up both hands. "Don't ask me why his mind works the way it does," he said exasperatedly. "Apophis is desperate, and desperate men do irrational things."

"But if he does call on you, Joseph, what will you do?"

Joseph closed his eyes. "Only what I'm already doing, my dear. I pray. I pray night and day for God to enter me once again, and speak through me, and tell me—tell us—what to do. These are very dangerous times. For all of us. And for all who come after us, as well."

Hakoris scowled and looked down into the half-empty bowl of wine before him. "Have you tried everything?" he asked. "Surely there must be some sort of nostrum—"

"Don't presume to tell me my business!" the magus retorted angrily. "I'm doing everything I can. I've given the boy everything you *can* give a child that young. There are stronger remedies, but they're for adults."

"Give them to the brat anyway," Hakoris said, not bothering to hide the contempt in his voice. "What do you have to lose? So the urchin dies. So what?"

"Easy enough for you to talk. You weren't there when Apophis threw that last tantrum. Gods! He's getting as bad as Salitis."

"Perhaps insanity is the Hai disease," Hakoris said. "All the more reason to wonder how long the Hai can hold onto a country they don't belong in and have no right to rule."

Neferhotep stared. "Well!" he said, a small and dangerous smile tugging at his lips. "We're getting bold these days, aren't we? Speaking open sedition in a public tavern, without so much as a by-your-leave. . . ."

Hakoris drank deeply, wiped his mouth, and made a face. "You forget. I picked the tavern. The landlord is as deaf as a post, and we're the only people here."

"And the slaves who clean off the tables?"

"Foreigners. More people who immigrated to Egypt to avoid starvation, and then wound up in bondage." He chuckled. "As Joseph and his family are doing, one day at a time." He held up one horny hand, grasping something invisible. "I'll have them in the palm of my hand—"

"Don't count your chickens before they're hatched," the magus warned. "Joseph is a survivor. He's lasted out a lot of crises before this."

"You believe in this mysterious, nameless God of his, then?" Hakoris's laugh was nasty, hateful.

"I just know he's lucky. Luck is more important than brains, or virtually anything else, for that matter."

Hakoris stared malevolently. "Use your head for a change. Let me tell you what's going to happen here. Apophis is about to cause his own downfall."

Neferhotep stared.

"Think," Hakoris said. "This military offensive of his. Even if it's successful, what will it accomplish?" He paused a beat, then went on. "For one thing, it'll bankrupt the kingdom, paying all those foreigners to soldier for us."

"But the idea is to take the Fayum. . . ."

"And a good thing, too. But you do not invite the wolf to help you tame the dog. He's filling this land with unmanageable mercenaries. He'll have to spend all his time trying to keep *them* in line. Look, man. What has kept the Hai in power all this time, eh?"

"The army."

"And where is the army now? Are they here, keeping the natives in line? No. They're up near the border, massing for an offensive against Baka. Coming here, through the streets, did you see any civil guards?"

"No."

Hakoris's tone was acid, biting. "There's no one guarding the city. No one but a token force. Eventually the populace will take notice. He tapped his forehead. *Think*. Is this place not ripe for revolution?"

"The—the revolution against the Hai? The one in Joseph's prophecy?"

"Does *anyone* in Egypt like the Hai? Approve of them? The country is filled with mercenaries who can't abide them and poor folk who came here to keep from starving and then ended up as slaves. With the born-and-bred locals grunting and sweating under the lash, their lands and properties seized by the Hai overlords, do you think anyone's forgotten that food production used to be in the hands of the Egyptians themselves, and not those of the Hai? That Egyptians used to be free? That Egyptian kings once sat on the throne of the Black Lands?"

"But the Hai have always been too strong to—"

"That's all a thing of the past. If Apophis wins this battle of his, it will be because of the foreigners. The soul of the Hai has been broken by their years of easy living. When they roamed the northern lands, driving their herds before them, living by fighting, they were a great people. But they weren't cut out for the soft life. They're no longer the Shepherd Kings, fierce and unyielding and invincible. Their time has passed."

Neferhotep's mouth hung open. How could he have failed to see it?

"When they fall," Hakoris continued, "I'll be here to pick up the pieces. And when I do—" he chuckled "—there's Joseph and that big Canaanite family of his. I have plans for them."

"But what if he should succeed with young Yahi where I seem to be failing?"

"You'd let him get by with that?" Hakoris challenged. "You wouldn't get to whatever nostrum Joseph prescribes for the child and make sure it's poisoned, so Joseph's blamed for the results? Or make sure that when Apophis calls Joseph to the palace, the great vizier doesn't get there. All manner of things could happen to a man on the way from that country house of his to the palace, particularly with the civil guard cut to the bone and bodyguards scarce. Who knows what sort of accident could happen?"

Neferhotep's eyes were wide open now, and his lips were set in a thin line. "I've underestimated you," he said with the beginning of a dark and secret smile. "I'll not make that mistake again, my friend."

II

By the time the crier, atop the wall half a block away, had called the hour, there were already over a dozen conspirators gathered in Mei's little apartment. Still Isesi resisted the temptation to call the meeting to order, and Aset went once more to the heavily curtained window to peek out into the street.

"No sign of her yet," she reported. "I wonder what's keeping her."

It was not like Mara to be late, and Aset was annoyed, having looked forward to showing off her handsome new friend, Neko, to the group in general and Mara in particular. Mara, as beautiful as Aset was plain, usually attracted whatever male attention there was, but this time, for the first time, it was Aset who intended to impress everyone with the dynamic young man she had brought to the meeting.

"We'll have to start without her," Isesi said, looking around at the seated conspirators. "I can't hold these people much longer. Some have other appointments tonight."

Aset stared, still annoyed. What a thing to say! What sort of appointment would one be making the night before their desperate and dangerous mission? Nevertheless, it was better to get the meeting over with, even with Mara absent. After all, she could always be filled in later on what she had missed.

"All right," Aset sighed. "Better begin."

She looked around and saw Neko sitting in a chair by the far wall, holding a place for her. He smiled and motioned to her to come, and her heart beat a little faster for it. How thoughtful he was! Blushing, she made her way to his side through the row of benches. The room was so crowded, it could hardly have held four more people; Mei must have borrowed every chair and bench in his building. She sat down, not quite daring to look Neko in the eye, still very conscious of her blush.

"Aren't you excited?" he asked.

"Yes," she admitted. "It's just that I was hoping to introduce you to a friend of mine who was supposed to be here in time for the meeting."

"Well, we'll all meet tomorrow. And after the day's business has been done, we'll all meet as old friends anyway, friends who have been through something together. That's always the best basis for friendship."

He reached out and patted the back of her hand lightly, and his touch was a shock wave that ran through her. This time she did turn her head a bit and smile shyly, and when she did, she thought she could see in his brown eyes just a touch of real affection. Her heart thrilled at the thought.

I'm the luckiest girl in the world, she told herself.

She had never been so excited. Or so happy.

Asenath came down the hall from her sons' suites. "This has been an exhausting, exciting day," she said. "A nice day."

Joseph smiled. "Come and sit with me." He made a place for her on the long couch.

"They're growing into such handsome young men. I wish your father could have seen them," she mused.

"He's not blind." Joseph snorted, sitting back against the

cushions. "He can see when he has to. Were you fooled by
his nonsense of not knowing which boy was the firstborn?"

"You mean he knew?"

"Of course. That business about giving Ephraim the
blessing instead of his older brother . . . it's getting to be a
tradition in our family. Believe me, Jacob knew what he was
doing. He whispered to me, 'I know, son. The elder one will
found a tribe too, and he'll be a great person in the world.
But the younger will surpass him and become the father of
nations.'"

"Goodness. And he meant that?"

"Yes. He also told me that he was leaving to me and my
line an extra portion of land, 'one I wrested from the Amorites
by force of arms.'" He chuckled. "Ultimogeniture rears its
ugly head again. Favoring the youngest son."

"But, Joseph. You'll never want, or need, an extra portion of land in Canaan."

"I know. But if he offers it, I'll accept and deed it over to
the boys. You realize what he's done, then? He's made our
line into not one tribe, the tribe of Joseph, but into two lines,
the tribes of Ephraim and Manasseh. He's passed my generation by and treated both my sons as the equals of my brothers." He whistled softly and shook his head. "They won't take
well to that! He's giving our sons Shechem, of all places.
Shechem! Where Reuben and the others put the citizens to
the sword. Shechem, where my brothers, years later, threw
me into the pit to die. Shechem, where the Ishmaelites took
me away to sell me into slavery."

"Poetic justice, I say," Asenath commented, surprising
Joseph. "If it's an affront to them, it's one they begged for on
bended knee."

"Now, Asenath," Joseph soothed, taking her hand, "you've
always encouraged me to forgive them. You must too. My
brothers are sincerely sorry for what they did to me. It is now
up to me to give them whatever absolution I can."

She looked curiously at him. "Sometimes I don't understand you," she confessed. "But even when I don't understand you, I've learned to trust what you say. You're a good
man, Joseph."

"I am a man of many failings," Joseph said. "Why else

would God not have spoken through me for such a long time." He sighed. "If only . . ." The second sigh was longer and deeper than the first. "But it is in God's hands, not mine. It is not mine to say when the power will come back, if indeed it ever does."

Asenath did not say anything for what seemed quite a long time. Joseph turned and looked at her.

"I . . . I've been worrying," she said into the void. "What if Apophis *does* call you in to help with his son?" Her eyes searched his. "If the magus is failing . . ."

He did not answer for a long moment. But when he did, it was with a sigh that matched her own.

Neko excused himself early from the meeting and went out into the night, having first arranged to meet his friends in the morning. As he went out the door, he noticed the disappointment on Aset's face; there was a tug at his heart, but he steeled himself and slipped out into the mild evening to walk briskly down the half-strange, half-familiar streets.

Where am I now? he asked himself. *Is this the Street of the Dry Well?* No, this was a different quarter altogether. And that up there, that was the opening to a bazaar. But which bazaar?

Yes, he did remember this one, he decided as he turned off into the now-deserted square and looked around. Even though he could not remember its name, he knew that there was a crack in the mud-brick wall of the building opposite, one nobody had ever bothered to fix. He and his mother had shopped here, back before—

He stopped, leaned against the wall, closed his eyes against the sudden pain, and wished that he had suppressed the memories before they had come full-blown into his mind.

Mother!

For so long he had avoided thinking of her, fearing the ache in his heart, the sense of loss, the guilt. If only he had been older, stronger, and more able to protect her, perhaps he would have been able to save her. Perhaps he would have been able to kill his father, Aram, or at least disable him so that the three of them—he, Mother, and Riki—could have gotten away.

But he had not. And he had seen her killed before his eyes.

Impotently he balled his fists and, in a moment of mad rage, smashed his knuckles against the wall. The blow sent a stabbing pain up his arm, and he immediately wished he had not given way to his emotions.

Yes. That was the way. Suppress your emotions. Discipline them. Letting them out like that only made you vulnerable. He had learned that in the years at the refuge. He had learned not to cry or to think about Mother or to let anyone know what he was thinking.

He looked at his hurt hand in the moonlight. It was bleeding a bit, but when he flexed it, no bones appeared to be broken. Good. He would have to use the hand in the morning—perhaps, to kill a man or two. And if his heart's desire was granted by the gods, it might be Hakoris!

Suddenly the bazaar seemed totally familiar to him, and he knew exactly where he was. With an odd gleam in his eye, his movements those of a man in a trance, he moved down the street, slowly at first, then picking up speed. He strode, single-minded, past dwellings, a storehouse, a tavern; past a pair of lovers coupling in an alley, past an aging whore standing in a doorway, still hoping to find custom for her wares despite the hour. He turned right, made his way down the long alley to the broad thoroughfare beyond—

And there it was. The Children's Refuge. Huge, imposing, windowless. Dark and forbidding, like the fortress it was. Walled, with great wooden gates that one of the conspirators would have to scale in the morning; the lock could not be forced with any implement they were likely to have.

It had been his home for more years than he cared to remember, and he had come closer to dying there than ever after, despite the violent and dangerous life he had led following his escape. Even now he bore scars received there, on both his body and his soul, and had dreams of still being a boy-slave there, owned heart and soul by Hakoris, dreams from which he would awaken screaming, covered with cold sweat.

Hakoris! And Sutekh!

He cursed below his breath, remembering the overseer's hated name for the first time in years. His hatred for Hakoris had stayed with him, but somehow he had managed to forget Sutekh, in name if not in deed. Now, effortlessly, he called back a white-hot memory of the evil overseer's scarred face, with its ugly white slash from the empty eye socket to the corner of his sneering mouth.

Sutekh . . .

When Hakoris had called for punishment, it had always been Sutekh who administered it.

Gods! Neko prayed. *Let him still be alive! Let his neck come within the reach of these two hands!*

As the meeting was breaking up, Mara finally arrived. Aset hurried to her side.

"Where were you?" the girl asked. "There was someone I wanted you to meet."

"Time enough for that, dear," Mara said. "Where's Isesi? Oh, there you are! Isesi!" Aset's brother drew near, one brow lifted in the mildest of reproofs. "I'm sorry I'm late. But I've good news!"

"What?" Isesi asked. "We can use some good news just now!"

"Another detachment of guards was ordered to the front tonight. They left at sundown. The civil guard has never been at this low a level before. It's our chance!"

Isesi beamed at her. "Wonderful! And I have good news, too: a new addition to our little cabal, and a man whose hatred of Hakoris is as great as your own."

"I'll meet him later," she said. "Right now I've got to hear what the plans are. That is, if you don't mind going over it all just this once for my sake."

Aset stared. Quite unconsciously the darkly beautiful Mara had drawn Isesi under her spell, and he was acting like a lovesick youth, hanging on her every word. Mara seemed to have no awareness of her effect on him, or indeed on any other man. What was it about some girls, Aset wondered, that they could wrap a man around their finger like that, while girls like herself—

Aset sighed. For the first time she was not sorry that Neko had not been here to meet Mara when she arrived.

III

That night the moon rose full and bright, hanging in the sky like a malevolent pupilless eye. All across the city the malign influence of the moon made itself felt on the young and old, rich and poor, powerful and insignificant—a mood of depression and disquiet, frustration and anger, paranoia and desperation . . . even violence and premonition.

The skeleton guard left in the city was hard pressed to handle the results. In taverns in the poor quarters, fights broke out, spread into the street, and polarized entire neighborhoods as first one neighbor, then another stepped in and took sides. The guardsmen who waded into the crowd to drive the combatants apart were in turn attacked and severely beaten.

Domestic quarrels quickly turned to major conflicts as husbands and wives went at each another with fists, feet, and household implements. Children joined the disputes in defense of one parent against the other. Atop the city wall, two guardsmen quarreled, and one man hurled the other down into the dark streets, breaking his neck. Alarm bells rang almost constantly in every quarter.

In the palace Apophis strode up and down the halls, bellowing at his staff. "Where is Neferhotep? Why is he not here when I need him? Mehu! *Mehu!* Is the magus here yet?"

The little servant, his heart in his mouth, stammered, "No, Sire. We sent a man—"

"Send another! Bring him here now! Do you hear me?"

Mehu blinked. "Yes, Sire." But he did not move quite as quickly as he could have. Eyes flashing, Apophis flung a

medicine vial at the servant's head; Mehu ducked barely in
time, and the little flask glanced off his head as he went
hastily out the door.

Apophis cursed and stalked back to the nursery, where
he found a servant on her hands and knees, cleaning up the
mess his incontinent son had made. "Is he all right?" the king
asked.

The servant looked up. "He's sleeping, Sire," she said
quietly. "He's exhausted, I think. As you must be, Sire. It's
been a long session this time, and—"

"That's all right. When the magus has come and gone,
I'll take a sleeping draught, perhaps. I just can't bear to see
Yahi this way. Falling on the ground, with his eyes rolled
back up into his head."

"I know, Sire. You had such high hopes for him. . . ."

His eyes flashed again. "Had? I haven't given up on him
yet. Yahi will be all right, you'll see. This is just a stage he's
going through. He'll outgrow it. I'll find a cure. I'll find one if
I have to bankrupt this country to find it."

The nurse stood up and went to the basin to wash her
hands. "It is in the hands of the gods, Sire," she said evenly.
"If they wish the boy to be cured, it will happen."

"Please!" he said in a voice more ruled by despair than
anger. "No defeatism. I can't stand to listen to that kind of
talk. There'll be a cure. There—"

He stopped in midthought, and a pensive expression
came over his face. "In the hands of the gods, you said. That
may be so, but I've finished with the priesthood of Amon.
They've been no help at all! And as for the gods of my own
people, no one believes in them anymore. But . . ."

"Yes, Sire?"

Excitement lit Apophis's face. "Call Mehu back, will
you? I want to send him on an errand."

"At this late hour?"

"*All* of his time is mine!" he exploded. "As is all of
yours!" His eyes flashed with a mad inner fire.

"Yes, Sire," the servant managed to get out. "I . . . I
didn't mean—"

"See that you don't," he said. "You, or Mehu, or the
magus, or anyone. Least of all that damned foreigner Joseph.

If he dares to complain, regardless of what time of day or night I may choose to call on him—"

"J-joseph, Sire?" the servant echoed.

Tossing and turning in the narrow bed Isesi and Aset had laid out for him, Neko, drenched with sweat on a cool night, became Kamose once again and lived through the horrors of a past best forgotten and the conjectural horrors of a future that might be.

In his dream's eye, his beloved mother had come back to life briefly, only to die again at her lover's treacherous hands. It was his fate to relive that night from years long past when he and Riki had barely escaped with their own lives by diving into the Nile and swimming to freedom with the terrifying sight of his mother's violent death still before his young eyes.

And in his dream's eye he once again lived through a scene that had yet to come to pass, in which he confronted Aram—Apophis, king of Egypt—and called him to justice. . . .

"Father!" the dream-ghost of himself called out angrily to the towering, black-bearded giant.

The shape of his father turned, glaring down at him from his nine-foot height. "Yes?" he demanded in a fierce, deep voice. "Ah, *you*, you insignificant puppy! You dare to challenge me, do you? Prepare for the death I was cheated out of, the night I killed your mother!"

Neko's dream-self tried to lift the sword in his hands, but it was as heavy as a huge boulder. Even using both hands he could hardly lift it, much less wield it. "Gods!" he implored. "Help me, please! Give my arms the strength to—"

His father charged. But there he stood, unable even to lift his weapon, unable to defend himself, unable even to force his leaden feet to turn and run. . . .

Mara, too, dreamed of confrontation, not so much against the hated Hakoris as her own paralyzing, irrational fear. Having driven Hakoris down a long, dark hall, she now found him turned on her like a cornered animal, his eyes blazing with hatred. And in the blink of an eye she was no longer armed, no longer a full-grown woman, no longer wearing a warrior's tunic and body-armor. Instead she was small, un-armed, weak, and naked—naked the way Hakoris had kept her all the time she had been his slave.

Slave! She was still his slave! The terrible thought burned its way into her half-sleeping mind. She had escaped after knocking Hakoris unconscious, and in any court of law she would still be considered his property.

"Come here, you little bitch," Hakoris growled in the dream. "You won't escape from me again. Here, let's have a look at you, now!" His terrible hand closed on her thin wrist with a viselike grip, and her heart froze with terror as her body suddenly transformed into its lush, womanly shape. "Ah!" he said, leering at her hungrily. "Perhaps before I hand you over to the soldiers, I'll try you myself. What's left of you the soldiers can have. The *Bedouin!*" He gave that word especial emphasis. Everyone knew how the savage Maaziou used women.

His hand reached down to clutch at her body—

Joseph sat upright. "He's sending for me!" he said in a stricken voice. The bedclothes fell away.

"W-what?" Asenath muttered, coming awake. "What's the matter, my dearest?"

"The king," Joseph said weakly. "He's calling for me. Suddenly I knew, almost as if his hateful voice spoke in my mind. He's sending someone for me, to take me to the palace."

"In the middle of the night, Joseph?"

"That makes no difference. It's Yahi. The magus has failed. Now it's my turn, and if I can do nothing for the boy, we're doomed—you, me, our children, my father and broth-ers, and all their families."

"No, Joseph! Surely—"

"If only God would speak through me! If only He would come into my mind now." His anguish was deep and heartfelt.

But even as he said this, he was once more aware of the aching emptiness inside him, which only one Mind, only one

Presence, could ever fill. Despair hung around him, draining his life, while suddenly the darkness in the room deepened, and the shadows seemed ever more black and menacing.

It had been many years since Hakoris had been able to sleep in a dark room; total darkness filled him with unreasoning terror. Thus, beside the guttering fire, on both sides of the great hearth, oil lamps burned all night long.

He sat up and looked around. There was a chill in the air, and he reached for the robe at his bedside. Once covered, he touched the headdress he wore day and night, pulling it down low over his brow.

At the foot of his bed, his lean, naked Tyrian slave lay stretched out, uncovered, near the fire. Even in sleep her limbs unconsciously fell into wanton positions.

A decade earlier, Hakoris would have felt his loins powerfully responding to the sight of her fire-warmed nude body. But now his perversions had taken their toll, and the sight awakened only interests of a different kind. Having known no restraints in the ways he used women over the years, he had tried many experiments. In the process, his desire for the normal uses of a woman's body had cooled, and now nothing could arouse him but the thought of giving pain.

He looked more closely at the Tyrian woman, at the burns he had left on her breasts and belly after he had tied her up and used the tongs to pick embers out of the fire, at the welts his whips had left, at the manacle on her ankle, and at the long, sturdy chain that kept her anchored permanently to within three paces of the fireplace. He wondered idly if there would be any eroticism in having her depilated, head and body.

No. The need for sexual release was not what had awakened him. Watching her now he felt nothing at all. Something else had disturbed his slumber. . . . Something about the refuge, a premonition of sorts. A fire? An insurrection? Something required his attention, something that Sutekh could not handle by himself.

He frowned. Yes, that was very likely. Sutekh was not the man he once was. In the last year two minor uprisings had taken place, and Sutekh had dealt with them with uncalled-for violence. The city guards had come, and that was unforgivable.

In the old days, when he had first taken over the refuge, he had attended to such matters himself. It had gone better then. But then he had tired of looking after everything himself. With Sutekh acting as his overseer, he had been able to develop his lands and possessions. As a result of that freedom, he was now on the verge of a great coup in Avaris real estate: Very soon Petephres would die, and Joseph, without his protector, would be deposed as vizier—and when that day came, all the lands and properties that Joseph's relations had been allowed to accumulate since their arrival in the delta would fall into his, Hakoris's, hands.

But now Sutekh seemed to be losing his grasp. It was time to get rid of him. And considering how much Sutekh knew about his operations—how much Sutekh, in fact, knew about him—that meant only one thing: Sutekh must quietly join the crocodiles at the bottom of the Nile. A new overseer must be found to take his place.

But first, a surprise inspection, in the middle of the night to set to rest his feeling of foreboding and to find out what other weak links there might be in the chain of his possessions and chattels. Yes! Now! While the world slept!

A cold smile on his face, he dressed quickly and armed himself formidably with sword and dagger. Then, covering his street clothes with a dark robe that would be almost invisible in the deep shadows of the streets, he slipped silently out into the night.

IV

Hakoris had gone no more than a block down the dark streets when the sound of approaching hoofbeats caught his attention. He came to an abrupt halt and, pinpointing the direction from which the sound was coming, stepped back into a darkened doorway.

Hoofbeats! Strange: The only horses allowed within the city limits these days belonged to palace couriers and the army or were beasts of burden that brought goods to market. But in the middle of the night?

The hoofbeats came closer. The bright rays of the full moon fell on beast and man alike, but the rider's face was hooded. The colors of the hooded garment, however, were those of the house of Joseph, vizier of Egypt. Now Hakoris knew. There could be only one reason that would bring Joseph out at such a time—the king must have called for him! Apophis's brat had had another one of his attacks, and . . . and the damnable magus had failed. Apophis had given up on Neferhotep and called in Joseph instead!

Hakoris's fists balled tightly, and a wave of black rage swept through him. Neferhotep and all his high-and-mighty talk! What a frail reed he had turned out to be!

Now an exciting idea came to mind. Here he was, guarded by darkness, razor-sharp dagger and sword at his belt, waiting for an unarmed Joseph about to pass. Nobody was around to see what might happen.

But as soon as he had been sorely tempted by the idea, the folly of it became clear. Joseph would be expected at the palace any minute now, and if he were delayed—

No. It was a foolish thought. Hakoris felt his bunched shoulder muscles relax, then his hands, which tightly gripped the two weapons at his belt. He let out his breath slowly. His heart was still beating wildly.

He flattened himself against the door in the darkness and, hand on his heart, watched Joseph pass by, sitting tall and straight on the animal's back.

The conspirators met at Mei's place, slipping in through the darkened rear door that led to the alley. One by one they gathered in the front room, where the benches were still lined up against the wall.

This time it was Neko who was late. Mara had arrived early, and as Aset and Isesi came in from the back room,

Mara was letting down her hood and shaking out her rich dark hair. Aset, as always, felt admiration and envy when looking at her beautiful friend. The moment she recognized her envy she was ashamed of it and went to embrace Mara. "I don't know whether I'm more excited or frightened."

"It'll be all right," Mara responded calmly. "We all feel that way. I even had bad dreams last night. But I know everything will continue to go well. I contacted several people who are going to shelter the children we free from the refuge. Everything's arranged and ready for us to move them to the hiding places. Then they'll be smuggled out of the city in produce carts tomorrow."

"But won't the carts be inspected? Won't everybody be on the lookout for us?"

"I've thought of that," Mara said. "The last thing Hakoris wants the outside world to know is the way things are inside the refuge. If there's not much loss of life or damage to property, the likelihood is that Hakoris won't report it at all. If he calls in the city guards, everyone will know what a hellhole the refuge is."

"But everybody already knows!"

"And pretends not to, because of Hakoris's wealth and power. If he calls in the guards and there's an investigation, however, all the people with whom he does business will also have to acknowledge the fact that they're cooperating in one way or another with a real monster. The tarbrush will paint them black, too, and they won't like that. But if Hakoris can keep this all hushed up, they'll go along with him."

"I see what you mean. Well, we'll hope for the best." Aset was about to take down her own hood when she looked over Mara's shoulder and saw a familiar face at the rear of the room, one that made her heart beat faster. She took Mara's elbow and steered her toward Neko. "Here's the friend I've been wanting to introduce to you. Come meet him right now."

She happened to glance at Mara's face and saw such a look of astonishment that she stepped back in surprise. And as her eyes went back to Neko, she could see that the eyes of her two friends had met and locked. Neko's eyes narrowed, then widened, and a broad smile came over his features as he

moved quickly across the room through the growing crowd.
Mara pulled her elbow from Aset's hand and moved to meet
him.

As Aset stared, Mara rushed into Neko's arms, and his
powerful hands gathered her in and pressed her to his heart.
Mara buried her face in his chest. Neko's eyes were closed,
and the expression on his face was one of mixed pleasure and
pain.

All the while Aset's own heart was sinking, sinking. They
looked like lovers! Lovers reunited!

After a long moment Mara deserted the comforting warmth
of his embrace to step back to arm's length and look at him.
"You look wonderful!" she exclaimed. "You're as handsome as
a god! You're so big and strong, and—" She smiled, blinking
away happy tears. "But Kamose . . . I'd have recognized you
anywhere! Anywhere! Oh, it's so good to see you! I've thought
of you so often. I was sure I'd never see you again. They said
you'd been killed escaping!"

His response was another bearhug and a happy smile.
Releasing her after a breathless pause, he steered the two of
them to an empty bench, oblivious to everyone but her in the
crowded room—oblivious, even, to little Aset, standing nearby
staring at them, a stricken look on her plain little face.

"Hakoris can't kill either of us," he declared. "We lead
charmed lives in that regard, you and I. There's a special
destiny that connects us, Mara. I feel it. I've always felt it,
from that first day we met, back on the river—"

"—when you and I and Riki were on Baliniri's island
planning our getaway," she finished for him. She could not
do without further contact with him, and she took his two
hands in hers, feeling a little thrill from his touch as she did.
"Oh, that seems so long ago . . . and yet it seems like yesterday. Gods, I've missed you. . . ."

"I thought of you for years," he said. "You're so beautiful, it hurts to look at you! And yet you're just as I remembered you. Mara, when we're done with all this"—his nod of
the head took it all in, the lot of them gathered there for the
morning's activities, the killing of Hakoris if it could be

managed, the freeing of the children—"just us, Mara, the
two of us . . ." He could not finish his thought and let out
a great sigh of happiness instead.

"But you and Aram," she said hesitantly, "I mean
Apophis—"

He looked around cautiously. "Yes," he said. "Aset alone
knows, unless she's told her brother. They're good people
and will keep the secret for now. But—it's true, Mara. I'm as
sure of it as I am of our sitting here." He squeezed her
hands, and another little shock went through her. "Oh, Mara,
I'm happier than I've been in years, just from seeing you
again and having you near me. I'm never going to let you out
of my sight."

But as he said this, he looked past her for just a moment
and saw Aset's face and the look of utter devastation on it.
And in that one instant he knew everything in the girl's
mind, knew the pain in her heart, the disappointment, heart-
break, and humiliation she was feeling just now. And yet he
knew just as surely that there was nothing at all he could do
to make matters less painful for her. When she turned away,
having looked into his eyes and realized that he knew, there
was a wrench at his own heart. His sympathy for and identification with her were complete.

". . . after the day's work is over. What do you think?"
Mara was talking.

"I'm sorry," he said. "For a moment my mind was somewhere else. What did you—"

"It doesn't matter," she reassured him with that lovely
smile he had remembered in the refuge, all those years ago.
How little she had changed, all in all, except to grow even
more beautiful in precisely the same way! "It's just good to
have you back. And you *will* be back for good, if I have
anything to say about the matter."

"What happened to Riki?" he asked. "When I escaped
and left the country, someone said you two had found your
way to Upper Egypt."

"Yes. He's a captain—or perhaps by now something
even higher up—in their army. It's his whole life. Everyone
kept wondering if, having been such close friends in our
childhood, we were going to . . . well, you know. But he had

his sense of what his life had to be, and I had mine. And you know what sort of hero worship he had invested in Baliniri."

He was holding one of her hands in both his own, and it felt so good, she never wanted to have him let go.

He nodded. "Mara, when we're done here, that's where we have to go, too. Upper Egypt."

"I've been there," she said. "I was lonely for the delta. But of course I had something to do here—something we'll do today, with any luck."

Yes, he thought, *there is the old hard gleam in her eye. Hakoris!*

"Why do you want to go to Upper Egypt?" she asked.

He looked right and left, then lowered his voice. "Mara. The Prophecy. It's real. I believe it now. I can't say how, I just *know*."

Her eyes widened, and her hand tensed in his. "The one about Aram? The one that says—"

He made a shushing motion with one hand, freed suddenly for the purpose. "The rest . . . I've told only Aset, and I don't think she takes me seriously. But I have to go to Upper Egypt. And the next time I come back here, I will be at the head of a victorious army."

She stared at him, incredulous. "But Kamose!" she said. "You—"

"Please. I'm known as 'Neko' to these people. A name I picked up on my travels. It's better this way."

"Whatever you say, my dear. But . . . *head* of the army? With Mekim and Baliniri and Riki and—"

"Trust me," he urged. "It's something I . . . I just know. I can't explain it, but when I escaped, I knew I was going to be able to fulfill The Prophecy. Just as I know that you and I—"

She put her free hand on his lips to silence him. Her smile was a warm and secret one, intended for his eyes only. "I trust you," she said. "You can explain to me later anything I don't understand. After our work is done." She stood up now, letting go his hand only reluctantly. "What a wonderful reunion—and on so auspicious a day! I can't wait to tell Aset! Imagine bringing us together like this, and not knowing about the ties we have with each—"

But then the truth struck home, and she looked at him, stricken. His eyes confirmed her suspicions. She scanned the room frantically, at last finding Aset in a corner, talking with two friends with a fierce, driven animation. Aset would not look her way. Her face was flushed and tense, and her nervous smile covered an abyss of pain and shame.

Joseph passed Neferhotep, who flashed him a look of pure hatred, going out the door. A blistering string of oaths, some in Egyptian, some in the gruff language of the Hai, came after the magus. The king called him a "charlatan" and "quack," and the hostility that emanated from the magus's tall, stiff body could be felt halfway across the room.

"All right, Joseph," Neferhotep said with a sneer and a quick glance back into Yahi's chambers. "It's your turn. Good riddance to the entire matter, say I. And good luck." His tone did not wish anyone luck at all. "You'll see. All too quickly, you'll see for yourself."

"Joseph!" came the enraged bellow from the inner room. "Where the devil is Joseph? Get him in here! What's keeping him? Mehu? Mehu, where are you, curse you! Bring me Joseph!"

V

The door stood suddenly ajar. By the light of the lantern held high on Hakoris's outstretched hand, he could see the two figures entwined on the oversized bed: In the flickering light the young boy's naked skin glowed and stood out against the white of Sutekh's night garment.

"So!" Hakoris said. He stepped forward into the room and placed the lantern on the high table beside the door. "*This* is what keeps you from your duties! Dallying with your catamite while chaos reigns in the refuge, while serious fire hazards are allowed to exist in—"

"Now you wait a moment," Sutekh said in a tight voice, shoving the boy aside and straightening his clothing. He got up slowly, unhurriedly, as if totally unafraid of his superior. "You, boy—be gone with you, now." He patted the lad's naked rump as the boy slipped out, past Hakoris's stiff form, into the hall, his garment clutched in his skinny hand.

"Now," Sutekh said, still unruffled and unrushed. He tied his robe, his bony hands like a vulture's claws. There was no discernible change in his expression, which was permanently twisted into an evil sneer by the terrible white scar that bisected his long face from the empty eye socket to the corner of his mouth. "What's all this fuss about? What sort of dyspeptic fit have you gotten into, that you break into my private life like this?"

"*Private*—!" Hakoris began. His eyes bulged; his mouth gaped. This was not at all like the scene he had pictured in his mind, in which he was the composed accuser and Sutekh was the flustered and incoherent accused, caught in the act and unable to defend himself. "You haven't got any private life as long as you're under this roof!" His hands shook with rage; he balled his fists, trying to get himself under control. "Every moment you're here, you're responsible for—"

"Oh, for the love of the gods," Sutekh said disgustedly. "Spare me your righteous rage!" He pushed his way past Hakoris and went out into the still, brightly lit hall with its long line of torches. He stretched long and hard, yawning—and leaving his back exposed.

For a moment Hakoris fumbled under his garment for the knife at his belt, considering. But Sutekh seemed to have had the same idea and turned now to face him.

"I wouldn't get ideas," he warned, his hand patting the protruding hilt of a wicked short sword. "Even in, uh, dalliance, as you call it, I am armed. I'm your master at the short sword, and you know it."

Hakoris's mouth worked silently, forming words he could not speak. Finally he succeeded in controlling his rage. "You left some of the cell doors open in the entire eastern block. In the western wing, the latch hung free, and all it took to open it was a hard slam with the side of my fist. They could all have got away. And the fireplace in the workroom was untended, with sparks—"

"I know all that," Sutekh said. "Don't you think I've got these sniveling urchins so frightened of me that they wouldn't dare try to get out? And as for the fire, there's nothing combustible anywhere near it. You're working up a rage without good reason. When you've calmed down, you'll realize—"

"I want you out of here!" Hakoris said in a strangled voice. "Right now! Don't wait until morning! If you're here by dawn, I'll have you—" He stopped, looking into Sutekh's mocking single eye, seeing the hateful sneer on the man's face.

"Listen to yourself!" Sutekh sneered, one hand still on the hilt of his weapon. "The moment I leave here—and it'll be when I want to, and not on any whim of yours—I'll take what I know to Apophis and denounce you. I've got enough on you to have you impaled a dozen times over. And that doesn't include what I could sell to your enemies, probably for a damned sight more than what Apophis would give me."

He now stopped, waiting for a response, his face fixed in a grin made even more hideous by the mutilation of his face. Hakoris gaped and fumbled for words that would not come. His hand gripped the handle of his weapon, hard. It was true what Sutekh said: The one-eyed man had enough on him to ruin him forever. It was best to make amends. There was no sense at all in starting a fight that he could lose.

Suddenly, down the long hall, in the cell blocks, chaos reigned!

Both men, taken by surprise, almost dropped their half-drawn weapons, and their heads whipped around toward the origin of the disturbance. At the end of the hall there was the sound of bolts being drawn, rusty doors swinging open, and the jubilant voices of children. The children were being set free!

Hakoris cursed under his breath and set out down the hall at a dead run, the one-eyed man at his heels. He tried to push the great door at the end of the hall open, but an obstruction had been wedged up against it from the other side. Hakoris backed up, rammed into it with his shoulder, and felt it budge—but not enough.

Sutekh joined him in a second assault, then a third. At last the door swung open, knocking over a heavy bench. Hakoris stumbled over this, falling to the floor. When, rising painfully to one bruised knee, he looked around, he could see the children of the refuge at the far end of the cell block jammed into the doorway, pushing and shoving to be first to get through. Between him and the children several adult figures loomed—men and women alike.

"You!" he screamed. "You come back here! When I catch you—"

Sutekh, meanwhile, had not hesitated. He had leaped over the prone Hakoris and rushed forward, blade bared, lunging at the nearest of the adult figures, a woman from the look of her. She parried, turned his thrust aside, stepped to one side and called out. "Neko!" she cried out in a high, child's voice. "Help me!"

The second figure was something else again, broad shouldered, powerful looking, competent. He had dark hair and cold, mocking eyes. There was something oddly familiar about him. "Get the children out!" he called to the two figures behind him, stepping between Sutekh and the girl. "Get to safety! I'll hold them off!" He smiled, saluting Sutekh with a wicked-looking sword of foreign make, a trifle longer than the Egyptian equivalent. "I've a bit of unfinished business with these two. . . ."

"Have at you!" Sutekh growled, lunging again after a lightning feint. His thrust narrowly missed the young man's neck and was turned aside at the last possible second. "Damn you, stand still and fight!"

"Neko!" the girl pleaded. "Leave them here!"

"Don't linger!" he responded, tight-lipped. "Do as I say! I'll join you in a moment!"

She gulped, looked with terror at the two of them, and shoved the last of the children through the door, following them out. This left the man she had called Neko, plus another figure, wearing a man's clothing but curiously womanly in form. And as Hakoris rose to his feet, favoring the knee bruised in his fall, the hood of her cloak fell back, spilling her thick, dark hair across her shoulders.

Hakoris recognized her . . . and in almost the same moment recognized the man the other girl had called Neko!

"Y-*you!*" he gasped. His hand trembled with wrath as he advanced to stand side by side with Sutekh facing the two of them.

"Yes," the woman announced defiantly. "It's I. Mara. Whose father you murdered. Whom you treated like dirt, and beat and tortured. . . ."

Now Sutekh's eyes narrowed in recognition. "Yes! And the other—I thought he was dead!"

"No such luck!" the young man responded in a hard voice. "Ah, yes. You know us all right, don't you? But you don't know who I really am. You only know the name I bore in the refuge, before I escaped."

"Who the—?" Sutekh asked. But the young man chose that moment to attack, and Sutekh, angry and bewildered, was driven back and back again, parrying desperately. Hakoris gaped; this young demon was a master of the sword. As he watched, the dark-haired youth feinted low and lunged high, catching Sutekh in the upper arm. It was no better than a flesh wound but made the one-eyed man nearly drop his sword.

And now the girl, Mara, attacked him, Hakoris, catching him unawares while he watched the others, and nearly knocked the weapon out of his hand. He gave ground, parried, battered her sword point back, counterattacked. She held her ground, turning his thrusts aside with practiced ease.

"Damn!" he said. It was time to use his superior male strength. Instead of thrusting, he swung wildly, battering her weapon aside, and hacked at her face.

She ducked just in time but stumbled and fell to one knee. Instantly he was upon her, hammering down the blade she held up to ward off his powerful blows. He poised for the coup de grace, hesitating to savor the moment.

But that gave her time to move backwards, roll away from him, and get to her feet before he could pursue her! She moved to a far wall, disentangling her limbs from her twisted garments.

He cursed and looked over at Sutekh. The one-eyed man had recovered and was giving the dark-haired youth a lesson in fencing. His blade licked out like a tongue of flame, hitting lightly here and there. Little red spots of blood were scattered over the young man's chest. Sutekh took more and more ground.

Suddenly the tide turned. With effortless ease and a mocking smile, the young man, iron-wristed, disarmed Sutekh with a supremely economical motion of the hand and ran him through! The sword was buried up to the hilt in the one-eyed man's middle! The youth paused, exultant, to let him fall!

Hakoris gasped. He forgot Mara altogether. With a bellow of rage he attacked the youth from the rear!

The young man half turned, having seen Hakoris's attack out of the corner of one eye. But he was too late. Hakoris's lunge caught him in the side. The youth staggered to one side, dropped his sword, and fell to his knees. Glassy-eyed, the blood spreading across his side, he weaved and pitched forward on his face.

Mara screamed with rage. She rushed forward, swinging her own weapon wildly just as Hakoris was about to lean over and hack Neko's head off. It caught Hakoris on the wrist and knocked the sword from his hand. But as he shrank away from her attack, she swung again and stabbed him in the hip. There was a sharp flash of pain—and the feeling suddenly went out of the leg and took all control with it. He crashed to the ground, howling with pain from his wounded wrist, clawing at the leg that would not obey his command, oblivious to both attackers, lost in his own world of agony and frustration.

Mara, still clutching the bloody sword, knelt beside Neko. There was no sign of movement. "Oh, gods!" she wept. "Any and all of you, help me! Don't let him die! I've waited so long. . . ."

Just then, however, Isesi stuck his head through the door. "Mara!" he said. "Come on! Someone got away and called the guards! There's—"

He saw Neko's huddled body on the floor. "Oh, no! Is he—?"

"No, but he's badly hurt. Where are the children?"

"They're being taken to safety, just as planned. Everything went well, except for . . ." He sighed. "Here, let me help you." The two of them got Neko by the arms and legs and heaved mightily. Mara, exhausted from the battle, could not quite lift her half. "Harder, Mara!" Isesi urged with a grunt.

They got him to the door, but then Isesi saw Hakoris at the far end of the room, clutching at his bloody head. "Hakoris!" he said. "He's still alive! He can inform on us!"

"You're right," she said. She put Neko's feet down and drew the sword she had sheathed to carry him. But there was the sound of scuffling feet outside, and she now knew how close behind them the guardsmen were. "We'll have to leave him. We have to get Neko to safety."

But as she picked up Neko's legs, she called out to Hakoris in a low voice. "You! Hakoris! Tell Apophis his son is back! His son! The one who's going to kill him and drive the Hai out of Egypt!"

Hakoris stared, his eyes largely unseeing, his face contorted with pain. "What did you say?" he asked in a tortured voice.

She did not answer. The two intruders had vanished through the door, carrying the limp body of the wounded man.

They could hear the guardsmen forcing the front door as they carried Neko into the back alleyway. Mei had a donkey cart waiting, the one he had used to carry the first group of children to safety. "Where are the rest?" he asked, glancing nervously around.

"Rest? What do you mean?" Isesi asked.

"The other children! There were twenty more in the other wing!"

Isesi made a face. "Curse the luck! I didn't know."

"Never mind!" Mara said. "Help me get Neko into the cart!" Sweating, the two of them managed to heave Neko's heavy body up into the back of the cart just as Mei flicked his little whip and the asses pulled the cart away. Mara bit her lip, looking after the wagon. "We'd better split up," she said. "I'll go to the halfway house and see to the children we did get out of here. You look after Ka—I mean Neko. And, Isesi. Take care of him. He's important. And not just to me."

"I know," he said. He smiled; this was a new Isesi, manly, decisive, one she had never seen before. "Now go, Mara! They'll be here after us in a moment!"

The captain of the guards knelt beside Hakoris. "Which way did they go?" he demanded. "Quickly! Before they—"

Hakoris moaned with pain and shock. "It hurts! It hurts so!" He hugged his injured hand to his belly. One leg stood out straight, not moving, while the other bent and flexed as Hakoris writhed in anguish.

The guardsman frowned. "What hurts? Your leg here?"

"No, you fool!" Hakoris said, his voice an angry whine. The truth finally registered in his mind for the first time. "I—I can't feel anything at all in it! It won't move! It's paralyzed!"

Paralyzed! He was a cripple!

VI

The rescued children had been delivered to three different houses in the neighborhood and would be transported from them one at a time to avoid suspicion. Aset had accompanied the second group, and now she hurried through the back alleys of the city toward Mei's house.

Her heart had taken quite a long time to slow its frenzied pace after the excitement and fright of the raid itself. Even now, as she made her way silently through the dark streets, she was acutely aware of the danger in which she stood.

She could hardly believe she had taken part in it! Timid little Aset, joining in a dangerous raid against the Children's

Refuge, in the very presence of the man some called the most dangerous person in Egypt! It was distinctly out of character for the person she had been all her young life. What had gotten into her?

And look at Isesi! He was a changed man altogether! Quiet, unassertive, as-dry-as-dust, scholarly little Isesi had been a very tower of strength, supervising the whole operation with competence and decisiveness. He had really come into his own tonight. What would become of him now? Could he go back to being the timid and unassertive fellow they had all known for so long? Could any of them, for that matter, go back to being what they had been?

A sudden sound interrupted her thoughts. Instantly alert, she shrank back into the shadows and flattened herself against the wall of a storehouse. Hardly daring to move a muscle, hardly daring to breathe, she waited as the runner jogged past—a guardsman, no doubt, on his way to the palace for reinforcements. She waited until his footfalls could no longer be heard before she moved forward again.

Out of the corner of her eye, as she had herded the freed children through the back door of the refuge, she had caught a glimpse of Neko and Mara, both furiously engaged in armed combat with two men she could not see clearly. Mara, fighting! But there you were. There was something different about Mara from the first: a hard streak, a—

But no! That was unfair! Someone had to take on the dangerous job of guarding the rear as they escaped with the children to safety. It was ungrateful to look down on Mara for undertaking a man's role, saving the lives of the poor little tykes and their rescuers.

All the same, a part of her mind now put Mara in a separate and different category for . . . well, for fighting like a man, with knife and sword. Women just didn't do that. They left that work to men.

On the other hand, it was a new world they were living in, and perhaps it had new rules. Once they had decided to strike back against injustice, it was also up to them to learn to fight. She could ask Neko to teach her the use of the sword someday. He certainly seemed to be a master with it.

Neko!

The thought tugged at her heart powerfully. Neko! She had lost him to Mara, had she not? She had seen how the two of them had paired off back at Mei's house before the raid. They had obviously known each other before, but even that could not account for the thing that had happened between the two of them, so suddenly, so obviously, back there.

And she must not forget that it had been Mara who had stayed behind with him to fight those two men. If anything could be counted upon to bind the two of them together . . .

Aset bit her lip and clenched her tiny fists. Well, it was the way of the world: Beautiful women with strong personalities and a powerful sense of their own attractiveness always had their pick of the men. Why should it be any different with Mara? Why should what happened tonight stand out as an exception?

But then, almost in answer to her question, something happened to make the night different, to mark it off as a time never to be forgotten. Up ahead, above the house at the end of the long street, a shooting star blazed an arc across the night sky. One, then another! In a moment the sky seemed to be full of them!

She froze in her tracks and stared openmouthed. *A portent!* she thought. But of what? What did it mean?

"You're right," Apophis said in a low, quiet voice, awed almost to the point of speechlessness. "He doesn't look the same at all." He gazed down at the tranquil figure of his son, sleeping peacefully now, his breathing regular and even. "It's a miracle. An hour ago he couldn't draw an even breath. What did you do?" The face he turned to Joseph reflected the wonder that he felt, openly and without artifice.

"I did nothing," Joseph answered wearily. "If the boy is cured—and I think he is—it is the work of the God of my fathers." He sank slowly into a chair by the child's bedside. "I have been in here praying, no more, ever since you called for me. That my prayers were answered has nothing to do with me." His voice, flat and dull, spoke eloquently of his absolute exhaustion. "It is apparently the will of God that your boy be made whole again."

"You're too modest," Apophis said. "Yahi, well again! I can hardly believe it! Joseph, my friend, we've had our differences in the past, I know, but no more. From this night you can draw on my goodwill as if it were as inexhaustible as the Nile itself. Ask what you will. Riches? Power? You shall have them! Dominion over your enemies? Just say the word, and any head in the delta will roll. Do you want Neferhotep killed? His goods seized and distributed among your relatives? Just say—"

"No, Sire," Joseph said. "Not on my account. The magus was doing his best. But I'm sure that the curing of Yahi was a thing beyond the strength and skill of any man on earth. Don't punish him."

"Then what?" Apophis said. "Name it! Say the word!"

Joseph closed his eyes and did not say anything at all for a long moment. Apophis wondered for one fleeting interval if Joseph had not perhaps fallen asleep out of sheer fatigue; then his counselor opened his eyes and looked at him, drained of all emotion, his face as expressionless as the soft voice that said, "If you could see fit to guarantee the safety of my father and relations . . ." he said. "My father is old. He will die soon."

"Done!" replied the king. "And Joseph, that business of seizing their lands and possessions—that wasn't my idea; it was the magus's. All will be restored to your family, who will be held in great honor here. I'll treat them as if they were my own blood."

Joseph's eyes stayed on Apophis's face for a long time, and the counselor said nothing. Apophis flushed when he suddenly remembered that Joseph had been privy to his earlier fears about "his own blood" and had heard him give the order to kill his own son Kamose on sight if the boy ever appeared on Egyptian soil. Hurriedly he changed the subject. "Come out onto the balcony, Joseph. You could use a bit of fresh air, I'm sure."

Joseph's eyes closed again. "Sire, I think what I need the most right now is sleep. I've never been so tired in my life."

Apophis was all solicitude. "Quite right! I'll have a bed made up for you in my own apartments. Mehu! Mehu, where are you?" His servant, never far from the king's side, scurried into view. "Put the noble Joseph to bed. He's done a splendid night's work. And as of this moment I want the greatest honor done Joseph. Take care of him, eh? There's a good fellow. And Mehu . . ."

"Yes, Sire?" The servant snapped his fingers, and two assistants came running.

"Come to see me in the morning. There's to be a proclamation: My son is well again.

"Yes. And great honor is to be done to Joseph, and to the god of the Canaanites, and to Joseph's father as his priest. Do you hear? There'll be a special feast, on the first day left open."

"That will be . . . *hmmm* . . . the end of next week, Sire."

"Wonderful. A feast day for the god of Canaan, for saving my son." He watched as Mehu's assistants helped Joseph into the neighboring apartment, half carrying him. "Ah, Mehu, it's a wonderful day!" He could hardly contain his joy, his relief. Pounding one fist happily into the other palm, he strode outside onto the balcony just in time for the meteor shower!

Wide-eyed, speechless, he stepped back, leaned against the wall behind him. "G-gods!" he exclaimed. "Look at that, Mehu!"

The servant pursed his lips. "Yes, Sire. It's well past the season for such things. A most unusual occurrence."

The shooting stars popped past, right and left. Dozens of them, all over the eastern sky!

"Mehu!" Apophis effused. "This is a great portent! A sign! The gods have given me a sign! Not only have they allowed this Canaanite god to cure my son—"

"*They* allowed, Sire?" Mehu asked in a quiet voice. But Apophis apparently did not hear.

"—but they've given me the signal I wanted. And look you, man, none of the astrologers predicted this! Not one! I want them all thrown into prison!"

"Yes, Sire," Mehu said mildly.

"Call the general in charge of the local garrison! Get him over here immediately! Have him bring along two of his best charioteers! Have them ready to go with his finest horses!"

"Yes, Sire." After the first glance Mehu had not paid the smallest attention to the astonishing display in the eastern sky. "You are sending a message, Sire?"

"Yes! To the armies at the front! It's obvious! This is the time I've been waiting for! What more auspicious moment could there be for my great offensive against the Egyptians?"

Now, just once, Mehu allowed himself one discreetly raised eyebrow. "The *great* offensive, Sire?"

"Yes! Yes! Well, what are you doing standing there? Get moving, man! Have the general here within the half hour! Be off with you!"

After the first shock Aset was all business. "Quick, Mei," she said after inspecting Neko's still-bleeding side. "Get me some water from the upper well. There isn't a moment to lose!"

"But the streets are sure to be full of—"

"I'm sorry," she said. "I didn't think of that. Of course you can't go out. But what can we do?" she looked at Neko's sweat-streaked face. The eyelids fluttered, as if he were about to return to consciousness. "I've got to close that wound before he bleeds to death."

"I can heat a sword blade," Mei suggested. "I've seen that work at the siege of Khem, when the Hai first annexed it. It's a shock to the system, and it must hurt terribly, but it works—at least it did when I saw it done. But if he cries out—"

"He won't cry out," she said. "Heat up the sword. Use the one Isesi gave me."

As Mei went away she gazed down at Neko's fevered face. It was shameless of her to think of a time like this as an opportunity, but if she were to nurse him back to health, waiting on him hand and foot every day and night until he was well . . . well, many love matches have begun just so over the years! Men often had a special feeling for women who tended them when they were ill.

Yes! That was just what she would do. She knew he had already come to care for her. He had given ample proof of that. The surprise of seeing Mara once again after all those

years had just thrown things a bit off for him. When he saw
how tenderly she treated him during his convalescence, showing him again and again the proof of her love for him, he
would remember that she, too, Aset, was a prize worth
coveting.

His eyelids fluttered again.

She bent over him, hearing his labored breath, empa-
thizing powerfully with his pain. *Oh, Neko! If you knew how
much I love you! First I'll make you well, then I'll make you
happy!*

His head rolled slightly: first left, then right.

Oh, don't worry, darling, she thought. *I'm here! Your
own Aset is here! I'm going to take care of you as no one, not
even your mother, ever took care of you. . . .*

But that was it, was it not? No one had *ever* taken care of
him, the poor dear. In his childhood he and his mother had
been dirt poor and his terrible father had tried to kill him.
And then his mother had been murdered, and he had been
thrown into the refuge and abused until he had escaped. He
had lived a rough life among sailors and pirates and cutthroats, and then he had been shipwrecked, and in all that
time no one had ever—

The eyes opened a crack. The cracked lips moved.

The voice was a hoarse, almost inaudible croak when he
at last spoke.

"Mara," he said weakly. "Mara, my darling. Is that you?"

CHAPTER
FIVE

The Border Below Lisht

I

Standing on the bluff above the Nile, Mekim peered anxiously upstream, shielding his eyes with a weathered hand. In the far distance the signal fire let forth one cloud of black smoke, then another. "Now what could that mean?" he said to no one in particular.

Baka, vizier to the great king Sekenenre, lord of the Red Lands, squinted southward and then turned away. "That means the message is for me. A single cloud means official army business, and two, in rapid succession like that, that's for the vizier. The message will be sent in a secret code, which only I, the king, and his communications officer know."

Mekim raised one eyebrow. He looked around; the other, more junior, officers seemed not to have heard. "And you tell me this?" he asked, his tone showing his mild puzzlement.

"Why not?" Baka said, smiling. "Look, my friend. I'm retiring as soon as I can decently contrive to do so. I've had the running of things long enough, and my heart isn't in it

115

anymore. When I retire . . . well, I've decided to recommend you as my replacement as vizier."

Mekim's surprise was total. He stepped back, eyes wide. "Me? You're not just having sport with me? Because I'd always thought—"

"You thought," Baka said, looking back toward the signal fire and taking in its message, "that your old friend Baliniri was the man for the job. I suppose that's what everyone has expected."

"That's right," Mekim said, still much taken aback. "I mean, everyone always assumed—"

Baka, however, held up one hand, interrupting him, eyes straining toward the signal clouds. "Just as I thought: The king himself is favoring us with a surprise visit."

Mekim shook his head. "I'll be damned. He has no secrets from you, then?"

Baka smiled. "None of which I'm aware. See those three dots on the river, way down there near the bend? That'll be the king's party. He thinks he's going to catch me by surprise, and I'm going to pretend that he has done so, as I always do. Never show His Majesty that you're really a step ahead of him." His smile was tinged with cynicism. "I'll teach you my whole bag of tricks, never fear. We have a few months yet before my resignation becomes official, and I expect the two of us to spend a lot of time together."

"I'm at your disposal day and night, as always," Mekim said with respectful humility. "But I can't get over the idea. I always thought Balinir—"

"Never even considered him for so much as a moment," Baka said. "Whatever he may have been back in your mercenary days, when the two of you were cutting such a swath through Mesopotamia and winning fame at Mari, he lost it a long time ago."

"But he's a brilliant soldier."

"He's an *indecisive* soldier," Baka corrected him firmly. "Look at how long it took him to leave Salitis's army before he came here. No, no. Something happened to him."

Mekim pondered this. Now he could clearly see the royal barges on the river, the great one in the middle flanked by the two military vessels, packed to the rails with heavily armed, handpicked warriors. "Maybe it was that woman he fell for, Ben-Hadad's wife. He went crazy for her, and when she threw him over to go back to her husband . . ." He scratched his head. "I'll never understand how a woman can get that kind of a hold over a man."

Baka's smile was knowing and tolerant now. "That's because you're not that kind of a man. You never will understand either, because women recognize the kind of man they want and head for him, as straight as an arrow's flight. They leave your type alone, the kind who can take them or leave them. They want the sort of man they can possess heart and soul. Baliniri's one." He sighed softly. "I am too. That's how I know."

Mekim looked around. The younger commanders were just standing around gossiping. "You!" he bellowed suddenly at them. "Don't you see the king's barge on the river? Get moving! Call out the garrison! Step lively now! Yes, you! Every damn one of you!"

Baka and Mekim watched as the junior officers and subalterns scurried away, shock on their beardless faces. "Well," Baka said, laughing, "you've just given yourself a reputation for omniscience. When the king's barges actually dock, the whole garrison will know you've spotted them before anyone else did, and that the king's surprise inspection hasn't caught you napping."

"I'm learning," Mekim said. "You'd be surprised how closely I watch you in everything you do. It's an old noncommissioned officer's trick."

"All the more reason to choose you," Baka said. "That, and the fact that you have several languages at your command. If we're ever going to get the Hai out of the delta and win Egypt back for ourselves, we're going to have to do just what they've been doing: hire mercenaries. And hire them from any damned place we can get them." He turned and looked Mekim in the eye. "I understand Musuri taught you his own tongue before he died."

"Yes. And besides Moabite, I picked up several of the Canaanite dialects from him. I could probably carry on a half-baked conversation with that Canaanite vizier of Apophis's."

"All the better. Any upriver dialects?"

"Nubian. You'll remember I translated when young King Nehsi came on the state visit three years ago. And Musuri taught me at least to hold my own in three of the languages from the lands beyond Nubia, including the language of the high mountains, the Mountains of Fire. I could command an army in that tongue, with some bilingual help at the lower levels."

"Splendid. You begin to see why I'm choosing you?"

"Vaguely. But Baka, I went so long as an officer's aide, I still haven't got used to the idea of being a general, much less—"

"You'll get used to the idea," Baka said with assurance. "And don't think that you have to know everything before you take the job. You'll just want to *look* as though you know everything. You'll spend the rest of your life learning the job. I'm still learning, and I've been vizier virtually forever."

"You reassure me," Mekim said. "But I doubt if I'll ever be totally at home in the civilian world, where a vizier spends so much of his time. Even now, after this many years on the fringe of the court, I feel a fool in formal circumstances."

"I understand," Baka said. "Come along, now. We've got to welcome our glorious lord to his border domains." He led Mekim down the long path that led from bluff to dockside. "I'm not exactly born to all this myself, you know. I spent my first years as a scribe, with my nose buried in a scroll all the time. I only became a soldier by necessity, when the Hai invaded Egypt and destroyed our standing army. I had to learn soldiering on the job."

Mekim caught the oddly wistful tone in Baka's voice and looked sharply at his superior, whose gaze seemed to be turned inward.

"Gods!" Baka continued thoughtfully. "I've spent almost my whole adult life at this, now that I think of it." He sighed deeply. "I sometimes wonder what my life would have been if the Hai hadn't come. I was young, deeply in love. I had wanted a family. I could have been quite happy going to work, coming home to Mereet and a couple of roly-poly little urchins tumbling about. Instead . . ."

Mekim eyed his superior sympathetically. "They told me the Hai took Egypt by surprise," he said.

"Yes," Baka said. "There was a civil war going on. Besides the military units fighting one another, there were robber bands roaming the countryside. It all started when one of our kings died. His wife married a commoner and tried to reign with him. Of course the priesthood and the nobility complained. One thing led to another. Dissent, then open rebellion, then armed camps hiring mercenaries . . . and all the great while, as Egypt squabbled, the Hai were flattening great Ebla to the ground, up north, and marching through Canaan."

"I understand they spared Canaan the usual destruction."

"Yes. As strange as it seems, the man who brought this miracle about is still alive, and living in the delta. He must be ancient by now. You've heard of him—Jacob—the one they call Israel. Joseph's father."

They were down at the landing now, watching the oarsmen steer the three royal vessels toward shore. Baka stood above the dock, arms crossed across his chest, squinting out across the river. "Jacob had somehow made friends with the Hai commander Manouk, so when the Hai invaders came through, Manouk spared Jacob's lands. Mereet told me about it: She'd been imprisoned with Joseph after he was brought here, and they got to be pretty good friends. But—that's strange, now that I think of it."

"What?" Mekim said. "Mereet and Joseph becoming—"

"No. The business about Jacob and Joseph. It seems that in some strange way, their destiny, and the destiny of their people, seem to be tied up with the Hai." He shook his head. "That doesn't bode well for them, I'd say. If the common people get to associating them with the Hai, they'll have a bad time of it when the Hai are finally driven out of Egypt."

"You mean the people will retaliate against them, too?"

Baka frowned. "I wouldn't be surprised. If they've any sense, they'll go back to Canaan while they still can. Jacob's getting on; he'll die soon. If Joseph's in good odor with Apophis when the old man dies, he'll be allowed to take the body back to his home country for burial—Jacob's people set great store by that—and all the sons will take the wives and children along and simply stay there. I hope for their own sakes they'll decide to stay. They don't deserve the slaughter that'll take place when the Hai leave. Mereet always said Joseph was a very upright sort, the kind you wouldn't wish any ill."

Mekim was going to comment, but the royal barge now shipped oars and began to coast majestically, shaving the dock close. Six burly sailors leaped to the dock and guided the boat to land. Mekim prepared to take out his sword and salute the arrival of the king, military fashion; but Baka stayed his hand. "Civilian-style honors," the vizier said. "You'd better get used to the changed rules. I'm going to announce my decision about you tonight, at dinner with the king."

"T-tonight?" Mekim asked, eyes popping.

Baka grinned at him. "No use putting it off."

The inspection took place almost immediately, as Baka had suspected it would. The underofficers had been busy, and the units, turned out on parade, were impressively immaculate. Young Sekenenre was highly complimentary. "Splendid work, Baka," he said after they passed the last soldier in line.

"Congratulate Mekim for this, Sire," Baka suggested. Mekim blinked but said nothing. "I'm only an observer at the front here, just as you are."

"Well, whoever's in charge deserves recognition," Sekenenre said. "There'll be a ceremony in the morning, before I leave. I intend to give away a couple of decorations. If you're the man responsible for this splendid turnout, Mekim, expect a Distinguished Order of Merit."

"I don't deserve it, Sire," Mekim said. Baka glared; Mekim winced. He would have to curb his tendency toward false modesty, he could see that now.

"Yes you do," the young king replied. "Anyone can see these units are combat ready. With troops like these, Sesostris III would have annexed the whole of Nubia, instead of stopping at Semna."

It was sheer hyperbole, of course, but the compliment was graceful and nicely turned. Mekim inclined his head, unable to find a proper answer. He hid his discomfiture behind a cough. He was about to force himself to say something when he saw motion along the road to the front: a lone horseman, coming at a hard gallop. He turned, frowning.

A subaltern saluted nearby and asked, "Shall I dismiss the men, sir?" he asked.

Mekim waved the idea away. "No, not just yet," he said. "I wonder what that's all about. Pardon me, Sire." He moved away, first walking, then jogging, and met the horseman as he pulled up hard fifty paces away.

"Begging your pardon, sir," the soldier said, gasping for breath. "There's activity along the enemy line. Lots of activity. You might want to have a look, sir. Something's about to happen. And—here we are, with half the army on parade and only a skeleton crew on the line. . . ."

II

Mekim and Baka exchanged looks. Baka's right eyebrow rose significantly, but he said nothing. He gave his subordinate the smallest hint of a nod toward the young king.

Mekim recovered quickly. He turned to Sekenenre, bowed slightly, and said, "Your Majesty, I think for the sake of your safety . . ."

The corners of the young monarch's face turned down in disdain. "Retire to the boats?" he asked. "But the one thing I most wanted to do here was inspect the front."

"I beg your pardon, Sire, but if there's even the smallest hint of danger, every precaution must be taken. As the gods' representative to the people of the Red Lands and the embodiment of hope for the enslaved of the Black Lands as well, everyone looks to you to cast out the Hai and retake the delta. If I allow your life to be endangered . . ."

He let it hang and looked quickly from the king to Baka. To his relief, the proper expressions came onto both faces; he had said exactly the right thing.

"You're quite right, of course," the king conceded. "But instead of retiring to the boats, perhaps I might go to the top of the rise, where I saw the two of you watching my approach. With a suitable guard close by and the boats made ready . . ."

For the first time Baka spoke. "Yes, Sire," he said thoughtfully. "As always you find precisely the right compromise between the imperative and the possible. As a matter of fact, there is an observation tower there, which I had constructed when I was in charge of the garrison here—before I had the good fortune to find the estimable Mekim to replace me. From atop the tower you can see all the way to the front. But, Sire, at the very first sign of trouble, you must retire under guard to the river and get well out into the channel, ready to sail."

Sekenenre, smiling, nodded. He would have agreed to anything now, given his first chance to see the enemy, even at a distance. "I understand. Now if you'll see that I'm escorted to the observation post, I'm sure you have other things to attend to." He graciously stepped back.

Baka nodded to Mekim, who barked a half-dozen quick, terse orders.

Mekim, freed for action now, hurried down the path toward the lines, with Baka at his side. There was in the back of his mind the nagging notion that something was very wrong, that he should have handled the situation differently.

"Baka," he blurted out suddenly, "you don't suppose the Hai might—"

"Of course they might do something. You know how it's been here for twenty years—they leave us in peace for the longest time, then they launch a sneak attack. Always we beat them back."

"But the reports we've been getting about Apophis bringing in mercenaries—"

Baka dismissed the thought with one wave of his hand. "Yes, but he's been doing that for years. Frankly, I think he's mired in inaction. Remember, Mekim, there's a standoff in his government. Apophis doesn't have the support of the priesthood of Amon for any major offensive, and he needs their support if he's to do anything at all. Petephres has been a real stumbling block. As long as nothing happens to disturb that balance of power—"

"But Petephres is getting old. What if he suddenly dies? Or if something else has happened recently to lessen the Amonite priests' power over Apophis?"

Baka made a face. "That would be terrible for us. But we've got a spy in Petephres's household. He'd let us know if something had happened."

"But what if something drastic happened before our spy could get away and get the message to us?" Mekim shook his head.

"There was that meteor shower the other night," Baka suggested in a troubled voice. "You know what store Apophis usually puts in soothsayers and signs from the heavens."

Mekim did not answer. For a moment the loudest sound was their own footfalls on the hard-packed soil. Then, suddenly, both men became aware of a high-pitched, faraway sound that seemed to drift, disembodied, over the leagues of land before them, from the far side of the long line of palms that marked the border between the two Egypts. It was the sound of male voices, crying out in falsetto:

"U-lu-lu-luuuuuuu . . ."

Baka came to a dead halt, stunned. "That's a battle cry!" he said. "I've heard that once before, when I was hardly more than a boy, at Athribis! The traditional cry of the personal guard of the Hai kings!" His mind was fixed on a time long past, searching, searching. "But if they're here on the border, they must be—" He stared at Mekim. "They haven't left Avaris in twenty years! If they're at the front—"

"Come on!" Mekim said, and set out at a trot toward the source of the sound, which, strangely, seemed to have suddenly doubled, even trebled, in volume.

"Steady there!" bellowed Yufni, captain of the first legion. "Archers, hold your fire! You can't hit anyone from here! The first man who fires without my command will be whipped!"

The archers, bows poised, held. The tense front ranks watched as the Hai advanced, screaming, across the strip of neutral ground before the line of palms that marked the beginning of Shepherd-held territory.

Beon, commander of the reserve troop, had come up from the rear to observe the attack. "Look how pale they are," he commented.

"They're Hellenes," Yufni said. "I fought them once in my own mercenary days. They're quite mad. Don't care if they live or die, so long as they get a chance to kill a few enemies in the process. If they win, they'll rape any women or boys they find—or any men if that's all that's left alive. If there's no one to violate, they'll get drunk and try to steal one another's boyfriends."

"But fearful fighters." There was tension in Beon's voice as he watched them advance, spears at the ready, shields held high.

"Expendable fighters," Yufni said. "That's how they're being used, anyhow. The Hai will let their damned foreign mercenaries get killed in the first wave. Their own troops will be saved for later, when we're tired enough to be vulnerable."

Now the Hellenes were getting close. "Archers!" Yufni called out. "Ready . . . fire!"

His hand swept down. The silent shafts flew high into the air, then fell among the Hellenes. Some staggered and fell; others turned the rain of arrows aside with their shields and continued the advance. They had now joined in with the high-pitched battle song of Apophis's home command, and the haunting falsetto hung in the air.

"Ready the front rank!" Yufni ordered. "Hold firm, now!"

He looked past the advancing Greeks and saw a second wave already behind them, moving across the plain. What sort of tactic was this? Did the Hai have so many men that they could afford to be wasteful like this?

The first wave was almost upon his lines. The second was already well out onto the plain. And now yet another became visible in front of the line of palms.

"Steady up front!" Yufni bellowed. "Archers at the ready!" White-faced, he turned to Beon. "Get me a runner!" he said in a low, tense voice. "A runner to Mekim!" He pounded a fist into the other palm. "Where are those reserves of mine? Why doesn't Baka get them up here on the double?"

The Hellenes, stabbing and hacking, engaged his own front line. The sound of metal against metal punctuated the shrill song of the attackers. And, across the plain, a fourth line of attackers rose and formed in front of the line of palms.

Atop the tower Sekenenre stood, hands clutching the railing, and watched, aghast, as the Hai's mercenary units advanced, one seemingly inexhaustible line after another. To the left the Greeks had battered his own men back; on his right the Maaziou Bedouins now engaged his troops, hacking mightily with their great curved swords.

He peered through the dust the mercenaries had raised at the line of palms that marked the beginning of Hai territory on the far side. A fifth line of foreigners stood and brandished their weapons, awaiting the order to advance.

"Baka!" he cried in a tremulous voice, searching the landscape below. "Baka, Mekim, where are you?"

And now as he watched, staring, openmouthed, the Hellenes broke through his left flank and turned an orderly engagement of two lines into a confused, disorganized mass of humanity in which the mixed ranks were distinguishable only by the Greeks' nakedness. He watched in horror as three of his own men were cut down, saw his own commander—was it Yufni? Yufni, to whom he had given a medal only last year?—run through by a Hellene sword and then beheaded, saw the dark head raised on a pike amid shouts of laughter!

His reserves, the men he had just inspected, joined the fight. "Hurrah!" he whispered. "Have at them, men!"

But the Greeks, joined by a Hittite unit, battered them back. The reserves fought mightily, but were overwhelmed. It was a rout! A rout!

For the first time the reality of war, conflict, began to come home to him. *I'm in danger! I'm personally in danger!* he thought. He looked at the guard Baka and Mekim had left behind. "P-prepare to retire to the ships!" he said in a quavering voice. "I'm coming down!"

*   *   *

Mekim, battered and bloody, peered through the all-enveloping dust. "Baka!" he bellowed. "Where are you? Baka, to me!"

Before him a naked Greek warrior, his pale body slick with blood, emerged through the dust. A snarl on his lips, Mekim drove forward, coughing, and ran the Greek through before the man could get his weapon up. Mekim spat on the huddled body on the ground.

"Baka!" he screamed.

Individual duels raged all around him, duels between grunting, half-exhausted men. He intervened in one, stabbing a Bedouin warrior in the throat and leaving him to die, then narrowly avoided being skewered by a foreigner's spear. Cursing, Mekim tripped the man with a hard kick to the ankle, wrested the spear away, and stabbed home. The fallen warrior's last cry was a low croak of pain and rage.

Mekim turned, the spear still in his hand, and almost tripped over one of his own fallen men, dead, with staring eyes.

"Baka!" he gasped, recognizing the corpse in the uniform of a field general.

For the first time, fear came upon him. Until now he had had time to feel none. But now, with the greatest Egyptian fighter of his lifetime fallen before him—

No! He dare not think that way! That was the way to become weak! To lose! To die!

"Come and get me, you sons of bitches!" he screamed, laying about him right and left with the spear until it struck metal and broke. He drew his sword and hacked fiercely at anything that moved before him. Dust and the red film of rage impaired his eyesight.

"Come and get—"

He had just begun the war cry again when a spear caught him in the lower back. The next word never came. He reeled; the sword fell from his hands. He saw the advancing soldiers through a red film that slowly turned gray, a dull and featureless gray. . . .

"Come, Sire!" the captain called. The royal ship stood at anchor; the rowers sat with oars poised. The sailors stood, each man holding one of the lines that would loosen the furled sail.

Sekenenre stared downstream through tear-filled, unbelieving eyes. "They've won," he said weakly. "They've broken our line. Baka, Mekim, all the rest . . . they'll take no prisoners, not even Baka. They'll have Lisht by tomorrow. And . . . the Fayum! Our breadbasket! We don't have enough troops to hold them out of the Fayum! We're lost! *The Hai have won!*"

But now gently insistent hands were pulling at him, and he let himself be led to the dock's edge and onto the ship. In shock he heard the order to cast off and watched from the railing as the foreigners swarmed down to the water's edge half a league away. He could feel the strong pull of the oars as the rowers jerked the great boat out into the current. Overhead the great sail billowed, as it filled with a brisk wind.

III

From well out into the main channel, as oars and sail joined forces to draw the king's vessel steadily, slowly upstream, it was possible to see the full dimensions of the rout. The Egyptian contingent along the border had been totally destroyed, and as Sekenenre watched in horror, the last mopping-up took place at water's edge—prisoners taken in the advance were slaughtered without mercy by the barbarian mercenaries after being subjected to the most appalling tortures.

Sekenenre swallowed hard and forced himself not to turn away. He steeled himself to the ordeal of sharing, as best he could, the pain and disgrace of defeat of his soldiers. If he looked away now, the poor devils on the bank might see their monarch turn away from their suffering. Knuckles white, he clutched the railing and looked on, tears streaming down his young face.

"Your Majesty?" a voice said at his side. He turned and

saw the ship's captain standing stiffly. "I think you'd better go below."

"You know I can't do that." Sekenenre wiped his eyes, firmed his delicate jaw, and stood a trifle taller. "My place is here."

"Sire, there may be fighting." The captain pointed downstream, to where three sleek fighting craft, all bearing the Hai colors, had eased their way out into the river and were pulling powerfully upstream toward them. "We can't risk exposing you to their fire."

"This ship isn't going to fight," the king said suddenly, with new authority. "Our duty is to warn the garrison at Lisht, then make our way to Thebes. If Lisht falls, the Fayum will fall with it. We've got to get to Thebes, raise an army, and prepare for invasion."

The captain stepped back and nodded. There was new respect in his demeanor. "Quite right, Sire. I'll put the escort ships to work to delay our pursuers." Without another word, he turned and shouted out half a dozen crisp orders, then turned back to his king. "Sire, I . . . I can't understand how this happened. How did they manage to take us so by surprise? Baka should have known."

Sekenenre stared angrily back toward the grisly scene at water's edge. "Yes. I suppose it's my own fault," he admitted. "I ignored the signs of his decline. The best of us grow old, beyond our most effective years, and lose the qualities that gave us distinction. I . . . I'd been raised on the notion that Baka was virtually infallible because my father had always thought so. And with that notion fixed in my mind, I ignored the evidence, when it came, that Baka was no longer the man he had been."

He did not continue for a moment but stood looking downstream, thinking, his eyes unfocused. He blinked the last tears away and shook his head angrily, his mouth a straight line. "Well, no more," he said flatly. "From this day our backs are against the wall. Lisht will probably fall in spite of any advance warning, and we'll lose the food-producing regions in the Fayum. We'll have to import food at terrible cost. I'll have to make a new treaty with Nubia and give away some mineral concessions in the bargain."

Once again he paused, and the captain, knowing the
turmoil in his sovereign's mind just now, held his peace.
When Sekenenre spoke again, his voice was low and full of a
new resolve. "Mekim was about to replace Baka," he said,
"and I suppose Mekim would have done as well as anyone.
Now I suppose I'll have to offer the job to Baliniri." He
seemed to be thinking aloud, so the captain remained silent,
listening. "That means I'll have to find a new general. And all
I have are old men and striplings, over the hill or without
experience. And none of them, not even the competent ones,
has that quality or charisma that inspires men to rally around."
He looked at the captain, the corners of his mouth turned
down. "We haven't had that kind of soldier in the army since
Baka became vizier. The closest we ever had was Musuri,
and by the time we got his services, he was overripe for
retirement."

"He did win the war against Akhilleus, Sire." The captain knew the moment he spoke that he was overstepping
himself, but he plowed on recklessly; Musuri had been one of
his mentors in his own youth and had recommended him for
his first naval command.

"Thanks to trickery: an iron sword and a timely defection
by Akhilleus's own wife and her women's army, the Black
Wind," the king said. "I'm not diminishing the old boy's
efforts. He was the right man in the right place at the right
time. But it was his last battle. He retired shortly afterward."
A thoughtful look came over his face. "I wonder whatever
happened to that sword, the iron one he got from Karkara of
Sado. Ah, if only our army had iron weapons! We'd have no
fear of the Hai or of any mercenaries they cared to hire."

"Sooner or later we'll have the secret. And when we
do—"

"Where are we going to get it?" the king asked bitterly.
"Shobai's dead, and he never taught the process to his children. Now his son, Ketan, has given up armsmaking, his
daughter has disappeared. Ben-Hadad never learned iron
making, and his son can't make fire with two pieces of flint."

"Ben-Hadad left a son, Sire?"

The king made a face. "Yes, yes. They say he's very
bright, but his head's off in the clouds all the time."

"But Ketan has trained assistants. We got a new shipment of swords from Thebes only last month."

"But by no stretch of the imagination can their quality be compared with the arms our soldiers bore during my father's reign." The king spat the words out bitterly. "Captain, all of this is my fault, just as the impending fall of Lisht is my fault. When the barbarians take the city, the deaths of the defenders will be on my head alone. I'm going to recommend a wholesale evacuation of the city—and of the Fayum as well—by all civilians." He angrily held up his two weak-looking fists and shook them at the enemy on the faraway bank.

"Evacuation, Sire?"

"I want them all safe at Thebes. I have to rebuild our defenses from them and what army we have left. I'm going to mobilize the whole country. I'll take command myself if I have to. I'll draft every man in the country. The Hai may take Lisht from me, but the only way they'll ever take Thebes will be over my dead body!"

This was a new side of the young king, one the captain had not seen before. He stole a glance downstream, where the royal barge's guard vessels had maneuvered in the channel for a flanking attack on the enemy ships. As he watched, one of the Egyptian vessels rammed a Hai ship broadside at full speed, its lofty prow biting hard into the pursuer's hull. The boarders swarmed onto the Hai vessel, hacking and stabbing amid cries of pain and rage.

"Somehow, somewhere," the king continued thoughtfully, "I have to find a real leader for the army. But where? If I bring in a foreigner, a mercenary with the necessary qualities, will our troops refuse to fight for him?" The king slammed his fist on the railing. "The key is iron weaponry. The Hittites, up North, prove that every time they go out to fight. If I could only find a Hittite mercenary who carried his own armorer with him when he went from army to army . . ."

The captain spoke up. "Sire, if Karkara of Sado knew how to make iron, perhaps he taught it to someone. Perhaps in Nubia."

The king, his young face hard and his mouth set, looked at him. "Karkara is said to have had some apprentices who

survived him. I've had spies up that way for some time now.
So far no luck."

The captain looked down at the king's hands. Funny how
difficult circumstances brought out a man's true character, he
thought. He had always taken the king for a shallow courtier
type, but perhaps there was more to Dedmose's son than met
the eye.

Well, there would need to be. It was a black day for
Egypt. And there would be harder and worse days ahead.

Suddenly he remembered the spectacular lights in the
heavens the other night. Could there be a correlation between the fact of that night's wild display of shooting stars
and Egypt's stunning defeat of today? Maybe it was all over
for Egypt at last. Maybe the Hai had won, once and for
all, and the rest would be no more than a mopping-up
action.

The men in the bow called out the arrival of an Egyptian
patrol boat, slim, light, and maneuverable. Its commander
boarded the royal vessel, and Sekenenre quickly snapped out
orders to him, covering the defense of Lisht and its probable
evacuation and the dispatching of runners to the Fayum
towns and garrisons.

"Yes, Sire," the stone-faced commander said. Only his
eyes betrayed his concern. "I'll pass all of this along to the
general in charge of the city garrison. But, Sire, hadn't you
better get under sail now?"

"My escort vessels have bought me time to escape with
their lives, poor souls," Sekenenre said. "You're right, though.
I must get back to the city. What a loss! The border area,
Baka, and Mekim at one stroke!" He had been about to add
"And Lisht and the Fayum as well," but had caught himself
at the last possible moment. He threw back his skinny shoulders and assumed a more military pose. "Well, Captain, good
luck. The lives of your people and the safety of Lisht are in
your hands. I'm sure you—"

He stopped in midsentence, seeing the horror in the
commander's eyes. He wheeled, squinted downstream, and

saw the plumes of smoke curling heavenward. "The ships!"
he said. "My escort ships! They're—"

The captain interrupted in a quiet, subdued voice that
spoke eloquently of the pain in his heart. "No, Sire," he said.
"There's too much smoke for just two ships. That's the border
towns. Houses, shops. Women and children . . ."

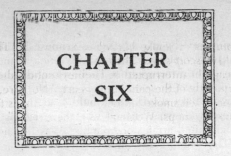

CHAPTER SIX

The Delta

I

The startling news of the amazing Hai victory came slowly down the great river. Messengers were dispatched both by land and by river the moment the rout became evident. The courier boats did not make stops at the riverside communities; where it was possible, their crews merely steered close to shore and shouted the news to fishermen on the banks. Meanwhile, the king's own couriers sped across the delta lands on horseback at full gallop, stopping to inform no one. The news was too important to be delayed even for the moment required to break stride and call out a few words to people by the side of the road.

Despite this, the news got out and was received with disbelief and utter chagrin everywhere. The citizens of the delta correctly saw the news of an early Hai victory as the beginning of the end for their own hopes of eventual liberation. And Baka dead? Baka, the only hope of Egypt these two decades and more? The border armies destroyed? Lisht, the

Fayum, menaced by the advancing armies? Surely it could not be. Surely Egypt would rally. Surely reinforcements would quickly be sent downriver from Thebes to crush the advance. Surely . . .

But with Baka dead, who would lead them? And with Mekim dead too, what chance was there against the fearsomely augmented armies of Apophis? Was this not, in fact, the end? The beginning of the last days?

In Avaris Jacob's sons had gathered for their last farewell to their father, now called Israel. The old man was sinking fast, but he had rallied for an hour or so, just long enough to speak to each of his sons, characterizing each of them in terms none the less harsh for the poetic turns of phrase in which they were couched (". . . Simon and Levi are a pair; their weapons are tools of lawlessness"), and speaking prophetically of those who had escaped his wrath ("You, O Judah, your brothers shall praise"). Given the differing nature of their father's words toward each of them, it was remarkable how alike their worried expressions were now as Joseph, the last to enter the old man's room, hovered at Jacob's bedside, beyond the closed door.

"I don't like this," Reuben said, pacing in the anteroom. "Once again he'll be giving away our inheritances to Joseph. And the moment Jacob is gone, Joseph will turn us all out with nothing. Once there's no Father around to protect us—"

"No," Issachar broke in. "I can't believe that Joseph will just throw us to the wolves, particularly now that he's regained the king's favor. He'll surely leave us with something."

"Hah!" Reuben said. His rugged face was all downward-drawn lines. "Joseph? Whom we sold into bondage? Do you think he's ever forgotten that—any more than we have ourselves?"

Issachar appealed to calmer minds. "You, Benjamin. Joseph still confides in you now and then. What do you think?"

Benjamin looked at him, and his eyes were filled with an even greater apprehension than were his brothers'. "Me?" he said slowly. "I . . . I wasn't thinking of an inheritance—I was thinking of Father, and that we won't have him anymore. I'm so used to bringing good news to him. Now I won't have anyone to bring it to anymore when he dies." His eyes went from one face to the next. He did not say anything for a long moment, and the shamed faces around him shared his stillness and silence.

In the little room Jacob lay propped up on an Egyptian-style bed, his weak hands folded atop the coverlet. His eyes stared sightlessly toward heaven. His breathing came in harsh, rasping gulps, uneven and audible.

Joseph sat by his father's side, looking down at the old man's wrinkled face. "That's how it stands for now, Father," he said. He felt empty, totally drained by the experiences of the past two days or so. "We're safe for now, while I enjoy the king's pleasure. I seem once again to be in the ascendancy, and the magus is out, for now at least. . . ."

His father's lips moved. Joseph broke off his discourse and anxiously leaned over, putting his ear close to the old man's lips, trying to hear.

". . . Manouk," the old man whispered. "I had him in the palm of my hand. I could have killed him." There was a thoughtful tone to the weak voice. "I wonder how that would have affected things."

"Manouk? Oh, you mean the leader of the Shepherd Kings when they entered Canaan. But—"

The old man's lips pursed again, and Joseph listened respectfully. "Of course, if God had wanted my hand to strike him, He would have made me do so. But . . ."

"Don't think about that," Joseph said. "Father, I've received permission to carry you home to Canaan. You'll sleep in the bosom of Abraham, in the cave near Mamre's Grove."

The old man ignored him. "My saving Manouk instead of killing him . . . it saved us, I thought, from destruction."

Joseph looked at his father, who seemed preoccupied with events from the far past. In fact, during a lucid moment he had told his son that the events of his long-vanished youth seemed more distinct than today's did. It seemed to bring him pleasure, more pleasure than he, Joseph, could bring with any new information he might possibly be able to impart. It would undoubtedly be best not to interrupt him.

". . . but if I had killed Manouk, I should never have wrestled with the angel of the Lord. Perhaps God would not have—"

Jacob broke off suddenly and opened his eyes, looking at Joseph for the first time with eyes in sharp focus. "My son. How good of you to come to me in my last moments." His weak hands clutched at Joseph's and held it. "So it is in Egypt that I am to die."

"I wanted to take you back," Joseph said. "But you were too ill to be moved. You would have died in the desert on the way. And Apophis would not have allowed my return."

"God gave Canaan to me and mine," his father said. "As He earlier gave it to Abraham, and to my father after him. I should never have left it—not to go to Haran, not to come to Egypt. I have the feeling that nothing but misfortune will ever attend my people, whom God chose me to bring into existence, whenever they leave the sacred soil He gave to my grandfather and to me."

Joseph's eyes showed his pain. "Have I done wrong by bringing you and the others here, then?" he asked. "I had hoped to spare you further hardships from the famine."

Jacob smiled for no more than the blink of an eye. "Don't worry," he said, his voice barely audible. "You did what God told you to do. We are always in His hands. Nevertheless, I think our people must return to Canaan soon. Ill fortune will attend a longer stay."

"But I can't protect them all if they—"

"You can't protect them here anyway from a monster like Apophis. He tried to kill his own son! No, get them out of here as fast as you can." The urgency in his voice belied his failing strength. "Otherwise the time will come when you'll all be vassals to someone worse than Apophis."

Joseph squeezed his father's hands gently. "I will obey my father's wise counsel," he said. But there was a note of doubt in his voice that he could not disguise, and that fact did not escape Jacob, for all his decrepitude.

"Ah," he said. "You do not wish to give up the lavish life you live here—the riches, the power. If you go back to

Canaan, you will no longer be the second man in a great kingdom. You will be one of many, the peer of your brothers, in a land without riches or pomp, without imposing civic buildings and pyramids and palaces and temples devoted to the worship of false gods. You will miss being a great man, respected and feared."

Joseph stared. His face fell. *How well you read me!* he thought. *I have grown used to the life I lead here as vizier to a heathen king, haven't I? How shallow and petty I must seem.*

"But, Father, in these unsettled times—"

His father tried to speak again. "J-joseph . . ."

"Yes, Father?"

The hands, as weak as a child's, clawed at Joseph. "Heed me. Don't wait until it's too late. Get all of our people back to Canaan."

Joseph closed his eyes. It was in his mind to answer once again that he could not return the family to Canaan in trying times like these; that there was an ever-suspicious Apophis to contend with, who had grown even more paranoid in the early stages of a renewed war; that the exigencies forced upon him by his present position would—

But he sighed and suppressed the thought. Jacob would not understand, even though he, too, had once been a man of heavy responsibilities. Once he would have understood his son's position, but now he was many years removed from that remote time and had forgotten how complicated life could get among foreigners with strange beliefs and customs.

He took a deep breath and began again. "Father, I understand what you're thinking, and—"

There was something wrong; the hands that had gripped his gripped no more. They lay back against the coverlet, not moving.

Joseph pulled his hand back in horror. He stared at his father's ancient face, at the look of peace that had come over the old man's visage.

"F-father!" he cried. "Father, come back! I need you! Father!"

Joseph's hands shook; his heart was pounding hard. He tried to speak, but his throat was constricted.

"F-father . . ." he began again.

But Jacob was past returning. There was none to hear. And so passed Jacob, son of Isaac, brother to Esau; Jacob, whom the God of his fathers had long ago renamed Israel, in a land far to the north, in the chill of dawn after a night spent wrestling with the angel of the Lord.

His brothers all could see by his face what had happened, when Joseph came slowly out of the inner room into the outer hall, dragging his feet like a man weighed down with a great and terrible burden. Nevertheless he spoke to them, in the voice of a man fatigued beyond endurance. "He's gone," he said.

"Joseph," Reuben said after he and Simon had exchanged glances. "There was something we all wanted to talk to you about."

Joseph stared at him unseeing. Outside there was a sudden commotion. Joseph blinked. "C-could someone see what that's all about?" he asked. "You'd think people could lower their voices at a time like this."

Reuben nodded to his brother Gad, who went out through the half-open outside door. "Look, Joseph," he said again. "We're all . . . well, we've been a bit upset, insecure, you know, because we know what you think of us, and—"

Joseph shook his head wearily. "Can't it wait?" he asked. "Didn't you hear what I said? Father's dead. Our father."

Reuben clasped his hands, unclasped them; crossed his arms over his chest, uncrossed them; balled his fists, and then relaxed them. "Joseph," he persisted, "it won't wait. We have to know what provision you'll be making for us now that Father's passed on. If you decide to throw us out into the cold—"

"Throw you out?" Joseph echoed, his face registering his shock. "What are you talking about? Reuben, haven't you any sense of propriety? Our father has just died, and here you stand talking about—"

"Now don't be that way," Simon said. "We're just as shaken up by all this business about Father as you are. After all, while you were in a foreign land becoming a big potentate, we were at home watching Father's slow decline. We've become reconciled to his eventual passing over a long, long time. We're willing to give you some time to recover; but sooner or later we have to know—"

Gad burst into the room, his eyes wide. "Listen!" he shouted. "The runners just came downriver! The Hai—they've broken through the Egyptian lines! They're heading for Lisht and the Fayum! Apophis's army has destroyed the Egyptian border guard! Baka's dead! The Egyptian army, it's no more! There's nothing but civilians between the Hai and Lisht."

The brothers looked at one another and then looked at Joseph. A moment before he had been at the point of absolute exhaustion; now his back was stiff, his eye alert, and his mouth set in a grim line.

"We'll have to talk about all this later, Reuben. I have to get to the palace." His voice was changed, too: tense, vibrant, the voice of a still-powerful commander. "Send the women in to tend to Father. I'll keep you informed on what's happening." His white teeth showed in an angry grimace. "I was afraid of this," he said. "This is bad news indeed."

"I don't understand what the Hai victory has to do with us," Reuben said.

"It has to do with everybody. Think it out," Joseph explained with elaborate patience. "If Apophis defeats the Egyptians outright, then for all practical purposes, he's master of the world!"

II

The news about the great military victory swept like wildfire through a city already tense from the conspirators' successful raid on the Children's Refuge. The city guards had been ordered out en masse to comb the neighborhoods for the missing children and the raiders.

The guards' invasion of the neighborhoods had created a mood of fear and apprehension. Homes had been broken into, sometimes in the dead of night; warehouses and out-buildings had been forced open, and their locks broken. One house had been burned to the ground by clumsy guardsmen whose torches had come too close to the thatched roof of the dwelling, and two deaths had resulted from the raids.

Now, with the stunning news from the front, the mood of the city had shifted to desperate depression. Very few citizens supported Apophis's bold move. Of course the parents of the boys impressed into Apophis's army welcomed the news, since a rout could be assumed to have resulted in fewer deaths to their loved ones. But for the most part the news was received as Joseph had received it: A final victory by the Hai was unthinkable, a total catastrophe. And when each successive courier came in every twelve hours from the upriver regions, citizens gathered around him, begging for news of loved ones at the front. Then each citizen quickly moved into the various areas of the city to spread whatever news the couriers had been allowed to report.

Thus one of these told Sem, one of the raiders of the refuge, and Sem hurried through the back streets of Avaris until he arrived at the drab hovel where Mara was in hiding. At the special sequence of knocks they had agreed upon, she hurriedly opened the door and ushered him inside, bolting the door firmly behind him.

"What's the latest?" she asked. "Have they taken Lisht yet?"

He took down the hood of his garment and looked at her dark eyes, which had a haunted look. "No," he answered. "In fact, Egyptian resistance seems to have stiffened. Evidently Sekenenre visited Lisht and made a speech that gave heart to the resistance. Lisht hasn't given any ground for a day now. The advance stopped well before the city wall."

The light came into her eye again. "But . . . there's more, isn't there? And it's not all good. Tell me."

He shrugged unhappily. A pity to drive the hope from that beautiful face! "No, it's not," he said. "The other arm of the Hai attack—the Bedouin legions—has driven way into the Fayum, where the Egyptian defense was less organized. It now appears that the Hai will control the whole food-producing region before week's end." His chagrin was obvious. "You know what that means. The end won't be far."

She bit her lip. "Gods! Is there no justice in the world? If the Hai or Bedouins take the Fayum, they will eventually starve Thebes."

"Perhaps," Sem said. "On the other hand there's some hope because Lisht is holding out and King Sekenenre is taking a hand in things. If he could rally Lisht—well, perhaps he can do something about building up the Thebes garrison."

She did not answer, and seeing the dark despair on her lovely face, he changed the subject. "What have you heard from the children?" he asked. "Have they continued to evade the raids?"

"So far we're all right," she said. "We've got most of them out of the city now, and we have them dispersed among families out in the farm provinces and on the islands. The last group is due to be moved out of the city tomorrow morning. With any luck, they'll all be safe in a day or two—or as safe as anyone gets under this horrible Hai regime."

Sem sat down and looked at her. "We have to move you as well, Mara, out of here, out of the city. As far away as possible."

"Why?"

He laced his fingers and stared down at them. "You know Hakoris recognized you the night of our raid."

"Yes. That's nothing new."

"And you had to tell him that Apophis's son was back."

Her face fell. "I . . . I couldn't resist that. I should have controlled my tongue."

"You should indeed. When Apophis heard that, it had the worst possible result: He was so grateful for the information, it cemented the already strong tie between him and Hakoris. Now, even though Joseph's back in the king's confidence and the magus is in disgrace, we've lost ground. The king has hailed Hakoris as a hero, as if the wound he took had been received in a good cause, and has had him moved into the palace to be looked after by the royal staff. He can't get around too well now. He's lost the use of the leg."

"I wish I had killed him."

"I wish you had too. Now the king gives Hakoris anything he asks for. And, my dear, you're a marked person. You can't show your face in the street. There's a reward out for you, one so large that even a person of good character might be tempted."

She frowned. "And—Kamose? I mean Neko?"

"We've had some luck there. Hakoris doesn't seem to have connected Apophis's son with the young escapee from the refuge who fought the duel with him the night of the raid."

"Thank heaven!"

"Yes. They'd like to find him, but they're seeking they know not whom. They do know what Neko looks like, even if they don't know that he's Apophis's son. So *both* of you have to get away."

"I see," she said. "But—he's hurt."

"Not as badly as we thought. He lost a lot of blood, and he has a broken rib—the one that stopped the knife thrust from killing him. He'll be well enough to travel very soon."

"Good! But where shall we go?"

"There's the problem. I went to see him today. He insists that he has to make his way through the lines and get over to the Egyptian side. He wants to join the Egyptian army."

Her eyes lit up again. "Yes!" she said. "Yes, Sem! Can't you see what it would do for the morale of Baliniri's army to have him coming over to their side? Everyone knows about The Prophecy and—"

"How?" Sem said, throwing his hands up in a gesture of hopelessness. "How can we get him there? Through the Hai lines, along a front where there's fierce fighting?"

She sat down now, too, and her shoulders slumped. "Let's see . . . we could go overland to the Red Sea and sail down the coast—"

"And get there two weeks after the fall of Thebes."

Her dark brows knitted in thought. "We could seek out the trade routes through the desert—"

"Even slower," he said. "The fastest way—perhaps the only way—remains the Nile. Which, I'll remind you, happens just now to be blocked by the Hai fleet. And three days from now, it'll be so clogged with the vessels Apophis is bringing up from the mouth of the river, that— "

She rubbed her temples. "There's got to be a way. But to save my soul I can't think of one."

"Me either."

"Sem, take me to him."

Sem hesitated, then agreed. "It's dangerous, but we've very little time. Let's go tonight. It's cloudy, so the moon won't be bright."

"Sem, I can't lose him again. We've got to get him out of here safely. When I first saw him again . . . well, I hadn't allowed myself to dream in so many years. . . ."

"I understand, Mara."

"Back in Thebes, Riki thought that something might have happened between us. It's understandable—I was the first girl he'd ever known really well. But I must have been a great disappointment to him. I never allowed myself to think about having a husband, a home, children."

"Children?" Sem raised a brow. "And you're thinking of them now? Children by Neko, a man whose destiny is war?"

"His destiny will go well beyond that!" she said, fire in her eyes. Then it died. "I suppose you're right. But for a brief moment, the dream came alive, the one I'd forbidden myself all these years, and I found myself beginning to think—" She looked at him, tears on her lower lashes.

Sem put a hand on her shoulder in comradely concern. To his surprise she leaned across to him, seeking his arms for comfort. As they struggled to their feet, he embraced her awkwardly, patting her back like an elder brother, while her body shook in silent sobs. At last she drew back, and her mouth was set in a grim line. "Very well," she said, dashing the tears from her eyes. "Tonight it is. As soon as it's dark."

Hakoris had been moved by the king's order to an imposing suite of rooms in the eastern wing of the palace, well away from Apophis's usual haunts. This alone emboldened Neferhotep to make his first call at the palace since his banishment from the royal presence. Even so, it required three substantial bribes to get him ushered silently and secretly past the guards and through to Hakoris.

Now, in stealth, the magus hurried down a long hall toward Hakoris's apartment, keeping close to the wall. He had no idea what would happen if he were to be surprised by someone close to the king . . . and had no wish to learn. It was with a great sigh of relief that he finally slipped through the last door to find himself in the large outer room of Hakoris's suite.

"Is he here yet?" came a sour-sounding, familiar voice from the inner chamber. "Well, damn you, show him in!"

Neferhotep noted the choked anger in Hakoris's voice and swallowed hard. For a moment he thought of running for the door, but then he straightened his back and, trying hard to assume some of his old dignity, forced himself to go into the bedchamber.

Hakoris was propped up in a broad bed twice the size of a normal one. Above the coverlet he was dressed in a light robe of expensive design; he still wore the distinctive headdress of another land. Below it his eyes blazed. "See what they've done to me!" he said in a voice full of sharp edges. "See to what depths I've fallen!"

Neferhotep asked, "Are you in pain?"

"Not now," Hakoris admitted. "But last night—"

"I'll give you something," Neferhotep said. He fumbled in the inner recesses of his robe, then brought out a curiously shaped vial, bell-bottomed. "Take this as you need it. When the vial is empty I'll send more." *Good thinking*, he told himself. *Keep him dependent on you—and addicted to the substance.*

Hakoris took it and frowned. "What's in it?"

"Extract of the poppy," the magus said casually. "It's like *shepenn*, only stronger. Keep yourself well fortified with this, my friend, and no pain can reach you. It's not common here. I'm not even sure it's legal. It costs me a pretty sum to bring it in, I can tell you. But it produces not just absence of pain, but a pleasant feeling of well-being."

"Good," Hakoris said gruffly. "I'm in your debt. I'll need something for my moods. I tell you, learning that you'll have to drag a useless leg around the rest of your life—that you'll have to walk with a crutch or a cane, maybe with incessant pain . . ."

"You have my sympathies," the magus said. "By the way, what do you hear about, uh, Joseph? Has he—"

"The news is mixed," Hakoris replied. "He's very much in the king's good graces and will probably remain so. His father just died, so he's asked permission to accompany the body back to Canaan for burial."

"He asked that before I left the palace," Neferhotep said. "That's not news."

"No. But he may want to change his mind now, with the uncertainty surrounding the news at the front. I wouldn't leave just now, let me tell you. But if he does—" He looked significantly at Neferhotep. "I'll keep you informed. You could regain lost ground. I could put in a good word now and then."

"You'd have my gratitude." He changed the subject. "And your attackers? The kidnapped children? Any news there?"

"No, confound it!" The powerful hands turned into claws, rending the air before him; then they relaxed and fell to the blanket. "The guards claim they've scoured the whole city, but the brats are nowhere to be found. And neither, it appears, are the boy and girl. I suppose you've heard who they were. Former slaves of mine, bearing a grudge. I should have—"

"There, now," the magus soothed. "Take some of the extract. No use getting yourself upset over something you can't do anything about just now."

"You're right," Hakoris admitted. But his reddened face was contorted into a snarl of hate. "If only Apophis hadn't siphoned off all the city guards for this attack of his. . . ."

"Just take the extract." The magus's tone had softened and bore the practiced professional sound of the doctor advising a patient: soothing, firm, full of concern and authority. "Take a nice strong draught, now. I won't leave until I've seen you take it."

Hakoris drank—timidly at first, then thirstily. He wiped his lips and looked up. "I can't feel anything."

"You will. I guarantee it. And when the smallest sign of pain or agitation returns, take more. I would gladly get another vial to you tomorrow, but it's dangerous for me here. . . ."

"I'll see to your safety. I'll make sure the king doesn't know. Trust me. And—"

"Yes?"

"I want my own people out there looking for those ex-slaves of mine. I want them! When I find them—"

"Relax, now. Do you want me to carry a message to anyone? Someone who could organize a patrol to look for those two?"

"Yes. As soon as you leave here . . ." Hakoris's face changed. "Ah. *Ahhh*." He sank back. "I see what you mean. It works quickly! Ah, yes, that feels *much* better."

"Tell me when you need more. Meanwhile, tell me what messages you want carried, and to whom. I feel we can both be quite useful to each other in the days to come. Don't you?"

III

Neferhotep managed to control his feelings all the way down the stairs and through the outer courtyard. But once free of the palace grounds, he could not resist a savage chuckle of triumph, and only his habitual dignity kept him from giving a little jump into the air as he made his way briskly through the city streets in the pleasant, invigorating cool of dusk.

What an inspiration! What a coup!

No doubt about it: The stars must certainly have been working for him today. He would have to consult the astrologers about it. If there were some fortunate alignment in the stars that created such great success, perhaps it would repeat itself someday. He would watch for the return with great interest.

Imagine! He had begun the day in total disgrace, his career in ruins, his future uncertain, his prospects bleaker than they had ever been. And in one moment he had gone from outcast to . . . well . . . he did not quite have the world in his pocket, but he did find himself in a position of power, covert though it might have to be at first.

What could have prompted him to stick the vial of the double-strength *shepenn* into his pocket before leaving home that afternoon? He did not know, but he breathed silent thanks to any and all of the gods for putting the thought in his mind.

His heart pounding triumphantly, he increased the length of his already robust stride. Passersby, taking note of the purposefulness in his demeanor, stepped respectfully to one side for him. He rewarded them with something like his old, habitual arrogant glare, head held high, back stiff.

What a coup! Now Hakoris was in his hands and would remain so. A man in constant pain would quickly find himself unable to resist the relief *shepenn* promised, or the permanent sense of heedless euphoria induced by frequent use of the stuff. He would quickly find himself needing more and more of the substance. And in all of Lower Egypt, there was no other source for the immensely potent, immensely addictive Cypriot variety of *shepenn* than he, Neferhotep the magus: despised, exiled from the king's presence, a virtual pariah . . . but, he thought with satisfaction, a man now indispensable to Hakoris!

He would have to stockpile the stuff. He had quite a sizable supply on hand already, having bribed a sea captain to smuggle it past the customs collectors six months before. But he would need a large and reliable amount every quarter or so, and he would need to make sure no other supply reached Egypt, so that he would remain the only man through whom Hakoris could obtain the substance.

Well! That was no particular problem. He had put aside a considerable sum of money in the time he had been assigned to the palace. He could buy out the right people and put them on his permanent payroll.

He looked up. The sun had fallen below the level of the city wall now, and darkness lay over all the eastern sky. He would be passing through a dangerous quarter of the city on the way to the modest quarters he had rented when the king had thrown him out of the palace—and he would be passing through it in the dark. He patted his pocket: There was still a good deal of money in his purse after the bribes he had had to pay to get through to Hakoris today. He had no wish to be robbed of it on the way home. And from the looks of things, there would not be much moon out tonight: a bare sliver, through the clouds, at most.

He stopped and looked around him. If he could hire himself a couple of big, burly fellows to walk him home now . . .

His eyes scanned the homeward-bound people around him, looking down on them from his imposing height, as the darkness intensified with every passing moment.

What luck! An off-duty guardsman, still armed to the teeth and all too obviously freshly off the day watch!

He raised one hand, called out. "Here, you! Officer! Over here!"

The guardsman looked up, saw him, started to turn away, then thought better of it and came toward him.

"Yes, sir?" he said politely enough, taking in Neferhotep's still-impressive mode of dress, the expensive weave and cut of his garments. "How may I be of help?"

"Officer, I have to traverse the thieves' quarter just now." He gave the address. "I happen to be carrying a modest sum of money, and I'd appreciate having an escort. Of course I'd be very happy to pay handsomely. . . ."

The guardsman bowed his head slightly. "I'm at your service, sir. Do you think one man would be enough?"

Neferhotep's brow knitted. "You give the impression of being able to take care of yourself." He looked around him. Various "professional escorts" had begun to gather in the square and were igniting torches for lighting their clients' paths to their destinations, and for a moment the magus debated hiring one of these instead: The price would undoubtedly be more to his liking. But no. Footpads knew better than to attack a man escorted by a guardsman in uniform. One man would surely be enough.

Suddenly he froze, eyes staring, mouth open.

Across the square, new light from a freshly lit torch had fallen on a face he knew and remembered. A woman's face, hidden now by her hood, but just a moment before illuminated by bright flames. Who was she, now? His eye followed her as she made her away across the bazaar. Some instinct told him not to let her get away. "Officer," he said, "would you come with me, please?"

"But that's not the way to the thieves' quarter," the guardsman said. Nevertheless he fell in step with Neferhotep, and the two of them pushed their way roughly through the crowd. As they did, the magus kept his eye firmly on the girl's retreating back.

"Her!" he said, pointing. "Just bear with me for a moment. You'll be paid well for this. Perhaps a bonus if she's who I think she is—and if we can catch her."

"Catch her?" the guardsman said, picking up the pace. "No problem, sir."

Neferhotep put his hand on the man's arm. "No. Not just yet. She can lead us to someone, I think. Just stay this distance behind her and make sure she doesn't get out of sight."

Yes! he thought triumphantly. *That's the one!* As he talked, he had searched his memory and was sure of it. Hakoris's slave! The one he was looking for! He never forgot a face, and while he had seen this one only years ago, when she was still an adolescent, it was the same face, all right. There were not two women of such natural beauty in all Avaris, and he was quite sure the naked little thing Hakoris had kept around his house in the old days to slap around and abuse would have grown up to look just like this.

And she had been one of the people in that raid on the refuge! She had been one of the ones who had let the children out, killed Sutekh, and wounded Hakoris! What reward would Hakoris not pay for her now!

Besides, the king had declared special interest in the raid and had fixed his own substantial reward on the heads of the perpetrators. Best of all, he had let it be known that the person who captured any or all of them would enjoy his favor. This was an excellent chance to recoup his failing fortunes—particularly if the girl led him to a hiding place for more conspirators!

The girl turned a corner up ahead. "Quickly!" Neferhotep whispered loudly. "After her! Don't let her get away!"

Sem sat glumly at a table opposite Neko, watching the operation. "I'm not sure that this is such a good idea, after all," he said in a sour voice.

"Tighter!" Neko said, gritting his teeth and ignoring Sem. "Don't worry about hurting me!"

Aset winced—but backed off a bit, the better to pull the white cloth tighter around Neko's chest. "That's as hard as I can pull," she said. "I'm not sure I should try any harder, Neko. I don't think this will do you a bit of good."

"The more immobile you make it, the faster the ribs will heal. Do as I say, please. It'll continue to hurt, whether or not you do it my way. But if you do as I ask, it won't hurt anywhere near as long. Pull, and while you're pulling hard, just walk around me, to wrap me up."

She complied, looking thoroughly unhappy. Only now did Neko take note of Sem. "I thought you said she was coming as soon as it turned dark," he said. "That was an hour ago. Are you sure—"

"I'm sure of nothing," Sem said. "It's very dangerous for her just now. The darker, the better. And it'd be most safe if she'd stay off the streets until the homeward-bound crowds had thinned. She'll be along soon." He fidgeted. "At least I hope she will."

"I do too," Neko said, teeth together, his face tight. Aset, having pulled the cloth tight around his chest, was knotting the two ends together, and the pain showed on Neko's face. "I've been thinking this over. We'll have to go by water, or not at all. And I don't think I can sail a boat upstream by myself."

"Not even a little one?" Aset asked, her misery compounded by Neko's concern for Mara.

"Particularly not a little one," Neko said. "They're more trouble than the big ones. I'll need Mara to shorten sail. All I'll be good for is manning the tiller."

"Well, if that's all you—" she began, but her words were

drowned out by a furious burst of highly painful coughing on his part and the cursing that followed it.

"But how will you get past their patrols?" Sem asked. "They're sure to see you unless you sail upstream at night—and with no more moon than this, that wouldn't be too wise."

"No," Neko said in a taut voice. "Believe it or not, we're going to do it in broad daylight, with all of them looking on."

"But they'll catch you!"

"No, they won't. The only dangers would be if they decided to try to sink us or simply turned their bowmen loose on us." He gritted his teeth as Aset pulled the knot tight at last. "On the other hand, they may consider it unlucky to have us killed. I seem to remember some superstitions about this."

"Oh, Neko!" Aset said suddenly, stepping back and looking at him. "I *knew* that would happen if I wrapped you that tight."

He looked down, and saw the red spot on his side where the sword had caught him. It seemed to be spreading slowly. "Damn!" he said hoarsely. "Well, there's nothing I can do about that now. I'll wear something over it. Don't worry. It isn't serious."

"How do you know it isn't serious?" she demanded. "I could have really hurt you. I *knew* I—"

When she saw the look in his eye, she stopped. She had learned better than to go on about something like this when he had made up his mind. "All right," she conceded in a small voice. "I . . . I wonder what time it is. I haven't heard the crier yet."

"The moon'll be high pretty soon," Neko said. "If Mara's here by then, we can go." He let his eyes go from Aset to Sem, and his face and voice softened. "Do say good-bye to Isesi for me, will you, Aset? I've come to respect him a lot during this. He doesn't look like the brave man he is. That deceptive appearance makes him all the more effective."

"He's come into his own, all right," Aset agreed with a shy smile.

"So have you," Neko said fondly, and for a moment she basked in his warm glance. "I'll not forget any of you. If things go as I hope they will and we can turn things around up in Upper Egypt and come back to drive the Hai out, my friends . . ." He sighed, then went on doggedly. "Should The Prophecy be something more than a lot of wishful thinking and should I come into the inheritance that's supposed to be mine . . . well, there's one thing the scribes will be instructed to write in every official history of our times: And that's the fact that the rebellion began right here, with you and me and Isesi and the others striking the first blow against oppression. It'll be your images on the walls, commemorating the day it began. Your names on the scrolls, as the people who first set the fire that finally burned down the Hai palaces and the heathen temples. You, the heroes and heroines of the revolution!"

Neko, exhausted already from the long speech, looked from the one face to the other as Sem and Aset exchanged shocked glances. In his own ear it rang like idle bombast, and he was a little ashamed of having stirred them up this way.

Mara! What was keeping Mara?

IV

"It's all arranged," Joseph said, taking off his outer garment and dropping it onto a bench. Before him, his brothers Simon, Levi, and Reuben stood, faces tense, eyes on his face. Behind his wife, Asenath, a servant stood by with plates of figs and olives, but nobody seemed interested.

"We've permission to escort Father's body back to Canaan for burial?" Simon asked. "The procession won't be stopped at the border?"

"No, no," Joseph said a little impatiently. "That hasn't been in question since I got back into the king's good graces. No, what I was negotiating was something else entirely. Father's to be buried with great honor and ceremony, with an escort of high-ranking officials of the court joining us."

"You mean nobles and officers and all that?" Reuben asked, incredulous.

Joseph nodded. "Representatives of every department except the priesthood of Amon. I talked with my father-in-law about that, and he agreed it wouldn't be seemly, given the different natures of our beliefs."

"This is splendid news!" Levi said, smiling broadly. "This constitutes official recognition of Father's status. It'll be received well in Canaan, and—"

"Oh, shut up," Reuben said, a sour look on his lined face. "Can't you see that Joseph has struck a bargain with the king?" He turned to Joseph, grudging respect in his dark eyes. "What did you have to give up for it? We'll be in your debt. As usual. It behooves us to know how much."

"Not much," Joseph said. "Only . . . well, as much as I would like to come along . . ."

"So you're to be held hostage for our prompt return?"

"Something like that. And your families. They'll remain here, too. Only the brothers may go to Canaan with Father's body for the burial. There's going to be a guard as well. The problem is that in Father's absence, the Canaanites have grown used to thinking they own the lands he used to reign over." His voice was flat when he added, "The lands promised to him and to us, his heirs, forever, by God. So you see, without a Hai escort armed to the teeth and the requisite cooperation from the Hai overlords in Canaan, you'd be subjected to all sorts of indignities there."

Levi's face had fallen halfway through Joseph's speech. "Then when we return to Canaan for good—"

"We'll run into a hornet's nest," Simon finished for him. "We'll have to fight our way into the country, as Abraham did when he came back from Egypt and had to raise an army to defeat the Four Kings."

"Very likely," Joseph said. "For the time being we have the might of the Hai behind us, and the Canaanites won't do anything to us while the Hai guards shield us from harm." He frowned. "I keep saying 'us.' Wishful thinking." His sigh was deep, aching, heartbroken. "Do you know how long it's been since my foot stood on Canaanite soil?"

"Now, Joseph," Simon said, "I thought you weren't going to bring that up again. . . .

"Be quiet," Reuben said harshly. "He didn't mean anything by it. Of course we're sorry you can't come." There was a thoughtful tone to his voice now. "This is hard for me to say, Joseph, but Father was right, favoring you. You're the best of us. None of us would have been as magnanimous, in your place, or as forgiving, with the rest of us turning up on your doorstep the way we did."

"Oh, come, now—"

"No. It's the plain truth. And you're smarter than the lot of us combined. That's why I'm sorry you won't be coming along. When we are able to return to Canaan with our families, we'll need you to run things. And—"

"Reuben, Reuben," Joseph said in a weary voice. "I despair now of ever seeing Canaan again. Somehow I know that when the move takes place, I'll be dead and buried. God has not told me so in those words, but I think that in some ways He's prepared me for this, to cushion any disappointment I might feel. The lot of taking our people back to our homeland will fall to another, I'm sure of it."

"But—"

"No. Think no more of it. Look. There are things you must do, Reuben. You'll want to milk this occasion for every bit of show you can get out of it. When you get to Canaan, hold a festival of mourning. Draw it out. A week would be fine. Make sure that the Hai guardsmen and the courtiers who accompany you all participate in some way, to show you're all united in honoring Father. Make sure that when it's over—and when the burial ceremony has taken place— the Canaanites take note of how much time and money have been lavished on the whole thing. This will raise our stock with the Canaanites. They have to be made not only to fear our Hai allies, but also to respect us."

"I understand. Tell me exactly what you want done, and we'll do it." Reuben's hands went up and closed on his brother's shoulders. And for the first time they could remember, the two embraced as brothers and friends.

Within sight of Sem's house Mara suddenly realized she was being followed, although she could not have said exactly how she knew. Certainly she had seen nothing, had heard no echoing footfalls behind her. But an instinct she could not name told her that in the darkness, there was someone who had been behind her a good deal of the way here.

She passed under a lighted torch jutting from a brick wall and suddenly turned right, into a dark alley that cut through to the next street. The last thing she wanted to do was lead anyone to Sem, Neko, and Aset. Rushing forward, she came to the end of the alley and turned to look back. Anyone following her would have to pass underneath the lamp.

Yes! There they were! Two of them! A uniformed guardsman and . . . who was it? It was the magus, Noferhotep! Hakoris's closest associate!

She turned the corner again and this time took off at a run down the next street. Her sandals tended to trip her up; she broke pace for a step or two to kick them off into the shadows and raced barefoot, heart beating madly.

As she ran, panicky thoughts raced through her mind in a hopelessly chaotic succession. The magus! Had he recognized her? But of course he had. And if he caught up with her, she would be back in Hakoris's hands, after ten years of freedom—but still a slave under the delta law, a chattel to be used any way Hakoris saw fit! For a moment the memory came back, clear and distinct: the years of humiliation and abuse, the beatings . . . All that had only ended when little Riki, her street-urchin friend, had raided Hakoris's house and taken her away to Upper Egypt. Was it to begin again? Only this time with the added disadvantages of Hakoris's grudge against her for having taken part in the fight that had lamed him—and, she had heard, left him in constant pain—and her being a woman now, instead of a child.

No! That was unthinkable, falling into his hands once again! Quick death would be infinitely preferable to the slow, drawn-out extinction she would know as his slave. She would never let herself be taken alive to him!

Up ahead! What was that in the shadows? One of them? Could they have doubled ahead and come up the next alley? She braked, stumbled to one knee, looked both ways. A transverse street began in midblock, leading between two warehouses; she dove for this and ran, head down, toward the dark end of the thoroughfare.

Behind her she could hear voices, several of them, now: They had apparently picked up reinforcements.

"There she goes! Don't let her get away!"

"Head her off! You two, go that way!"

Panting, gasping, she ran as fast as her legs would carry her. There was some sort of light at the end of the next alley, and she made for that. A lantern!

Could it be one of them? Stunned by the thought, she almost tripped and fell, but then, halfway down the short block, she recognized the face. Sem! She opened her mouth to cry out! *Sem! Run for it! Get away!* But she held her tongue. No! She could not call out to him now, with the lot of them this close behind her! She knew her own capacities, knew she could hold up under torture, would refuse to give away the locations of the hidden children, the addresses of her coconspirators; but she did not know that of Sem. Perhaps, subjected to enough pain, he would—

At that very moment the footfalls caught up with her, and rough hands closed on her arms. For the bare blink of an eye she could see Sem's face turned her way; then he covered the lantern with something dark that blotted all light out, and the worried-looking face disappeared.

Captured! Her heart sank. But at least the rest would get away; she had seen to that. Neko, or Kamose, would make it to safety and fulfill his destiny. That was the important thing. Even if she, Mara, did not live to see it.

Good-bye, she thought. *Good-bye, my darling.*

"There now," Aset said. "Just sit there for a moment. When you start feeling dizzy again, try sticking your head down near your knees. I'll help you."

"Damn the luck!" Neko said from between clenched teeth. "What a weakling I've become, fainting like that."

She sat close beside him, their thighs touching. "It happens to everyone sooner or later," she said. "Don't let it concern you, dear Neko. Just sit quietly. You'll be stronger in a moment or two. I know about such things."

"I'm sure you do." His voice was tight with anger and frustration. "Damn it! A fine time to feel the weakling, when I've got to get out of here. What time is it?"

She put one thin arm around his back and held him close, thrilling at the touch of him. "There are still a few minutes until the crier calls out midnight, I think."

"Curse it!" he said, hardly opening his mouth at all. "If I'm not at the gate by midnight, the guard will have changed. And we haven't got the next watch bribed. But if I try going out there in this condition—" He cursed again softly under his breath. "What's keeping Mara?"

As if in answer there was a sharp knock on the door, then a pause, then another knock, then two more. "The signal!" Aset said. Giving him a last timid pat, she went to the door and unbolted it.

Sem, hugging the covered lantern to his bosom, slipped inside furtively. "Quickly!" he said. "Close it behind me. There's not a moment to lose! If they've followed me here—"

"Followed you?" she said, pushing the door firmly and shoving the bolt home before continuing. "Who?"

Sem looked at her in anguish. "The guards! They've got Mara! Half a dozen or so of them!"

Neko stared openmouthed, then tried to rise, but fell back. "No!" he said. "Not now! Not just when we're—" The sharp pains hit him again, and he felt the sick vertigo again, and he almost fell forward on his face. Aset and Sem barely caught him in time and held him erect. "M-mara!" Neko said in a sick, weak voice.

"How did it happen?" Aset asked when Neko was once again seated. She held him to her, patting his back gently.

"The magus!" Sem said. "He was with them. He must have recognized her! There's a reward out for all of us. I took a desperate chance and talked with one of the guardsmen. He gave me a precise description of you and Neko."

For the first time it was beginning to dawn on Aset how dangerous the little game was she and her brother were playing. "But what about Mara? If she—"

"She was literally surrounded by them. It's hopeless. I thought of trying to get her free—but the folly of that became immediately evident. There were at least six of them. There may have been more."

"But I can't go without her—" Neko began.

"You must!" Sem said. "Look, my friend, if you're who you say you are—and I've never doubted you—it's of the utmost importance that you be got to safety, with or without Mara."

"But with her here—"

"You've only got a few minutes left, my friend. You've got to go if you're going to deliver us from these Hai pigs." Sem looked at him, at the stark whiteness of his face.

"Sem," Aset said quietly, "he can't go like this, not by himself at any rate. We were counting on Mara to be able to help him."

"Well, what do you suggest?" Sem asked irritably. "I have duties here. I can't just slip away."

"No," she said in a surprisingly firm voice, "but I can."

"You?" Sem said, startled. "Do you know how to sail a boat?"

"I grew up near the seashore. Father taught both Isesi and me. And besides, I have no choice—there's a price on my head too. You just said so. I *have* to go."

Sem and Neko looked at her. There was a serious look on Neko's face, as if he were seeing her with new eyes. At the thought, hope sang in her heart once more. Perhaps the two of them, alone together on a desperate mission, sharing dangers and hairsbreadth escapes . . .

"All right," Sem said. "Get your cloak!"

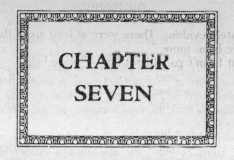

CHAPTER
SEVEN

Upper Egypt

I

Upon Sekenenre's hurried return to Thebes, the city and surrounding areas were plunged into intense activity as Upper Egypt, in desperate circumstances now, began the total mobilization for all-out war. Anyone not urgently needed for the production of weapons or basic foodstuffs—virtually every male above the age of puberty—was immediately drafted into the army, and Baliniri's officers set to work marching them, drilling them in the use of arms, teaching them discipline.

Of the regular garrison only a skeleton cadre of experienced and blooded troops was kept in Thebes to train the new recruits. The rest—tough, battle-hardened veterans—were organized into an elite striking force and sent downriver with the fleet, in increments of two hundred or so men each, to shore up the valiant and surprisingly stubborn defense of Lisht, which continued to offer stiff resistance to the stalled Hai advance.

Commander of the unit was Riki, although, in the hope

of talking Baliniri out of more troops, he held up his own departure until the last unit was ready to leave. Now, with every ship ready to draw anchor, he paid Baliniri one final visit at the training camps where the army's supreme commander now lived night and day. Nodding curtly at the guard before Baliniri's tent, he strode inside, feeling tense and ill at ease.

Baliniri sat behind an improvised table, studying reports from the couriers who, on Sekenenre's orders, sailed upstream from Lisht twice daily to keep Thebes informed. "Riki," he said, "I'm glad you came by. I did want to see you before you left."

Without ceremony Riki sat down in the chair opposite his. "Is there anything new?" he asked.

"Only that the Fayum is lost," Baliniri answered with a dispirited sigh. "But of course we were expecting that."

"I wonder that Baka wasn't," Riki said. "How could he have been caught napping like that? Or Mekim, either? I hate to speak ill of the dead, but—"

"Baka was squeezed dry by his experience. Mekim was an underofficer raised above his abilities. I don't mean to denigrate him. He was a comrade, and a good one. There never was a better underofficer, not in any army anywhere. But Baka promoted him beyond his capabilities."

Riki frowned. "I sometimes think you may have done the same thing to me," he said gruffly. "Am I up to this command? I ask myself every night, unable to sleep."

Baliniri leaned forward. "I don't care how many such questions you ask yourself at night before the battle," he said in a flat voice, "as long as you forget them the next morning, when you're putting your sword belt back on. And who, might I ask, trained you for the job? Do you think I don't know my business? Am I that poor a judge of men?"

Riki blushed. "All right. You can count on me. It's just that—"

"Don't qualify the statement. Tell me that I can count on you and leave it at that. Stop the bastards in their tracks if you can. If you can't, protect the evacuation, and then fire the city. Don't leave them anything they can use. Make them pay for every step they take forward. You're buying us time to arm for the final defense. I'm sure I don't have to tell you how important everything is. This is it. Either we win and drive them back, or—"

"I understand," Riki said, rising. "You can count on me."

"Good. Now hear me. Sekenenre is getting his own reports"—he waved the papyri before him—"but I want my own, for my eyes alone. You'll send them, sealed with my own seal." He pulled a battered old Mesopotamian ring off his finger and handed it over. "This they'll find difficult to forge. And if the seal's broken by one of the king's people, I'll resign and go over to the other side. I want none of your messages interfered with or read by anyone but me. And in them I want the truth, and none of this official twaddle." He waved the papyri again, this time with utter contempt. "They're telling him what they think he wants to hear. And for the love of heaven, man, even Sekenenre isn't stupid enough to want that."

"I don't think he's stupid at all," Riki said. "Look how he rallied the Lisht garrison before coming home."

"Right," Baliniri said, rising and coming around the table. "I didn't mean to sound flippant. He's young and inexperienced, but it does begin to look as though there were more to him than any of us thought. That's beside the point. I want *you*, my friend, to tell me the truth. And when something arises too quickly for you to consult with me before acting . . . well, try to remember what I've taught you, and act on it." The two men embraced as father and son might have done. "Bring me a victory if you can."

"Yes, *sir*!" Riki's salute was smart, by-the-rules, respectful. He turned on one heel and marched out of the tent, head held high, shoulders squared, looking confident.

Ketan had received his own notice almost immediately. When the letter came he had gone into a rage. How dare they? How dare anyone call him back into military service just when he was beginning to make a little money for himself at last, making jewelry for the rich and for the international trade?

But after the first anger had left him, he admitted how

unavoidable the whole thing was. This was not a matter of
arming for some faraway war. This was a matter of defending
Thebes itself, of keeping the Hai away from his own home,
from the homes of his friends and neighbors. And with his
first child due any day, the immediacy of the problem quickly
came to him. Grudgingly he closed his little shop, sent his
regrets to his clients, and went back to the forges he had
abandoned months before.

There, in his absence, total chaos had set in. Scowling,
cursing, he had kicked the sloppy forges to pieces, ordered
two subordinates fired and another whipped publicly, and set
about rebuilding the whole armsmaking for Baliniri's army.

To this end he had pressed into service several young
men brought over from the artisans' village at Deir el-Bahari,
men who had demonstrated some ability to work with their
hands but who had disabilities that would keep them out of
the fighting army. Two of these had worked out well so far.
So on the fourth day after the king's return, Ketan was able to
leave the forges for a night and come home to Nebet, his
wife. Ketan had, in the press of work, sent messengers home
daily to find out about her condition, but he had longed to
see her and talk to her.

Now his first opportunity had come, and he hurried
through the city streets in midafternoon. Already the compo-
sition of the city seemed changed; the bazaars, the streets,
and the main thoroughfares were either full of women or
empty altogether. The king's order had affected virtually
every male, and such of these as still roamed the streets were
subject to being stopped by roving guardsmen and asked to
produce reasons for not being in camp with the rest of the
army. Already he had been stopped this afternoon by a
guardsman brought in from the provinces, a man who did not
know him.

Along the way to his house now, he passed the Market of
the Four Winds, looking especially empty. At the fruiterer's
stall he recognized Cheta, Tuya's servant, and catching her
eye, stopped to talk for a moment. "Greetings, Cheta. My
best to your mistress. Is everything all right with her?"

"Yes, sir. Except . . ." She hesitated for a moment, uncertain whether or not to trust him. "Well, perhaps it's nothing."

"What? Get it out, woman!"

"Well, sir, there's this strange woman who keeps asking about her. She sometimes has a young boy with her. I don't think she's up to any good, I don't."

"Do you know anything about this woman? Or is it your instinct that makes you distrust her?"

"I wouldn't know her from the queen, sir, except . . . well, her dress isn't of the best. She looks like a bit of a tart, if you ask me. I think perhaps she used to be pretty, about twenty years ago. But I don't like her hanging about, you know."

Ketan pondered the matter. "I don't know what I can do, except have one of the guardsmen look in now and then. But that might be difficult to arrange now. Everyone's time is pretty well committed. But I'll see what I can do. How's everything else?"

"Master Seth has disappeared again, been gone the best part of a week. Mistress hasn't started worrying about him yet. You know how he is."

"Yes, I do. Did I hear something about Tuya having a new interest in life? A man, perhaps?"

"Well, sir . . . I shouldn't talk, but with you being family, sir, there's Master Kedar. Master Seth's old tutor. Mistress has had him to dinner once or twice. They are very good together. He seems to be good for her. A calming influence, you know, sir. She's had a bequest made up for him, so no one can say he'd be marrying her for money. And . . . well, sir, it is worth mentioning . . . he *is* past the age for bearing arms, and these days virtually nobody else is."

"Yes. I think I met him once or twice. A sound chap, quiet, well-spoken. A foreigner. I remember he was good with Seth."

"Yes, sir. And might I ask, has the child come yet? Mistress is sure to ask me when she hears I've seen you."

"I'm going home to find out," he said with a smile. "In all this mess, I haven't been home in three days. Any day now. Give my best to Tuya, will you?"

*   *   *

In warm weather like this, guests of the tavern tended to take lunch outdoors on the patio, under the grape arbor. Most stopped only briefly for a plate of figs, olives, dates, a loaf of flat bread. Business, with all the men gone off to camp, was atrocious; thus the innkeeper of the shabby tavern at the Bazaar of the Four Winds found it expedient today to break his standing rule and allow Tamshas, late of Avaris, to enter and eat unescorted by a man, in .defiance of all custom. Ordinarily the only women allowed in his place were his own waitresses, his professional nude dancers (and these only at night), and carefully screened prostitutes hired for closed parties.

Now, having eaten her olives and gone through two small bowls of palm wine, Tamshas found the strong drink was beginning to calm her. She picked up the third bowl and sipped from it, shuddering as the fiery liquid went down. Replacing it on the table, she nearly spilled it. *Damn!* she thought. *Getting clumsy there. Too early in the day for drinking this much. Better watch your step there, old girl. . . .*

What was keeping the boy? She looked up through the dappled light of the arbor at the midafternoon sun. Did he not have any notion of the passage of time? If he waited any longer, they would not be able to catch the woman at home. Did the brat not have any idea how important this was? If they could pull this off, she, Tamshas, would have a nice lump sum to live on for the next couple of years or so, and in some style—and the boy would have a rich mother to take care of him.

Sometimes, she thought, sipping again at the wine, *I think he's not very bright.* Maybe he could not imagine what it would be like to be well off, safe, sheltered, with never a care, knowing always where his next meal was coming from. He had always been poor, for all she knew. The gods knew that when she had found him wandering in the back alleys of Avaris a year ago. Orphaned, naked, scavenging for scraps of garbage to eat, he seemed never to have known much better than this.

Well, *she* had known better, that was for sure! She had been a rich man's daughter, the eldest child of Wenis the trader, well fed and richly dowered, ready to make a fine marriage with young Ben-Hadad, for whom her father had had high and mighty plans . . . and then all her world had come crumbling apart in one horrible night. And all thanks to this bitch Tuya, who had come along on the raid that had killed her father and burned his house to the ground and beggared her forever! Who had taken Ben-Hadad away from her, along with the fortune she would have come into, and ruined her life!

Well, look what the slut had done! She had turned Ben-Hadad into a sniveling, drunken fool in only ten years with him. When he had run away from this nasty wife of his and turned up in Avaris, years later, he had tried to hire her, Tamshas, as a prostitute—but he had been unable to consummate his act of infidelity. Disgusted, Tamshas had thrown him out, naked and drunk, into the street, and in a day or two he had gone out and got himself killed.

Well, she had had her revenge on Ben-Hadad for abandoning her; she had humiliated him good and proper. But her fortunes had continued to fail as the years passed, and from a well-paid whore she had become a poorly paid one, and in time her body had begun to show signs of age and gravity, and the dancer jobs had dried up once and for all. She had been on the verge of suicide.

And then she had stumbled across the boy, Meni, scavenging in the street, and she had seen in his face the totally fortuitous resemblance to the young Ben-Hadad, and the idea had been born, and from that moment once forlorn hope had begun to grow in her desolate heart. The two of them had found their way across the border, and she had whored for their passage upriver to Thebes: From asking around she had learned that Tuya, Ben-Hadad's widow, was a rich woman . . . a rich woman with many regrets about the past, mistakes she would like to have the chance to rectify.

If she, Tamshas, could convincingly present herself as the mother of Meni, the bastard son she had had from her brief liaison with Ben-Hadad ten years before, and work on Tuya's conscience . . .

But just then the boy came in by the side door and approached her. She glared at him through bloodshot eyes. "Where have you been?" she rasped.

"I couldn't help it, Tamshas," the boy said, his face set in that innocent look she despised so. "There was nobody home."

"Curse you!" she said angrily. "Don't call me Tamshas! Call me Mother! How many times do I have to remind you?"

II

For perhaps the tenth time since the runner had left, Nebet went to the window and looked out over the busy streets below, wondering what had happened to Ketan. The runner had come by more than an hour ago, to say that her husband, having organized his forges, was taking some time off to spend with her. What could have detained him?

Idly she placed one hand on her swelling belly, feeling the life inside her. Suddenly the great extra weight pulled at her, making her feel weak, heavy. She moved away from the window and sat down on the bed, looking across at the opening, with its warm pool of sunlight and the patch of blue sky above the buildings opposite.

Ketan had built her the house shortly after they had come together, before even their marriage intentions had been made public. It had high walls, an interior garden, and a second story, where doors and window shutters could be adjusted to let the cool breezes into their bedroom and sitting room. She had always loved this room, which opened onto the roof with its cool, shaded arbor. How like Ketan it was to have built such beauty and comfort into his house!

Strange: She had never had any idea how well-off he had been when she had first met him at the tavern where she worked as a dancer. She had only known that he was young and decently dressed, but solitary and unhappy. Inexperienced in the ways of women, he had fallen into the icy hands of a courtesan with an eye to the main chance. The courtesan— what was her name, now? Well, perhaps it was not worth remembering—had got her claws into Ketan and led him a merry chase before Nebet herself and Ketan's cousin

Tuya had exposed the courtesan for what she was and saved Ketan from himself. Only after she, Nebet, had wound up with him had she learned that he was the wealthy scion of a family of famous armorers.

The marriage had worked out very well over the past ten years. They had a fine relationship, marred only by their childlessness. She let her hand once again stray to her belly, feeling the reassuring bulk of the warm life within her. Perhaps this time . . . But no—let there be no "perhaps" about it! This time she was going to give him a baby, an heir, a Child of the Lion to continue the family's distinguished traditions.

Even as she thought this, a cloud passed across the sun. The skies became gray and subdued, and the bright colors of the buildings opposite her house turned drab and ugly. And her mood changed, as it had done, horribly, interminably, at odd intervals during the past week. Despair replaced hope.

What if . . . ? What if the child died?

"No!" she said, clasping her hands tightly over her belly. "It's going to live! It's going to be beautiful and healthy and bright and happy, and it's going to live to a ripe old age!"

Now, with great suddenness, the dark premonition came into her mind, as it had two days before: *The child will live. It will grow tall and strong and handsome. A son! A son for Ketan! But you and Ketan will not live to see him come to adulthood. He will be raised by others. He will not know either of you. He will have to ask others to tell him who he is, and who you were . . .*

"Stop!" she cried out, covering her face with her hands as hot tears blinded her and sobs shook her body. But as quickly as the evil thought had come, it vanished, leaving a great void inside her. Then the fear rushed in, with its desperation and loneliness.

I'm going to die. We'll both of us die. My child, my little son—raised by strangers.

She wept inconsolably now. *Ketan! Come to me! Where are you, Ketan?*

*   *   *

As his unit filed onto the ships, Riki, standing at dockside, looked up and down the long quay beside the river at the passing parade of humanity. This was the only part of Thebes that continued to operate much as it had before the mobilization: Longshore workers were always needed, and cargoes had to be loaded and unloaded, whether or not a war was going on.

Down the quay, a long, slender fishing boat docked and disgorged half a dozen burly fishermen, hard-muscled, sun-bronzed, and, of course, stark naked. Why wear anything when it would only get wet immediately and remain binding and uncomfortable? Beyond them, slaves, bent nearly double under their burdens, loaded grain. These wore loincloths in the Theban fashion, covering the behind, while baring the genitalia. Riki shook his head. Odd priorities, these, especially since the slaves wore one more item of clothing than the freemen. What an eccentric, fascinating place Thebes was!

Riki continued to believe what his mother had told him, that he had originally come from here. He had searched for proof of this, but without success.

Who am I? he thought. *Was my father really a man of consequence, as Mother always hinted? Or was she lying to me, and perhaps to herself as well?*

It would be nice to be the son of a great man. A nobleman, perhaps, or a general, or perhaps even a member of the royal house. Riki was certain that his father was not an artist, scribe, or member of any of the guilds of skilled tradesmen, since he himself had no talent with his hands, unless one counted the talents at fighting that Baliniri's instruction had brought out in him . . . and at sailing.

He had gone out with friends in the navy from time to time and been taught the art of sailing. An apt pupil, he had turned out to have a good fist there; under his hand, the tiller of a boat came alive. Under different circumstances he might have been a great sailor.

He sighed and looked at the fishermen again, their sweaty bodies scarred. They probably stank horribly of fish and were obviously exhausted from the day's work.

Gods! he thought. *What sort of airs am I giving myself?*

*Most likely my deftness at the tiller comes from being the son
of a poor laborer like one of those.*

What would he do with a damned pedigree anyway,
even if he managed to find himself a well-born father? His life
was a soldier's, one in which pedigrees meant nothing. He
had earned the respect of his men through strength, cunning,
and valor. No, a noble father would do him no good down at
Lisht a day from now.

He spat into the water at his feet. What did it matter?
When it came to the business of making war, the lesser
warrior had to give way to the better. Look at Baliniri, look at
Baka, look at the king. Baliniri had worked his way up through
the ranks and become a famous soldier by being in the right
place at the right time. Baka, trained as a scribe, a scholar,
had taken command of a troop of irregulars when its leader
had been killed and had learned on the job. The king, who by
blood outranked all of them, had yet to learn the first thing
about war.

But no. That was unfair. In a way, Sekenenre had had
his first blooding at the border and had not faltered or run
away. He had been moved to safety, but that was expected of
him; his capture would have given the Hai an even greater
victory than they already had earned, and the king had done
correctly to retire to safety. But he had valiantly insisted on
making a dangerous stop at Lisht to address the garrison,
making a fiery speech that stirred the blood of his troops. By
doing so the king had probably saved Lisht by stiffening its
resistance and had bought him, Riki, and his reinforcements
valuable time to move into position and strengthen the Egyptian line. That had required a bravery unexpected from
Sekenenre—a mild-looking, soft-featured young fellow raised
in the lap of luxury and married off as a child to a woman old
enough to be his mother. No, there was something to this
king.

Maybe we're of the same blood.

He dismissed the thought contemptuously. It was easily
the silliest idea he had had today. But the anguish continued
to nag at his mind as he watched the last of his soldiers file
aboard. He prepared to join them and called for the captain
to draw anchor.

Who am I? Why am I here? Whose blood do I bear?
What day was I born, and what stars rule this destiny of
mine that I do not and cannot know?

Spread across the great clearing, eight separate troops
drilled, each ignoring the existence of the others. One unit
practiced marching in a long column; the next had formed
into a square for spear drill; the last did limbering exercises
in jerky rhythm.

Smendes, underofficer in command of the Fifth Troop,
scowled at the raw recruits before him, looking each one up
and down. He cursed under his breath. These? He was
supposed to turn these ill-assorted louts into something uni-
fied? Something that could work together, fight together, and
march together? They could not even walk in a straight line,
and as for learning to march in rhythm and in step with one
another . . .

Look, now! One of them was about to fall asleep on his
feet! "You there!" Smendes bellowed. "Straighten up! Shoulders back! Belly in! Chest out!"

The man did not move but looked at him curiously for a
long moment, unblinkingly. "That's a very bad posture you've
just described," he said thoughtfully. "If everyone did what
you just said, we'd all go to bed with terrible backaches.
Frankly, I think—"

Smendes's eyes shot sparks at him. "What the blazes are
you muttering about, you diseased spawn of a baboon? No,
don't answer! Stand up straight there!"

Lips pursed, the recruit thought about the matter for a
moment, and then looked at the sharp-tipped spear in his
hand. "After all, if I throw my chest out and pull my shoulders back, as you say, I'll poke myself in the armpit with my
spear. Surely it would not be considered rational for you to
ask me to do that. Therefore, I can only conclude that you
mean the order only in a sort of general way. In which case,
perhaps a more precise order might be more effective under
these conditions."

Smendes spat on the ground and strode to the line,
stopping just close enough to blow his alcoholic breath di-

rectly into the young man's nostrils. "Look here, you!" he said in a snarl that would wilt papyrus plants in the royal pond at half a league's distance. "I don't know what sort of latrine trench they dug you out of in order to send you to me, but—"

The young recruit's face was as mild as before. And as fearless and heedless as well; if anything, heedlessness was the thing Smendes hated most. "I recognize that scent," the young man said. "Ugh! Not pleasant at all. You've been drinking at the Inn of the Lame Horse, in Madu. Millet beer, if I'm any judge. I wouldn't do that if I were you, really. I did an analysis of a jug of that stuff some time back, and I can tell you that the landlord is on his way to getting in real trouble with the brewers' guild. The standard of cleanliness is being flouted, and that's a very dangerous thing in a brewery. You could die or be struck blind. If very substantial bribes hadn't been paid on all sides, someone would have gone to prison by now for—"

"Silence!" Smendes screamed. "One more word out of you, and I'll have your head on a pike, decorating a whorehouse closed for disease!" The young man winced at the bad breath being blown in his face. This was insolence intolerable, and Smendes's voice rose another tone or two. "You!" he said. "What's your name?"

The recruit just looked at him. He had the curious faculty of being able to stare without blinking for a longer time than anyone Smendes had ever seen. The young man did not speak. One eyebrow rose, thoughtfully.

"I asked you your name," Smendes growled. "Speak up, or I'll—"

"All right," the young man said mildly. "Quite obviously the second command cancels the first. I thought it was a trick question. When your men picked me out of the street—quite arbitrarily, I must say—and brought me here—"

"Enough!" Smendes shrieked. "I don't want to know! Guards! Have this idiot run three laps around the parade ground and bring him back here!" He spat on the ground again. His eye was like a serpent's, cold and hard. "And you, you puppy, you'd better be standing right back here before my shadow's as long as I am tall, or so help me, I'll—"

The young man closed his eyes for a moment. When he reopened them he said, "I think that can be managed. Perhaps with a moment or two to spare. That is, if the rough estimate I've made of the perimeter—"

"Get him out of here! Out of my sight! Before I kill him!"

III

Coming back through the city from the office of the city recorder, Tuya impulsively turned her steps toward the Market of the Four Winds. Her intention was to ask about Seth, who seemed to have disappeared several days ago, but she had a feeling that going to the market would benefit her somehow. She had learned to trust her impulses, they so often led to delightful surprises.

And, true to this tendency, the first face she saw when she passed the ornate well and moved out into the sparsely populated bazaar was that of Seth's former tutor, Kedar, poking about the market, looking into the scrolls the vendors had for sale, unrolling one to peer at it with his fading eyes. Her heart warmed at the sight of him, as it so often did these days, and she hurried over to the far side of the square to greet him. What a fortunate meeting!

Hearing her footfalls, he looked up, blinked, and let his serious, lined face work its way into a slow smile. "Ah!" he said. "Madam Tuya! What a pleasant surprise." He was about to launch into an elaborate Damascene greeting when she broke in.

"I was looking for Seth, Kedar. I wondered if you had heard anything." There: That was a good start—plausible, not too forward.

"Seth? No, madam. As a matter of fact I did inquire about him not more than a day ago. I had a mathematical problem for him, something troubling a colleague of mine at the palace. It seems to have an application in the construction of siege machinery. But no one has heard from Seth for about a week." He smiled again, indulgently. "You know how he is. The last time he disappeared, he was found living with a Bedouin tribe, studying diseases of horses."

"I suppose I shouldn't worry about him," she said. "But how good to run into you." Her heart beat a little faster now, and she found herself short of breath. The elaborate story she had constructed to bring Kedar back into her life seemed so embarrassingly transparent in the clear light of day. She plunged into it, regardless. "I have what I hope is good news for you."

"Good news? For me?" he said with mild incredulity. His words came out slowly, with the strong Northern accent. The Egyptian tongue was still not totally his, even after all these years.

"Well, yes. My . . . my late husband's estate recently came into a substantial bequest." She mentioned the sum she and the scribe had worked out: just enough to qualify as "substantial," not enough—she hoped—to scare Kedar off. His eyebrows lifted, and for a moment her heart sank.

Hurriedly she continued. "Under provision in his will, income from this particular source was to go to an educational fund that is no longer in existence. The bequest thus reverts to me and Seth. And . . . well, I've had a number of conversations with my son over the years. As you know, to him—and, yes, to me, Kedar—you're like one of the family"—here he made a polite half bow—"and acting for both Seth and myself, I've asked the scribe to transfer the bequest to you." There! She had managed to get it out!

He stared, then blinked. "My word," he said. "Madam, of course I am honored, but—"

"Now, I won't have no for an answer. That's all there is to the matter. Seth would surely want it this way, and so would my late husband if he'd lived to know what you've meant to his son all these years."

"But, madam—"

"When are you going to start calling me Tuya, Kedar? I'm not your employer any longer. Old friends like us should no longer stand on ceremony. Our status has changed. To be frank, I was very sad when you moved out of the guest wing in the first place. It's a big house, and I'm very lonely in it with both Seth and you gone, and only Cheta to talk to. I'd thought that our having dinner together a while back would have clarified my feelings for you in this regard."

"But, mad—I mean Tuya—I don't know what to say."

"Then try saying, 'Thank you, Tuya. I accept the bequest, and I'll call tomorrow at the office of the city recorder.'" She watched him standing before her, for the first time looking like the befuddled scholar some thought him. "If that's too complicated, just nod your head."

He stared, then he smiled and bowed graciously. "I have never been able to refuse your requests, mad—Tuya. But you must let me adjust to the idea. A 'substantial bequest,' as you say, is beyond my deserving and beyond my wildest dreams—back in the years when I dared to dream."

Her heart went out to him, and she impulsively seized his hands. "Oh, Kedar! Don't tell me you've given up on dreaming. I haven't, and I won't let you give up either! You're independent now! You can do virtually anything you want with the rest of your life if the Hai leave us alone. Surely there are things you want—books, a nice house, people to look after you, companionship . . ."

Their eyes caught, held. He was alone with his thoughts, but he did not let go of her hands, as she had expected him to do.

"You *what*?" Tamshas demanded, advancing on the boy menacingly. His dancing image was double now; she shook her head angrily, trying to get Meni's face in focus. When she could see him clearly, she could not help but notice his fortuitous resemblance to Ben-Hadad, and for some reason this made her all the angrier. "How *could* you at a time like this? You're within a step or two of getting rich, or having a secure future for the first time in your life. *I'm* within a step of getting some of my own status back after all these years. Don't ruin this for me, you little bastard."

"I didn't mean anything!" Meni whined, putting the table between himself and her. "And I didn't get caught!"

"You didn't— Then what were you telling me about that old man?" The boy paused off guard for a moment; she reached across the table and barely missed grabbing his arm. He danced away.

"He let me go! He didn't tell anybody! He's a nice man! He wouldn't turn me in!"

"Bastard! You're not going to foul this up, this late in the game." She lunged across the table; this time her hand caught his loincloth and held it. He yanked free, and the front of it ripped and hung in ragged streamers.

"Tamshas, I was hungry! I haven't had anything to eat since yesterday! You never remember to feed me!"

There came an angry pounding on the door. "You there!" a rough male voice said. "If you can't keep it down, you're going to find yourself out in the street! Understand?"

Tamshas made a face at the door, but when she spoke, her tone was softer than before. "All right," she called in her hoarse, alcoholic voice. "I hear you. I hear you." She spoke to Meni in an even quieter voice. "Why didn't you tell me you were hungry?"

Meni did not move from behind the table. His eyes were slits, and there was a wary expression on his face. "You were drunk," he explained. "You slept until noon, and then you started drinking again as soon as you got up. When you do that, you never think to eat. And you never think of—"

"All right, all right," she said sourly. "Have you eaten? I mean, since—"

"The old man bought me some figs. He told me that if I ever found myself in that situation, I should try to find him. He said, 'Don't steal, son. Ask around for me. Usually people around here will know where to find me.' "

"Huh! I know *his* kind."

"No, he isn't that way at all. I know, Tamshas. I've had to fend off that crowd all my life. No, he's just . . . well, old and kind."

"Well, you stay away from him! You hear?" Her voice was hardly more than a loud whisper now. "I don't want you getting close to anybody. We're strangers to all these people, and we're going to stay that way. From now on, you stick close to me. You understand? Real close."

"Yes, Tamshas. But could I have something to eat now? I'm hungry. The figs weren't enough."

"All right, all right." She reached into the bag atop the table and handed over a one-*outnou* coin, a copper ring. "Here," she said. "Go out and get us something to eat."

He looked at her, and it was as if he could read her mind. "And a jug of—"

"Yes, yes. Now go! And don't let them fob off any of that half-fermented stuff like they gave you the last time! I was as sick as a dog for two days!"

"Yes, Tamshas."

"And for the love of the gods, call me Mother! You've got to get into the habit. We don't want any mistakes when the time comes to make our move."

"I don't know about all this. Do you really think—"

"Do you want to have a home or not? A nice rich 'mother' to raise you? Or do you want to spend the rest of your life with me? Or out on the street, the way I found you, without a rag to cover your behind, eating whatever you could scavenge from the garbage heaps, sleeping before somebody else's fire in an alleyway in the winter, shivering, sick with fever?" She took note of the doubt in his eye. "Ah! That does get through to you, doesn't it? Already it's a little better than it was, and even though you hate me, you wouldn't want to go back to that, would you?"

"I don't hate you, Tamshas. But if you only wouldn't—"

She wasn't about to listen to any recitation, however brief, of her own failings just now, though. "Enough!" she said with a vague wave of her hand. For some reason, his eye fixed on her broken nails, the thickening at her waist. "Go along, now. Get us something to eat."

"All right," he said, opening the door.

"And no more escapades! No more stealing! No more—"

But the door closed behind him, and he was gone.

Ketan, his mind elsewhere, came around a corner suddenly and ran into someone. The stranger steadied himself by gripping Ketan's upper arms—and when the two looked each other in the eye, it turned out they were not strangers after all. "Ah! Master Ketan!" Kedar said in his slow, accented voice.

Ketan blinked. The light of recognition flickered in his eye. "Kedar, isn't it? You were my cousin's tutor, right?"

"I am flattered that you remember me. You've dropped your parcel. Here, let me. . . ."

Ketan stooped first and retrieved his package, though. "I was just bringing home a gift to my wife. She's . . . well, we're expecting a child any day now."

"How fortunate. May the blessings of the gods be on the both of you." Kedar made motions to brush the dust off Ketan's parcel.

"Here, you don't need to do that."

"Oh! I'm so sorry. Force of habit. A lifetime of teaching, of being a substitute father to so many young people. I sometimes offend. My apologies."

The very real humility in the older man's manner came through to Ketan, and he softened. "Don't mind me," he said kindly. "I've been jumpy lately. What with Nebet's pregnancy . . . and I've been yanked back into military service. I'd hoped to be free of it all. . . ."

"Ah, yes. This Egyptian invasion. Tell me, Master Ketan, are we really in danger? I've been presented with a rather difficult choice, one that could change my life altogether. And if there's a real chance of our being overrun by—"

"It's possible. Very possible. Baliniri wouldn't have ordered this complete mobilization if there weren't great danger, I know that."

Kedar pondered that a bit. "I see. I suppose I should go off for a while and think this out. Perhaps I could visit my in-laws in the country. My dear departed wife, may she find peace, had a brother and sister upriver who . . . ah, but I'm taking too much of your time—"

"Quite all right," Ketan said. "Look, it's been nice running into you, Kedar. Give my best to Tuya when you see her, will you?"

"Yes, sir. I suspect I won't be seeing her for a week or two, though. Not if I do what I—"

Ketan clapped him on the arm familiarly and smiled, wanting to get home but taking his leave as courteously as he could. "Good luck to you, Kedar."

*   *   *

For some time Kedar stood in the middle of the thoroughfare, thinking. Not until it was apparent that he was blocking the path for others who wished to pass did he mutter an apology and step to one side.

Very well, he thought. *That's what I'll do. I'll go away for a few days and think this over.* But not to the in-laws; he would head upriver to Edfu, perhaps, and get away by himself while he pondered the prospect of a companionable marriage to Tuya. He could easily find shelter at the school for scribes—they always had a spare room for a brother in the craft. And then, in peace and solitude, he could sort out his thoughts.

If he were thirty years younger, it would all be so simple. Tuya was attractive, in spite of the hard emotional life she had led with her now-deceased husband. She was wealthy, but not arrogant or haughty. There was magnanimity in her, too: Look at how she had created that fictitious bequest for him to give him a measure of independence from which to ponder her offer. There was real delicacy and maturity in a gesture like that. Then why did he hesitate?

He sighed. Perhaps he was just used to the life he was leading, comfortable with the dull, reassuring routine, knowing in advance what every day would bring. A life without surprises.

But that was not entirely correct. Even his quiet life had its little surprises and irregularities. Look at the boy he had caught stealing today—a decent lad, but one forced into bad ways by circumstance. Without thinking, he had taken the lad aside to keep him from being caught by the storekeeper and turned over to the authorities. He had given the boy a talking to and tried to steer him onto the right path. Kedar smiled to himself. There was always the chance that one could do someone some good, after all. The boy was an orphan and lived with a woman of the streets who was no relation to him. She had some plan for him, which the boy disapproved of and dreaded. More than that, the child would not say.

Think, his mind told him, *about how many such children*

you'll be able to help once the bequest is settled upon you. And how many more you could help as the husband of a wealthy woman. You could establish a fund for them; buy a place to house them; provide for apprenticeship or education for them.

Ah, idle dreams . . . But were they idle, after all? Had he not just been presented with the opportunity of a lifetime? One worth giving up his independence, his privacy, his autonomy for?

He shook his head. "Vexing question," he said under his breath. He would have to think it over very carefully.

IV

As the shadows lengthened and the sun sank low, Riki's flagship overtook a pair of wretched vessels heading upriver bearing wounded from the fighting at Lisht. Riki called to one of these and interrupted his flotilla's downriver progress just long enough to ask for news of the battle. "Give it to me without nice-sounding lies," he said to the commander of the unit guarding the hospital ship.

The officer frowned. "You have how many men coming to our relief in this shipment?"

"Six hundred," Riki answered.

"Nowhere near enough," the man said. "We need twice that today, and as many again the day after. You haven't any idea how many of them there are, or how good they are. Those damned Greeks! I'd rather fight wild leopards with my bare hands." The officer sighed deeply. "We're putting up a good fight, sir. Better than Baliniri has any right to expect. But . . ."

"Go on."

"It's a losing cause. If it weren't for Baba of El-Kab, sir, we'd have been overrun altogether by now."

"Ah! Baba of El-Kab!" Riki said. "Baka's right arm all those years, down in the delta?"

"I don't know what his record was in the old days, but he's the best man in the world on the short end of a siege. As tough as nails, and the people—army and civilian alike—love him like their father. For all that he's no older than Baliniri. He has everyone working happily in harness." He hesitated.

Riki waited. Then he had to ask the question. "But?"

"But . . . we need an *attack* leader, somebody who can lead a charge against the bastards and drive them back. We're hoping you'll turn out to be one."

"Or whoever Baliniri can find. Very well. I understand the situation. I'm glad you're not undervaluing Baba of El-Kab. He's been the right man in the right place so far."

The officer smiled wryly. "But if you can *win* a skirmish now and then, or at least make them pay dearly for anything they get from us . . ."

"I'll see what I can do." Riki's eyes narrowed. "Baba of El-Kab," he said thoughtfully. "I'm looking forward to meeting him."

The old soldier's name was known throughout all Upper Egypt, and the Nubian soldiers who had been put up in the Thebes garrison during their king Nehsi's last diplomatic mission had spoken well of him. Baba, on loan from Sekenenre's army to Nehsi's on a special mission, had helped the Nubian officers throw back a particularly vicious invasion by a young hothead from far up the Nile who had decided to contest Nehsi's right to the kingdom. To hear the Nilotics tell it, Baba of El-Kab was blood brothers with half the Nubian army now, a man the black soldiers would gladly follow to the death.

Why then was this Egyptian commander describing Baba as a man valiant in a defensive position but lacking in the ability to strike quickly and viciously at a stronger foe and drive him back from captured ground? Curious! Riki couldn't wait to meet Baba.

But would Baba be resentful about being commanded by a man—himself, Riki—half his age or less? A man with less experience? Would there be friction? Baba of El-Kab was widely known as a tough, salty old officer of the old school, a man who, like Baliniri, had risen through the ranks to his present position by sheer ability and valor.

Stop that! he told himself. *Don't go anticipating trouble where there isn't any!* He stiffened, stood tall. "Well," he said, "I've held you up long enough, my friend. Go in safety!"

"You, too!" the officer said. "Bring us a victory or two! We need one—and soon!"

Ketan arrived home at sundown to find Nebet, red-eyed from weeping, sitting disconsolately before a cold stove, wringing her hands. "What's the matter?" he asked, rushing to her side. "Nebet!"

"Oh, K-ketan," she said, leaning against him and clutching at his encircling arm. "I . . . I keep having the most horrible premonition. I didn't mean to tell you. But with the baby so near now . . ."

He fell on his knees beside her and looked into her eyes, holding her hands in his. "Tell me about it," he urged gently. After listening patiently to her terrible fears about his death and hers, and of their child growing up without either of them, an orphan in another's home, he patted her hands reassuringly. "I . . . I know it's silly of me," she said with a sob. "But it keeps coming back again and again."

"That settles it," he said. "I'm going to call the midwife now and have her stay with you until the child comes. You're alone too much. I'm going to be home for a few days. I worked extra hard and got a bit of time off. But even if I have to go out for only an hour, I want someone here with you."

"I don't want a midwife, Ketan. I want you."

"I know, my darling." He pulled her to him and kissed her forehead, rubbing her back warmly as he spoke. "And as for that dream . . . Nebet, women have had fears about their children's safety and welfare ever since people have had children. You mustn't give them any credence."

She was still stiff and withdrawn under his caressing hands. Quickly he changed the subject. "Oh, I have some news! I ran into Cheta. She said that Tuya is thinking of marrying again. Imagine!"

She pulled away and looked at him teary-eyed. "Tuya?"

"And to a man twice her age! Well, no, that's exaggerating. She's what? Forty or so? He's over sixty if he's a day. You'll never guess who."

It was just the right approach. Already she had forgotten her troubles, lured into a new mood by gossip. "Ketan, I haven't the faintest idea."

"To Kedar! Seth's old teacher! She doesn't know what Kedar will say when it comes right down to it, but my feeling is—"

"He doesn't have an *outnou* to his name."

"He does now. That Tuya, she's a sly one. She's had some sort of bequest registered in his name. Now when he makes the decision, it'll be from a position of independence."

"And it won't look as though she'd bought a husband. I'm surprised she's considering a man so much older."

Ketan rocked up off his knees to sit beside her, one arm around her waist. "You know Tuya's had a hard life. Too many ups and downs, too many unpleasant surprises. I think she'd appreciate a more restful life these days. And Kedar's a very quiet, comfortable chap to be around, as I remember him."

"Of course Seth will approve. Kedar's been as much of a father as Seth ever had, really."

"Yes. Curious you should bring Seth up. He seems to have disappeared again."

She smiled wanly. "Well, that's not uncommon."

"This time is different. In the past there's always been someone in the bazaar who has some idea where Seth could be found. This time he seems to have vanished as though he'd never existed at all."

"Well, he'll turn up." Now her smile was a warmer and more accepting one. "Oh, Ketan. Look at me! I feel ever so much better. Will I really have you home with me for a couple of days? Or are soldiers or court messengers going to come in in the middle of the night again and—"

"Even if they do, I won't go with them," he assured her. "This is too important a time for us. Besides, there's nothing left for me to do until the beginning of next week. Riki's units left today for Thebes, and my forges are working night and day and doing quite well without me, thank you."

Her smile wavered. She clutched at his arm. "Please, Ketan! Don't leave me! Not for so much as a moment!"

"What the blazes is *he* doing here?" Smendes demanded, looking the troublesome recruit up and down. The boy was covered with red dust from head to foot, and his issue garment hung in rags.

The soldier in charge of the human scarecrow made a face when he turned to Smendes. "You put this one to work at digging a latrine trench, sir. And to be sure, it was the damnedest latrine trench you ever saw, sir, for all that this recruit doesn't know one end of a shovel from another. It looked like someone was going to bury a pharaoh in it, instead of a pile of—"

The boy's caked lips opened. "It was structurally sound," he explained calmly. "If someone hadn't driven a double-ox team so close to it, pulling a wagon full of dirt from the excavation next to the—"

"I see," Smendes said, the "s" hissing like cold water on red-hot coals. "And the casualties?"

"Three oxen. One axle from the wagon. Two recruits and a subaltern in hospital."

"That does it!" Smendes roared. "Throw this—this oaf into the dungeon for a week! Bread and water!" Then a sudden thought struck him, and his tone took on caution. "Which subaltern?" he said suspiciously.

"The little pipsqueak from Edfu, sir, who—"

Smendes almost smiled, then caught himself. "A week's too long. Make it four days. In hospital, you say? Anything broken?" His voice hinted of barely concealed delight.

"His jaw's dislocated, sir. He won't be able to talk for —"

"Make it three days." He glared at the prisoner. "You! Get out of my sight! And if they bring you back here before me, your next stretch in the pits will be for a month, and I don't care how many subalterns you disable." The prisoner, as bland as ever, turned to go obediently. "You!" Smendes called after him. "When you come out, show me your design for the trench, eh?"

The prisoner nodded his head respectfully. As he turned

away it was obvious that his mind was elsewhere, and that a three-day stay in the dungeons of the Thebes citadel would likely have as little effect on him as would any command. Smendes, eyebrows raised, pulled off his helmet to scratch his bald head. And at last he permitted himself a grin so gleeful as to be unseemly, given the circumstances.

Tuya sat, stunned, looking at the two of them. Her eyes went to the boy, and then settled once again on the woman, on her weathered skin and baggy eyes and dowdy clothes. Try as she might, Tuya could not conjure up any memory at all of Tamshas, the wealthy merchant's daughter she had seen only once in her life, during the raid by Baka's little band so many years before. Tuya did remember that the merchant's daughter had been very beautiful and pampered. What had turned her into a coarse woman of the streets, bloated, her face shapeless and indistinct from drinking and debauchery?

"I . . . I'm sorry," she said in a shaken voice. "I'm having a hard time grasping it all. I don't mean to be rude, but . . ."

The woman who called herself Tamshas looked around at the unostentatious affluence in which Tuya lived, at the tasteful wall hangings, the understated furniture, the imported plants. "I understand," she said hoarsely, her voice gravelly from years of hard drinking and cursing. "Living in fine circumstances like these, you'd easily forget how the other half lives. The idea of responsibility for your actions, and the actions of others in your household . . . it's all so easy to look the other way, not having to worry where your next meal's coming from—"

"You don't have to tell me about it!" Tuya said in an anguished voice. "I know! I was poor back when you were rich—that is, if you're who you say you are."

"If?" the woman asked ironically. "Look at the face of your husband's son and tell me you still doubt me, my friend. This is the son I had by Ben-Hadad. I worked and slaved and scraped to raise this boy. Look in his eyes and tell me you're not sure. Is that Ben-Hadad's face or not? And *then* tell me you refuse to take him in! Tell me you don't owe me for raising him and returning him to you safe and sound and healthy!"

Tuya stared at the boy in horror. The eyes . . . that round face . . . the curly hair . . . the open and guileless look on his face . . . Tears came to Tuya's eyes. Ben-Hadad had looked just so when she had met him. He had been about eighteen at most, and this boy was what? Ten? The timing was about right. Ben-Hadad had disappeared about ten years back, and she had later heard of his death in the delta; and at great expense Baka had pulled strings to get his body returned for burial.

"Come here," she said to the boy. "Let me look at you." He moved to almost within arm's length and stood before her, half-afraid to smile. "What's your name?" she asked in a strange, forced voice.

"Meni," the boy said. Timidly. Hopefully.

CHAPTER EIGHT

On the Nile

I

Several miles below Lisht, in Hai-held territory, the Nile was at a lower level than it had been since the worst days of the great famine. As a result, the river had narrowed disastrously, and many sandbars and small islands that normally lay well below the surface were now exposed, and the channels between them were shallow enough to allow a man to wade across and not get wet above the waist.

This enabled the Hai commanders to maintain almost absolute control over river traffic. And while the great battles on the west bank of the river raged a couple of miles upstream, the Hai sentries stood guard at the narrows, making certain that no Egyptian patrol slipped past them.

It was lonely, boring work. The island manned by the two bowmen was flat, featureless; the view from atop it, no more than a few feet above the level of the water, was dull and boring. Each watch brought its own food and water, so there were no authorized visits.

Making the monotony even worse was the fact that the sentries' control had not been challenged by so much as a stray fisherman in more than two days. Under the circumstances Teherhu, the senior of the two, was bored beyond belief midway through the watch. He had given his partner, Isheb, permission for a swim an hour before; now, out of sorts, he called Isheb in. "All right," he said, "that's enough." He backed up the order with an impatient wave of the hand.

Isheb, naked and darkened by the sun, reluctantly waded to shore. The water here was barely up to midthigh. "Do you want to take a dip?" he asked. "I'll gladly watch out for you."

Teherhu sat cross-legged on the islet and glared at Isheb. "No," he said irritably. "Put something on. You never know when someone might come to inspect us."

Isheb yawned and stretched but made no immediate move to don his uniform. "If anyone comes, I'll pretend to be one of the Greeks. You know how they are about running around naked. And mind you, they're the fair-haired boys of the Hai command just now, after the service they did at the border, breaking the Egyptian lines. They're so popular with the upper echelon that I wouldn't be surprised to hear of a general order to discard our loincloths altogether."

"Fat chance of that," Teherhu said. "The Bedouin are so prudish, they'd never put up with such an order." He yawned this time; the habit was catching. "You served with the Greeks for a bit, did you?"

"Yes. They're crazy." Isheb sat down atop his discarded kilt and wiped the salt water out of his eyes. "Personally, I think their mode of dress makes sense. Nothing to get torn or dirty. The southern units of the Egyptian army fight wearing nothing but a sword belt." He shook his head. "The Greeks are good to fight alongside, but you wouldn't want to get to know them much better than that."

Teherhu squinted up and down the stream; nothing out of line as far as the eye could see. "Quarrelsome, then?"

"Yes, but mainly just crazy. For example, they've only got one thing on their minds once the fighting is over. And when that happens, nothing's safe. Not a man or boy or girl or horse or stray dog or—"

Teherhu made a moue. "Don't be disgusting."

"I'm just telling you how they are. They'd do it to a hippopotamus if somebody would hold the thing down."

"Ugh. Stop. I don't want to hear any more. And put on something, even if it's just your loincloth. Someone might come."

Isheb stood up, yawned again, stretched mightily, and reluctantly reached for his kilt. But as he did, he looked downstream. "Someone *is* coming," he said, "believe it or not." Unhurriedly he buckled the kilt and sword belt around his waist. "You see? Down there? Two of them. In some kind of silly-looking little sailboat."

Teherhu stood and squinted northward, shielding his eyes with one hand. "Well!" he said. "I was wondering if we were ever going to be asked to earn our pay out here. I wonder who they are."

Isheb stood beside him, fists on hips. "Whoever they are," he said, "they're overdressed for this weather. Long robes! Hoods over their heads!"

"Huh," his superior said. "Not priests of any cult I know of, either—none of the proper colors in either robe. Well, if they're spies who don't want to attract attention, they're sure going about it the wrong way."

The little vessel came closer. The two soldiers reached for their bows and quivers. They still could not see the passengers in the boat. "All right, there, you two!" Teherhu called out in a voice of command. "Come aground and identify yourselves!"

Hands made invisible by the long, baggy sleeves of the garment stayed on the tiller and steered the little coracle into the narrow channel. There was not a sound from either of the hooded figures. Teherhu reached for his bow and nocked an arrow. "Did you hear me?" he shouted. He repeated his words in each of two Lower Nile dialects, with no results. "Isheb!" he said. "Wade out to the boat. Stop them. I don't want to have to kill anyone, but—"

The words hung menacingly in the air. Isheb moved toward the little boat and blocked the channel. One of the invisible hands yanked hard on the lines to shorten sail. The other figure turned the tiller toward land.

As Isheb approached the stern, Teherhu drew the bow

and aimed at the first of the two hooded figures. "All right, now," he heard Isheb say. "Let's have a look at who we have here—"

He reached for the arm nearest him; reached, in fact, inside the baggy sleeve and pulled out a hand—and stood suddenly as if glued to the spot, his eyes wide, his mouth hanging ajar! He released the stark white hand as if it had been deadly poison.

"Get back!" Isheb shrieked. "You! Get away from me!" He recoiled, stumbled, fell back in the water.

The two in the boat were quick to respond, giving the little craft full sail and steering hastily out into the channel once more. Teherhu slacked his bow, staring after them, as Isheb struggled to his feet and frantically washed his hand in the Nile.

"Gods!" Teherhu said. "Was that what I thought I saw?"

"Yes," Isheb said, cringing. "And I *touched* one of them. Lepers! Stinking lepers! Here, now! No! Don't shoot! Don't you know how much bad luck it is to kill one of them? Let the Egyptians have them! Good riddance, too! I hope they give the disease to the whole city of Thebes!"

Teherhu looked at his subordinate with horror. The bow hung limply by his side now; the arrow had fallen to the ground. Beside him, Isheb washed the offending hand again and again, his features fixed in an expression of abject fear. He looked upstream and saw the pariahs pass the bar and turn out into the broad river, tacking out past the main channel into calmer water, heading ever southward.

The battle lines had been stabilized for two days within sight of the very walls of Lisht. After the first mad dash from the boats when the combined armies of the Hai and their mercenary associates had taken firm control of the northern access to the river, the defenders had wisely chosen their time and place and, within an hour of seeing the Hai make camp, had suddenly swooped down and hit them with a vicious attack that had decimated a full two troops of Maaziou warriors and destroyed the entire right flank of the invading army. The defenders of Lisht then quickly returned to their city with minimal casualties.

As the Hai line re-formed, darkness had come on quickly, a night of no moon and few stars, with drifting clouds. Baba of El-Kab had chosen the opportunity to lead personally a devastating raid, which had penetrated the invaders' half-formed defenses and struck deep into the center of the line. Three captains and one foreign general had fallen before the knives of the assassins, and when the dawn shone bright and early, the heads and the distinctive helmets of these warriors decorated pikes atop the walls of Lisht, and the morale of the city troops was higher than it had been before the Hai attack had begun.

In the next two days the Hai and their allies had quickly come to know, respect, and hate the sturdy, bald-headed figure of Baba of El-Kab, clearly visible just beyond their bowmen's range, striding confidently from unit to unit, haranguing his men, shoring up their confidence, joking coarsely with them, occasionally bellowing a taunt across the lines at his enemies, and—when an attack finally came from the Hai lines—leaping eagerly into the fray, hacking lustily away with his deadly battle-ax of gleaming bronze, a legendary weapon said to have been made personally by blind Shobai, last of the great armorers of the line called the Children of the Lion.

In battle it quickly became evident that Baba of El-Kab was first and foremost a fighting general, one who would batter his way through a whole squad of the enemy, with or without help, grinning, even laughing all the while!

For some reason he had captured the attention of the naked Greeks on the Hai side. They spat when they said his name and called him "the Toad," referring to his blocky physique, bald head, and bowed legs. They cursed him when he threw back their attacks, and they shouted threats at him across the line—threats in Greek, in Egyptian, in the Hai tongue, and for all anyone could tell, in half a dozen other languages—when there was a lull in the fighting. But they respected him as they respected no other general, save for a few of their own. The Hellene who killed him would not only win that famous battle-ax, he would earn rich booty when the city finally fell: five men's portions, plus his pick of the slaves that the city's demise would provide.

Now, after a morning's exchange of minor assaults designed to test the other side's line for weak spots, Cepheus, commander of the first Greek troop, spotted his nemesis beyond the lines, inspecting a unit of green recruits newly brought up from the reserves. "There he is!" he called out in his powerful bass voice. "There's the Toad, inspecting his children! Trying to decide which one of them to commit incest with tonight!"

Across the lines, the round face of Baba of El-Kab poked up from behind the row of spears, breaking into an insolent grin. Up went the burly arm, and the broad hand made the ancient sign of the fig, an insult understood instantly by all men of all countries. "Come over and join me!" he said in a voice full of good-natured raillery. "I promise you, boy-lover, you can molest any one of them that you can disarm. But you'll find that harder on this side of the line than on that one, I'll wager! Our recruits don't bend quite so easily at the waist, the way yours do!"

Cepheus's thick lips curled in a snarl. "You talk bravely," he said, "for a man who won't meet me in the space between the lines in single combat!" The reference was to a challenge many times made, many times laughed away.

"If you could fight," Baba of El-Kab said in a voice that carried every bit as well as Cepheus's, "it might be worth taking you on, just to teach the recruits a few easy parries for use against a foe so inept he might just as well be unarmed. But I could teach the lesson quite as well using a blind, one-legged beggar with a withered arm and a bad case of palsy. Why should I spend my time wasting the lesson on a perverted indigent who can't even afford a rag to cover his rear end, and who insists on exposing his, uh, shortcomings to the shocked gaze of every passerby?"

At the insult to his manhood, Cepheus reddened and fumbled for adequate words to answer Baba. But it came out as incoherent bluster when he finally spoke, and it was evident to his whole line that he had lost face once again. Down the line one of his own warriors chuckled—and spent the next night chained to a wagon wheel, lamenting his own impulsive nature.

* * *

In the morning the Hellenes attacked once again. No one was surprised that Baba of El-Kab, superbly prepared, personally led the defense—a stiff one, in which the Egyptians lost not so much as a stride of ground—and the counterattack that followed, in which a well-placed flanking unit suddenly struck in perfect coordination with Baba's advance, catching the Greek unit in a pincer movement and mowing down the entire squad on the left of the Greek line.

In a trice the Hellene unit was surrounded, and the Egyptians closed in on them. Towering half a head taller than any of his remaining men, Cepheus cursed and squinted through the dust in search of his old nemesis, the man he called "the Toad."

"Baba!" he bellowed. "Baba of El-Kab! Where are you? Come to me, Toad!"

His words had hardly been uttered when the familiar bellow cut through the surrounding lines. "Ah, there he is!" said Baba, grinning broadly. "Let him through, boys! Do whatever you like with the rest, but this one I want, to find out once and for all whether his fighting heart is as small and insignificant as his—"

With a bellow of rage Cepheus hacked his way through the still unmoving Egyptian circle around his unit and to the side of his old enemy. "Stand and fight!" he said with a wry and ironic salute.

But as he saluted, Baba of El-Kab, smiling, ran him through. It took no more than that. He looked down at the naked and bleeding form of the man who had attacked him, and sighed. "Talk's cheap, boys," he told his unit. "Finish them off cleanly, now. No prisoners today. You know the rules—odd-numbered days only. Prisoners tomorrow: We'll need them to carry away the wounded. None today."

With that, he turned his back on the whole scene and walked away, pausing to retrieve the feathered helmet that had been Cepheus's only article of clothing. This he used to wipe his sword clean; then he tossed it away as if it had been a bone gnawed white by a lion.

II

Enraged by the loss of an entire unit of Greek shock troops, the Hai commanders immediately called for a retaliatory strike along the section of the Egyptian front personally supervised by Baba of El-Kab, and word was passed through the Hai lines that promotions and substantial cash bonuses would go to whomever killed or captured the man called "the Toad."

When the sun was high, the Hai armies struck. A bow-and-arrow barrage preceded the charge, causing little damage. But when the charge came—wave upon wave of Hai-hired mercenaries falling upon the Egyptian lines—even the splendid morale and high spirits of the defenders were not equal to the task of holding the line. The Maaziou warriors struck just to the right and left of the Egyptians' center unit and drove the defenders back a hundred yards or so before being stopped in their tracks by a stiffened resistance led by Baba of El-Kab himself.

This left a salient in the line. Baba solved the problem by falling back to reduce the risk of being surrounded and captured; his retreat was a model for all such withdrawals, and by the time the line was straight again, he could look across his ranks and smile, having lost not one soldier in the maneuver.

Nevertheless, he had lost valuable ground, and in the distance he could see new and fresh troops coming up from the rear of the Hai lines. More troops! He kept his round face impassive, but inside his heart sank. Would they never run out of money with which to hire new mercenaries? And how long could the Egyptians hold out here, even losing only one man to the enemy's three, as they had been doing since the siege began?

It was in this mood that he received the runner from his headquarters. Sourly he rasped, "What is it, son?"

"Sir," the runner said, panting, "report from the right flank. We've captured a captain from the other side and thought you might want to be present when he's interrogated."

"Right you are," the commander said. "Take me to him."

Baba barked orders to the unit commanders nearest him, then set out along the path after the young man, matching the boy stride for stride, looking as fit and fresh as if he were thirty years younger and had not been fighting all morning.

The Hai captain was spread-eagled on the ground, hands and feet tied to stakes driven into the earth. He managed to raise his head long enough to see who it was they were bringing to watch him undergo questioning. "Ah, the Toad," he said. "I'm flattered. I didn't think I rated a visit from the supreme commander himself. At least I can die with a bloated opinion of my own worth and importance." The battle-weary nihilism of his tone made the Egyptians standing around him shake their heads.

"You don't have to die," said Baba of El-Kab with surprising blandness. "You don't even have to suffer the torture. Just tell us what we need to know."

The captain's hands pulled at their bonds feebly; then he slumped again, and his head, raised for another moment, fell back to the ground. "Perhaps I could," he said, his voice quivering with self-loathing. "What the devil do I care if Apophis wins Lisht and Thebes? I'm not even a soldier by choice. I was impressed into service at the last moment to fatten up Apophis's army and was made captain because my relatives have a bit of influence."

Baba of El-Kab motioned the others away and knelt by the young captain's side. "I see, son. You have no particular quarrel with us, and I have little quarrel with you—except that Apophis sent you upriver to try to take my town away from me. What's your name, son?"

"Nushin. I'm the great-grandson of one of the warriors who rode with Manouk and conquered Syria and Canaan and the delta. I was but a scribe at Apophis's court. A student of Hai history, can you imagine it! Not that I was allowed to dig very deep, most of the time. Students of history are limited to researching genealogy for some parvenu who wants to prove he always had a pedigree. . . ."

"Here, you must be uncomfortable," said Baba. He looked up at the two guards still standing above the captured soldier.

"I'm going to cut him loose, boys. No use making him miserable. Here, pass me your dagger." The guard blinked but passed it along; his commander swiftly cut through the thongs restraining the captain's wrists and helped him to a sitting position. For a moment Baba looked the prisoner in the eye, and then looked down at the dagger in his hand; finally he shrugged and tossed it back to the guard. "He'll be all right," he said. "I left the leg fetters on. He can't go anywhere. If you boys could step back, I'd like to ask this fellow a few questions."

He waited until they were out of earshot, then sat cross-legged next to the prisoner and spoke in a conversational tone. "I hope that's better. Now, you say you were a scholar, eh?"

"Yes," The young man rubbed his wrists. "I was allowed to read the testaments of some of the old-timers who came here in my great-grandfather's day. I learned some things I'd never suspected, given the official version of events we're taught around here when we're young."

He was beginning to warm to his subject. *There's a real, dyed-in-the-wool scroll-roller for you*, thought his captor. *If I were roasting him on a spit, he'd be trying to lecture me on some obscure reference in his specialty.* "Later, son," Baba said gently. "I need more immediate information first. I don't know how many reserves you have and how quickly they can be brought into battle. . . ."

The captain flexed his wrist, wincing. "I can tell you that," he said. "But—did you know Apophis himself was coming here to lead the final charge on Lisht? He may be here already, for all I know."

Baba of El-Kab stared. "Here?" he said. "Now?"

The prisoner tried to move one cramped knee. "Do you mind if I loosen one of these bands?" he asked. "This is extremely uncomfortable."

Baba reached down and untied both ankles. "I'm going to ship you upriver to talk with Baliniri after I'm done with you. Under guard, of course. You'll be treated all right, never fear. Now what were you saying about Apophis coming here?"

"He may already have arrived. If so, he'll be well behind the lines. We've set up headquarters about two leagues downriver. There are reinforcements there—as many as we have on the line here and then some. More are coming up daily. Apophis is counting on wearing you down by attrition, throwing one wave of reserves after another at you until your own forces are exhausted and his aren't."

"I had more or less pegged it that way," said his captor. "Thank the gods for the high hills on our left flank. If your boys could go around us and hit us from the side . . ." He made a face. "Apophis probably thinks we've about had it, then? Then there will be a big push in a day or two?"

"That's what I've been given to understand, sir. If you don't mind my saying so, Apophis doesn't put much stock in the force at Thebes. He undervalues Baliniri, as he underestimates you."

"Well, of such stuff are successful defenses made, my boy. You can't imagine how pleased I am to have made your acquaintance. You've given me half a dozen ideas already. If I can use so much as one of them, my day will have been made. Here, let me help you up. Guard! Would you be so good as to escort us to headquarters?"

Coming downriver on the Nile, sails were seldom necessary because of the strong water current, but for speed Riki had brought along a force of powerful oarsmen, fresh and rested. His flotilla had made record time down toward Thebes and now negotiated the current within sight of the first pickets on the hilltops. "Up oars!" called the second mate as the two burly sailors who manned the tiller oars steered the fleet's flagship toward shore.

Riki, in the bow, turned to the captain. "We'll be docking a few minutes from now, I suppose."

"Yes, sir," the captain verified. He smiled. "We may have broken the downriver record for deep-draft vessels, sir."

"Whether we have or not, I intend to send a letter of commendation for your efforts back to court by the next messenger. You've done well. Our arriving on time may make the difference between keeping Lisht and losing it. Here!" he broke in suddenly, noticing something out on the water. "I thought the evacuation of the city was completed. What's that little boat doing out there?"

The captain looked where Riki pointed. Then he called out a quick series of orders, and within moments a long-boat had been lowered over the side, manned by hard-muscled marines. Bowmen from the flagship fired a warning salvo across the tiny vessel's bow and forced it toward shore.

Riki looked at the hooded figures in the boat and frowned. "Those robes and hoods . . . could be lepers. It's a way they have of dressing, to keep from offending the eye."

But as the longboat approached the small coracle, the two figures threw back their hoods, proving themselves unmarred by the dread disease, and began yelling something that neither Riki nor the captain could understand. The captain motioned to his longboatmen to take the two figures to shore; then he set about the serious business of steering his great vessel toward the long docks up ahead that marked the southern limits of Lisht.

At dockside, surrounded by soldiers, sailors, and guardsmen, stood a figure Riki had been hoping to see ever since setting foot on board: Those bowed legs, that bald head could only belong to Baba of El-Kab. The seasoned soldier stood on the quay, his hands on his hips and feet placed well apart like a sailor's, as he watched the ships bear down on him. Riki forced himself not to smile; this, then, was the hero of the siege of Lisht, the man who had thus far stopped Apophis's great expeditionary army in its tracks despite overwhelming odds!

The moment the ship came into the slip, sailors swarmed ashore, tying up and securing the lines. Riki waited until the gangplank was securely in place, then strode down to the quay. He saluted the blocky commander and said, "Riki of Thebes, sir, reporting for duty with reinforcements from the main garrison!"

In response the toadlike man clapped him on both arms soundly, laughed in a booming bass voice, and embraced him as though they had been old friends. "Riki! I'm glad to see you. I've heard a lot about you, most of it good."

Riki was taken aback. Was this a way to greet a man less experienced than yourself, perhaps, but technically your superior? But he grinned a little nervously and nodded.

"Come on!" the burly commander said, taking Riki by the arm. "I've just captured a Hai captain, and he's spilling his guts to a couple of my men. We have the whole Hai order of battle. And can you believe it? Apophis himself is here to direct our final annihilation! *Apophis!*"

The famous voice, one that could shout across no-man's land and be heard distinctly, carried across the water, even in the wind tunnel of the Nile Valley. As they marched along, Riki noticed the two robed figures from the small boat struggling with the guards who had taken them prisoner; the taller and more powerful-looking of the two perked up his ears at the name Apophis and looked their way.

"What's that you said?" he yelled at Baba of El-Kab. "Did you say Apophis himself was here?"

The commander stopped before him. "I did," he said seriously. "We do have that honor. And who is it that asks me, Baba of El-Kab? Wearing the robes of a leper, for all that you don't seem to be afflicted?"

The robed man pulled loose of his captors and shook the robe to the ground, standing before them in only a narrow loincloth. His body bore the scars of warfare and of whipping: old ones, except for the recent knife wound in his side, scabbed over and healing. "As you can see, I'm clean. I had to get upriver some way or another, and our disguise got us past the Hai guards in the narrows. My companion's clean, too; I'd appreciate it if you could let her leave her robe on for the time being."

Baba of El-Kab, intrigued by this bold stranger, waved the guards aside. "Let him speak."

"Thank you," the stranger said. "So you're Baba of El-Kab! Well met! I've heard much about you!"

Now, though, for the first time, his eye lit on Riki, and he stopped, and a puzzled look came over his face. Something in the stranger's visage awoke memories in Riki, whose face split in a broad grin, and the two embraced as if the same thought had occurred to both of them in the same blink of the eye. There was much hugging and thumping on the back, and a lot of half-finished sentences no one else could quite make out.

"What's this?" asked Baba. "A meeting between long lost brothers? Riki, you could introduce me, I think."

Riki stepped back, smiling. "Of course," he said. "This is Baba of El-Kab, commander of the Lisht garrison. And *this* . . . I have the pleasure of presenting none other than the unacknowledged heir to the throne of the Golden Pharaohs, the eldest son of Apophis!"

"What the devil are you talking about?" exclaimed Baba. "You mean to say this is—"

"Kamose, son of Apophis," finished Riki. It was suddenly very quiet at dockside. "The child of The Prophecy."

III

In the commotion that followed, Aset was largely forgotten for many minutes, left to look on from a distance as the soldiers and guardsmen gathered around the man she knew as Neko, asking questions, talking in heated voices. This suited her dislike of being in the center of things, and she moved back toward the quay's edge, watching the longships disgorge the rank upon rank of soldiers on board. The men peeled off the long lines to file silently down the gangplanks, their faces serious, their young bodies hard and lean.

So this was the war zone! Thus far she had been spared from seeing any violence; their only close call had occurred when the two guards on the sandbar had tried to detain them and been driven away by the leprosy makeup Neko had put on his body. But now she was in Upper Egypt for the first time, and from now on, she would have to live with war constantly.

She looked at Neko and sighed. He was standing tall in the middle of them, looking—even dressed in no more than a loincloth—every bit the leader, singled out by the gods for a special purpose. Look how they treated him, from the lowliest soldier to the commander of the entire garrison!

Neko! She would have to get out of the habit of calling him that, if he was at last going to reveal his true identity to the world. It would take some getting used to. Ever since she had found him on the beach, the name Neko had been on the tip of her tongue and had hung in her mind, even in her dreams. No: *particularly* in her dreams.

Suddenly her heart sank, as it often did these days. To be sure, Neko—Kamose—was a man chosen by destiny for a lofty role. A king's son and the subject of a prophetic tale that concerned nothing less than the long-awaited final removal of the hated Hai dynasty from the lands of Egypt!

Would such a man have a place in his life for the small and commonplace likes of her, Aset? When he came into his own, would he remember her and the things that they had done together, been to each other?

Not that anything much had happened on the trip south. He had treated her like a younger sister, one for whom he felt affection and concern, but no more. Even when they were in danger together, the fact had not drawn them together in the special way she had hoped for when she had first volunteered to bring him south to Egypt.

And now, for perhaps the fortieth time, she contrasted this with her fantasy of what it would have been like if it had been Mara, and not herself, who had accompanied Neko—Kamose—on the trip through the lines. They would have become lovers on the first night, and each day would have brought them closer together . . . and when the ships docked, he would have introduced Mara proudly to the lot of them—captains, generals, whoever—as his lover and companion.

Instead, here *she* was, left standing on the dock, totally forgotten. A wave of shame and despair swept through her, and she turned away to face the river.

But not before catching another glimpse of the young officer who had first recognized Kamose and embraced him. This, then, must be Riki, the young man he had told her so much about, the one who had helped Mara escape from Hakoris and her slave's life so many years ago. Well, he looked nice enough: tall, strong, with a good honest face, and a look in his eye that . . . She turned to look at him again. He had noticed her! He was turning Kamose around and pointing at her, and they were all motioning to her to come join them.

"Gentlemen," Kamose said, steering her into the little circle and peeling the hood back to reveal her newly close-cropped hair, "May I present Aset, one of my best and dearest friends?" He smiled the smile of a proud brother. Aset winced inside but managed a timid smile. "Don't be foolish—to look at her you'd think she was frightened to death. You'd be wrong. She has the heart of a lioness."

"Oh, Nek—Kamose . . ."

"No, I mean it. Riki, this adorable child not only risked her life in the attack on the Children's Refuge, she was one of the prime instigators and planners."

Riki grinned, and there was friendship in his eyes, instant, unreserved. He made a slight bow. "My compliments, Aset. That was a blow well struck. And you must certainly know how close such a project must be to Kamose's heart."

"She does," Kamose assured him. "She and her brother, Isesi—they've been my right hands ever since I landed in the delta. They saved my life. Took me in when I was shipwrecked, and I wouldn't have made it here without her." He looked at her sadly. "How I wish Isesi could have joined us! Gentlemen, he's another one of those people by whom you could be easily fooled. Looks like a quiet, retiring scholar, but he's brave and true like his sister. Unfortunately he couldn't come along; he's needed where he is. And Mara—"

"Mara?" Riki said, a new light in his eye. "What have you heard from Mara?"

"I'm sorry to say that Hakoris's people have recaptured her," Kamose answered. Neither man noticed how Aset's face fell as the conversation shifted focus. "Getting her back will be a high priority once we've driven the Hai back—"

"Easier said than done, my friend," said Baba of El-Kab. "I captured a Hai captain today, and he says the plan is to bleed us white up here. When they've exhausted all our reserves, there'll still be plenty of them, and they'll just walk into Lisht without opposition."

Riki nodded. "The only thing we have going for us has been our friend here from El-Kab, who has got our morale very high, from all I hear—"

"Splendid," Kamose said. "Would you like to lower *their* morale?" He looked Riki and Baba in the eye. "An idea struck me on the way through the lines. Did I hear someone say my father was going to be in the Hai camp today?" Riki nodded. "The Hai are getting cocky and careless. Aset and I shouldn't have had so easy a time of it, getting through the guards on the river. If one were to . . ."

Ovannes, commander of the Hai legions, met with Learchus, ranking commander of the Greek mercenaries in the delta army, well apart from the lines. Both men had left orders with their runners to come after them in their hiding place if any pressing developments occurred, but they agreed that it was imperative they discuss the campaign well away from any eavesdroppers, particularly Apophis's sycophants and informants.

It was sundown; shadows from the western hills lay halfway across the shallow Nile. Ovannes, shiny in distinctive Hai body armor, watched as the naked Greek paced at water's edge, his hairy body that of an old lion's. He did not speak for a moment or two. Then he said, "*He's* here, you know." His voice, sour and sarcastic, left no doubt who "he" was.

"Ah, yes," the Hellene said, spitting into the water. "Our august employer. Tell me, does he always travel in such state? Among the Greeks, a king would be ashamed to put on that much pomp if he were bluffing his enemies. We're not much on ceremony back where I come from, you know."

"There was a time when we Hai weren't, either, my friend. We were simple people, called the Shepherd Kings, nomads who carried everything we owned wherever we went. When we conquered Syria, we drove our herds before us. We did so all the way to the Sinai desert, and then we lost them all crossing those hellish wastes." He made a moue.

"We've grown soft and weak. Too proud to be called 'shep herds.' Our ancestors—Manouk's generation—would have taken Lisht already."

"You underestimate the Upper Egypt boys," the Greek said. "I lost a damned good troop to them today. The same men, mind you, fought with me at Ilios. This Baba of El-Kab is a soldier's soldier, and he's not leading weaklings. Don't be so hard on your own side, my friend."

"Be that as it may, we now have Apophis to deal with. He has fantasies of leading us in the final push against the Egyptians before we go upriver to take Thebes."

"So you've asked me here to talk, figuring I didn't like Apophis any more than you do. You're right! I don't. But what can we do?"

"I'd *like* to assassinate the son of a whore, of course. He's wrecked this country, and my people. I knew him back when he was still called Aram, you know. He'd steal the maggots off a dead dog. Gods! What a record! First we have Salitis, a madman king with his brains addled by the pox, then this dolt."

"You realize," the Greek said dryly, "that we don't need to take Lisht. We've taken the delta *and* the Fayum. I've two troops of mercenaries guarding the last decent-sized source of grain the Egyptians had. We could just sit back until they starve to death. When they're all dead, *then* we could start farming the Fayum again."

Ovannes stared. That idea had not occurred to him. Its sheer audacity and breathtaking simplicity impressed him. "I confess, my friend, that until this moment I'd still had some reservations about you, about the wisdom of Apophis in tak-ing you boys on. But if you're capable of straight thinking like that . . . well, my compliments. You go right to the heart of things."

"Quite so," the Greek said, scratching himself. Ovannes blushed and averted his eyes. The Greek yawned, a bit boorishly. "Now that we've figured out what needs to be done, we should get started before more good men in both our units get killed for no reason."

"If I thought that Apophis's vast entourage of sycophants would let us get close to him, I'd vote for staging a military coup of our own. Tonight. Slip in there and cut the pig's throat and declare—oh, just *any* damned body king. Pick a name out of a hat. Draw straws."

The Greek did not speak for a moment. He stood looking out over the water, burly arms crossed over his chest. Ovannes noted the fine network of scars on his back, his buttocks, his stout legs. Was there a place where the man had not been wounded? "Why don't you throw a big feast in his honor?" he suggested softly. "Make a fuss over him. Surround him with your own people, under the pretext of lionizing him. Haul a bunch of lambs and fowl over from the Fayum farms and butcher them, then feed him as if you were stuffing a goose. When he's eaten his fill and as drunk as a lord, lying there in his vomit and giggling to himself about what a wonderful fellow he is . . ." He looked up at the sky above, at the tiny moon already visible over the low eastern horizon. "Then we carve the goose we've stuffed. Simple as that, my friend. Would *you* like to be pharaoh? I wouldn't. I like to be out and about. I like to fight too much. Now, you, you might make a good king. No worse than this popinjay from Avaris, at any rate. Be a pleasure to serve someone who can tell fat cow from lean bull for a damned change." He grinned venally. "Of course, I'd expect a rather substantial fee for acting as your, uh, consultant in this, for providing, as it were, valuable legal and career advice."

Ovannes pursed his lips and knit his brows. Finally he rasped, "I'm trying to think of holes in your argument."

"And you're not doing very well at it, I'll wager." The Hellene's grin was mocking, cynical—and at the same time oddly friendly. "Go on. I'm waiting. I won't rush you."

IV

For the first time in several days there was a quiet night along the Hai-Egyptian line. Riki, Baba of El-Kab, and their captains braced themselves for a dawn offensive, but none came. And as the day advanced, Riki's leaders strode up and down the ranks, setting the men to tasks like polishing their weapons and body armor—anything to keep them busy and alert in case the Hai attack was launched.

But the quiet was not disturbed, and by midday two of Riki's captains conferred and drew straws to see which one of them would have to ask the crucial question. Deser, of the third troop, lost the draw and was faced with confronting the new commander in chief. "Sir," he said now, standing stiffly after an impeccable salute, "we think there's a good chance for doing damage if we attack just opposite our unit. Things are very lax in their lines there just now."

"Stand easy," Riki said. He looked across the headquarters area at where Aset sat with Baba of El-Kab. Locking eyes with Baba, he winked. "Your suggestion's a fine one, Captain, but I'm not going to take you up on it." He took a seat on a building block left behind by some construction crew centuries before. "I'm going to tell you something in confidence. Not even a word to your dearest friend in the lines."

"Mum's the word, sir."

"Very well. We slipped a man behind the Hai lines. Apophis is in the camp now, you know. If our man can get close enough . . ." He waited for the look of understanding, then went on. "Ordinarily, starting a scrap along our lines to divert attention from our man is usually a good idea. Tonight it won't be necessary; we sent out a patrol in the night and kidnapped one of their pickets, and word is that a big feast is planned for tonight, to honor Apophis. Operation is shut down in the Hai camp for the time being. The picket was also . . . persuaded to tell us a rumor he'd heard, that someone in the Hai camp is planning a coup tonight. As you can imagine, he didn't want to give us this information. It took until midmorning today to extract it from him, poor fellow."

Deser winced. "I understand, sir. How does this affect our man?"

"It makes things very sticky for him." Riki shook his head. "He insisted on doing this. I never would have ordered him to do it—particularly not when he's the best friend I ever had in the world, other than Baliniri, perhaps."

"Do you think he has a chance, sir?"

"It's in the hands of the gods. If anyone in the world can get through, he can. But I wish he'd known about this coup before he went behind the lines." Riki rose again, dismissing the young officer. "Now, remember—not a word of this to anyone."

"No, sir!" Deser's salute was as faultless as before. He turned on one heel and went away.

Riki went over to Aset and Baba of El-Kab. "That young captain is a good man. He had the right idea, actually. I haven't given up on the notion of causing a little ruckus on their lines before the day's out, as much to make it look like an ordinary, run-of-the-mine day as anything."

"Oh, I wish Kamose hadn't gone!" Aset said miserably. "I'm so frightened for him."

"And well might you be," remarked Baba. "But remember, my dear, that we sent one of our best men with him to be at his back. And Kamose is a resolute and resourceful fellow, with plenty of experience." He patted her on the shoulder in a fatherly gesture. "I wish I could talk you into going inside the city, Aset. Let me send you in with our next messenger to Lisht. The battling could break out at any time, and it could be very dangerous for you to remain here. You wouldn't be deserting Kamose."

She wavered visibly . . . and then reluctantly nodded her head. "I suppose that is what he would want me to do. I'm certainly not doing him any good hanging around here. And I'm in your way."

Baba embraced her impulsively, patting her back reassuringly. Behind her back he returned Riki's earlier wink. "A wise decision, my dear. Riki, get one of the messengers up here, will you?"

When she was gone the two commanders moved up to the observation point and silently looked out over no-man's land for a time. Riki spoke at last. "It's awful to watch. She's in love for the first time, and I don't think the notion has even occurred to him for so much as a moment." Baba nodded somberly. "You should see the woman he does love. Ah! I haven't seen her in years, but she was magnificent even as a child. She must be one of the great beauties of the world now. A lioness! I don't know why I didn't . . ." He shook his head. "Yes, I do. At a certain point something told me she was not for me. In the first place there was that savage obsession of hers. Hakoris! Gods! Imagine him capturing her again!" He shuddered with revulsion.

"You don't want to share a woman with anything else, then? Not even an idea?"

"I don't know. I have the strange feeling that her smoldering intensity was one of the things that made her so attractive to me in the first place." He bit his lip. "But it was a thing she didn't want to share with *me*, you understand. It was to be her crusade alone." He sighed. "But she shared it in the end with Kamose. I have the feeling that if I asked the astrologers about the two of them, I'd get a very interesting story. Destiny picked her out for him, not for me." He smiled ruefully. "I just hope the fates have someone equally fascinating reserved for me, one of these days. When I do meet the love of my life, I hope she isn't a terrible-tempered hunchback with a sty in one eye and a big wart on the end of her nose. If, as Baliniri says, a man doesn't have much choice when these things come along—"

There was a deep, appreciative chuckle from Baba of El-Kab. "Don't worry. When the time comes, you'll find her beautiful whether she is or not, my boy. And most likely she *will* be, too. I have the feeling that destiny holds a few rewards for you down the road. You're a man marked by the stars. And you tell me you don't come from a military family? You certainly seem to the manner born."

"I haven't any idea. Mother only told me that my father was somebody big. She wouldn't say who. She was sorry she'd told me as little as I did get from her. She only leaked it out when some of the boys on the block were calling me a beggar's bastard. She'd say, 'Oh, if only I could tell you who you really are!' But she wouldn't reveal any more than that. And then she died in Avaris, and I was on my own, living by my wits in the streets, without so much as a rag to cover my bottom. Not that I did too badly. It was a world I knew and understood and could survive in, you see. There are a lot of places I prefer it to. Court, for instance."

"Ah, a man after my own heart. Give me a field garrison any day. But—after Mara? No girls of your own? No great love affairs?"

"Oh, I've had women here and there. And I enjoy them as much as the next man. But Baliniri used to tell me of what it was like, being in love, and if that's what it's like, it's never happened to me."

"It will. It catches up with all of us. Just because it never happened to you down in your home country in Avaris, don't think it won't happen here in Thebes. Why, I could tell a pretty tale myself, if I were minded to."

"Avaris?" Riki said. "I was born in Thebes. Mother had to leave for some reason she never would explain, when I was tiny. She had a relative near Avaris, and we lived with her until she died. Then we had to go into the city, and . . . well, Mother didn't last long there. I used to wonder what she died of. Since then I've figured it out, I think. She gave me all the food. I think she was starving to death slowly. Then, in her weakened condition, she showed signs of lung disease. That's what finally killed her." He shook his head. "I used to try to dream up her face, going to sleep at night. But now it's pretty much gone. I think she was pretty once, before she got so terribly thin."

There was a strange look in the eyes of the old warrior next to him. "Ahhh!" he said. The word was one long sigh of pain at the waste and loss of life, at the cruelties of existence. "A sad tale, lad. One that strikes me to the heart. But never fear. You'll find your destiny. Perhaps you'll find this father of yours someday, too. But if you don't, I have a piece of advice: The only name a man can bear that makes any real difference is the one he makes for himself."

"Be that as it may," Riki said, "I'd still like to know who I am. I've been nobody so long."

"You've *never* been nobody. That one thing I can assure you, young man. And you're not one now. You're my respected comrade in arms."

"Thanks for the reassurance," Riki said. "Coming from you . . ." He grinned. Compliments came hard to his thick tongue. "How about you?" he asked. "Has your life always been camps and battlefields?"

"Pretty much so," said the old trooper. "Except for . . ." A sighing sound, wistful, almost tender, came into his voice. "I was kind of nobody too, in the sense you're talking about. I was sold to the army when I was a boy. I don't know what had happened to my parents. I think they had too many kids and couldn't afford to raise me. But when I fell in love . . ."

Riki's smile held great affection already. "Another old war story, eh?"

Baba ignored him. "This, you understand, is not for public consumption. You pass it along to anyone, and I'll have your gizzard cut out with a dull knife while you sleep." His eyes twinkled as he said this. "Try, if you will, to imagine me young and handsome."

"I'll imagine a square moon overhead while I'm doing it, but go on."

"No, really." The older man laughed. "I wasn't always bald-headed and frog faced. Nevertheless, I'll ask you to imagine this impossible thing, just for the sake of argument. I was assigned to guard a princess of the blood. Ah, my young friend! She was as beautiful as the full moon, with skin like a baby's, and big dark eyes as deep as the Nile at floodtide, and long slender limbs that . . . ah, Riki, my lad, she weighed no more than a child. Hands as soft as flower petals!"

"She weighed no more than a child! In a word, you had occasion to weigh her in your arms?"

"Would you believe it? It was she who fell in love with me. I wouldn't have had the effrontery to fall for the likes of her, let me tell you—not if she hadn't made the first move. And the second, and the third. And so on. One day she asked me to stand guard while she bathed in a little pool, with nothing but a gauze curtain to hide her from my view, and the gauze might just as well not have been there. She began to talk to me. Her voice so soft, so intimate. . . . I was embarrassed. I turned my back. And then I had the odd feeling that the voice was getting closer. And when I turned around, there she was on my side of the curtain, not a handspan from me, all pink and soft and deliciously damp from a bath scented with rose petals, and she put those soft little hands up to my face and drew me down. . . ."

Riki looked at him, hard. The older man's eyes were

damp. The memory, even this long after, of a moment of his lost youth, moved him so deeply. Riki neither smiled nor spoke.

"It couldn't last, you know," continued Baba. "Word came through one of her handmaidens that there was some suspicion in the official circles, you know, that something untoward was happening. But they couldn't prove anything. So I gave her up. It was the honorable thing, you know, the only honorable thing. But it was like cutting the heart out of my chest. I went to my superior and asked for field duty. I've never been back to court. Not when it was moved to Lisht. Not when it was moved back to Thebes again. When Dedmose called in all of the princes and princesses of the blood and moved them to his new capital at Lisht, I asked for duty along the Nubian border and got it. Nobody asked why. They just thought I was a glutton for punishment."

"And when the capital was moved back upriver?"

"After Akhilleus's invading force was turned back, I asked for duty up here. On the line."

"She's still at court? And you've never seen her again?"

Baba of El-Kab visibly fought to impose rigid control on his emotions now. His back straightened into a military brace. "Never," he said. "And you couldn't get her name from me if you lashed me to a wagon wheel and flogged me until your arms were tired." The softness returned to his voice. "There hasn't been a day since that I haven't thought of her." He stiffened again. "I don't know what the point of this story was," he said in an entirely different voice, "except perhaps that the old were not always old and the ugly were not always ugly, lad. And that this love business has a way of catching up with all of us sooner or later." The twinkle struggled to come back into his eye. "Including you, my young friend."

As he turned his head back toward the front line, something in his manner indicated that this part of the conversation was over forever. "Look," he said. "Bonfires over there. They'll be roasting lambs on a spit, and we'll be stuck here with damned front-line fare and having to smell what they're cooking."

Riki took in a deep breath and blew it out through pursed lips. "May the gods go with Kamose," he said. "May they put power in his arm and cunning in his heart."

V

Behind the long line of wagons bearing provender, the stragglers staggered along, bent nearly double under their burdens of dressed meat, bags of grain, and baskets of olives and dried fruit—human beasts of burden too poor, too humble, even to own donkeys or other livestock to bear their heavy loads for them. The guards let them pass with hardly more than the most cursory inspection, chuckling and muttering halfhearted insults as these, the lowest of the low, brought up the rear of the hastily improvised caravan.

Near the end of the line was Kamose, his face half-hidden under the towering reed basket of dates he carried. He wore only a loincloth he had deliberately dirtied with clay dust and ripped to ribbons, making him look like the other wretched laborers bringing supplies for the feast.

He had worked his way up from the very end of the line, where he had waylaid a half-starved worker, brained him with a rock, and taken his place. As the unfortunates staggered through the lines, Kamose had attracted hardly more than second glance; the singularity of his lean, hard, fit body was more than made up for by the pattern of whipmarks, commonplace among the ill-fed laborers, still prominent on his back this many years after his escape from the refuge.

Now, as the laborers one by one began to stack the food they had brought to the Hai encampment, he looked around and tried to get his bearings. He had taken great pains to memorize the Hai's order of battle, which Baba had outlined for him, but it took a moment or two to find enough landmarks to establish where he had come in this far behind the lines.

Yes: There were the main, native, Hai lines far over to the left side of the line, and next to them the Maaziou units. The whole right side of the line seemed to be Hellene, and a new Hellene troop, quartered until today a mile downstream, seemed to be moving into place from the rear ranks to replace the unit decimated by Baba and his men in the day's fighting.

Yes! And the royal units were over *there*. And the place

where the feast was to take place . . . it was situated just behind the Greek lines. All right, he knew where he was. There was an advantage to be gained in the fact that an old unit had been slaughtered almost to the last man and a new one was moving into the gap thus made. Change meant confusion. . . .

Hmmm, he thought. *My Greek wouldn't pass muster if I tried to pass for a mainlander. But if I told them I was from Ilios, perhaps, or, better, from somewhere farther down the coast . . .*

It might just work. He had served with Greeks before, in his own years of mercenary wandering, and he knew their ways and their language, although he spoke it with an accent. If he could pass for one of them, it would put him very near the center of the evening's festivities. He might even manage to get fairly close to Apophis's tents.

"You, there!" a voice said nearby. Kamose spun, looked into the eyes of a Hai guardsman. "What are you loitering around here for? Get along with you!"

"Pardon me, sir," he said in the accent of a Fayum peasant, learned years before from a fellow slave at the refuge. "I was wondering where we went for our pay."

"Pay, you insolent wretch? Your pay will be a hot meal for the first time in a month, you ungrateful bastard! Report to the commissary. You'll get a chit for dinner. Now get along with you, and be quick about it!"

He nodded meekly and set out down the long row of tents. But after fifty paces he turned his head and saw that the guardsman was no longer watching him. Quickly he ducked behind a tent and stood thinking. The Hellene replacements were straggling along in three files through the rows of tents. Some wore a different color of plume in their helmets than others, and the ones with the red plumes had helmets that covered their faces, leaving only the noses free.

Almost without thinking, he obeyed the sudden impulse, reaching out and grabbing the next Greek soldier who wandered past. His hand got up under the side of the helmet and yanked the man's head to one side violently; so violently that a snap was heard and the Hellene crumpled like a rag doll.

Kamose looked around warily and hurriedly dragged the

Greek inside the empty tent beside him, wincing at the pain from his broken rib.

In the far corner of the tent were a number of pillows piled high. This was evidently an officer's tent, owned by a man who liked cushions and comfort when he slept. Kamose relieved the dead man of his sword and helmet, then dragged the body into the corner to cover it with the pillows. *Better you than me, my friend,* he thought sourly. *You've bought me a few hours' time, perhaps. . . .*

On second thought he retrieved the scabbard as well, stowed the sword in it, and hung it about his neck after the Greek fashion. Savagely he ripped off his loincloth to stand in the full nudity of a Greek warrior of the line. Then he donned the helmet and stepped out into the fading light.

He fell into step with another Greek sauntering down the line and asked in a thick Samian accent, "Hey, friend, where was the first troop's place in the line? Cepheus's?"

"Right up here," the man said in a Mycenean lilt. "My unit's replacing 'em. Appears they ran into the Toad, and he gave 'em what-for."

"Good. I think I'm assigned to your unit. I was with Cepheus at the beginning of the fight, but he sent me back as a runner to headquarters, and when I got back, there was nobody to give the message to."

The other soldier gave him a sharp look. "Runner? You're pretty able-bodied for a runner. In our troop we give that work to the feeble."

Kamose thanked his lucky stars for his half-healed knife wound; the scar was still visible in this half light. "I got this when we broke Mekim's line," he explained. "I didn't ask for light duty. Cepheus looked at the wound and sent me back with the messages. It was pretty humiliating. But Cepheus was that way. If the Toad hadn't killed him, one of his own men might have done it sooner or later."

"Well, you'll get no easy duty under Tereus, who leads your new troop, my friend. The old bastard'll have you whipped for a slacker if you ask for it." He looked at Kamose's naked back and grinned. "Although it wouldn't be anything new to you, I'd say."

"Whipping?" Kamose said with a shrug. "That one was

for insubordination, and for breaking an officer's jaw when he made fun of me." There was steel in his voice when he said this, but he thought the matter over and took a lighter tack. "You served in the unit I was with, you bore whip scars. They were a tough bunch of bastards."

"So I see. Well, friend, welcome to the ninth troop. My name is Palamedes."

"I'm Nikos," Kamose said, assuming the Greek equivalent of the false name he had given Aset back in the delta. "By the way, what's with all this fuss they're making back here? Some feast of the Hai, maybe?"

"Haven't you heard? His royal nibs is in camp. *Apophis.*" He said the name the way a man might say an obscene word and spat after saying it.

"You don't like him either? You should have heard Cepheus talk about him."

"None of us can abide the bastard. There's a rumor— But I'd better not say. . . ."

"Come on. You can trust me. Well, you can if it's something derogatory about Apophis, anyhow."

"Not a word to anyone." Palamedes turned his head to look Kamose in the eye. "But word's out that there may be more going on tonight than just eating and getting drunk and fooling around with the whores they've brought in for our amusement." He drew his hand like a knife across his throat. "If you get my meaning."

"Eh? His royal worship?"

"I say no more. But don't be too surprised at anything you see tonight. The Hai commander's on our side. He has certain . . . ambitions."

"And what part do the likes of us play in this?" Kamose asked.

Palamedes frowned. "The smaller the cabal, the cleaner the coup. I asked the same question and was told that if push comes to shove, I should join in. Otherwise to stay out of their way—and don't let the loyalists interfere."

"Well, I'm your man, whatever they decide to do. I have no love for Apophis. For my money, he's responsible for the death of my old unit, the first troop. I had a particular friend in that outfit. I'll miss him."

Palamedes's brow lifted. "That sort of thing, eh? Well, I quite understand. It's a long time in the field without girls. A man has to make do with what he can find." But Kamose noticed that the Greek's friendly manner had appreciably cooled with his last words. All to the good: It would keep him at arm's length just long enough to —

To what? he thought suddenly. Just what was he going to do, now that he was privy to these startling new facts? Wouldn't this complication make his own plans for Apophis's assassination unnecessary? Was there a chance that he could use this volatile situation to his own advantage?

He frowned, chewing on his lip. How did he, Kamose, fit into all this?

The generals doubled the guard along the Egyptian line, prepared a second line to fall back to in case of attack, then went to the area provided for the feast. The bonfires blazed high in the starless, moon-starved sky. The wagons full of tall amphorae of wine and palm wine came first; then the wagons of whores pulled up, to thundering cheers from the units gathered around the fires. There were the strong smells of roasted fowl and mutton. A band of kitharas and flutes and drums and shawms had appeared, and musicians tinkled and wailed. Naked dancing girls, their slim bodies glistening with sweat, undulated deliciously before the fire, bronze bracelets and anklets and stomachers jingling merrily. One of the girls was ravishingly beautiful, with generous lips and firm breasts; as the soldiers watched, laughing, one of the Greeks, every bit as naked as the girl, joined in the dance, matching her intricate footwork, brushing her soft body with his hard-muscled form as they circled and spun. From time to time he would grin, reach out with a practiced hand, and pat her suggestively on the rump. She only smiled and danced all the more suggestively.

At the far end of the long line of fires the ranks finally broke to make room for the king's party, and those closest to the Hellenes' end of the line could see the tall plumes of the royal guard, and among them the stocky form of the god-king, the so-called Golden Pharaoh himself. The guards took up their places on all sides of him, and he sat down at a jeweled chair someone had brought up.

The music and dancing did not stop. If anything they grew louder, more furious. Broad-shouldered soldiers threw dried palm fronds on the fire, making the flames leap ever higher. Slaves turned the spits slowly as the cooks hacked half-cooked meat off the sheep and oxen that had been slaughtered for the feast, and half-grown boys, staggering under the heavy weight of their trays, carried the meat to the units spread fanwise around the fire.

Slowly, slowly, Kamose circled through the crowd, moving from unit to unit almost totally unnoticed, moving ever forward toward the king's private area. Weapons had been stacked by the campfire, his with them; but he carried three slender, tough leather thongs with him, each as long as his arm, knotted loosely at their ends and worn around his neck like some sort of lightly braided necklace. He had learned this trick from a sailor, out on the waters of the Great Sea. The garrote was silent, drew no attention, and could be easily disposed of. But it would kill a man as dead as any knife would, and with less blood and fuss. Tonight, if fortune favored him, he would leave it knotted around the neck of the man he hated most in all the world, Hakoris not excepted. His father, the king.

VI

"I know Apophis," said Ovannes. "He can't hold his drink. He'll become incoherent almost immediately, say he's feeling a bit under the weather, go back and sleep for an hour, and when he gets up, he'll be fresh and rested and will go right back to the same old thing. He's done this at every national feast day since he became king."

"Then that's the time to strike," Learchus said. "Slip back to the royal tents, take the guards by surprise—"

"Not so fast," Ovannes said. He looked sourly down at

his half-consumed drink. "There'll be layers and layers of guards. You won't be able to get in there without rousing the whole camp."

Learchus frowned. "Then what do you suggest, my friend?"

Ovannes held up his bowl, sloshing the drink around idly, but did not drink from it. "He likes," he said in a soft, slow voice, "to be awakened at the end of that hour of rest." Learchus stared. Ovannes went on in the same thoughtful tone. "If just one man were to get the job of awakening him . . . hmmm. He likes it to be someone of consequence."

"Like yourself."

"Like myself. I'll have to get close to him first. I'll have to drink with him for a while, cuddle up with the bastard over palm wine, and listen to his damned stories."

"Surely you could make that sacrifice for the good of—"

"Maybe I could even be the one who walks him back to his tent so he can take his little nap." He made a face. "The more time I spend near him tonight, the more chances I'll have."

Learchus looked at him gimlet-eyed. "Go on," he said. "You're making more sense the longer you talk."

"What are you talking about?" the officer demanded. "Cepheus's whole troop were wiped out to the last man. There were no survivors."

"But . . ." Palamedes gulped, blinked. "There was a runner. He was sent back to headquarters with messages. When he got back, there wasn't anyone left. *He* survived. I know. I met him today. Name's Nikos. His accent's from Cos or Samos or somewhere like that. Rustic."

"Nikos? I don't remember any Nikos, and I was assigned to Cepheus's troop for two weeks. What did this fellow look like?"

"A burly chap. Lots of marks of the whip on his back, as if he'd been in a lot of trouble. Fairly recent wound in his side. He said he had a broken rib or two. You could see him wince from it now and then."

"Doesn't ring any bells. Are you sure—"

Palamedes looked into his wine bowl and then lifted it to drain it in one gulp. "No," he admitted, putting the bowl down. A sour look spread across his face. "I'm not sure of anything. Except that this fellow stacked his arms with our unit's, and that he's out here in the crowd somewhere now."

"From Samos, you say? I don't remember any Samians at all. Cepheus didn't like islanders. Thought they were a bunch of ignorant bumpkins, untrainable and cowardly, with two left feet."

"Then what was he doing here?"

"Good question, Palamedes. One that the security people would probably like to ask you right about now."

"The king's in camp," Palamedes said slowly. "He has a lot of enemies. There's that business about the coup." His eyes widened suddenly, and he dropped his wine bowl. "Gods!" he said. "I *told* him about it! What if he was one of Apophis's spies? I'm ruined! My life isn't worth—"

The officer stared, cold eyed. "I think you'd better do some quick thinking, my friend. And you'd better come to some right conclusions—fast."

In the shadows behind Palamedes and the officer, Kamose stood, unmoving, listening, thinking. *They're onto me*, he reflected. *Well, good enough. It forces my hand.* There would be no opportunity for vacillation now; he could only go forward, do what he had come to do.

But what was that, precisely? He had never quite made up his mind. Assassinate his own father? There would be real satisfaction in that, but from the sound of things, he would have to stand in line. There were people all over the Hai encampment who wanted to murder Apophis, and they had more opportunities for it than he was likely to get.

Besides, he had dreamed about their final confrontation— the false king and the son he had tried to kill—so often, he knew how he wanted it to happen! He wanted it to take place in broad daylight, under the expanse of sky, with thousands looking on! He wanted it to be the sort of thing they composed songs about, to sing for many generations! Not a grubby, cowardly matter of sneaking up on someone in the dark and choking him with a leather thong!

No! He wanted to meet Apophis—Aram, his father—in

the open field, with both men armed. And he wanted to make the man who had murdered his mother beg for his life, before the assembled armies, where no one could miss it. And that meant . . .

Gods! he thought. *I've got to hurry!* And, cat-footed, like a wraith in the deep darkness of the starless night, he slipped back into the shadows and made his way toward the fatal confrontation.

"I . . . I'll take my leave o' you now," said Apophis, still leaning on Ovannes's arm. "I'll be awright in jusht a while. I'll lie down for a bit an' be good ash new again. J-jusht you wait an' shee."

Ovannes looked around them. Three guards stood with spears at the ready. *Not now*, he thought. *Later, when I come to pick him up.* "As you wish, Sire," he said. "I'll come back in an hour or so." He bowed, accepted the guards' salutes, and went away.

Apophis blinked, trying to get the guardsmen into focus. "Very well, gentlemen," he said. "He'll be b-back for me." He hiccuped, covered his mouth, blinked again. "Resht eashy." Weaving unsteadily, he moved back inside the dimly lighted tent, casting strange shadows against its walls by the flickering light of the single candle.

He managed to make it all the way to the pile of cushions in the far corner before collapsing. Almost as soon as his head struck the pillow he was asleep.

Suddenly he came awake. His hands were tied tightly behind his back. He could not move! He could not speak for the gag in his mouth!

Terrified, he looked up. Beside him a tall pile of stacked pillows masked the glittering candle. Over him knelt a naked man. The face . . . where had he seen that face?

"You never believed you'd see me again, did you, Father?" the man asked in a voice hardly above a whisper. "I'm Kamose, whose mother you murdered. Whom you tried to have killed. I'm back. I'm back in Egypt to fulfill The Prophecy."

"*Hmmmfff!*" Apophis protested through the gag. Struggling only made it worse; he almost choked.

The kneeling man who called himself Kamose . . . could it be? The face . . . yes, there was something of himself and something of the mother.

"They took my weapons back at camp," Kamose said. "All but the thongs that bind you . . . and this one." Smiling coldly he held up the one single leather thong, dangling it from two fingers. "I was taught the use of this by an assassin from beyond the Indus, Father. I can cut your head off with it if I want. Or I can tighten it just so much that every time you swallow—"

"*Mmmmmph!*"

"But that would be too quick, Father of mine. Your life's in my hands. What shall I do with it? Yes, I know. Ovannes will be back for you in a few minutes. But he's coming to kill you. He and the Greek leader, Learchus—they'll assassinate you tonight and put Ovannes himself on the throne of Lower Egypt. They can do it, too. And after the first moment or two of shock, everyone will sympathize with their cause. You have no idea how many people hate you, Father."

"*Mmmmm-mmmmmm!*"

The soft, deadly voice went on. Apophis's heart was beating wildly. He was crazy with fear. And he could do nothing, say nothing.

"That gives me two options: kill you or leave you for Ovannes." Swiftly his hands slipped the leather thong around Apophis's neck and tied it in a loose knot. Then he yanked on the cord! Apophis could not breathe!

But the pressure was abruptly relaxed, allowing Apophis to breathe once more.

The king tried to get the hateful face in focus . . . but the figure was gone! Gone! Leaving him here, helpless, trussed up like a pig on a spit, easy pickings for the assassin when he came. Ovannes! Ovannes would show no mercy at all! Ovannes would cut out his tripes in a moment and laugh at him as he bled to death!

The moment he spotted the Hai guard, Kamose called out, "You! I've got to see your captain! Where is he?"

The guardsman brought his spear to the ready position

and fixed him with a suspicious glare. "Here, now! What business would a drunken Greek have with the captain of the guard?"

"I overheard! I was standing in the darkness, behind the officers! You've got to hurry!"

"Hurry? Hurry about what?"

"There's a plot! They're going to kill the king! You've got to go get help! I heard them talking! The king's in his tent. They're going to kill him when the man comes to awaken him!"

The guard's eyes widened. "Why would a Greek want to—?"

"I'm not Greek! I'm Egyptian! I was off in the bushes at play with one of the whores they brought from the Fayum! When she wouldn't play anymore, I tried to find my uniform. While I was looking for it . . ." He waved his arms wildly. "Save him! You could be a hero!"

The guard stared. "Should I believe you?" he asked, still uncertain.

His hand on the knife hilt, Ovannes slipped inside the big tent and looked around. Where was the king? And why was that great slash in the far wall of the—

"Grab him!" ordered the angry voice in the shadows. "Don't let him get away! And don't kill him! I want him alive!"

Strong hands closed on Ovannes's arms before he could turn the weapon on himself.

In the pink predawn light the Egyptian picket peered downstream toward the shore. "Who goes there?" he called. He drew his sword and bellowed for his comrade, who was sleeping lightly six yards away. "You! You in the water! Come out with your hands held high!"

The exhausted man struggled out of the water on hands and knees. "You!" the young soldier said once again. "Stand up there!"

"I . . . I'm not sure I can," rasped the castaway, collapsing onto his side. "C-can you g-get me a blanket or something? The river's like ice."

"Friend or foe?" the picket said, striking a heroic pose.

"Oh, for heaven's sake," the hoarse voice said. "This is no time for that. Help me get to Riki. Now. There isn't a m-m-moment to spare."

Apophis's revenge was savage and sweet. By dawn he had drawn and quartered Learchus and Ovannes before a strangely somber crowd. Both heads had been hoisted high above the Hai ranks on pikes as a grisly expression of the king's wrath.

Still Apophis was not satisfied. Eyes red rimmed with rage, he called his generals in and ordered an attack in force in one hour.

"One hour, Sire?" echoed one of his advisers. "But, Sire—"

For answer, Apophis had him gutted and impaled and left for the crows. As the unfortunate one was being dragged away, the king screamed again so that all could hear: "One hour! Hit them all down the line! Hit them with everything you've got! Drive them back! Annihilate them! Take no prisoners!"

VII

"There's activity over there," the soldier commented. "They're getting ready for something big. My guess is they'll come at us at several places at once."

"You're almost right," Kamose said in a flat exhausted voice. "But he'll hit us *everywhere* at once. Bring up the reserves, Riki. You'll want to be as deep as possible all along the line."

Riki raised a brow but nodded, looking his old friend up and down. Someone had found a clean loincloth for Kamose, and a sword and belt had been taken from the body of one of the fallen. He looked like a man who had not slept in days, but incredibly the dark eyes still flashed with intelligence and understanding. "Right you are," Riki said, then nodded to an aide nearby to implement Kamose's strategy.

Baba of El-Kab had remained silent. He was still thinking about Kamose's venture into the enemy camp the previous night. Now he spoke. "I don't mean to criticize," he said, "but you had him in your hands and could have killed him."

"And why did I not?" Kamose finished for Baba. He sighed deeply. "It's The Prophecy. The way it came down to the people is the way events should take place. And the people believe that the promised deliverer of The Prophecy will vanquish the hated king, his father, on the battlefield—not assassinating him in a tent, quietly and neatly."

Baba was skeptical. War was war. "I understand that part well enough, but—"

"I could have just thrown a scare into him and then let it go at that," said Kamose. "As it was, I did you a favor—his top commanders' heads decorate pikes."

"My concern is that in a moment or two I'm going to lose some men who might have stayed alive if the coming attack hadn't been called," retorted Baba.

Kamose rubbed his temples, an act of utter exhaustion. "But do you want only to win this battle or do you want to win the whole war? Do you want the help of a civilian rebellion, or do you prefer to go it alone like this?"

Baba of El-Kab looked at him thoughtfully. "Go on."

"The people have accepted the Hai oppression without resistance because they believed any rebellion to be futile. But," he said, his eyes blazing again, his voice sounding more alive, "what if they suddenly found a leader chosen by the gods? Not only the gods of Egypt, but the pagan gods of that country up north where Joseph came from? Wouldn't they rise and join the fight? And think, man—what damage they could do just now, with Apophis's supply lines extended the way they are?"

"The story *will* get around," Riki acknowledged thoughtfully. "It'll put heart in our men."

Baba frowned, then smiled good-naturedly. "All right,"

he conceded. "You've made your case. And who knows? Maybe there is something to all this. Even if there isn't, it won't matter as long as everybody believes there is." He winked. "Everybody but me." There was no hostility in his tone, just the bald fact of his own skepticism.

Kamose looked up as the old soldier stood and squared his shoulders. "I see I've got my work cut out, converting you." As he himself stood, a great sound swelled far down the line, the sound of voices uplifted, male voices bellowing battle cries in half a dozen tongues. Kamose loosened his sword in its sheath and, his eyes mere slits now, opened his mouth in a tight grin. "Here they come," he said quietly. "May the gods give power to your right arms, and to mine."

Sailors had brought up from the boats the framework of a tower Apophis had had built back in the delta, a tower to be assembled here, and from which he could watch the progress of the battle. He stood there now, peering out across the battlefield in the thin morning light, surrounded by aides, guards, runners, and staff. "A breakthrough on the right flank!" he said. "Smite them! Cut off their heads!"

At his elbow an aide spoke. "Those are the Hellenes, Sire. Even with their leader dead, they fight like animals. If we could only get that spirit to spread to our own—"

Apophis ignored him. He turned to the guardsman nearest him. "You!" he said. "You brought the news last night about the revolt. You saved my life."

"Yes, Sire."

"You say it was a *Greek* who turned the conspirators in? You're quite sure about that?"

"No, Sire, I'm not sure. It's difficult to tell one of them from anyone else—except he was naked like a Greek. And, well, they have this sort of arrogance about them."

"Describe him again for me," the king said, his eyes on the battle below. The guardsman did so, in almost the same words he had used earlier. The description fit exactly the man Apophis had awakened to find kneeling over him, the man who had called himself Kamose, his son. Apophis scowled but said nothing. Fool that he was, he had blurted it out

when the guards had first come to untie him. How could he
have been so stupid? It had already got around the encampment, but he did not need to confirm it by talking about it
anew.

Yes, he thought, his lips set in a grim line, *in that first
moment I could have corrected my error. I could have had
this chap killed, and with him all who had heard.* But he had
not thought fast enough, and the word had got around: Someone the king thinks is his son has been here! His son! The one
who—

Below, on the battlefield, the Egyptians counterattacked
and drove the Greeks back. And on the left flank the Egyptians had actually gained ground. The middle held. Apophis
gripped the tower's railing and squinted through the dust.
"There," he said. "That one down there. Is that the one?"
On the field the man who had called himself Kamose fought
shoulder-to-shoulder with a squat, bowlegged figure who could
only be the Toad. "There! Next to Baba of El Kab! Is that
the man?"

The guardsman frowned. "He . . . *hmmm.* It could be.
It could be, Sire. But I can't be sure. I can't see clearly. The
one I saw last night had scars all over him. Whip marks, knife
cuts. But there *is* something about the way he holds his
shoulders, Sire."

"Is that the man who turned them in last night or not?
Answer me!"

"Well, Sire, I think so."

"You!" Apophis bellowed, that sudden tone of mad rage
back in his voice. His finger pointed at an aide chosen at
random. "Get me an archer up here! The best you have!"

The first attack had broken. The Egyptians had actually
gained ground, not lost it. In the first skirmish Riki had
comported himself well enough to allay his fears about his
first day under fire; he had killed three men in single combat,
wounded another, and held his part of the line. He had
shored up the fading confidence of his men after the first
Greek breakthrough and had inspired them to turn and fight

back and push back the Hellene advance. He felt good about himself.

He had had ample chance, between duels, to watch both Kamose and Baba of El-Kab in action. They were as different as two brave men could be, even in the degree and type of their bravery. Baba was steadiness personified—unflappable, smiling, unhurried, and deadly, a man with a joke always on his lips. The perfect hands-on leader and the ultimate under-officer. What a soldier! No wonder Mekim had placed such confidence in him!

Kamose was something altogether apart—a man possessed! A man with a demon inside him! A man not altogether human once the sword was in his hand and the fever of war was upon him. A man, perhaps, with a touch of the gods in him, or demigods. And from the moment the fight began, a man the other soldiers looked up to and took their cue from. He seemed to imbue them with a touch of his own mad frenzy when he tore into an opponent. Seeing his savage fury, they also became savages.

For one fleeting moment Riki, watching him, had thought of The Prophecy, fervently wishing he could believe in it with all his heart.

But the thought had been interrupted by a new wave of Greeks coming at him, bellowing in their strange tongue, their bodies stained with blood and dust. Gritting his teeth, he had caught a brief glimpse of Kamose at his side, and he had actually found himself taking on a bit of Kamose's madness, diving into a glut of struggling bodies and hacking right and left with his sword.

Now, though, there had been a lull in the fight for a full five minutes. Riki looked about him. Baba strode far down the ranks, clapping one man on the shoulder appreciatively, exchanging jokes with another. To his own flank Kamose stood, fists on hips, peering across toward the enemy side.

"Look," Kamose said, nodding at the tower. "There he is. At the top. Imagine that. There's no wood like that in all the delta. That thing had to be made from wood cut down across the Great Sea somewhere, brought here at horrible expense. . . ."

"He's a bit fatter than the last time you and I saw him,"

Riki noted somberly. "The night your mother . . ." He let it hang, seeing the quick flash of hatred and anger cross his old friend's face. "I'm sorry. I shouldn't have mentioned that."

"No, no, it's all right. I want to keep that moment always before my eyes. It'll be in my mind the day I kill him." He shuddered and shook the thought away now, though. "Your man Baba is quite a fellow," he said with an appreciative grin. "He reminds me of what people used to say about Mekim. The perfect underofficer." Kamose looked at him, and there was an odd expression on his face. "I hope you won't take this wrong, old friend, but if you take away the bow legs and the years and the too many rich meals over palm wine, he could be a close relative of yours. There's something about the bone structure in your face. Now, don't go getting your back up at me. I'm not saying you look like a toad. But—"

"I'd be honored to be a relative of his," Riki broke in. "Who knows? I still don't have any idea who I am. He could be a cousin."

"Look at the son of a bitch up there," Kamose said, his eyes again on the faraway tower. "Generals and bowmen to right and left. What a coward! When I think of being the son of such a man as *he* . . ." He spat into the dust angrily.

"Don't dwell on that," Riki urged. "Think instead about your mother. I remember her pretty well, and I think you took after her. You could tell she had been a good-looking woman, before all the neglect and hard work and illness."

"You remember her!" Kamose said suddenly, and the look he gave Riki was sorrowful, full of longing. It made him look young and vulnerable. "Please. Do whatever you can to keep the memory fresh. *Someone* should remember her, someone besides me. Otherwise it would be as though she'd never existed. There were no services, you know. No embalming, no ceremonies to see her across the other side to the Netherworld."

"You believe in that stuff?"

Kamose wiped his eyes with a dusty hand. "No. But she did." His voice was tight, controlled. "And she was denied all of it." He could say no more.

Riki was about to speak when Baba of El-Kab came striding toward them, a grin on his broad face. "Gentlemen!" he said. "Do you see what they're doing over there? They're falling back! The Hai attack's failed! We've held them!"

It was true. The enemy was regrouping, falling back to prepared positions. Riki looked up, saw Apophis atop the tower, gesticulating angrily while one of the bowmen at his side handed the king his bow and quiver. "Look," Riki said. "He's probably going to shoot one of his own generals for failing to crush us."

"Forget him," said Baba of El-Kab. "We've earned ourselves a drink today, boys." His delighted wink removed that sting from the total lack of formality in his words when addressing Riki, his commanding officer. "You've fought bravely and well, both of you. I'm proud of you and the whole unit. I'm ordering an extra ration of palm wine for the entire army tonight. And you two are going to share with me a jug of something special, something I've been saving for the right occasion. Have you ever had any of that wonderful stuff the blacks brew up in the Sudd? Mekim gave me a jug after—"

Baba happened to look up as he spoke, and saw, in one single blinding flash, the spent bow in Apophis's hand, the shaft flying swiftly through the sky! "Down!" he cried out suddenly in a voice of command. Moving almost too swiftly for a man of his years, he seized Kamose by the arms to shove him out of the way.

As Kamose lurched forward, Baba's square body shook as with the palsy, and the hard grip on Kamose's biceps became the faltering grip of a child.

And, wordless, Baba of El-Kab fell into Kamose's arms.

Riki rushed to his side. The two of them held Baba.

The part of the arrow that stuck out of his broad back was half the length of a normal Hai arrow. The rest was deep inside him.

Riki and Kamose lowered him gently to his side. His eyes were already fluttering; but for a moment, the mere blink of an eye, they came into focus, and fixed themselves on Riki's face.

"S-sssss . . ." he said. Only the sibilance. A last surge of
breath, and the sibilance. The word that was to have followed
had no voice behind it. And no breath. The light died in the
brown eyes. And Baba of El-Kab was no more.

VIII

Kamose's eyes locked with Riki's over the body of their
fallen comrade. Neither man spoke for a long, long moment.
Then Kamose closed his eyes, and his lips came together in a
grim line. His hands clenched. Riki could see the great
muscles of Kamose's forearms tighten and grow hard, hard.

With a shudder Kamose opened his eyes, glimmering
with a dull fire. "The men will have seen this." His voice was
low and hoarse. "Baba of El-Kab, the finest leader they
ever had, felled by a coward's arrow." He spat the word out.
"*Apophis*'s arrow."

Riki's mind reeled. He felt dizzy, stricken. "I—I don't
know what to say."

Kamose's powerful hand shot out and gripped his arm.
"Then I'll tell you what to say," he said in an enraged half
whisper. "Call a counterattack. Right now. Before the men
have time to react. Before the shock of it has time to set in.
And before Apophis's men have time to set up a decent
second line." His voice throbbed with urgency as he added,
"Before Apophis has time to climb down to safety. If we hit
them hard, right now, without hesitation, maybe I can face
him myself—just the two of us."

Riki, squatting beside the body of his fallen subordinate,
let his body fall forward onto his knees, and his shoulders
drooped. "Attack? Now? But—"

"The sheer audacity of it will have a certain effect,"
Kamose said. "Call Elset. He's ranking officer under your
command now that Baba is gone. He was Baba's right arm.
Make the command sound like the best damned idea you
ever had. Make it sound resolute and authoritative, as if the

gods had just dropped victory in your lap, and all you had to do was obey." He did not wait for Riki's reaction, but turned to the circle of aides and officers around them. "You!" he said to the first runner his eyes lit on. "You! Call Elset! Get him here on the double!"

"Yes, sir!" the aide said, turning smartly on one heel.

"And don't say anyth—" Kamose began. But the soldier was already out of earshot. Kamose lowered his voice and, rising, helped Riki to his feet. "It doesn't matter. They'll all hear in a moment or two. The thing to do is keep them nice and busy just now. Get hold of yourself. You look like a child who's lost his father."

"How strange," Riki said, stunned. "That's just how I—"

Kamose scowled and barked new orders to the waiting aides. "Alert the men! Prepare for the charge! Get down to all the units, and make it quick! Tell them to be ready to move the moment Riki gives the signal! *You!* What are you standing there for? Get moving! *Now!*"

Only when they were alone did Kamose turn back to Riki. He put one hand on Riki's shoulder. "I have a feeling about today, an idea that this is going to be a day we'll look back on with awe and astonishment. Today will be used as a point of reference—people will reckon dates from today's date as if it were a festival day or a king's birthday. If you and I are alive at the end of the day, I know where Baba kept that jug of palm wine he was telling us about, and I think he'd want us to have it and drink to his memory. But first we have a battle to win. Get yourself together! Shoulders back! Chest out!"

Riki stared—and suddenly let his face show hope. "Right you are!" he said, loosening his sword in its sheath with a practiced hand.

Ten minutes later the Egyptian army stood poised at their positions. Riki fretted, waiting for Kamose to return. Finally his friend came striding up from the river, where he had gone himself to the docks rather than entrust his message to someone who might garble it. "All right!" Kamose said. "The boats are launched! Let's get to work!"

Riki nodded and raised his sword high. "Ready!" he said in a powerful new voice, a voice of command. "All units . . . now!"

The strong and lusty roar that answered him came up from a thousand throats. As the now blooded and battle-hardened troops under Riki's command eagerly fanned out across no-man's land toward the enemy, Riki dismissed the overwhelming odds against him. There was none of the raw terror commonly experienced just before the first engagement. He felt only the raw power in his arms, exhilaration, readiness for whatever the afternoon might bring. And when the two lines clashed—his own men resolute, fearless, full of new vigor whereas the enemy's were faltering, undecided, acutely feeling the loss of the two leaders Apophis had had executed the night before—Riki's sword hewed through flesh and bone as if it had been no more substantial than sea foam.

Miraculously, the Hai lines broke! The Egyptian attackers sliced deeply into the enemy lines, stabbing, cutting, killing; here and there a Hai unit collapsed and ran pell-mell from the fray, defying the enraged officers who tried to beat them back with the flat of their swords into formation. The native units were the first to buckle under; it was common knowledge that the Hai had lost the spark that had made their ancestors great warriors. But when a Greek unit was destroyed outright and even a Bedouin troop had to fall back to high ground before re-forming and making another stand, Riki knew the day was won.

Finally the enemy fell back on the last reserves; this time the new positions held, and the Egyptian advance was halted. Here, a half mile behind the battle lines, the weakened, embattled Hai managed to stalemate the great onward rush of the Red Landers. And only then, looking up at the now-abandoned tower from which Apophis had loosed the fateful arrow that had killed Baba of El-Kab, did the commanders of both sides ask the question they had not, before this, even had time to consider:

Where was Apophis? Where was the king?

* * *

Sword at last sheathed, Riki squinted through the dust. "Kamose!" he bellowed. "Kamose, to me! Where are you!"

His comrade suddenly materialized at his side. "Come with me!" he said, grabbing Riki's arm. "Drop everything! Don't worry: Elset's doing just fine! Just come with me!"

Riki let himself be led through a field full of dead and dying Hai soldiers and mercenaries toward the great wooden tower Apophis had erected. Only when they were quite close to the structure did he pull back. "Gods!" he said, flabbergasted. "Did we come that far? Have we gained that much ground?"

"Yes!" Kamose said. He virtually shoved Riki up the first few steps of the ladder. "Up you go! All the way to the top!"

Riki obeyed. When they reached the top, he looked around. "Gods!" he said again. "Is that all there is left of them?"

"Yes!" Kamose said, laughing as he joined Riki at the railing. "It's the greatest victory of the war." But as he looked out over the plain, his eyes did not focus on the battlefield, but toward the river. "Now where can they have— Ah! There!" He pointed eagerly. "Look! The Hai boats out on the river, heading downstream!" He punctuated his words with a raucous, vengeful, triumphant laugh. "That's Apophis himself on the lee rail of the lead ship!"

Riki gawked. "Running from the fight!" he said incredulously. "Leaving his troops in the field! They'll never fight for him after this! They'll never let him live this down!"

"Yes they will," Kamose replied seriously. "He'll find new leaders who'll put guts into them. He'll hire new troops, tough bastards to whom this day won't mean a thing. He'll come back at us a few months from now with a fierce army twice this size. All we've done today was buy ourselves some time." His voice was brightened. "But we've also given ourselves a victory to rally our spirits. Now Baliniri will be able to instill new spirit into the recruits and woo Nubian mercenary help. Before this I was sure Nehsi would turn us down when we went to him—as we'll have to—for help. Now I think he'll listen."

Riki looked at Kamose with a new eye. "I still can't quite believe it. And you! *You're* the one who did it for us! If you

hadn't foiled the coup in Apophis's camp and got two of his
best generals killed . . . Kamose, for the first time I really
begin to believe The Prophecy. Maybe you *are* the deliverer."

Kamose regarded him with a dispassionate eye, then
turned back to the scene below. He looked out over the field,
where the Egyptians had soundly defeated the Hai and their
experienced, battle-hardened allies, had driven Apophis in
disgrace from the field, and had proven their mettle against
overwhelming odds. "The deliverer?" he repeated in a faraway
voice. "I suppose I am, if anybody is. We need something to
rally around, and a foreigner's prophecy is as good as anything.
I do know I've always felt I had a mission—but I always
thought it was to avenge Mother's death and all the poor
bastards I grew up with in Hakoris's frightful refuge." His
voice tightened, and his eyes narrowed as he added, "To avenge
Mara, now. To avenge her and free her." He closed his eyes
and shuddered.

Riki said nothing, watching him.

Kamose went on in a thoughtful voice: "Apophis will go
back and try to reorganize his armies. He'll stop at nothing.
He'll get his native troops, and he'll get the money to scour
the entire world for new mercenaries, but the unrest will
grow—he long ago reached the limit of the oppression the
people could stand. I see a role for my friend Isesi, Aset's
brother, in all this. He reminds me of Baka: the quiet scholar
who goes to war because he can't get anyone else to do it,
and quite in spite of himself becomes a great warrior and a
great leader. Isesi won't want to start the rebellion, but he'll
have to do it, just as he had to organize the raid on the
refuge. And with him and his friends pecking away at Apophis's
home front . . ."

Below, they could see Elset approaching, preparing to
scale the ladder. "Riki," Kamose said, "encourage everyone
to believe that I'm the promised deliverer of The Prophecy."
He watched the officer climb up toward them and said in a
louder voice. "We'll go back to Thebes together, and we can
meet with Baliniri. Ah, here's Elset. Good work! You've
won a famous victory today, my friend!"

"The army has, sir," the young officer responded. "There

are a lot of heroes here today. Not the least of them the two
of you . . . and my late superior."

"Baba of El-Kab," Riki said sadly. "I feel fortunate to
have known him even this long. I was looking forward to
knowing him better."

"And he you, sir." Elset said earnestly. "He spoke of you
just before the battle, sir. He wanted me to tell you. I think
you were looking for information about your parentage, sir?
Yes? Well, my master told me to tell you, if anything happened to him and he hadn't time to tell you himself, that he
may have known who your mother was."

"Oh, yes. I told him. We had a talk shortly before—"

"*And* your father, sir."

Riki stared. His head reeled. Words would not come for
a moment. He swallowed and tried again. "What did he say?
Tell me!"

"Only that on your return to Thebes you must seek out a
woman named Maryet, the widow of a scribe named Setesh.
Baba thought she could be found living in Deir el-Bahari.
Now, of course he was not sure about all this and hesitated to
bring it up without further proof, which he said *you* would
find when you spoke with Maryet. He liked you very much,
sir, if you don't mind my saying so."

Riki, his eyes glazed over, stared into the distance. Forgotten now were the scene below, the sight of Apophis's fleet
retreating in unseemly haste with the Egyptian ships in laugh-
able pursuit—with their three tiny ships to Apophis's nine—
and the fact of the great victory he had won today in his first
real battle of any size. All he could think of was Elset's words.

My father! he thought. *What if he's still alive? What if I
could meet him? What would he say? What would he think of
me?*

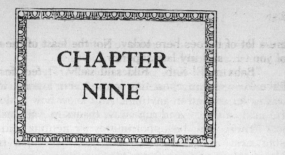

CHAPTER
NINE

The Delta

I

The news about Egypt's stunning victory and Apophis's craven retreat from the field traveled downriver on the wings of the wind. The sight of the returning ships was at first greeted from the banks of the Nile with chagrin, as a sign of victory; but there was none of the usual accompanying ceremony that would ordinarily announce victory—no flags flying, no martial music, no cheers from the sparse guard on board— and this set people to wondering.

Then a soldier on the flagship fell overboard—some said he appeared to jump voluntarily— and, as luck would have it, was picked out of the water by a passing fisherman. The soldier told the full story to his rescuer. "I'm through with soldiering," the young trooper said in disgust. "The king made cowards out of us all yesterday. Imagine running away, leaving the army in the field!"

"Well, now," said the fisherman, "so you're quitting.

Does this mean you're going to be needing a job?" There was an impish grin on his face as he said this.

"I obviously can't go back home. Are you offering me a job on your fishing boat? As you saw, I'm a poor swimmer. I was never trained in anything. All I know how to do is fight." He made a face. "*And* run away, thanks to Apophis."

"There may be opportunities for fighting and *not* running away as the days go by," the fisherman suggested. "Don't give up so quickly. Meanwhile, you can earn a few meals in the next few days by doing nothing more than what you're doing right now—shooting off your mouth."

The ex-soldier scowled. "Boasting about my bravery? Telling old war stories about the famous victory at Lisht?"

The fisherman's fist landed none too lightly on his knee. "Get your wits about you," he said. "Listen to me. There's a revolt brewing, one that can use the talents of a man who prefers fighting to running away and honest Egyptian blood on the throne to Hai by-blows of doubtful ancestry and questionable character." He let this sink in for a beat, then went on. "Meanwhile, we're recruiting very quietly, out on the fringes of things. There's supposed to be a chapter of our order in Avaris, running things, but I don't know about that. I do know we're growing by leaps and bounds here in the outer districts."

"I see. You want me to help recruit people for your order by telling about what happened at Lisht."

"Yes."

"What do you stand for?"

"We want the Hai out of Egypt. A man's lands in his own hands. Foreigners out of high positions. We call ourselves the Brotherhood of Shai, the god of destiny."

"Sounds good. Count me in."

"Not so fast. We have to test you. You could be a traitor." There was a mischievous grin on the fisherman's face. "There are rituals you must go through."

"I don't have any money."

"That's all right. You can pay your way by talking. Come home with me. Tomorrow we'll go down to the docks, and you'll talk to the workers there. Some of them are still on the fence."

The sailor shrugged. "Suits me. What have I to lose? I'm sure there's been a price on my head ever since I fell overboard."

"*Fell* overboard?"

"All right, jumped. I wouldn't have tried it if you hadn't been working so far out in the channel."

"Quite obviously the gods wished us to meet. Then it's arranged. Come home and I'll have my wife fix you something to eat. In the morning we'll have work to do."

In Avaris the news was sometimes delayed twenty-four hours before it filtered into town, but by the noon of the day Apophis returned, all the bazaars were buzzing with gossip. The returned guardsmen included men who had been part of the rear guard that attended the person of Apophis and those who had fought in the line. The line soldiers knew; the word had got out: "Apophis's son, he said! He calls himself the promised deliverer! He managed to creep all the way through the lines into Apophis's tent, then spared the king! The Prophecy said the Hai tyrant would be killed on the field of battle! And when this son of the king came to the Egyptians' camp, they all grew stronger, braver! They lost their fear of us! You should have seen them! It was the way Egyptians used to fight, back in the days of our fathers!"

Miraculously, the rumors spread without much hyperbole. They did not need to be amplified; they were shocking enough as they were. Shocking and inspiring. One by one, despite the civic prohibition against people gathering in crowds, the word passed from person to person. The guards walked uneasily through the squares and marketplaces, eyeing every small conversation suspiciously. Behind their backs the people of the city winked at one another and smiled.

Sem heard the news first and hurried to Isesi's hiding place in the loft of a boarded-up granary. He waited until he was quite sure he had not been seen, then slipped in through an unguarded door. "Isesi?" he said in a hoarse whisper. "Are you there?"

"Come on up," said his comrade. Sem climbed the rope ladder to the loft and was handed up the last step or two by Isesi. Breathlessly he told the news; Isesi heard him out silently, eyes bright, nodding here and there, then said, "We have to get word to Mara. Don't ask me how; Hakoris has the place guarded as if it held the gold reserves of the nation. But she has to know. It'll give her hope."

"Before we even call a meeting of the order?" Sem asked.

"Before even that. Tell you what: I'll try to get the word through to her somehow. Meanwhile, you call a meeting for tonight, at the usual place."

"The island?"

"Yes. I'll be there by the time the moon is high, whether or not I've succeeded in talking to Mara." Only now he let himself indulge in a thin smile. "That Kamose! I didn't see the greatness in him at first. Aset could tell from the very beginning, but I thought him just an adventurer. And look what effect he has in one day—one day!—on the Egyptian army."

"You don't think this has . . . that the Egyptians have *won*?"

Isesi frowned and shook his head. "Not a chance. It'll strengthen Apophis's resolve. But every new oppression back home will drive another hundred converts into our camp, and our dozens of new members can peck away at his supply lines, raid his granaries and armories, and make life as miserable as possible for him." He looked at Sem, his face animated. "For the first time, I almost think we can win. Not today, not tomorrow or next week. But down the road . . ."

The hand that balled into a fist at the end of his thin arm was still that of a scholar, a wielder of brushes rather than weapons. But as Sem looked at his companion now, he recognized the new spirit in him. Isesi seemed to grow visibly in strength and resolve as he spoke. Could this still be the old Isesi? Or was a new man growing up right before his eyes?

Joseph uncharacteristically came home in the early afternoon, looking wan and tired. Asenath met him at the door and embraced him. "Oh, Joseph! You look terrible. Has it been so bad, then?"

"I don't want to be around him today," her husband said, sinking onto a couch in the great central hall of the house, his shoulders drooping. There was still youth in his face, but his red hair had grown quite gray in the stressful times of the past year or so. The uncertain political climate had aged him considerably. "He's taken a terrible beating, and he's taking it out on everyone."

"Poor Joseph! Let me bring you something to—"

"No, no," he said, with a weary wave of his hand. "Come sit here by me. I need company more than anything." He tried to smile as she joined him on the couch. "I had a letter by the courier from Canaan. From Reuben. Father's funeral and interment were completed with great ceremony. It seems we're not all quite so forgotten in the old country as I'd thought."

"Are they coming back quickly?"

"I told them to mend fences first with everyone there instead." He looked at her now, and there was fear in his eyes. "I wish we could leave here tomorrow. I'm very concerned about the way things are going just now. Not just with Apophis, with the Egyptians as well."

"What do you mean?" she asked, taking his hand soothingly in hers.

"My spies have infiltrated a new nativist movement dedicated not only to the removal of Apophis and the Hai, which would in general be a good thing, but to the removal of all, uh, 'foreigners' as well. That means us. They see us as leeches, living off the lifeblood of Egypt—"

"Oh, no, Joseph! You and your family are—"

"I know. On the whole we've been a fairly benign influence. Nevertheless, the Egyptians are starving, and we 'foreigners' are viewed as holding property, living very well by their standards—"

"I see why you're worried. Can't Father help? Does the priesthood of Amon carry no weight with them anymore?"

"Your father would like to help, but he's a very sick man. I'm not sure he'll ever recover his strength. And his successors won't have reason for helping us. It's a bad situation. If only we could leave tomorrow, but the families, the wives and children, are being held hostage here for my brothers' return."

His shoulders lifted and fell. Asenath's heart sank. If there were only something she could do! He had carried this heavy burden so long, so very long!

Hakoris hobbled painfully toward her on his crutch, his bad leg trailing uselessly. "Curse you!" he shouted. "Shut up that termagant's tongue of yours!"

Mara, naked, her thick, beautiful hair cropped short and her neck chained at the end of a long tether to the wall behind her, stood in a defiant attitude, hands on hips, and glared at him. "That's it," she taunted. "Come within my reach, won't you?" Her smile was a harpy's, merciless and unforgiving. "Come hopping over here on the end of that stick of yours and try, just once, to beat me again. Whether it's a stick or a whip that you wave at me, you'll find, as you did before, that I'm faster and stronger than you. I'll grab it out of your hands and knock you senseless with it before you can get away. And if you don't let go of it quickly enough, I'll use it to drag you to me, and I'll choke you until you turn blue. You'll be a dead man."

He stopped just beyond Mara's reach and glared at her. "I don't know why I don't just have you killed and have done with it," he said. "Slowly."

She laughed. "It's because you're even sicker than I thought you were when we were younger. I'm the only person in the whole world with whom you have any relationship at all. Isn't that right, Hakoris? If you killed me, you'd be totally alone. There wouldn't even be anyone to curse at."

"I could take you out to the edge of town and sic the feral dogs on you."

"I'd win them over to my side. Animals always like me. And then I'd come back in the middle of the night, some night, and kill you."

He raised the crutch and tried to hit her with it but lost his balance and almost fell. She grabbed for the crutch and yanked it out of his hand. She tried to swing it and hit him in the face with it, but he scuttled crabwise out of reach. Disgusted, she hurled it at him. He cringed in the corner as it bounced harmlessly off the wall beside him. And, trying desperately to climb to his feet despite the bad leg, he looked just once into her eyes, shuddered, and wondered briefly to himself: *It's almost as if I were afraid of her, and not the other way around. . . .*

When he was gone Mara sat down on the cold floor and rubbed the sore spot on her neck where the manacle chafed. If only she were stronger and could force the two ends of the manacle apart!

From above and behind her, from the latticed window, a loud whisper came from the garden outside: "Mara! Are you there? Is he gone?"

Instantly she was on her feet, straining upward toward the unseen source of the sound. "Isesi! Is that you?"

"Yes. We're still trying to get you out. But in the meantime, you ought to know that Kamose joined up with the Egyptians, and they beat the Hai at Lisht."

"They did! Tell me!"

"He was brilliant. He drove Apophis back to Avaris in disgrace, with half his army dead or captured. The king's mad with rage and fear. Kamose announced himself as the promised deliverer. Mara, for the first time I believe! I believe we can win!"

Mara closed her eyes and pressed her balled fists to her mouth. Her heart was beating fast. She did not answer, for she could find no words to describe the feelings running through her mind.

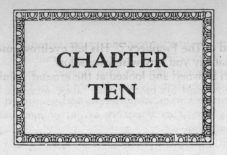

CHAPTER
TEN

Thebes

I

The news traveled equally quickly upriver, and more openly. Even before Kamose and Riki shipped back to the capital to report to Baliniri and King Sekenenre, the supply packets that ran incessantly up and down the river had carried the news of the Egyptian victory to all the lands south of Lisht. The instantaneous reaction was universal jubilation. And when the second packet carried a letter from Riki to Baliniri telling the whole story and announcing that he was returning to Thebes with the promised deliverer, Baliniri consulted with the king in private before making any announcement.

Sekenenre listened silently as Baliniri read the document aloud. His face betrayed no hint of what he was thinking. Finally, the king spoke quietly. "I thought that the news of a victory, large or small, would raise my spirits immeasurably. That was before . . . this other business entered the picture. Now I don't know what to think. 'Promised deliverer'? 'Child of The Prophecy'?" His left eyebrow rose sharply. "Well? What say you, my wise counselor?"

Baliniri frowned and looked at the ground, thinking. As a child, Kamose and his mother had taken refuge at Baliniri's island home. "Could be a double-edged sword, Sire. There is a proverb in my country that says you do not invite the wolf in to help you control the dog. This chap Kamose could very well have been the one Apophis was looking for when he ordered the killing of the ten-year-olds. If he is, Riki would recognize him in a moment. They were close childhood friends. Riki was there when Kamose's mother was killed."

"And?"

"This is no final victory. Apophis will regroup and hire new mercenaries. Let's hope he doesn't talk the Hittites into breaking their long tradition of neutrality and nonintervention. When he's strong enough, he'll hit us again, but this time he won't be overconfident and stupid." He scowled blackly. "Unfortunately, I had a hand in training him, and I think he'll remember what I taught him."

Sekenenre rose from his seat and walked to the window to look out over Thebes and the river. "And in the meantime what should we do? Particularly with this two-edged sword in our midst? This Kamose will have designs on my throne once he's driven the Hai out of Egypt and killed his father. I don't see any room for myself in this, and a kingdom can't tolerate two claimants to the throne. What do I do with a pretender sitting right here in my lap?"

"I've been thinking about that, Sire," Baliniri said, joining him at the window. "When he returns with Riki, it'll be to a hero's welcome." He crossed impressive arms over his big chest. "We welcome them with all the royal dignity we can muster, Sire. We announce a feast, even though we can't afford it just now. We make a personal appearance with both of them for all the people to see. Largess, sir. Be big about it. The king welcoming his loyal and faithful servants."

The pause was heavy with unstated meaning.

"Then?" Sekenenre asked.

"Then, Sire, we send each of them off on a mission. In different directions."

A small smile crept onto Sekenenre's face. Then the

smile became a conspiratorial grin. "And these 'missions' . . . you will send our 'deliverer' friend where?"

"Upriver, Sire," Baliniri answered. "To Nubia, as envoy to Akhilleus's son, Nehsi, who, I think, has stayed out of this fight quite long enough. After all, if we were to fall, there'd be no one to keep Apophis from scaling the walls of Kerma. There comes a point where Nehsi has to help look out for his own interests. My sources say that Kamose has a golden tongue and much charm. If anyone can get through to Nehsi, it may be this chap. Kamose will be kept busy and *quite* out of the way."

Sekenenre gave a mock-polite bow. The expression on his face, merry and mischievous, mirrored his delight. "All right," he said. "And Riki? What shall we do with him while all this is going on? Obviously we have to keep him busy too."

"My thought exactly, Sire. I have plans for him, Sire—special plans." Baliniri's own smile did not invite further questions. Sekenenre thought the matter over for a moment and decided against pressing him. But the king fervently wished he could read the look in his vizier's eye.

The door took a long time to open. When it did, the face that peered out at her through the crack looked so unlike Ketan that Tuya would have had difficulty recognizing him without the context of standing at the doorway of Ketan's own house.

"Ketan!" she said. "I came as fast as I could." He opened the door wider, and when a ray of sunlight fell on his stricken face, she feared the worst. "Nebet! Is she—"

She knew the answer even before he got it out. "The midwife just left," he said dully. "There was nothing more she could do."

"No! No, Ketan!"

He leaned back against the wall, eyes closed. All the lines of his face dragged down; his shoulders drooped. "It was a breech birth. Nebet was so small. . . ."

Tuya impulsively hugged him to her. She was so short, her head came only halfway up his chest. He accepted her embrace passively. She could feel his big body shake suddenly in a shuddering sob. "She wanted a child so badly," he said. "We tried so many times."

"The baby!" Tuya said. "Is it—"

"It's in the other room, with the wet nurse." His voice was flat, stricken. "It's a boy. The midwife told me it had the birthmark. It's a Child of the Lion." He was just reporting the facts, without joy or pride. "I haven't looked at it."

"Oh, Ketan!" She took his big hand in her two small ones and led him inside. "If only there were something I could say, something I could do—"

"Tuya," he said, looking at her almost for the first time. "You knew, maybe better than anyone, about me and Nebet. You were there from the first. She—" He could not finish the sentence. He seemed to fold in on himself and sank slowly and wretchedly to the bench behind him, where he sat hunched forward, his body shaking uncontrollably.

Tuya looked down at him and put her hand on his head. "I'll go see the baby," she said. Giving him one last despairing look—what could she say to him, anyway? What could she do for him at a time like this?—she went away into the small room that Nebet had lovingly prepared for the nursery.

In a small pool of light from the open window, the young wet nurse was giving the breast to a lusty, naked boy-child. He sucked vigorously, his little arms waving reflexively. Tuya smiled. "I'm Ketan's cousin," she said. "Is there anything I can do?"

"The child is all right," the girl said. "I'll stay with him. I can move into the next room. I just lost one of my own. My, what a strong, vigorous little one this is!" She looked down almost proudly at the child in her arms. "Too bad about the birthmark on its back . . ."

"Oh, no," Tuya said, looking at it—the angry red mark of the lion's paw, clearly visible even from here. "It's a proud family tradition. It'll make the boy rich and famous someday." She paused, thinking. It wouldn't do to keep on calling the little dear "the boy." "We'll have to give it a name. Has Ketan thought of this?"

"Oh, no, ma'am. He doesn't even want to see it. Not

yet, anyway. I'm sure he'll change his mind." She smiled down at the tiny bundle cradled in her arms.

"No, he can't go on ignoring his son. Ketan's broken up over the mother's death. He'll come around. You just stay on the job and take care of the baby."

"Someone will have to look out for the master, too," the girl ventured. "He's dismissed all the other servants."

"Oh, dear." Tuya looked back through the open door toward the big central room, where Ketan still sat slumped over, his head dropping almost to the level of his knees. He looked as if he were about to topple over, except that his tense body was rock-hard, frozen in place, quivering from time to time with sobs.

What can I do? she thought desperately. *If only I could help him. But I have my own problems just now. That woman! That Tamshas!* She had fastened on to Tuya like a leech, preying on her guilt feelings over Ben-Hadad, always accusing her of one thing or another, keeping her off balance . . . and now Tamshas was stealing from her, Tuya was sure of it. Stealing money, jewelry, taking them to be sold. It would serve no purpose accusing Tamshas because she always denied everything, while at the same time making veiled threats to make public exposure of Ben-Hadad's shame, to tell everyone about Meni and about Ben-Hadad's last degrading, humiliating days.

Oh, if Seth were only here, or Kedar! But Kedar was away on a visit to his family, and nobody seemed to have any idea where Seth was. She was so alone with all this!

And now once again, as it had so many times before, the thought invaded her mind: There was one person who could help her in a minute, but he was the one person in the world she could never force herself to approach. Baliniri, the vizier to Sekenenre, the second most powerful man in the entire country! But there was no way in the world that she could take a problem to him. Not after all that had passed between them, so many years before!

Deep in her heart she knew she had to solve the problem herself, if only to keep the boy, Meni, Tamshas's son, from being hurt. If Tamshas fell, her son would be ruined too, and somehow, despite growing up with such a mother, he had managed to become a bright and decent child, likable and kind.

There must be something to the story, she thought. *It has to be true. Meni has to be Ben-Hadad's son. He's so like the way Ben-Hadad was when he was young: honest, trusting.* Time after time she had tried to tell herself Tamshas was lying, that it was just a scheme for extorting money from her, for worming her way into Tuya's house so that she could connive and steal. But then she had looked into Meni's face and seen Ben-Hadad there, and all her defenses had crumbled.

What can I do? she asked herself again. She looked across the room at Ketan, and the sight of him—crushed, helpless—drove the despair out of her own mind for a moment. She had to deal with Ketan first. Then perhaps she could figure out what to do about Tamshas.

"They'll be letting you out today," said Nushin, the captured Hai soldier, standing at the barred door and looking up the dark staircase toward the only light source. "Don't forget me, eh? Just tell them what I told you."

Seth nodded. "I'm sure you're right about it being very important, although I'm not sure exactly what the significance of the information is. I wonder if there are any other Hai-born slaves here, people who would know something more about this."

"Get them to let me out and I'll find them for you!" Nushin promised, his voice rising. "I'm going crazy in here. I'm not a soldier, I'm a scribe! I was kidnapped and pressed into service. I'm not a fighter. I don't belong in this hole with the rats."

"Nobody belongs here," Seth responded calmly. "I'll see what I can do. I don't guarantee anything—so far they haven't paid any attention to anything I've said. Not listening to the private soldier—even when he has something of importance to say—appears to be a general policy. Strange turn of mind, that. You'd think a good idea would be welcome, and that it wouldn't matter who its father was. When I'm let out, I'll refuse to be a private soldier anymore. I think I'll be a captain at least. That's about the lowest rank they ever listen to. Yes, that's what I'll do."

Nushin stared at Seth's bland face. "You'll 'be a captain'?" he echoed. "Just like that? And they'll let you? Oh, gods! I've wagered on the wrong horse once again. The man's mad. A complete lunatic!"

II

The inn was a new one. Tamshas had been barred from every one she had frequented in the past, for public drunkenness, soliciting, creating a disturbance, or merely for failing to bribe the owner to let her stay in defiance of the usual customs of the city, which prohibited the making of assignations by women not employed by the house.

The present inn—she could not have given its name to save her life; she could find it only by landmarks—was one in which, to date, she had minded her manners. Thus, when the traveler wandered in just past dinnertime, saw her sitting alone at a table in the darkened corner of the room, and ventured to join her, the landlord had raised a brow but had not intervened. Instead, the landlord watched with interest as the traveler began buying her drinks. The woman seemed to be well enough fixed; perhaps the issue of the bribe could be delicately broached some time later.

Finally, as the evening wore on, as the dancers finished their last set and the musicians were paid off, the landlord decided to make his move. He sidled up to the table and leaned over it, the fingers of both hands splayed on the wood, and spoke. "Begging your pardon, ma'am, but city regulations won't allow me to let unescorted women—"

That was as far as he got. The traveler's hand came out of his dust-stained garment so swiftly, it could hardly be followed. Something flashed in the dim light, and there was a solid *clunk!* on the wooden table, and when the landlord looked down, blinking, at his hands, a razor-sharp dagger was embedded in the wood precisely between the second and third fingers of his right hand!

He blanched, pulled back, and rubbed his hands. When he looked down at his attacker in disbelief, there was pure and undistilled menace glittering in the traveler's eyes.

"The lady isn't unescorted," the harsh voice growled. "She's with me. Let that be the last we hear of regulations. The city also prohibits selling poisonous pig urine, which you call millet beer."

It was the most chilling thing that had ever happened to the innkeeper. "My apologies!" the landlord said, recoiling. "Please accept a jar of my finest palm wine, with my compl—"

"Leave us," the traveler said. His voice was still deadly, all the more so for being hardly above a whisper. "Bring the palm wine. Put it right over there. But don't bother us again." The eyes fixed on him seemed to glow in the near darkness. The innkeeper retired in unseemly haste.

"There, now," the traveler said. "No more interruptions. What were you saying, my dear?"

Tamshas had recovered her composure by now and sat a bit more stiffly beside him. She was trying desperately to remember something of the formal manners of her youth, the small talk and protocol that distinguished quality from riff-raff. "Goodness," she said in a slightly affected voice. "You certainly have a forceful way about you, Apis."

"Don't waste any coquetry on me, my sweet," the traveler said roughly. "I'm not buying it. If you want to please me, tell me more about this rich bitch you're gouging. Your little swindle might be improved upon with the benefit of my expertise and experience. I never saw a racket that couldn't be made better, once like minds look at the matter from several angles."

Tamshas's mind was deeply divided. One half of her consciousness told her to bolt and run; she was in over her head, suddenly the pawn of a man who would always be two steps ahead of her, outbluffing and outflanking. The other half of her consciousness . . . she looked into those darkly hypnotic eyes and melted, as if she were a timid virgin in the hands of her first man. "Oh, Apis," she pleaded, "can't we go somewhere else and talk about this? I'd like to get into something comfortable. You're just in off the road, and you must be tired and dusty. Come up to my place and let me give you a warm bath—"

"Later," he said. "Business first, fun later. Always. Come on, now. Get it out. Tell me everything."

His hand gripped hers, hard. She gulped, shuddered. *Gods!* she thought. *This is going too fast for me!*

The boat had been held up all night some miles downriver from Thebes because Kamose, accurately reading the visceral needs of the public, wanted the triumphant arrival to take place around midmorning, when people were up and about— and wanted there to be time for signal fires downriver to announce their coming.

Now, however, the sun was high, and they had passed the great curve of the river, where the current divided around the central island and one could see the sentries standing tall atop the high hills watching then.

"Look, Aset," Kamose said, standing beside her at the rail. "Unless I miss my guess, that'll be Thebes."

"Right," Riki said. "You'll like Thebes, Aset—particularly the artists' village on the far side of the river. Everyone up there is involved with the visual arts, even if they're only engaged in cutting stone blocks for the sculptors. They're a different sort of person than you'd meet elsewhere. I used to go over there all the time when I was off duty. Now there's a chance that my mother came from Deir el-Bahari."

"And perhaps your father too," Kamose added. "If there's anything to that business Elset was telling you. What was the name of the woman you were supposed to look up, now?"

"Maryet," Riki said resolutely. "Widow of the scribe Setesh. I've got it memorized."

"On the other hand, Aset," Kamose continued, "the artists' village has been affected by the war. Every male has been conscripted for military service unless he's under ten, over seventy, or crippled."

Riki looked out over the river, looking for the first sign of the city proper around the bend. "It may not be quite that bad. But you'll find it a bit subdued." He patted Aset's arm. "But however it is, you'll be welcomed there as a heroine, Aset!" Suddenly his eyes widened, and he pointed upstream. "There it is!" he said as their boat moved slowly around the bend. And, indeed, they could all see the first buildings, the tall temple, the palace, and . . .

"Good heavens!" Aset said.

It looked as if the entire population of the city, civilian and military alike, was lined up on the two banks of the river to welcome the victors home! Now the cheer began. It built slowly, then grew and grew, amplified by the cup of hills on the west bank.

Hail the victors!

Aset found herself weeping shamelessly. She had never been so moved by anything in all her young life.

Tuya heard the cheering, the roar of the many voices, as she wearily closed the door of Ketan's house behind her to begin her slow, exhausted walk home. *The victors*, she thought dispiritedly. *The heroes of Lisht*. Perhaps at some other time she might be able to join in the celebration, but not now. She was too tired and depressed for that. She was too tired and depressed for everything. Spending the night there watching Ketan through his time of trial, she had got no sleep at all. She had never felt so totally depleted, not even in the desperate days of her childhood, when she had seldom known when or where she would find a place to sleep more than an hour before the time when she found it.

She had managed to find someone to send after her own physician, and he had come to examine the infant first and then Ketan. The still-unnamed child had been pronounced perfectly healthy and normal, and Ketan had been given a quite strong sedative to help him sleep.

Now, stumbling tiredly homeward through the streets, Tuya wondered if there might have been something that the doctor could have given her for her own ills. What was she going home to? That terrible situation, with that villainous woman coming in at all hours, badgering, stealing, bullying.

The cheer rang down the streets. She was blocks away, but it sounded as if she were no more than a few yards from the festivities. Well, she supposed it was a good thing. They had won, had they not? They had kept the Hai out of Lisht and presumably Thebes and bought Baliniri some time to rearm and outfit his army and seek out new allies for the fight. Rumor had it the rout was so complete that units of the Lisht force had been sent over to the Fayum to reclaim the food-producing areas from Hai control. That would be very important.

So why could she not join in the jubilation? Was there something missing inside of her, that she could not rejoice? She had, it seemed, reached once too often inside herself for a new reserve of strength and belief and renewal. Now she found only emptiness. If only there were someone older, stronger, and wiser for her to lean on, tell her troubles to, and ask for advice!

Kedar, where are you?

"So this is the girl you've been telling me about!" said the lord of Two Lands, Sekenenre. "Approach, my dear."

Aset's heart was in her throat. She was embarrassingly aware of the simple shift and straw sandals she wore, her wigless and unkempt hair. Poor turnout indeed for a girl meeting a king. She felt like a fool, like a dirty little ragamuffin, but she could only obey the king's words, after all. Thankfully he was young, with a kind face, very human and accepting. Surely he would forgive her appearance. She bowed humbly.

"It is I who should bow to you," the king said graciously, reaching out to take her hands. "Our royal thanks, and those of a grateful people, my dear. While you reside with us, the protection of my own hand will be upon you, and you shall have whatever your fancy dictates." He smiled, released her hands, and actually did give her a tiny bow, one that was not missed by any of the court nobles nearby. The audience was over. And Aset, once she had been ushered out of the royal presence, stood stunned. None of it had seemed real at all.

* * *

"What shall I say?" the king said, beaming first at Riki, then at Kamose, and finally at Baliniri. "Can any reward be great enough, Baliniri? If this kingdom were as rich as once it was, or as it shall be in time to come . . . But as it is, I can only reward these heroes with my royal confidence. Therefore"—here he turned to the other two—"know that from this moment you both carry the rank of general, with all perquisites appertaining."

"Sire!" breathed Riki. Both he and Kamose bowed. Kamose did not speak.

"And," said the king, "to you, Kamose, whom the gods have sent us in our hour of need, I further offer the rank of ambassador plenipotentiary, with all the rights and dignities thereto appertaining, and so on, and so on." Kamose's eyes gleamed oddly, but the king went on, obviously not requiring answer just yet. "You shall speak with my voice . . . in Nubia, where I charge you with the task of bringing over to our side, once and for all, the strong right arm of Nehsi, son of Akhilleus."

"Your Majesty!" Kamose said in a voice whose precise tone none of the others could read. He bowed. "I hasten to obey in all things."

"Very good," Sekenenre said. "After a thorough briefing, you will leave immediately. It is imperative that Nehsi be brought into our camp. Without the reinforcement of his superb troops, it is highly unlikely that we can withstand the assault that Apophis will now prepare. Thus I cannot over emphasize the importance of your mission. And I thank you from the bottom of my heart, both personally and in my capacity as the voice of the Egyptian people, for what you have done and for what you have agreed to do." A wave of the hand; the audience was over. Kamose bowed his way out.

Riki remained. "You, General," the king said, and Riki blinked at the term. "I have an equally important mission for you. Baliniri will explain the details. I can only tell you that your assignment will be arduous and perhaps even dangerous, but the whole of our success rides on your shoulders."

"I'm yours to command, Sire, now and forever," Riki said. "What is it that I'm supposed to do?"

The king waved a hand at Baliniri. Riki looked at the vizier expectantly. Baliniri did not speak for a moment. Then he said in a quiet and decisive voice: "Bring us weapons of iron."

III

"Well, look at this," Kamose said with a smile. "The king seems to have meant what he said." He looked around the great central room of the apartment Aset had been assigned to in the palace and whistled long and low. "You'll be a great lady of the court." His eye twinkled as he went on. "Much too great to hang out with dusty, battle-weary soldiers like Riki and me."

Aset looked ruefully down at the beautiful gown and expensive buffalo-leather sandals she had been given. There was an entire closet full of these sorts of things in the next room. How had they guessed at her size in everything? "I don't want any of it, Kamose. Not if I have to be separated from you. And, uh, Riki."

Kamose gave no sign of noticing her last-minute emendation. "Look at those tapestries!" he said admiringly. "I'd feel ill at ease with such affluence. After years at sea without a roof over my head in all weather—"

"Oh, Kamose, do you have to leave me here? I don't know anyone at court. I'll be out of place." He turned and took her hands and spoke in the voice of an older brother, which she hated. "It's too dangerous," he said flatly.

"Dangerous?" she repeated, pulling her hands away— and immediately wished she had not. "After all we've been through? A raid on the Children's Refuge? Escaping from the delta one step ahead of Apophis's soldiers? The great battle at Lisht? You call a mission to a peaceful country too dangerous for me?"

"It was the king's decision," he said with a shrug. "He won't let you go. Not even on Riki's mission, much less on mine. I can't do anything about it. Young Sekenenre is a forceful young man when he gets his mind made up. I'm pleasantly surprised to see he has as much backbone as he has. I'm sorry, Aset. I'd like to have you along, if the truth be known."

She looked desperately into his eyes and saw the confirmation of the reserve underlying his tone. "No you wouldn't," she said. "You're just as glad to be rid of me. And why shouldn't you be? I'd just be underfoot. I'll bet if I were Mara . . ."

The moment she said this last, she wished she had not. But it could not be called back. He stepped back, a sad look in his eye. He did not say anything.

"Put something on," Apis retorted with a frown. "Or get away from the window. You're going to get the guards down on us, running around like that."

Tamshas's hands immediately covered her nakedness. She reached hastily for her robe. "You didn't feel that way about me half an hour ago," she said resentfully. "You couldn't wait to get my clothes off. You said—"

"I don't care what I said. That was then. This is now. And I've been looking over this inventory you did of her assets. You've done a pretty thorough job. Of course you couldn't be expected to itemize her real properties or credit on deposit with the merchants and bankers—not until you start living in. For that we'll have to get the boy to do some spying for us. Have him steal records from her house in the morning—"

"No!" Tamshas said. "He wouldn't be any good for that. He's too young!"

"Nonsense," Apis retorted in that maddening flat voice of his. "I was lifting purses in the marketplace when I was half his age. Besides, we'll get the stuff back to him before she comes home in the evening. Only a few scrolls a day. I suppose about a week ought to do it."

"You can read them?"

"Of course. I failed out the school for scribes, but not for lack of talent. Actually I never failed out, not really. There was this difference of opinion about whether or not you should be allowed to go around—"

"Spare me," she said. She was fully clothed now except for her shoes, and she was frustrated and full of sharp edges. "Did they send you to prison for it?"

"They would have if they could have caught me," he said. "But they didn't. Nobody ever does. And stop worrying. Nobody will catch the kid, either. Particularly if we get to work on this immediately. If we wait until that schoolteacher chap of hers comes back from his little vacation, it'll be a lot harder. I asked around about him—he's pretty sharp and will be hard to fool."

"Don't make me bring the boy into this," she said. "I won't have it."

She was about to say something else, but his hand shot out and grabbed her hard by the lower jaw, so hard it hurt. She tried to pull away but could not. "Stop!" she tried to say. "You're hurting me!" But the words were a pained garble.

"Don't you ever say *don't* to me," he warned quietly. "Not now, not at any time in the future. Never."

"Well," Riki said, bringing up his bowl of palm wine in a mock salute, "that was quite a performance you gave in there for the king. Baliniri, the man of mystery. But we're alone now. Just what were you getting at?"

"Just what I said. You're going after my secret weapon. Bring me back a sword of iron, the finest. I've been putting this moment off for years, until there was someone fronting the army who could wield the thing. But that Kamose fellow has the stamp of greatness on him. I think he's the man." Baliniri looked him in the eye. "I mean no offense against you, my friend. You're the best. I ought to know—I trained you. But the finger of the gods has not touched you to reign. Not as a king, although you may wind up as a vizier running a kingdom. I intend to train you for the job; it'll be the only way I can exert any control over whoever my successor turns out to be."

"I'm sure you're right," Riki said with a shrug, "although I haven't given up on the notion that I come from better stock than you might expect. Baba of El-Kab said—"

"I heard about that! Good hunting, over in Deir el-Bahari! I hope you find out someone's estate owes you a fortune—just so long as you don't inherit enough money to make you quit my army."

"Fat chance!" Riki responded, laughing, and drained the bowl. "You'll not be getting rid of me that way. Not even if it turns out I'm a nobleman. Still, it'd be nice to know I wasn't just the bastard son of a drover by a woman with delusions of grandeur."

"Just you wait," Baliniri said with a sigh. "When you do learn, it won't make a bit of difference. You'll say, 'Well, I'll be damned,' and then you'll toss your pedigree off into the corner and go about your business as if nothing had changed in your life."

"Maybe," Riki said, but there was wistfulness in his voice. "But maybe you only say that because you know who your father was. Well, enough of that. When do I leave? And where am I headed?"

A mischievous look came into Baliniri's eye. "Into the desert, to meditate and learn," he said. "Your fortune will seek you out. You will undergo tests, as befits a man seeking a great secret and its answer. If you pass the tests—"

"Oh, come on. Don't give me this silly song and dance, Baliniri. I deserve better than that."

"You'll have to prove whether or not you're the true bearer of the great news that the promised deliverer has come."

"Then why doesn't Kamose come with me?"

"Because I want you to go. You have another role to play here, an important one. When the time comes, you'll know. The thing I'm sending you after has great power and is all-important to our victory and to the future of Egypt. I want you to be the one who brings it, and Kamose to be the one who wields it."

"Come on. . . ."

"Look," Baliniri said, leaning forward. "One thing I'm sure of, my young friend: Of all the men in the world who could be seeking the secret of forging iron, you're the only one who could bring it back." He stood and clapped both hands on Riki's broad young shoulders. "And you will. I'm sure of it."

Riki stood up . . . and suddenly realized how much wine he had put away. He weaved and almost fell back onto his chair. "Huh!" he said. "Some world saver I am! One minute all assurance and soldierly competence, and the next I'm falling on my—"

"You're fallible and human and vulnerable, and there's not the smallest trace of a god or demigod in you, my young friend. Precisely because of these things and not in spite of them, you're probably the best man in the world you move around in, including myself. For what I am asking you to do, you're precisely the right person to ensure once and for all that the Red and Black Lands of Egypt be saved from the heavy hand of the Hai, and that their curse be lifted for all time. I don't know whether you're the most important person in the world just now, but I wouldn't bet the future of my immortal soul against it."

"W-what sort of nonsense are you talking, Baliniri?" Riki asked, trying once more to rise. "Important? Me? I could be replaced by any one of a hundred sol—"

"Not so," Baliniri interrupted. "For the job I'm sending you on, only one man in the world will do. And you're that man."

Riki stared. And slowly sank down again, blinking.

Barefoot, Tuya tiptoed up behind the boy. She had left her sandals at the door. Meni, on his knees, leaned far out over the little pool in the atriumlike inner room, blowing softly on the sail of a tiny boat he had made from a twig and a leaf. The leaf, spread lateen style, caught the soft gust of his breath and sent the little boat out across the water. She looked down at the unobserved innocence of the child's smile and a harsh hand grabbed at her heart.

He heard her little sob and drew back, eyes wide. "I . . . I didn't mean to make a mess! I'll take the boat off the pond! I'll clean everything up! Please don't—"

She knelt beside him and affectionately mussed his dark hair with one gentle hand. "It's all right. I was remembering how my Seth used to like to play with boats in the same pool. He looked much as you did just then. I looked down, and it was as if I had my little son back again."

Meni struggled with a smile, a timid one that threatened to give way to tears at any moment.

Before going across the river to Deir el-Bahari, Riki had dressed more appropriately for the occasion. No use showing off his soldierly status; it might very well scare off the very people of the back streets he needed to talk to. Now, in mufti—a plain robe, which, given his muscles and his soldier's deep tan, probably fooled no one—he headed for the ferryboats at the river, pausing now and then to acknowledge a salute or other greeting from one of the soldiers he had trained here in Thebes.

Truly, he thought proudly, they did not look too bad, particularly given the short time he had had to train them in! Drilling like this took precision and attention, and you could not usually expect that from a bunch of raw farmboys and fishermen's sons.

Ah! *There* was an exception! Look at that fellow, now! Could not keep in step at all, and there was his superior, cursing him out about it.

It was some sort of prison detail, headed either to jail or back from it, he knew from the plain, raggedy clothing they wore. And the tallish one who could not get in step, who kept stumbling over his own feet, was . . . Riki changed step, set out at a light jog toward the little work detail.

"Seth!" he called. "Seth, is that you?"

All it took was the general's word. Seth's career as a private soldier in the army ended the moment Riki took him in charge. The administrative scrolls would be altered to show Seth's new status as personal adviser to Riki, and from that moment the retrograde movement of Seth's life changed inalterably. Arm in arm, the two friends sauntered down to the first inn they could find on the crowded waterfront; Riki ordered food and drink and led Seth to a table by the parapet overlooking the quay below.

"I'm not hungry," Seth said.

"Eat anyway," Riki said. "I know you too well. People always had to remind you when to eat—"

"No," Seth responded, looking him in the eye. "That's over. I've been living in a dream world. I've been lost in my own mind, trying to ignore the everyday world. And what happened because of it? The world got fouled up terribly. So much so that it eventually invaded my safe little sphere and started wasting my time."

Riki raised an eyebrow. This was the first time he had ever heard the young savant talking in so down-to-earth a manner. "You're coming back into the world, then? I'm liking what I'm hearing."

"Yes. Somehow I hadn't noticed what desperate times these are. I have to do something. And I don't mean carry a spear—not that there's anything wrong with carrying a spear, if that happens to be something you're good at."

"I understand." But imagine Seth being sensitive to the feelings of the person he was talking to! "Go on."

"No, *you* go on. You were talking about this trip Baliniri wants you to go on, to look for iron. Why would he want you—"

Suddenly he stopped, and for a moment he seemed the old Seth again, lost in his own world. "And sent Kamose to Nubia, too. Nubia, which is quite rich in ores of all kinds. Doesn't want him in the way complicating things. And in the meantime . . . but wait. There was that thing I learned from the fellow in prison. That could be very important. But no. That can wait, can't it? Meanwhile there's plenty of work to do. And you're just the right man for it. Yes. Baliniri knows what he's doing. And even before there's a sword, there has to be *the* sword. Good! Good!" One of his weak fists banged on the table, surprisingly decisively. He looked at Riki with a smile. That was uncharacteristic too: Seth *never* remembered to smile.

"What are you talking about?" Riki demanded in a voice that leaked annoyance.

"Nothing," Seth said. The new tone to his voice was

back again, calm and resolute. "I'm going with you into the desert. There'll come a point where you'll need me. It's settled. When do we start?"

Riki, wide-eyed, motioned ineffectually for the innkeeper. "Landlord!" he said in an odd voice. "Where is that wine I ordered?"

IV

"Ma'am," Cheta said, forcing resolve into her voice, "I've been meaning to talk to you. If you could spare a moment, please?"

Tuya's head jerked around. "What?" she asked sharply. "What is it now?"

The harsh tone took Cheta aback, and her heart sank. It was touchy enough trying to bring this up in the first place without having to run it past one of Tuya's increasingly frequent bad moods. She swallowed hard, though, and tried again. "Ma'am, it's about Tamshas."

"I know," Tuya said warily. "I *know*. I don't like her at all myself. But what can I do? There's Meni, after all. I have an obligation. I can't just abandon him because she—"

"Ma'am," Cheta said, forcing herself to break in, "are you sure? *Please*. Couldn't you talk this over with someone? Isn't there someone we could bring in to . . . well, to ask some questions? Find out a little more about—"

"The boy. I don't want to hurt the boy. If it was just Tamshas it would be different."

"Ma'am, she's going to drive you crazy. She's up to no good."

"I know." Tuya threw up her hands. "If only Kedar were here! He'd know what to do. But what with the mail service breaking down and couriers not allowed through—"

"They would if you went to Bal—" Cheta got the first syllable out, then knew instantly that she had overstepped herself. "I'm sorry, ma'am. I know I'm not supposed to bring up—"

"Oh, just leave me alone! Leave me alone! Can't you find something to keep yourself occupied with?"

Deir el-Bahari was a changed place. No longer was the main street a bustling avenue of vendors' stalls, rich with the sounds of bargaining and dealing, fragrant with the smells of food-merchants' wares. Some of the same businesses were still there, to be sure, but there were few buyers. The desperate buildup of the army in recent days had decimated the shops, the workbenches, even the quarries themselves. The arts of peace were in short supply.

Seth looked to right and left, shaking his head. "I haven't been over here in some time. Has it been this way long?"

"No," Riki answered. "I hate the way things look. I'd hoped this place would be spared in the general mobilization. The art village here was the sort of thing one fought to preserve. It wasn't something you were supposed to be able to raid for manpower in a war." He let out a long, long sigh. "The war has pushed its way into everything, my friend." He smiled ruefully. "Even into that crowded mind of yours, it appears."

Seth nodded. "It's as if a veil has fallen from my eyes. I've been a parasite all these years, living off the land, giving nothing back to the community. People like you have had to sacrifice, to lay your lives on the line, to protect the likes of me. Well, no more of that. I'm in the world now, and I'm in the world to stay."

He paused in his progress down the street. Riki, looking back, stopped a few paces ahead and watched where Seth's gaze was fixed. Seth was looking down at a jeweler's stall. The jeweler was eyeing him—Seth was still shabbily dressed— with suspicion.

"Look here," Seth said. "This is better work than most." He bent over to examine more closely an expensive ceremonial dagger. "Take a look at this."

Riki joined him and inspected the dagger. "Oh, it's pretty enough."

"It's not a real weapon, sir," the jeweler said. Riki's air of authority inspired a grudging respect in the vendor's voice. "It's for show only. But look at the workmanship. It's by Ketan, a Child of the Lion." He said this with pride.

"Ah, Ketan! My kinsman!" Seth said. "The one who took after my grandfather, Hadad of Haran. The artist in the family."

"You, sir?" the vendor asked in a changed voice. "You're a Child of the Lion too?" He looked at Seth's soft hands skeptically, but he did not dare let the doubt creep into his tone.

Seth's attention was still captivated by the dagger. "Look at this, Riki. It's not bad at all. But he doesn't get the kiln hot enough. The last stage in granulation requires really intense heat. The little granules haven't fused all the way. I'll have to speak to him when we get back. It's very pretty, though. He does have the touch."

The vendor bristled at Seth's patronizing tone. " 'Does have the touch'!" he said. "Well, I never! The very—"

But Seth had turned his back and was walking down the street with Riki, talking rapidly and animatedly. Riki chuckled and lengthened his stride to match Seth's longer steps.

Meni backed away, hand to his face. "Tamshas!" he cried in a hurt voice. "Don't let him hurt me! He has no right to hit me!"

Tamshas, all nerves, looked rapidly from one face to the other. When she spoke, her voice had lost all its resolve. "Apis," she said tentatively, "don't you think another approach might—"

"Shut up!" said Apis coldly. "You, boy. You'll do as you're told, and no damned backtalk. Do you hear?"

Meni backed all the way to the wall, holding his hands before his face. "I don't want to do it," he whined. "She's been very nice to me. How can I repay her kindness by doing something like that?"

Tamshas approached Apis timidly. "Apis, isn't there some other way? If he's nervous and frightened, he'll give himself away. He won't do a good job. He'll get us all caught."

"No, he won't," Apis threatened. He turned his deadly eyes to the boy. "He knows what will happen to him if he brings the law down on us, don't you, boy? I took some pains to explain it to him in detail while you were out of the room."

"I don't want to hear about it," Tamshas said with a shudder. "Be practical, Apis. I can sneak in through a window at night while she's out. Meni can leave one window open. The servant, Cheta—she sleeps very soundly most nights."

"You, you fat cow? You'll go blundering in and knock over things like a clumsy oaf, and you'll rouse the guard. They'll be down on you before you can get that huge behind of yours back through the window."

"You don't have to be unpleasant."

"Shut up. You, boy. Did you think about what I told you? Did you think about whether you wanted that to happen to you? You're still very young. If someone does that to you when you're this young, you grow up a sort of monster, fit only to guard somebody's harem for him. You'll be a great bloated blob, with bosoms like a woman's, and you'll talk in a high voice—"

"Don't!" Tamshas cried out. "You've no right to talk to him that way!"

His whole arm moved, so quickly it could hardly be followed with the eye. The back of his hand caught her on the forehead and smashed her backward against the side wall. Her head hit the mud-brick wall with a loud crack. She sank to the ground in a heap, dazed.

"Now, boy," Apis said, as if she had never been there in the first place. "Let's go over what it is that I want you to do again, now? Eh? Repeat it after me."

A series of questions asked in the craftsmen's village had led them to a withered crone. Toothless, bent over, she glanced nervously from one to the other. "Yes," she admitted in a quivering voice, "I knew Maryet." She volunteered no more. "Begging your pardon, sirs, it's customary in such cases to—" She let it hang, looking expectantly at Riki.

"Oh? Oh, yes," Riki dug out two coins and pressed them into the gnarled old hand. "Go on, please."

"Maryet," the old woman repeated. "She moved away. I think she may have gone back to El-Kab. Or was it Edfu? Yes, I think it was Edfu. That was the year of—"

"Tell me," Riki said a little exasperatedly. "How about another woman named Net? I think she used to live here. I'm really looking for her. I only asked about Maryet because I heard she might know something about Net. She was . . . oh, about so tall, I think. She had a little son. This was about twenty years—"

"Ah, young sir. You're jesting with me. I ought to return your money. I can't help you if you're jesting with me. You shouldn't fool an old woman like that. It isn't kind."

"I'm not jesting!" Riki said in frustration. "For goodness sake, it's my mother I'm trying to find. I lost her when I was very young. She died in the delta. I grew up an orphan in the streets of Avaris, fending for myself." He ran his fingers through his hair in exasperation. "Look, lady, I grew up not knowing who I was. All I knew was the name of my mother, who had led me to believe that I was the son of somebody important. I know, I know. Every orphan likes to think that sort of thing about himself. It helps keep him going. But somehow I believed her. She wasn't the type to lie."

"No," the old woman said slowly. "That's true. Maryet wasn't the type to lie. I'll give her that. Not in anything but the best sort of cause, and certainly not to a child."

"What are you talking about?" Riki asked. "I'm not talking about Maryet. She's not my mother." He shook his head in frustration. "Look, old lady," he said, trying to remain patient, "I'm leaving in the morning on a dangerous mission. You're very old and frail. I may not make it back here, and even if I don't get myself killed, you may have passed over to the Netherworld yourself."

"This is all very true," the old woman agreed. "Then what is it that you want of me?"

Riki swallowed a sharp retort. "Information about my mother. And no, my mother wasn't Maryet. I'm Net's son. Net. Did you perhaps know her?"

The old woman smiled a terrible, toothless grin. Her

hooked nose and protruding chin nearly met. "Net? Why, of course I knew Net. Bless your heart, young man, I knew her well. Her mother and I were children together. Of course after Net lost her first child and couldn't have any more, I lost track of her, and sh—"

"You can't be talking about the same Net I'm looking for information about," Riki said.

"Why not? It's quite an uncommon name in these parts. How many parents in Thebes would name a child after the partroness of a faraway town like Saïs? Answer me that, young man."

Riki's mouth was a thin line now. "It couldn't be the same woman. Not if she had me. For heaven's sake, I'm her son!"

The old woman looked at him with a suddenly thoughtful eye. "No, you're not. She didn't have any son. She couldn't. That first birth, the child who died—it fixed things so she couldn't bear any more. She may have *raised* you, young man, but—"

Riki stared. "Then . . then what . . . ?"

"I'm afraid I can't say more, young man. I gave a sacred oath a long time ago, and I'm at the end of my days now. If I'm to find my way to Paradise, I can't go breaking any vows at a time like this."

"But—"

"Now, Maryet, she's another thing. She didn't come along until a bit later, when there was nobody to give an oath to. If you can find her, she can tell you more. I think she's in Edfu, if she hasn't moved away by now. Or died. Let's hope for your sake that she'll still be alive."

Riki, his face filled with anger and frustration, looked at Seth. "But I've got to leave at dawn! If only . . ."

Seth, in a quiet voice, said, "If you're meant to know, it will keep. If not, it won't."

Riki did not answer. Instead he pressed another coin in her hand and moved slowly away with Seth in tow. "She knew," he said helplessly. "She knew, and she wouldn't tell."

"It speaks well for you that you didn't try to force her to

tell," Seth said gently. "Or could it be that, having come this close, you're not sure you still want to know?"

Riki turned his head, stumbled, recovered, and came to a halt facing Seth. "I . . . I do want to know," he said hoarsely. "I do!"

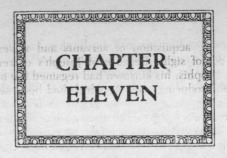

CHAPTER ELEVEN

Avaris

I

Everywhere there were soldiers: drilling, marching, making a nuisance of themselves in the taverns and public squares. And such soldiers! Swarthy, fair, tall, and squat; hair kinky or straight, noses flat or hooked. In body armor or long, gaudy robes; in brief loincloths or startlingly naked. Soldiers who kept to themselves and sought out only one another's company; soldiers who picked fights with the citizenry, raped their women, beat up their striplings and their old men.

It was a time of trial for the people of Avaris. Having that many soldiers inside the city meant feeding that many additional hungry mouths, turning out the granaries to supply the encampment outside the city, and removing the already scarce provender from the city's civilian markets. No complaints were allowed. Anyone who spoke up would wind up in prison or worse before the day was out.

During this time, the sons of Jacob and their large entourage—which had swelled alarmingly through marriage, births, and the acquisition of servants and slaves—stayed prudently out of sight. Because of Joseph's current ascendancy over Apophis, his kinsmen had regained the ownership of their food-producing acreage, which had been seized earlier. This made them the only group so favored and the object of much envy and hatred among some segments of the population, however quietly it might be expressed.

Reuben and his brothers had returned from Canaan with news that conditions were ripe for their return, but in time of national emergency all exit permits had been rescinded, including those of the vizier's kin. It was a time for lying low and making long-range plans—but nobody, least of all Joseph himself, could have any idea how or when those plans might be brought to fruition.

To make matters worse, Petephres, Joseph's father-in-law, had become visibly senile and incompetent and in his fading days had been replaced as official head of the religion of Amon by a younger priest named Hap, a man who had long resented Joseph's friendly association with Petephres. Hap was now openly calling for a purification of Egypt, a casting-out of all "pagan" influences and foreign gods. Daily Joseph's position at court grew more precarious, and by now the only friend he had in the palace was Apophis himself.

Unfortunately, Apophis, stung by defeat and humiliation on the battlefield, vowed to return with a larger and better army and crush Thebes outright. He pressed Joseph for a new prophecy, a new vision, one that would foretell his own final victory and his consolidation of Hai power over both Black Land and Red Land.

In vain did Joseph assure the king that the gift of prophecy was not a thing one could order into operation by mere mortals. Apophis had his mind made up, and it became increasingly evident that the vizier's present position would soon depend upon his ability to predict a desired future. Joseph prayed constantly, asking the God of his fathers for counsel on what to do. But for now the voice of God seemed to have deserted him. Daily he grew more haggard; daily Apophis became more importunate; daily the situation of the Children of Israel deteriorated. But there was no escape through the thick clot of soldiers clogging the streets of Avaris and surrounding the city to block off all unauthorized movement through the neighboring countryside.

The Brotherhood of Shai held a meeting inside a boarded-up former granary building in the dark of the moon. Isesi's stout guards at the door demanded the secret sign, the password, and allowed no one to pass who could not show the signs of initiation.

Thus the guards at the door were taken aback when Isesi himself, coming in from outside, showed up bringing in tow a complete stranger. The guard in charge looked at the towering hulk, a misshapen giant with a huge head and enormous hands. The giant smiled an idiot's smile but said nothing.

"Does he speak our language?" the guard asked.

"He doesn't speak at all," Isesi answered. "Or hear. What the gods gave him in strength, they took away in the ability to communicate. I'll vouch for him. In my own way I've run him through the ritual. He's honest and trustworthy and true. That's all that matters. His name is Buchis, after the bull god."

"If you say so, sir."

"I do. Come, my friend," he told the unhearing giant. His words were accompanied by a gently guiding hand, pushing the behemoth forward toward the seats in the dimly illuminated room. Indicating to the giant that he could sit to one side, Isesi then moved to the middle of the room and looked around.

"It looks like a pretty full house," he told the crowd before him. "There may be a few more stragglers, but I think I'll get started. Can everyone hear me? I don't want to risk talking too loudly."

He raised both hands. "Greeting!" he said. "First I'll bring you up to date on what's happened: Three days ago we raided a caravan carrying the month's wages for the Ninth Legion. There were a few casualties on our side, but we got away with enough money and weapons to outfit a legion of our own. More importantly, a sizable portion of the legion itself declared its loyalty to our cause. This rather large fellow you see here, Buchis, was personal bodyguard to the legion commander who, let's say, is no more, thanks to Buchis." He clapped the giant on the shoulder and watched as the big man basked in the attention. "The legion is hiding out on the islands now, awaiting our call."

He looked around. "There's more!" He recited a quick list of recent accomplishments of the Order. The impulse of the crowd was to applaud, but due to noise considerations, they contented themselves with nods of approval.

"And now," he said, "I've a special need for volunteers. A very dangerous job. I need six men—"

Twenty hands shot up enthusiastically. Of these Isesi picked five—adding, at the last moment, the giant Buchis. "Thank you!" he said to one and all. "Keep up the good fight! We shall prevail! The promised deliverer will come!"

At the palace, Apophis interviewed a new general. His name was Rasmik, and like all the inner circle of Apophis's high-ranking officers, he was a true Hai, a direct descendant of one of Manouk's warriors and a Shepherd noblewoman. He was new to an Egyptian command, having served only in the occupation forces left behind in northern Canaan; but his reputation for ferocity—earned when Hai forces, responding to an uprising at Megiddo, had leveled the town and later rebuilt it after the Hai fashion—had preceded him. He was, witnesses said, a stern and unforgiving man: no mercy shown, no prisoners taken. The burning of Megiddo had broken the last Canaanite revolt once and for all.

Now he stood before his king, his cool demeanor easily concealing the contempt he and all the other soldiers of his command had felt for the ruler who had deserted his own men at Lisht, leaving them to their fate. Apophis eyed him nervously, suspecting something of the sort, but he elected to say nothing of this. "So, Rasmik," he said. "You have a plan?"

"Yes, Sire. Based on reports I've heard and the official records to which I've had access, it would seem—"

"Get it out, man!" Apophis cut in irritably. "Say what you want to say."

"Very well," the soldier said, his eyes all ice. "The Egyptian king, Sekenenre, showed some mettle in the border incident. It would seem he's got a bit of a backbone after all, in spite of reports describing him as a weakling raised by women and ignorant of the use of arms."

"Yes, yes!"

"Sire, challenge him to a one-on-one duel. Appeal to his newfound pride. Surely he'll fall before your sword." A thin smile played upon Rasmik's lips. "And if he doesn't, the moment you have him out there on the field of battle, we'll have bowmen strategically placed. . . ."

Apophis glared. At first Rasmik thought he had over-stepped himself. Then a small gleam appeared in the king's eyes. "I see. Take no chances. You're a man after my own heart, I can see that. I'll start sending him insulting messages—personal ones, reflecting on his doubtful masculinity. I'll insult his mother and sisters. I'll speak to him as I would to a child and make a mockery of his bloodlines. He ought to be quite vulnerable there; his father's line had few real claims to the throne."

Rasmik stared but did not say anything. Apophis's own lineage was known to be suspect, and he was a usurper to boot.

"Yes, I'll do as you say," Apophis continued, warming to the subject. "I'll make it a point of honor to meet me." His hand pounded the table. "You're in command of my expeditionary force as of this moment. When can we attack?"

"I can have the troops licked into shape in a week. I can deliver them on the line a week after that, ready for battle."

"Done!" Apophis said. He looked down at the table before him, where his own sword lay unsheathed. He picked it up, brandished it. "Did I hear you say something about a deadly poison the Greeks sometimes use on their arrows? Or, perhaps, on a blade like this?"

It was all Rasmik could do to keep his lip from curling in utter disgust. "Yes, Sire. A distillation from black hellebore. It comes from Epiros, I think. One of the Greek commanders we hired has a small supply of it."

"Good," Apophis said. "Send him to me." He turned the blade this way and that, watching how the sunlight took it. "With Sekenenre dead, their resistance will be broken."

Rasmik let the words out before he thought about the

effect they might have Afterwards he would have given anything to recall them. "Sire," he said, "there's this deliverer fellow to think about, the one who——"

"Enough!" Apophis hissed in a voice that dripped venom. "The interview is over. Have your units ready to move upriver in one week."

Joseph's spy entered through the back gate of his villa after dark and slipped unseen through the dark passageway behind the storerooms. None but Joseph had ever seen his face or known who he was, and even now he was careful to avoid being seen by the servants. The guards had been instructed in advance to let the visitor through the gate at a specific time without getting a look at him. He rapped three times on Joseph's wall and was let inside by the vizier himself.

"Good to see you," Joseph said. "Have you eaten? Shall I send for wine?"

"No," the spy answered. "There's no time. I have to be somewhere. I'm going along on one of the Order's secret missions tonight. My guess is that we're going to raid Hakoris's house and free Mara."

"Good. Could you contrive to kill Hakoris while you're at it?"

The man flashed a quick grin. "If he's there, I'll make a point of it. Then we'll get Mara out of the city. Too dangerous for her by far. I'd like to get her upriver before Apophis's next troop movement. Rumor has it she's this deliverer's right arm, besides being his lover."

Joseph nodded. "I'll do what I can to facilitate it, but that won't be much. My every action is circumscribed these days."

"Sir, I wanted to report on something that concerns you directly. If the Brotherhood of Shai ever comes to power, you, your family, and entire entourage are in trouble. There's an unhealthy hatred of foreigners being encouraged, and you've been specifically named at their meetings. There's talk of 'cutting the throat of that damned infidel vizier.' That sort of thing."

Joseph stood and walked to the window. "Well, I'm not

too surprised," he said, gazing out into the dark night. "We're all seen as children of privilege. Go on."

"Worse, sir. This deliverer—he's apparently sworn to driving the Hai into the sea to die and to rid Egypt of all outsiders."

Joseph's sigh was long and deep. "I'd hoped that our shared interest in getting rid of the Hai—"

"Apparently it doesn't hold much weight with him, sir. He sees you as just another foreign oppressor."

Joseph shrugged and came back to the table to sit down. "Well, if that's the case . . ." He blew out through pursed lips, thinking. "My brothers want me to take them home. I'm beginning to think it's a good idea. Maybe the time has come to give up the pomp and influence I've grown so used to. While Apophis and the army are upriver attacking the Egyptian lines—"

"Apophis is doubling the border guards."

"I know. I relayed the order. And since my orders are assumed to come from Apophis himself . . ." He smiled.

"Ah. You can relay another order, of your own, which will allow you and your family to pass unmolested through the border guards. Well, sir, that's a good idea, but one you can only use once."

"Yes," Joseph agreed nervously. "I pray once will be all the times I need." He shuddered. "Imagine escaping from the clutches of the Hai into the Sinai desert, my friend. With women and children beside me." He gave another shiver. "I'll pass the word along to my kin."

II

Neferhotep held the door while the hunchback hobbled through the doorway. He turned to Hakoris and nodded. "Here's the seer I was telling you about," he said. "The astounding Tchabu. He comes from Sile. He'll be able to tell you things about the future that will amaze you. Tchabu, meet the noble Hakoris."

The hunchback's beady eyes glinted in the dusk light. "Ah. Hakoris. Yes," he said in a singsong voice. "Strange mark on forehead. Much anger. Much pain. Lame like me. Yes. Yes."

Hakoris's face was flinty. "Well, he's direct, I can say that of him." He looked the little man's crooked body up and down. The hunchback, in turn, inspected him through his one eye; the other was a dull white from lid to lid. His ugly face broke into a toothless grin. "Well," said Hakoris, "bring him into my office. There's nobody here."

But when he ushered them into the big room, the naked young woman chained to the wall was immediately evident at the far end of the room. Even in the dim light of the torches they could see the hatred in her angry eyes. She stood facing them, her arms folded over full breasts, as if they were not men but animals, before whom one need observe no modesty.

"I thought you said no one was here," Neferhotep said, his eyes drinking in the sight with a hunger uncommon in the usually celibate magus.

"She doesn't matter," Hakoris said.

But the hunchback was looking at her now, his brow knit, a puzzled expression on his face. "Great lady," he said respectfully. "Great like queen. But much anger. Much."

"Great lady?" Hakoris echoed, sneering. "She's a *slave*. She's spent most of her life as my slave, without a thing to call her own." He turned to Neferhotep. "Gods! And *this* is the seer you intend to use in deposing Joseph? Why do I waste my time with the likes of—"

"Hold your tongue," Neferhotep warned. "We don't need to insult one another. I tell you, he has real talent. I've never seen such a gift. And with him it operates all the time. Joseph has to pray for months to go into a trance, then spend hours, even days, analyzing his dream—and even then it doesn't always work. While this fellow—"

"He's right, you know!" Mara interrupted in a loud, mocking voice. "He said, 'Great like a queen,' and that's what I'll be, while you two lie forgotten in paupers' graves. Just watch and see, you leeches!"

She stood defiantly, fists on those ample hips, flaunting her nakedness at them, her feet planted firmly. She took note of Hakoris's angry yet hungry glances, as well as Neferhotep's, and ignored the pained and confused expression on the hunchback's twisted face. "See something you like, gentlemen? Look your fill, because look is all you'll ever do. It's a body fit to be a queen's, your own seer told you that. And none but a king will ever touch it! Do you think I'd cohabit with a snake like Neferhotep, a failed and probably false magus who has to hire another man to have his visions for him? Or play the beast with a slug like Hakoris, a branded thief who pimps for child molesters?"

"Shut up, you bitch!" Hakoris shouted. His hand automatically went to the turban on his head in a telltale motion, and as he looked Neferhotep in the eye, he could see instantly that the magus already knew the secret he had killed more than once to hide. "Shut up or I'll murder you!"

"Come ahead," she taunted. Her tone was pure acid. "Murder me or caress me. It doesn't much matter which you try, because you'd fail at both. Remember when you tried to rape me, Hakoris? I bloodied your nose for you and blackened one of your eyes. You had to call in two of your servants to subdue me, and even then I bit the arm of one of them to the bone. And in the end you couldn't get it up, could you?"

"*Silence!*" Hakoris whined hysterically.

"It wouldn't help," the girl continued. "You couldn't do it to me when I was gagged either. You've never managed to have sex with me, have you, Hakoris? And you never will."

"So much pain, so much hurt," the hunchback whimpered. "For you, Hakoris, much pain . . ."

"That's no deep insight," Hakoris spat out. "I'm always in pain."

"Not same. Slow pain go on long time. Quick pain very sharp, very sharp, but not last long. Over as soon as start."

"Bah!" Hakoris said. "Neferhotep, why do you waste my time? This misshapen little mountebank—"

"*Danger!*" the hunchback said suddenly, sharply. "*Much danger! Very close by! Very close! Very soon!*"

There was a loud sound.

Hakoris wheeled.

The huge paneled door to the office rocked under a powerful assault. It splintered, broke, and swung wide!

Through the opening rushed half a dozen men, followed by the hulking, elephantine form of the largest man Hakoris had ever seen in his life!

The hunchback cowered back against the wall, whimpering. He sank slowly to the ground and lay there in a dismal, twisted heap, moaning pitiably. "No! Not hurt. Not hurt poor Tchabu!"

The party advanced, spread out. They were fully armed, all except the giant. Hakoris limped to the wall, pulled down two swords, tossed one to the startled magus. "Defend yourself!" he cried. "Assassins!"

The magus's first defense was his dignity. "I'm an official of the court," he announced. "A physician. You have no business with me. Really, gentlemen—"

"Take him." The slim form of the leader waved several of his men into place before the magus, while he himself drew a sword and faced Hakoris. Then he waved an arm wildly at the giant and pointed at Mara. The behemoth moved past him toward the girl in the far corner.

"Isesi!" Mara cried. "Look out for him! He's tricky! He's taken some lessons with the sword since—" She was going to mention the raid on the refuge, but Isesi cut in.

"So have I," he said, a new confidence in his voice.

"So!" Hakoris said, testing the edge of his sword with a crooked finger. "That's where I've seen you before! The refuge! Well, you won't get away so easily this time!"

"There's where you're wrong," Isesi asserted. "This time you're through, Hakoris, once and for all. When I'm finished with you, the world, as well as the land of Egypt, will be rid of you forever. And those pitiful few children left in your Children's Refuge will be set free. If we've time, we'll torch the building. Nothing will be left of you but a bad memory!"

As he spoke he stole a glance at Mara. The giant Buchis knelt at her feet and pulled mightily at her fetters. She was free. Almost before she had moved, Isesi instinctively knew what Mara was going to do. She leaped gracefully to the wall and pulled down a light and gleaming bronze sword. "No, Mara!" Isesi said.

But she had already lunged at Hakoris and caught him with a light blow high on the chest with the razor-sharp point of her blade. At the sight of his own blood, Hakoris shrank back, and then counterattacked. He battered her sword aside, disarming her!

Moving forward, however, meant using that paralyzed leg, which could not bear his weight. He stumbled and almost fell. The weapon flew from his hand and to the stone floor. He fell to the ground and grabbed for it, scuttling like a crab toward safety, but came against Isesi's blade, which lightly touched the tip of his nose, enough for pain, enough to draw a drop of blood.

Hakoris's sword came up but was deftly battered out of his hands. He fell backward and looked up at his opponent. "Can we perhaps talk this—"

Isesi spoke with great seriousness as he looked at his prey. "A month ago, six months, I'd have listened to you. But I've changed. You have nothing to say to me."

Isesi threw back his cloak, and newly acquired muscles, the fruit of desperate training and exercise, gleamed in the light. The blade in his hand flashed, almost too quickly for the eye to follow, and the reclining figure was headless, spouting gouts of dark blood, collapsing like a puppet with its strings cut!

Isesi wheeled and faced the trapped magus. But as he did, Neferhotep reversed his sword and drove it into his own vitals with a single, final effort.

Mara struggled into Neferhotep's outsized tunic and belted it. "What shall we do with this one?" one of Isesi's companions asked, pointing at the softly whimpering hunchback on the floor.

"Let him go," Mara said. "He wasn't part of this and is harmless." But then she watched as Isesi helped the little man to his feet, and an afterthought struck her. "Wait," she said. "Tchabu? Is that your name?"

"Tchabu, yes. Not hurt little Tchabu, please, great lady. No harm. Please . . ."

"We won't hurt you. We're your friends. We'd like you to come with us. We'll feed you and protect you."

Isesi—who had been issuing orders to the others to go to

the refuge, break the doors down, liberate the refuge's remaining prisoners, and burn the place to the ground—stopped and stared. "Mara," he said, "we have to travel light."

"Wait," Mara said. She looked down at the horrid severed head of Hakoris, its eyes staring. The turban had fallen away, uncovering the felon's brand on the forehead. "Tchabu," she said, turning back to look the little man in the eye. "You said I was a great lady, a queen. When I'm queen, there'll be a place for you in my court. Would you come with us?"

The hunchback's frightened eyes shifted back and forth between the two of them. Then something seemed to happen in his mind, something that allayed his fears. "Yes," he decided. "Yes. Tchabu go with great lady. You give Tchabu safe house with soft bed in it, all food he want. You keep Tchabu safe."

"Very well," she said. "You're one of us now."

Isesi stared. "But, Mara—"

She smiled. "Think, Isesi! We've got our own seer now! One who can tell us when to attack and when to run away!"

The fire blackened the skies over Avaris, and only with difficulty was it contained. The residents of that quarter seemed only interested in keeping the flames from spreading to other buildings, so when bucket brigades brought water from the wells of three bazaars, precious little of it was wasted on the refuge itself.

The news reached Joseph quickly, even before the refuge, with the fire totally out of control, had been pronounced beyond saving. The spy came in by the usual route. "Mission accomplished, sir," he said in a breathless voice.

Joseph's eyes were alert. "Then Hakoris is dead?"

"And decapitated, sir. Neferhotep fell on his own sword."

"I can't believe it. Shamir ben-Hashum! My old friend Ben-Hadad's stepbrother—and murderer!" He shuddered. "And the magus too . . . Well, that's one less enemy for me to worry about. You say they got the children out too?"

"Every last one. Then they set fire to the refuge. I doubt if it's out yet. There was another fellow with him. A little hunchback named . . . what was it, now? Tchabu?"

Joseph's eyes brightened. "Tchabu? Tchabu the seer? He has a cast in one eye? Crippled?"

"Yes, sir. He seems simpleminded and harmless enough."

"I know of him. He's got a very great gift. He's not quite right in the mind, though. But harmless? Not in the hands of someone like Apophis, he's not. You did right to take him with you. The Order will make good use of him in keeping Apophis's hands tied. With any luck I can take my family and . . ."

"You were saying, sir?"

"Never mind. Good work! Very good work! There'll be a very substantial bonus quietly paid into your account tomorrow morning, under your real name. Meanwhile, maintain your cover, do as they tell you, and continue to report to me."

"Very well, sir." The spy stood. Joseph's eyes went up, and up, and up; the man's head almost touched the ceiling as he attained his full height. "I'll be going now, sir."

"Very well, Buchis," Joseph said. "Go with God's blessing. May His hand keep you safe."

CHAPTER
TWELVE

The Western Desert

I

Once there had been many roads into the desert, connecting the valley of the Nile with the great string of desert oases in the west. The great El-Kharga oasis, which the Nile dwellers variously called the "southern one" or the "inner one," was a deep rift in the earth. Some hundred and twenty-five miles long and from eighteen to twenty-five miles wide, its floor lay beneath the level of the faraway Great Sea. In the ancient days before the first dynasties, foot tracks had led from El-Kharga to such Nile ports as Abydos, Hu, Gebelein, and, less reliably, to El-Kab in the east and to other oases in the south such as Salima, El-Shab, and Dunqul.

Now, after a century of neglect, only the natural routes from Abydos and Hu were still maintained. Since both of these lay well north of Thebes, Baliniri had recommended the more direct, ancient route that led from Gebelein, just south of Thebes, to Edfu. For this a guide was necessary, however, so Riki's party had taken on a towering Nubian woman named Sakhmak. A guide, scout, and interpreter, Sakhmak lived in an ancient colony founded centuries before by Nubian mercenaries in the service of the early pharaohs.

Sakhmak was laconic, unperturbable, indisposed to communicate beyond the minimum required to keep the party on the road. Her family's long residence in Gebelein had led her, like the other Nubians, to adopt Egyptian dress, so she looked like a taller, darker Egyptian; nevertheless, Riki had the feeling that the woman, given the smallest encouragement, would have abandoned the more effete ways of the Egyptians in a moment and continued the march dressed as scantily as the naked warrior-women of Nubia who reportedly made up the elite guard—the Black Wind—of King Akhilleus's widow, Ebana.

During the first days of their slow march into the trackless wastes west of Thebes, Riki tried repeatedly to make friends with Sakhmak, but to no avail. The only member of his party whose efforts in this line met with any success was, surprisingly, Seth.

The young savant had a remarkable gift for languages, and his congenital inability to march in step with anyone led him to march ahead of the entire column with its towering Nubian guide.

Riki, keeping pace with the rest of his troop, could see Seth, strong legs flashing, staying abreast of the tall Nubian woman and conversing with her. Meanwhile Riki turned his own attention to the strange and exotic world through which they were passing. Considering the great heat and general desiccation, it was surprising how much wildlife there was in the bone-dry hills. Where did they find adequate nourishment? There were hares, oryx, antelopes, even an occasional ostrich to be seen at some distance, beyond the range of their bows, plus their traditional predators: jackals, lynx, and striped or spotted hyenas. The leopard and the lion, objects over the years of many a royal hunt, which had by now reduced their numbers to insignificance, were nowhere to be seen.

It was thus a shock for Riki to notice, toward the end of the first day, that the caravan had picked up a solitary follower: a full-grown cheetah, long-limbed and lithe and lean. Sakhmak's chosen path lay for the most part through the clefts and arroyos and wadis, whereas the animal chose the high ground, staying well above their party at all times. The remarkable thing about the cheetah was that it stayed with them. From time to time its surefootedness and greater familiarity with the terrain allowed it to get ahead of them, but when this happened it always stopped to await their coming, looking down at them with a regal aloofness only mildly tinged with interest.

Once the animal disappeared for an hour and turned up not ahead of them but behind them, easily passing them afterward. Riki could only guess that the animal had caught, and fed on, some sort of small game; master of its chosen ground, it seemed totally at home in the barren landscape and was obviously quite capable of finding nourishment in circumstances in which a man would starve or die of thirst. Looking around, Riki, who had never poked about in the western desert much farther than the hills behind Deir el-Bahari, felt more than ever an intruder in this harsh and inhospitable land.

At dusk he called a halt and ordered the troop to make camp. Clustered around a succession of well-spaced small campfires, he and his party ate and prepared to bed down for the night after posting sentries on the heights above camp. After darkness fell, he fancied for a time that he could see the glowing eyes of the cheetah, watching him, thinking such dark thoughts as he could not force himself to imagine.

After a time Seth joined him, and Riki told his young friend about the cheetah. "Yes," Seth responded, "I have noticed it. I don't think this is natural behavior, do you?"

"Well . . . no," Riki said, "but I don't profess to know much about wild cheetahs. You don't suppose it's some sort of evil spirit, do you?" His tone was light, bantering, but there was an undertone of half-seriousness to it. "I've had to snarl a bit at the men for their speculations since we made camp. All sorts of superstitions have been invoked."

Seth laughed. "I think that the answer's a lot stranger than that." Riki was about to ask Seth to elaborate on that when Seth abruptly changed the subject.

"Riki, I've been chatting a bit with Sakhmak. I picked up a smattering of her tongue back in Thebes from the mercenaries

in the king's elite guards. They use a different dialect in
Gebelein, but we can make ourselves understood."

"And you've learned what?"

"Quite a bit about the area. For one thing, the road from
Gebelein was closed off only fairly recently, under Baka's
orders, which Baliniri has continued to enforce. The order
seems to have been Baliniri's idea in the first place."

"Baliniri's? I don't understand."

"I don't either," Seth admitted. "It doesn't make any
sense. Considering what's out here, you'd think he'd want us
to have easy access. Much of our food supply used to come
from farms in El-Kharga. The southern towns, like Gebelein,
have been living off food from El-Kharga for years."

"Food? Farms? Here?" Riki asked. His hand waved away
all of the barren land around them.

"You'll see. Sakhmak said the El-Kharga oasis alone has
over seven hundred lakes."

"*Lakes?* In this?"

Seth nodded slowly and folded his arms. "Seven hundred.
Maybe more if you include the seasonal ones. Nobody knows
where the water in the wells come from. Maybe as far away
as the Sudd marshes."

"But those are a thousand miles away! And—underground
rivers that don't surface—"

"They *do* surface. As lakes and wells in the sinks. The
oases are so deep in the earth that you don't see them until
you're right on top of them. You come upon them suddenly,
looking into a deep hole full of greenery that the delta would
be proud of."

Comprehension began to dawn on Riki. "A lost world of
sorts. One that the desert caravans have the free run of—but
that ordinary citizens of Thebes are not encouraged to visit."

Seth nodded. His face, in the light of the dancing flames
of the campfire, had a thoughtful look, and his eyes were
bright. "Yes. These ten years or so."

"Damn," Riki said. "And nothing to satisfy our curiosity
but the cock-and-bull stories the desert sheiks tell when they
bring the odd caravan into market on the Hu road—drivel
about warrior-women and—" He spat into the fire. "Bah. I
can't even figure out what *I'm* doing out here. Searching for

iron? Not bloody likely. Even the tall-tale specialists from the caravans never claim there's iron ore in the western desert."

"But El-Kharga *is* on a good desert route to Nubia and Kush and the mountains, you know," Seth suggested softly. "And that area's very rich in iron ore. Iron to make weapons with, and gold—gold in unbelievable abundance, mind you—to pay soldiers with."

Riki stared. "Gold that isn't ours," he said truculently. "How will we pay for that iron ore?"

"I think I know," Seth said. "But I also think I'm not supposed to tell you."

Try as Riki might, that was all he could get out of Seth on the subject. As annoyingly as ever, Seth had switched topics and could not be induced to speak of things he did not want to discuss. After a time a few of Riki's officers joined them, and there ensued a heated discussion of El-Kharga wines, the most popular product of the oasis, which managed to make it to Thebes in spite of the restrictions on travel.

In disgust Riki took out the map Baliniri had given him, a sparsely detailed papyrus roll giving only the approximate locations of various oases in relation to one another and rough indications of the routes that connected them. Drawing apart from the others and huddling close to the fire, he inspected the chart with a perspective enhanced by his conversation with Seth.

"This is odd," he suddenly said to himself in a low and puzzled tone. He held the papyrus to the light. Here was the long, narrow rift of El-Kharga; the Dunqul and Salima oases to the far south; the Farafra oasis, sacred to Hathor and jokingly called "the Land of the Cow," far to the north and, halfway from there to the Fayum, the smaller Bahariya oasis . . .

Where was the El-Dakhla oasis? The one people called "the outer one"?

He blinked and looked again. The long, curved route sliced through the desert from El-Kharga to El-Farafra, but where there should have been an intermediate oasis roughly halfway between them along the great arc, there was nothing. Nothing at all.

He searched his memory. He and Baliniri had had a

conversation just before Baliniri gave him the command. He
had spun that crazy story about warrior-women roving in
bands, preying on the caravans. *Hmmm*, Riki thought. *I'm
sure he mentioned El-Dakhla then, so there must be an
El-Dakhla oasis*.

On the other hand, he had mentioned it virtually in the
same breath with that ridiculous warrior-women story. He
could not cite that in favor of anything.

"Look," he said, raising his voice. "Somebody tell me. I
have this map Baliniri gave me." He tossed it to Seth across
the fire. "I can't find the El-Dakhla oasis on it. Can you tell
me what's going on?"

The subaltern nearest him looked up from the papyrus in
Seth's lap. There was a blank look on his face. "El-*where*?"
he asked.

Seth looked up. When his shoulders rose in an eloquent
shrug, Riki began to wonder if reason were perhaps beginning to desert him.

Riki tried to sleep. His eyes would not stay closed.
Above, the timeless stars blazed forth in the sort of insane
profusion seen only this far from the haunts of men. He
stared, his face fixed in an angry frown.

Why all this secrecy? Why would Baliniri send him out
here into the desert with only the sketchiest orders and a
map that he could not have used to find the River Nile, even
if he happened to be sitting hip-deep in it? Without the
faintest idea why he was here and what he was looking for?

He snorted. Iron weapons indeed! Here in the western
desert, where any kind of minerals were hardly to be found at
all, where was he to find anyone to work the ore, even if it
could be found?

Wait. Wait. There was this fellow Karkara of Sado, whom
everyone used to talk about back when he had first come to
Thebes. Could he still be alive? Could he perhaps still be
making weapons?

Sado had been in Nubia, and Nubia was on the trade
route that ran through El-Kab. And Karkara had been in
retirement *then*.

He looked up. The fire had guttered long ago, and only the stars above and the half moon lit the sky.

Not ten feet from him the lithe body of the cheetah stood. The beast was looking down on him from an overhanging rock. Riki's hand fumbled under his sheepskin robe for his sword.

But the animal stood as still as a statue, betraying no plans either to pounce on him or to run away. Riki's hand relaxed on the sword but kept contact with it.

The cheetah locked eyes with him. The two of them stared. Riki was the first to blink.

His eyes were closed for the smallest fraction of a second. When he opened them, the animal was gone.

II

In the morning the march resumed, and the little column moved slowly out across the rocky wastes. The track had not been maintained by frequent caravans, and rockfalls had made it impassable in places. Riki cut new trails here and there under Sakhmak's direction, but in other places obstructions had to be physically removed. This slowed the pace of the troop through the western wastes, and there were two lengthy halts that had Riki fretting and cursing impatiently. During each of these delays, he could look up and see the lean form of the cheetah on the rocks high above, watching them.

As morning wore on into afternoon, though, a new sensation became noticeable. It was a vague feeling of unrest, of insecurity, of vulnerability. It persisted all through the afternoon's long trek, and he grew more irritable and testy, to the point of snarling at the men when the smallest thing went wrong.

As sundown approached he picked a sheltered, easily defensible place beside the trail, flanked by large rocks on which lookouts could be stationed. He posted pickets and ordered the men to make camp. Only then did he look for Seth, who, as before, had spent the entire day marching beside the stately Sakhmak. As he walked toward Seth, he happened to look up at a rock outcropping overlooking their camp; the cheetah looked down, eyes unblinking, lithe body relaxed but ready.

"Baliniri taught you well," Seth said approvingly. "You could hardly have picked a better site." He cast a single glance skyward. "We still have our observer, I see, but the last time I heard, cheetahs can't hold bows or spears."

Riki blinked. This was the closest Seth had ever come to banter in his presence. "I confess to being a bit troubled though—anywhere a cheetah can go, an assassin can follow."

"Ah," Seth said, "then you've noticed. I was wondering if it was only me. Sakhmak won't admit to feeling it."

"What do you mean?" Riki asked, knowing very well what he meant. But he wanted Seth to be the one who said it.

"That we're being watched by unseen eyes. I haven't caught sight of a single one of them yet; they're very good. But we've been watched at least since this morning. Perhaps longer."

"Good. Then I'm not going mad."

"No. And it's not the animal. It's human eyes. While they haven't given any sign of hostility, I find it unsettling. I wish one of them would show himself."

Riki shaded his eyes and looked off to the west. The sun was very low indeed, and the shadows very long. It was no more than a matter of minutes to sunset, the brief afterglow, and then darkness. He frowned. "You there!" he bellowed suddenly to an underofficer nearby. "Get the campfire detail to work immediately!"

"You're jumpy," Seth said in that bland voice of his.

"Yes." Riki looked around, scanning the distant ranges. "There are things about this mission that bother me. I'm brave enough under normal circumstances. I can stand up to a charge as well as the next man, and I can even sleep soundly the night before a planned attack, but not knowing what I'm doing, or where I'm going, or why, or when I'll get there, or what I'll find there, or whom I'm supposed to meet when I get there —

Seth nodded and once again almost smiled. "I understand. I probably know a little more than you, and I can guess at more than that, but a similar feeling still gets through to me, despite everything."

"I find it irritating that you won't share with me what you do know," Riki said with a definite edge on his voice. "I'm responsible for your safety as well, if you need reminding."

Seth looked at him with calm eyes. He did not say anything for a moment. Then, "The day we left, Baliniri drew me aside and told me a thing or two. Not enough to clarify all this, to be sure, but I can guess some of the rest. I'm not sure why he confided in me to the extent that he did. But he did swear me to silence, at least until a certain point in our journey. By the time that point arrives, you'll probably have figured out most everything for yourself." He paused. "Except, perhaps, why *you* were put in charge of this expedition in the first place." Now he did smile, if minimally. The effect, in Seth's habitually bland and unemotional face, was shocking. "It'll all work out. You'll understand by and by."

Riki glowered. He looked away and let his eyes once again take the long focus, scanning the horizon on two sides. "More mystery," he said testily. "If someone were ever to think, for so much as a moment, of the effect of all this—"

He stopped so abruptly that even Seth looked quickly at Riki, took in the sudden tension in his face and body, then looked where Riki was looking. "What do you see? I can't see anything."

"A silhouette against the sky, sharp and clear. Then it was gone."

"A silhouette of the cheetah?"

"No," Riki answered. "A human being, outlined against the setting sun." His face was flinty, and his voice taut and tense. "Tall and lean and fit. Carrying a bow and quiver." He paused for a long moment, then went on. "All I made out was the outline. No sign that it was wearing anything at all, other than the quiver."

Seth looked at him with bright and interested eyes. "There's more, isn't there?"

"Yes," Riki said in a clipped tone. "It had breasts and hips. It was a woman."

Inspecting the campfires and the outposts required the first hour of darkness, as Riki went from fire to fire, from picket to picket. Only when all was secure did he go back to his own fire and eat a simple dinner of bread, olives, and dates. For a long time he sat staring into the fire, the light of the dancing flames playing merrily on his face.

After a time Seth sat down beside him, faced the fire, and poked at it with a slender stick. "I spoke with Sakhmak," he began. "Have you ever heard of the Black Wind?"

Riki looked at him. "An elite unit of Nubian warrior-women in the service of Akhilleus's wife, Ebana, right? They were crucial to the victory at El-Kab, if I remember correctly, when Ebana came over to our side and forced Akhilleus to accept Musuri's challenge to single combat."

"That's right. Ebana organized the band during Akhilleus's original takeover of Nubia. Her women took the river forts." Seth let it sink in for a moment, then added, "They fought naked. With spears and bows."

Riki's voice had some of the old tension in it. "Yes, I've been thinking about that, actually. The Black Wind. It fits. I remember Baliniri telling me about naked warrior-women preying on the caravans out here. But I was sure he was kidding me."

"And now you're not so sure."

Riki stared at the fire. "No. But if that was one of the Black Wind women, Seth, what was she doing this far north? Nubia's border is many days' march to the south. Have we made an agreement with Nubia that allows them to police our trade routes? Have they perhaps *taken* our trade routes by force? Are we besieged from the south as well as the north? If that's the case, we're sunk—we can barely mount an offensive against the Hai."

"If that were the case, would Baliniri be sending this troop into the desert to talk to anyone?"

"No," Riki admitted. "That wouldn't make any sense.

Besides, Kamose is the emissary to Nubia, not I." He spoke through clenched teeth. "What am I doing here?"

Just as he spoke he happened to look up again, into the darkness beyond the fire. For the merest blink of an eye he thought he saw the tall, naked form of a dark-skinned—and undeniably female—figure out at the farthest edge of his field of vision. She stood looking at him, her hand resting on the cheetah's head.

He turned quickly to Seth. "Look! Over there!"

But when both heads turned to the scene, she was gone, and the cheetah was gone with her.

Riki doubled the guards. He gave the near pickets the worst tongue-lashing they had ever received. By the time he was done, he had a camp that none but a phantom from the Netherworld could have penetrated. The night passed without further incident, but it was also a night during which he did not get a wink of sleep.

The next day's trek took them through new country, crossing a towering pass and emerging upon a new, higher, tableland. Then, without warning, the track plunged into a deep valley. A long-ago rainy season, before the terrible droughts of recent years, had rearranged the valley floor; it was the bed of a dried-up torrent, fine sand strewn with fallen stones. The walls of the valley were perpendicular, but the harsh sun had destroyed the ridge and the upper strata, and the loosened rock had crumbled into long banks of rubble. Seasonal rains had undermined the banks during the winters, and the current had dragged the rubble away block by block, throwing the rocks farther down the plain.

The gorge was fairly wide at first, but it soon narrowed. It was divided in several places by beds of harder stone, which the seasonal water could not wear away; these formed steps over which the rains had flowed in angry cascades. Dry now, they formed a gargantuan staircase fit for the feet of a race of giants, down which Riki's men clambered carefully.

At the bottom some evidence of moisture yet appeared—stray shrubs and even a stunted palm or two. Succulents gathered near the roots of the palms. During a pause as the last of Riki's men made their perilous way down the stone stairway, Riki set two of his men to digging, and they struck not water, but rather damp soil only a few feet beneath the surface. It was obvious that more vigorous digging would uncover water, and soon, but Riki was eager to reach the highlands again by dusk, so the project was abandoned and the long climb up the far side of the valley begun in earnest.

In all this there had been no time at all to look for the cheetah or the naked warrior, and Riki had abandoned trying to find either of them. But as his party emerged from the valley and the track once again wound along the side of a hill and narrowed to single queue, Riki looked up and saw the silhouette of the warrior-woman, the big cat at her side, against the setting sun. It was amazing how quickly the figure could appear from nowhere and disappear as easily a moment afterward.

But this time as his eye scanned the hillside, he caught sight of two more women, standing atop rocks to either side of the trail. He tensed and was about to bark out an order, but the women disappeared. He let the order choke in his throat, and he cursed the figures roundly in his mind—but remained silent.

In the night Riki dreamed he was attempting some sort of journey, alone and under enormous pressure to reach his as yet unknown destination. Someone was behind him, someone he feared, but he did not know who it was. Similarly, his objective, his destination, was a thing he feared. As he traveled this unknown road he was constantly aware of being in terrible danger.

Now he came to a sheer cliff above a seemingly bottomless gorge. On the far side of the abyss lay a pleasant tableland, green and peaceful. Spanning the chasm was a swaying rope bridge, ancient, rickety.

He looked back. Only a matter of yards away a faceless demon, huge and threatening, loomed. Its eyes burned into his. Horrid claws flexed; hungry jaws yawned, revealing razor-sharp teeth. It drew nearer, nearer.

There was nowhere to go but forward, across the horrible void, across that delicate span that swayed so frighteningly in the wind.

He looked across the bridge.

A sight greeted him that was so beautiful, so awesome, that he could not look directly at it. . . . A female figure, golden, nude, commanding, stood at the other end of the bridge. She was all women—mother, lover, daughter.

Glowing, at once soft and strong, powerful and yielding, she was everything he had ever wanted—and everything he had ever feared to find

He rushed to the bridge, dashed out upon it.

The soft wind of only a moment before became a gale. The bridge swayed, threatening to throw him off. He hung onto the rope rail for dear life, trying to move slowly across the chasm, trying to keep his eyes on the beautiful figure of light. Behind him he could hear the heavy footfalls of the fiend.

The bridge beneath him bucked and swayed horrifyingly. He struggled forward, terrified. As the bridge twisted underfoot, he caught a heart-stopping glance of the abyss below, beckoning, screaming its fearful threats wordlessly, soundlessly, inside his mind.

Behind him the fiend advanced mercilessly. Before him the golden figure beckoned yearningly.

The bridge beneath him began slowly to dissolve under his feet—

He awoke in a cold sweat, the scream choking in his throat. He sat bolt upright, looked about him.

The coals of the fire still glowed.

Just beyond the soft light he could see one of the warrior-women quite clearly. She had small breasts, a flat belly, and legs both long and strong. The dark eyes regarded him without emotion.

He reached out to her, his mind still half in dream. She vanished into the night.

He sat looking after her, trying to clear the confusion of sleep once and for all from his mind.

The vision he had had of her kept trying to meld into that of the shining figure of his dream but would not do so. Both of them, so sharp in his mind only a moment before, began slowly to fade, until after a few minutes, he found he could not recall either of them.

Only three things of them remained: the dream figure, her golden aura, and the knowledge that she had been, in one person, everything he had ever wanted. Of the warrior-woman, only the knowledge that, whatever she had been, live human being or phantom from the Netherworld, she had not been a woman of the Black Wind.

She had not been Nubian.

The close-cropped hair had been the straight hair of a Semite, not a Hamite.

The skin, bronzed by the sun or no, had been white.

III

Their march resumed the next day, and as Riki moved doggedly along the ancient track behind Sakhmak and Seth, he scoured his memory for more details about the woman—the real one, not the vision—he had seen the night before.

To no avail. All he could bring back after an hour or two of mulling it over was the impression of leanness, fitness, a perfect warrior-woman's body: long-legged, small-breasted, flat-bellied. Of the face, with its somberly noncommittal expression, he could recall nothing at all.

But no! There was one other thing: The woman's hard-muscled young body had gleamed with gold—a necklace of the simplest design, bracelets, anklets, and earrings. They were all she had worn other than the quiver, and even that had glinted dully with golden ornament here and there.

Evidently, too, the warrior-woman had disdained foot-wear, preferring to toughen her soles against the hard rock underfoot. Here he quite approved; shod soldiers became totally useless when their sandals wore out. Even the idea of

fighting naked made sense; no uniform to get dirty, torn . . .
It was nothing new in the abstract; some elite Theban units
had fought that way for years, and one of the heroes of the
battle of El-Kab had been a young man—what was his name
now?—whose unit had worn only a sword harness and, draped
over one shoulder, the blanket in which they slept at night.

It *was* different, seeing women in this kind of dress! It
was at once erotic and the farthest thing from erotic. Idly he
wondered if the warrior-women spurned the opposite sex, as
the Amazons of the Black Sea shores were said to do.

"Riki!" Seth called over his shoulder, "Look!"

Riki looked around him and almost broke step. They
were marching up the side of a hill, with tall rocks towering
to the right and left of them. Atop each rock stood one of the
warrior-women. All were fit and lean and stood as straight as
cranes. All were naked except for the gold bands on arm and
ankle. All were armed. All were unmistakably Egyptian.

He let his hand steal to his sword hilt, but after a
moment's tension, he made himself relax.

They did not seem to be doing anything, after all. They
were just watching, watching him and his companions as they
worked their way up the gradually steeper hillside track.

All this time the imperturbable Sakhmak had said nothing; had, to Riki's surprise, largely ignored the whole phe-
nomenon, as if the warrior-women had been part of the
landscape. But now she had reached the top of the ridge and
came to an abrupt halt, signaling the column to halt with her.
She spoke rapidly to Seth. Riki warily put his hand back on
his sword hilt. "What is it?" he called testily up the hill.

"Come on up!" Seth said.

Riki nodded to the underofficer beside him to take over
and jogged up the steep hill to the top.

He looked down.

Prepared for the unexpected as he had been, the sight
below was still quite a shock. Here, in the middle of this
barren, forbidding, waterless country, the great gash below
them was something he could hardly have imagined. The
steep cliffs descended perhaps a thousand feet, baring the
reddish walls of the valley, before the first sign of green.

Below this it was *all* green.

Riki blinked. It was like looking at a green version of a mirage. Everywhere, shrubs, trees, palms, grew wild; groves were set out in regular, planned rows; and, most incredibly of all, water roiled up out of the earth as springs, rushed over rocks as streams, and emptied into fresh-looking, bright-blue lakes!

"Gods!" he breathed. "Why didn't anyone ever tell me about this? I'd have requested duty here! It looks like Paradise!"

But if it was Paradise, it was a heaven not everyone was invited to enter. To all sides the warrior-women now stood, bows at the ready, long arrows already nocked, watching them silently, with an air of unspoken menace.

He raised his arm in the universally recognized sign that meant "We come in peace." There was a brief, tense moment in which nothing happened; then the woman with the cheetah, the one he had seen the night before, motioned him and his troop down the long path toward the green oasis below. Sakhmak looked to him for confirmation.

"All right," he said. "Go ahead. But keep your eyes open, all of you."

As they descended, Seth spoke. "This can't have been the original path," he said. "For some reason Sakhmak has taken us here by another route."

"Why do you say that?" Riki asked, clambering down a rock-strewn track.

"This is no caravan route, that's a sure thing. Neither porters nor pack beasts, loaded the way a caravan would be, could make it down this path. No. This was chosen to make us vulnerable. At any time, if the warriors choose, we can be picked off by their archers—or they can just kick down an avalanche on top of us."

"Wonderful," Riki said. "I see what you mean. This can't have been a mistake. Sakhmak was too confident of the path for this to have been any accident. She knew this route. She's taken it before. And I'll wager she knows the other, older path, the one the caravans used to take before the road was closed off. There's a plan behind this."

Seth was about to answer, but at that moment Sakhmak

turned back to them, looked Riki in the eye, and said, in the perfect Egyptian of a woman of Thebes, "Yes. You are right. I had my orders. But do not fear. You *have* been watched over all the way, since the first night. But it is for your protection, not your harm. Put your minds at ease. There will be a feast in your honor tonight. You are expected. And you are welcome."

At the foot of the path there was a paved road through a long avenue of date palms and, incredibly, a city, with houses, temples, civic buildings, landscaping, and canals and pools fed from the underground springs! The streets were full of people, the same sort of people one might see in an ordinary Egyptian city, but there were also foreigners from the desert caravans, travelers, men and women speaking strange tongues and wearing strange garb. The tall, naked female warriors were everywhere, always in pairs. More surprisingly, some of them were Nubian, frizzy-haired, coal-black, and totally bare even of the gold adornments the Semitic women had worn!

Riki pulled up alongside Seth and Sakhmak. "Those Nubian women—the Black Wind?" he inquired. The woman nodded. "But I thought—"

"You will see much of them now. They mingle with the Daughters of Aker." She hesitated, then went on. "Those were the women who watched over us as we crossed the desert."

"Aker," Riki repeated after her. The lion god who guarded the gate of the dawn through which the sun passed every morning. An apt name for an elite guard policing all routes to the oasis from the east. "Pardon me for my astonishment. How have I never heard of all this? How could I have lived this long in Thebes—ten years—and never have heard of . . ."

He stopped and thought. But he *had* heard! Baliniri had told him, and he had not believed it. He sighed. "Never mind. Lead on. I gather we've someone to meet here. Someone who was behind our mission here in the first place."

He hesitated, waiting for an expected reply. But Sakhmak was done with speaking for now

*   *   *

Incredibly, at the center of the city was a beautiful landscaped pond, surrounded by parkland and flowering shrubs: jasmine, chrysanthemums, mandrakes, oleanders. A loggia flanked the lake, and at the end stood a grape arbor. Here waited a towering, statuesque warrior-maid, with two hard-eyed female spear-bearers at her side.

Sakhmak motioned to the troop to stop. She bowed before the tall woman. "This is the noble Riki and the sage Seth," she told the woman. "Gentlemen, this is Weret, commandant of the Daughters of Aker in the oasis of El-Kharga."

Riki obligingly bowed but kept his hand near his sword hilt. Seth's bow was perfunctory, and his eyes stayed on the tall warrior-woman's face. "Greetings," he said. "We come as emissaries from Baliniri, vizier of Thebes, and from—"

"I know why you came," she said. "I sent for you. If you had not been wanted here, you would not have reached here, I can assure you of that. No, don't bristle at me, please. We mean you no harm. Relax and enjoy yourself. There will be a feast in your honor tonight. In the morning your troop will be given the grand tour of the oasis and its positions. Baliniri requested this."

"You said 'your troop.' Then you have other plans for me?"

Her face remained emotionless. "For you, and for your companion Seth. The others will remain here. You two will accompany me to the El-Dakhla oasis, where—"

"Ah!" Riki said, pounding his left fist into his right palm. "I *knew* something was wrong! El-Dakhla has been removed from all the maps! This is by design, am I right? It's some sort of special—"

She smiled coolly. "It is a place *no one* is allowed to visit. You both are to be accorded a great honor." She let them wait a beat, then added, "In ten years no man has been allowed to visit there."

Seth and Riki exchanged glances. "And we will meet there—whom?" Riki asked warily.

"That is a thing for tomorrow to provide," Weret responded. "Meanwhile, divert yourselves tonight. Feast and

make merry. Accommodations will be provided for you and
your men—"

"Wait," Riki said. "Not indoors. My men will sleep in
tents, on the bare ground. I don't want them getting soft.
When we go back to Thebes, they'll have a war to fight. I
want them lean and tough, unspoiled by city comforts, even
such as your city may be able to offer."

For the very first time Riki could see approval on the
warrior-woman's face. "So be it. But my women do not often
meet male warriors their own ages. Surely you will not be-
grudge them the right to meet your men and . . . uh . . .
fraternize?"

Riki stared. *That settles one of my questions,* he thought.
And he smiled. "We'll see. First we'll encamp, then attend
your feast. And then we'll see what happens."

Six hours later the feast was in full swing. The music
played, and the torchlight gleamed on the bare bodies of the
dancers, male and female alike. By Riki's dispensation, the
men of his troop—minus the pickets he had posted, armed to
the teeth, around the little grove beside the lake—had been
allowed to shed their garments for the dancing, and from
time to time one couple or other would vanish, hand in hand,
into the olive groves that lay just beyond the ornamental
shrubs that ringed the lake. The meal they had been served
had been at once plentiful and simple, a soldier's kind of
feast. Everyone would eat his fill, but no one would grow fat
or feel bloated by morning.

He watched the festivities with a critical eye, holding
himself aloof. Seth, scorning the feast, had gone off with
Sakhmak to meet the leader of the Black Wind detachment,
leaving Riki alone here with Weret. While there was nothing
hostile about her manner, he got the instant impression that
there would be no pairing-off between himself and Weret.
He shrugged and put the time to use asking questions but
received answers to no more than half of them. Particularly
taboo were questions about the El-Dakhla oasis and what he
might find there on the morrow.

Just as he was preparing to go back to the tents, however, he happened to look down at the battle gear laid out neatly beside Weret's seat before the fire. The light of the flames danced oddly everywhere but on the unsheathed blade of her sword. It did not take the light at all. Curious, he reached down and touched it, hefted it; shocked, he put it back down.

It was made of iron.

CHAPTER THIRTEEN

Thebes

I

Kedar had considered it to have been a relatively uneventful journey, given the frequent stops to show credentials to the patrol boats that dotted the Nile. It had also been a fairly quick journey, as trips downstream on the strong current of the great river tended to be. Nevertheless, the sun had been hot, and Kedar, arriving at the docks in Thebes, felt sun-baked and tired. He was certainly in no mood to shop at the markets for food to take home and prepare for his lonely meal.

Thus, despite his usual distaste for the atmosphere of inns, he looked about him at the cluster of taverns that lined the waterfront and, after a few moments' hesitation, chose the least offensive.

Once inside, it was immediately apparent that the habitués of this particular tavern would, if he remained long, wind up being as unhappy with him as he would be with them. Hostile stares from the heavy drinkers in the middle of

the room drove him out onto the balcony, where at least the
air was clean. The wait for service was a long one, but
eventually he was brought wine—heavily watered—and allowed to place his order.

This attended to, Kedar relaxed a bit and looked around
him. The rooftop balcony was only one floor above the street
below, and there was a pleasant view of the Nile and of the
lively traffic on and beside the great river.

As he idly watched the passing parade below him, his
mind once again turned to Tuya's proposal, as it had done so
many times in recent days. It was strange, he thought: So
generous an offer should have been the sort of thing he could
easily make up his mind about. But here he had been away a
week, and he was no closer to knowing his own mind.

Furthermore, consulting his relations had been no help
at all. It had been immediately evident that their concerns
and his were at odds. They perceived the situation simply as
a quick and easy acquiring of power and money. "What need
have I of a great deal of money?" he had pointed out. "What
would I want with power?" They had actually grown angry
with him. Money acquired by him, by whatever means, was,
after all, money they might inherit on his death.

He had in the end sadly turned away from them and
gone back to his own mulling.

Suddenly, he became aware of a conversation on the
dining patio just below him. Two men were talking. Kedar
frowned, irritated, and at first thought of moving to another
table, but for some reason the clearly audible conversation
intruded on his thoughts and captured his interest. There was
a deep voice, cutting, cynical, sophisticated, and educated.
The second, higher-pitched, voice belonged to a man obviously of the poorer quarters. It immediately struck Kedar
as odd that the two would be sitting together having a
conversation.

". . . said that you were a man who wasn't afraid of
danger if there was money to be made. He said you could be
trusted."

"Well, that depends, now, sir. Depends on how much

money we're talkin', how much trouble, and who you are, and what you're wantin' me to do."

"Fair enough. I'm engaged in nothing less than plundering an estate, and it's going to be dangerous. You and I could wind up decorating a sharp stick or two if we're caught—but it's a *very* big estate. My name is Apis. Ask the boys on the waterfront. I'm known here and there, although I haven't been in town long."

"And the job, sir?"

"It involves doing whatever is necessary to extort from a rich widow everything her husband left her. And that's a great deal, I assure you. He was personal armorer to the king, a job that pays extremely well."

Here Kedar sat up, choked on his wine, blinked, and listened all the more closely.

". . . that people with that much dough usually have the bucks to protect themselves against people like me and you, eh, Apis?"

"Yes, they do. This woman appears to have influential connections—she was once the lover of the vizier himself, while her husband was still alive. She has a son, but he's never around. He's one of those deep-thinkers who haunts the marketplaces answering questions. He's not quite living in the same world as the rest of us. And he disappeared several weeks ago. No one has the smallest idea where he is."

"Well, Apis, this is interestin' me, the more I hear of it."

"I've got one accomplice already, a woman, who came here with a plan of her own. She was going to swindle this widow by claiming some street-urchin she picked up was her illegitimate son by Tuya's husband. She showed up on Tuya's doorstep some time back and started using the kid to extort money."

"Huh. The woman, the kid . . . how many people are we goin' to have to split this with, anyhow?"

"Just you and me, Imiut. That's the correct name? Imiut?"

"It is in Thebes anyway."

"That's good enough for me. The urchin and woman are dispensable the moment we've got a line on just where everything is. Meanwhile, I'm manipulating the woman. Tuya's being encouraged, let's say, to liquidate as much as she can right now. And the urchin has been smuggling her papers out to me in the evening and sneaking them back in again before morning each day. I've been going over them."

"You read, then, Apis? A useful knack."

"I'm full of useful knacks. I went to scribes' school a long time ago. A little trouble with the law kept me from working except outside the guild. And I unfortunately have expensive tastes."

"Me too, Apis. I could develop even more expensive ones, if I come into the means."

"Since we understand each other perfectly, let's get down to particulars. My woman associate thinks there's more to be extorted from the widow. Unfortunately, I'm getting tired of my associate. She's a fat drunk, with delusions about being an adorable young thing. Frankly, that alcoholic breath of hers, coupled with her cowlike stare . . . if it weren't for the pecuniary possibilities here, I'd sooner mate with a water buffalo."

The man Imiut laughed coarsely. "You paint quite a picture, Apis. All right, she goes, when the time comes. You want me to be killin' the kid too?"

"Yes. He knows too much."

"When do we make our move?"

"Soon. Let's go somewhere less public to discuss details. Do you have a place nearby? If we go to mine, the woman is likely to break in at just the wrong moment."

"Sure, Apis. I'm over the butcher's market at the Market of the Four Winds. I moved in last week. Come along. I want to hear some more about this."

Kedar shrank back behind the palm until he could hear their footfalls outside on the street. Only when the voices began to fade did he try to lean over the balcony railing and get a look at them, but as luck would have it, two strapping guardsmen came out from behind the building and cut off his view.

Curse it! he thought. *Now I can tell them by their voices, but I can't tell them by their faces.*

He stood gripping the back of his chair, his heart pounding. What a thing to have found out!

What could he do about it?

* * *

With Cheta and Tuya at the market, Tamshas made the agreed-upon signal at the door, three knocks followed by silence followed by a single knock, and waited impatiently for young Meni to open the door. When finally he appeared, she brushed him aside and pushed her way in. "Shut the door behind me," she said brusquely to the boy. "Damn you, why did you wait so long? You know they'll be back soon."

"Tamshas, you shouldn't be here. This isn't the day when they go to several of the markets one after the other. They—"

"Shut up and show me where she keeps the records. Apis said you left out the one about the country holdings."

"I can't tell one from the other, Tamshas. I can't read. You know that. Please don't do this. Tuya's already given you a lot of money. Can't you just let it go at that?"

Just for a moment there was a vulnerable look on her face. "You know there's nothing left of that. You know how Apis is. . . ." The sentence ended in a long sigh.

"Yes, I know," the boy answered. "You've got to get away from him. He's a bad man. He *hurt* me last night."

"I *know*," she said in a dejected whine. "He's rotten to me, too. You should see the bruise I—" She shook her head and closed her eyes . . . and when she opened them her face had the old, hard look on it. "I was raised in a place like this. Raised in the lap of luxury, with maids and slaves everywhere to do my bidding. I never wore the same gown twice. And look at me now. And all thanks to her and that stupid foreigner she married." Her eyes were cold, angry. "Is it any wonder that I would want to pay her back for what she did to me? The conniving bitch! She was nothing more than a raggedy street-urchin like you. Why should *she* have a good life? Why should *she* be rich?"

"Please, Tamshas. Just go away. If you'd like, I'll go with you. But leave Tuya alone. She's a good person. She's kind to me. She's very lonely, and—"

"Where's the room where she keeps the records? If I

don't bring this thing back, Apis will beat me until I can't stand. Get a move on, you little—"

"Please, Tamshas!"

Only after the knocking at the door had gone on a very long time did Ketan finally respond. The wet nurse had taken the child to her own house for the day. Ketan had had a bad night and day of it; for solace he had turned to *shepenn*—the distilled sap of the poppy—and after taking much too large a dose had finally lapsed off into sleep. But it had been unpleasant, troubled with horrid dreams, and when the knocking finally came through to him he was almost glad to be drawn back into the world he had tried so hard to desert only a short time before.

He opened the door, and the sunlight streamed in. Ketan shielded his eyes. "*Agghhh!*" he said. "Here, come in, wh-whoever you are." His voice sounded like a drunken man's. He caught a sight of himself in the reflection of the black marble molding around the door. He looked like a man hauled up from a river after three days. "Who is it?" he asked, blinking, rubbing his eyes. "I can't s-see you just yet."

The voice that answered was soft. "Master Ketan, it's Kedar. Seth's tutor. I came by because someone told me of your loss. I wanted to tell you how sorry I am."

"Sorry?" said Ketan. "Everyone's sorry. Did you know her? Not well, I'll wager. No one but me did, really. She was the tenderest, gentlest—" His voice broke. Savagely he forced himself not to weep, not to break down. "Well, you don't want to hear about that. Thank you for coming. I don't feel well. If you'll excuse me—" He staggered back and fell weak-kneed into a chair.

But the older man made no move to leave. "Master Ketan, I would not presume to intrude upon you, especially at a time of great loss. But something quite out of the ordinary is going on with Tuya, and you are probably the only person who can help her."

Ketan looked up at him, trying to get the old scholar into focus. "What's this you're saying? What about Tuya?"

*   *   *

"Evidently Tuya and the boy are getting along well," Apis said. "She's lonely, and Meni reminds her of her husband."

"Pass the wine," Imiut said.

"The way I see it," Apis continued, "if she's that fond of the kid, we can use him to get to her. Threaten him with death or mutilation, and we ought to be able to talk her into letting go of some of those big assets. Most of her money is in real estate," he said, slurring the words.

"Huh. And you think—"

"I think. I don't know for sure. There's always an element of improvisation in these things. One thing doesn't work, you try the next." He hiccuped and reached over to retrieve the wine jug he had given away only a moment before. "I hope the woman gets the scrolls I sent her after. If she doesn't, she'll regret it, I can tell you."

"What do you want me to do with her? And the kid?"

Apis held up his powerful hands and blinked at them drunkenly. "Give me the wine." He took the jug, drained it, and held it up, both hands on its slender neck. "*Crack!*" he said. "Just like that." And, lip curled, eyes mere slits, he tossed the broken vessel contemptuously into the corner, where it smashed into fifty pieces. "Little bastard. Talk back to me, will he?"

II

Ketan was still a bit shaky, but he thought he had himself under control. As he and Kedar passed through the marketplace, Ketan stopped at the well and washed his face once more. He shook his head, and the water droplets flew off his face. "I feel horrible," he said in a hoarse voice. "Let's go to a tavern just a moment. A little wine would freshen me up, I think."

Kedar hovered nervously. "Are you sure, Master Ketan? The effects of mixing *shepenn* with strong drink—"

"Just one drink won't do me any harm."

Kedar glanced around at the faces passing by, then he looked back at Ketan, who looked like a man who had just got up from his deathbed. "Oh, well, perhaps just one. But I really think that under the circumstances—"

"I know what the circumstances are," Ketan said. "Look, Tuya's my cousin. I won't have anyone doing this to her. I'll stop these people, never you fear. But I've been through a great deal lately." A note of annoyance crept into his voice. "What am I doing here justifying myself to you? Come along. One bowl of wine, and I'll be a new man. Then we'll deal with these people."

Kedar went along. And despite all Ketan's promises, it took two bowls of wine, not one, before he was ready to talk hard sense. "Look," the young man said at last. "The problem is this: She has these leeches on her back, but she won't go to the authorities because she'd be embarrassed. It'd be a scandal if everyone found out about her husband fathering a bastard on a drunken street whore. And for obvious reasons she's touchy about taking things to Baliniri. Well, I can get through to Baliniri any time I want. After all, I'm still official armorer."

"Yes, Master Ketan. But these men are extremely dangerous, and they're about to move any time now."

"I heard you," Ketan said. He held up the wine bowl and shook the last drops onto the floor. "I'm going to go investigate them right now. Innkeeper!" He signaled for the landlord, who came running; whatever his present condition, Ketan gave the impression of being a man of money and power. "Innkeeper, bring brushes and papyrus. I want to write a letter."

"But, sir," the fat landlord said, "there's nothing of the sort on the premises now—"

"Very well. Send out to the square for the scribe. Bring him here, with his equipment. There's a coin in it for you if you get right back here."

"Yes, sir!" The innkeeper hurried away.

"Now," Ketan said to Kedar, "I want you to take the

message directly to Baliniri. I'll put my seal on it, which should get you through to him immediately. Meanwhile I'm going to find these people, learn who they are, and stop them."

"Alone? But isn't that dangerous?"

"Oh, I'll be armed. A man who makes swords knows how to use them. I've been trained by the best. Don't worry about me. Just you get my message through. I'll take care of the rest."

"Please, Master Ketan—"

"I'll hear no more about it. Ah, here's the scribe. Over here, fellow! Bring all your things! Now lay them out on the table here. Don't you have a better brush than this? Ah, that's better. Now, let's see. 'To Baliniri from Ketan, greetings. I have just learned . . .' "

In the street, though, coming around a corner of the Temple of Amon, Kedar met the one person he least wanted to see in all the world just then: Tuya, strolling in the city with a ten-year-old boy who could only be the one the two men had been talking about. A wave of mixed emotions ran through him: The boy was one of the enemy, after all, but whether he knew it or not, he was in even graver danger than Tuya. Kedar squinted. Why, this was the same lad he had caught stealing in the bazaar not long ago, who was being forced to—

"Kedar!" she said, smiling broadly. "How nice to see you! How long have you been back?"

He gripped the papyrus in his hand and forced a smile onto his lips. He was not good at the polite lie. "Two days, Tuya. I had a touch of indigestion when I came in. I'm only just out of bed from it. Otherwise—"

"Oh, that's all right. I understand." Her smile was warm and accepting, for all the underlying tension in her. "Here, I want you to meet a young friend of mine. Meni, this is Kedar, a very wise and learned man. He was the very able tutor to my son, Seth, and if I can at all persuade him to undertake your own education, I'll support it." Her eyes locked with Kedar's and said things her words did not. "I think I can persuade him. Kedar, after all, is a very dear friend of mine."

"I'm glad to meet you, sir," the boy said, averting his eyes. The words of polite address did not come easily to him, but he was obviously eager to please Tuya. Kedar had taken note of the affectionate glance that passed between the two of them and stifled a pained sigh.

Over the boy's head Kedar and Tuya locked eyes again. "Kedar, come to dinner tonight. That is, if you're quite well. I have the accounts relating to your inheritance, and I want to show them to you."

Kedar smiled nervously. "I have some errands that should take most of the rest of the day," he said uncertainly. How to keep her away from her own house? Keep her away from danger? "Look, Tuya, my lodgings are modest, but I do have facilities for preparing dinner, however unpretentious. Would you come there instead?"

"But I'll have Meni. Please, it'd be more convenient all around. I have maids, a cook—"

"Meni can come." He forced a smile for the boy. "If you'd be so kind—"

"Please, Kedar. Later. I really do want to show you the accounts. I just got them back from the bankers. And I don't want to have to carry them through the streets."

Kedar clenched his fists. He could feel the papyrus crackling under his fingers. Better not do that! Fearful of breaking Ketan's seal, he hurriedly relaxed his grip. "I'll make a deal with you. If you'll come to my place for dinner tomorrow night . . ."

"Certainly." She smiled, pleased.

"But in the meantime I have an enormous number of errands to do, and . . ." *Think quickly! What can you say to keep her away from the house until Baliniri's guards arrive?* "Perhaps you would be so kind as to help me by taking over one of my errands? That would free me to come to your house tonight with a clear mind." She nodded. His mind raced. *What will occupy her the entire afternoon? Quickly, now!* "I need something from the Great Hall of Records. A problem I was working on before I left. If you will please do me the kindness of going to the chief scribe and asking him in my name for . . ." He improvised a slow, time-consuming, and boring problem. It would annoy the chief scribe, and he would have to apologize afterward and perhaps slip the official a bribe to get back into his good graces. But after all, this was a matter of life and death. He had to keep her away from her house until evening. "I know that's a great deal to ask," he said. "But if it isn't done today . . ."

She put a small, warm hand on his own. "I'll be glad to do it. It isn't often that you ask anything of me, Kedar. I know how self-sufficient you are, and I'm flattered that you ask me. But you know, you'll have to get used to the idea of turning to me when you have a problem and need help with it, my dear." She squeezed his hand. He looked helplessly at the boy, at his clear and honest-looking young face, and wondered how deeply the lad was involved. Was he at all a willing accomplice? "Consider it done," Tuya said. "But I'll expect you at the house at sundown."

"It's settled," Apis said. "We'll hit the place tonight."

"But I thought you were going to wait until that business of the country property was settled," Tamshas whined. "That's a lot of money to pass up."

Apis ignored her, continuing to speak directly to Imiut. "Maybe this afternoon," he said, "just when she's coming home. The money's on the premises, I'm sure of that. The bankers say she withdrew quite a large sum very recently. She apparently intends to use it to bribe this old dotard Kedar to marry her." He let out a nasty chuckle. "Imagine that, my friend. A woman still fairly attractive, and rich—and she has to bribe an old fool of an ex-scribe to marry her. She must have quite a low opinion of herself. Well, all the better. If she were of a more normal turn of mind, it'd have been a lot harder to extort from her what we have to date."

"Apis!" Tamshas pleaded. "Wait a bit, and we can get some of the country property transferred to us—"

For the first time Apis addressed her, and his voice held an acidity that chilled her. "I thought that one over," he said. "Transfer of property includes such matters as having to establish legal identity and residence. Next thing you know, the courts have records on you and you're tied to the damned property."

"Not for long, Apis! Just long enough to sell it."

"Long enough to allow the guards to trace you back to your humble beginnings. No thank you! I like jobs where we make the hit and get out quickly—escape into the desert, perhaps. But as for staying around while legal records are investigated and titles are cleared—no, forget about it."

Imiut snorted. "Sound thinking," he said. "But you're sure the dowry she's bringing to this bloodless little marriage of hers is in the house?"

"I asked the kid. He reported that she spent the day yesterday in the western wing of the house, with orders to the servants to stay out. Him, too. But before she ordered him out, he admitted catching her unawares in the west wing. She had stacks of money before her on a table, counting them."

"Ahhhh!" Imiut and Tamshas sighed together.

"Then there's a hiding place I missed so far!" Tamshas said.

"Yes," Apis said. "I suppose I shouldn't expect you to have found it by now. The servants haven't, after all, and they've had the free run of the house longer than you."

Tamshas, used to abuse, brightened at being let off. "I'm glad you understand. I never know when she or Cheta will come barging in. I'm sure Tuya has some secret cache. If we had time, we could bribe someone inside the office of the chief architect, who built the place—"

"No!" Apis shot back. "That's final. No more shilly-shallying around, now. Today it is. We get in there before dark, and if the servants get in the way, the worse for them. Then when she gets home, if we haven't found the money by then, well, I have ways of getting people to talk. Or to do anything in the world I want them to do."

Tamshas winced. "I know. But don't you think—"

"That's all! No more! Get ready, now!"

On the way across town Ketan's private demons had begun to torment him again, and he stopped off at two more taverns to exorcise them. There came a time when his eyes started to blur, and concerned, he paid his bill and lurched out into the afternoon sunlight, hand touching the fine bronze sword at his side. His head hurt. He wished he had stopped by home for a little jar of *shepenn*, to quiet the horrid voices inside his mind.

This was an unproductive train of thought, though, and he drove it from his wine-addled mind. He straightened his back, firmed his jaw, and quick-marched down the narrow street on unsteady legs toward Tuya's house.

Tuya! He had never thought of her in this connection, to be sure—kin was kin was kin, after all—but now the thought of tiny Tuya brought to mind his own equally tiny Nebet, whom he had lost forever. He remembered how, when he had fallen into the hands of that dancer girl—what was her name, now? Fortunately he could hardly remember—Tuya and Nebet had saved him. For quite some time after that Tuya had taken a kinswoman's interest in him and Nebet, and after their marriage, Tuya had been Nebet's only real friend. And had Tuya not helped him through those terrible first days of his bereavement after Nebet's death?

Well, he would show these ruffians! He would drive them away from her forever! Even before Baliniri's men arrived, he would confront them and tell them to go away and leave her alone! He would show them a thing or two!

III

"That's the most idiotic thing I've ever seen," Sekenenre said. "If I hadn't read the letter myself and seen the royal seal of the Hai kings on it, I'd think it was some sort of hoax."

"No, Sire," Baliniri said. "That's just the kind of thing I would have expected from Apophis. As a matter of fact, I was a bit surprised that he didn't do something like this long before—back when he first decided to move against our garrison at Lisht, for instance."

Sekenenre held up the papyrus and read the clear writing, the work of a master scribe. "It's so stupid. So vulgar.

These attempts at irony and sarcasm: 'Your pet hippopotami
in the eastern canal are making too much noise and keeping
me awake.' This from Avaris, deep in the delta, mind you.
Baliniri, there's room for hope in this. If his spies at my court
haven't informed him yet that I moved the menagerie six
weeks ago, he needs help with his intelligence-gathering."

Baliniri made a face. "It may have taken him this long to
get the news that I caught three of his best spies and had
them impaled. I'm not sure there are any left now. When he
took the running of the intelligence network out of Joseph's
hands and started supervising it himself, the quality went
way down." He shrugged. "I wouldn't give the thing a second
thought, Sire. You knew some sort of personal challenge was
coming. The main thing is to continue rearming and be aware
of the danger and prepare for the worst."

"Then you don't think the Lisht garrison will hold next
time?"

"No, Sire." Baliniri strode over to the wide window and
looked out over the lovely view of the broad Nile and the red
hills beyond. "It was a miracle it held last time. All we can
hope for—particularly now that Baba of El-Kab is dead—is
that Lisht can buy us enough time to rearm and get ready for
the assault on Thebes."

Sekenenre's face showed the strain. "Then it'll come
down to a siege here."

"I think so, Sire. If Riki's mission is successful—and
Kamose's too—we'll have a chance. We've got a good army.
All they need is the extraordinary motivation that Kamose's
return will provide, particularly if Riki—"

There was a knock on the door. Baliniri wheeled. An
officer of the palace guard stood stiffly at attention just outside the doorway. "Yes, Captain?" Baliniri said.

"Sir, there's someone to see you. An old fellow named
Kedar. He has the manner of a scribe, but a rather seedy
one. He says he has something of importance to tell you."

"Tell him to wait, will you? His Majesty and I have some
things to discuss."

"Quite right," the king said. Baliniri turned to face him.
"If it comes down to a last-ditch battle here, do you think
we've a chance?"

"Sire, I've anticipated virtually everything Apophis could possibly do. He won't be able to outflank us or starve us out—not unless the siege lasts more than six months."

"But a frontal attack?"

"We can hold them, Sire. Whether we can drive them back is another matter. That'll depend on Riki and Kamose."

The knock on the door sounded again! Baliniri turned in some annoyance. "Captain, didn't I tell you—"

"Yes, sir," the officer said. "But he says it's of extraordinary urgency."

"I don't care what he says," Baliniri said. He was about to turn away, but something stopped him. He stood blinking, a frown on his face. "Wait. What did you say his name was?"

"Kedar, sir. A scholar, he calls himself, and he said to tell you 'Seth's teacher.'"

Baliniri and the king exchanged glances. "Why didn't you say so in the first place?" Baliniri asked. "Bring him in."

Cheta let herself in, suspecting nothing. Instantly strong arms grabbed her from behind, and a big hand went over her mouth. She struggled and tried to cry out, but the door slammed shut behind her, and Apis and Imiut dragged her, heels trailing, across the floor to an inner room, leaving one fallen sandal on the marble floor before the door.

"Tie her up," Apis said to Tamshas. "And you, boy, keep an eye out the window. Let us know when the woman is coming."

"But I don't want to—" Meni began. A hard cuff across the face knocked him to his knees, and when he struggled to his feet, his mouth was bleeding. "Tamshas, don't let them—"

"Shut up!" Apis demanded. He stood over Tamshas, supervising the knots. "Tie them tight. Gag her."

"But, Apis—"

"Shut up! Do you want me to break your nose for you?" He raised a fist; she cringed and once again bent over her work. "Come on, Imiut. Let's search for that money. We'll check the wall tiles. I'll bet one of them comes off."

But as Imiut joined him, two unexpected things happened: The front door opened, and a stranger stood in the door, silhouetted in the warm sunlight. And simultaneously through the back entrance strolled Tuya, mistress of the house!

Tuya instantly took in the scene. She saw the abandoned sandal Cheta had left behind, and the two strangers, and Tamshas coming out of the side room. She did not make out the identity of the figure standing in the open doorway for a moment. "Tamshas!" she said. "What are these men doing in my house?"

"T-tuya," said the figure in the doorway. He kicked the door shut behind him and drew the sword at his side. "It's Ketan! These men are here to rob you!" But his voice was slurred, and he was swaying unsteadily on his feet. "Look, you," he said in a quavering voice meant to sound menacing, "the guardsmen are on the way! They know everything! If you lay down your arms now—"

Apis was closest. With a snarl of red rage he drew his own sword and lunged with one fluid motion. Ketan tried to raise his own weapon in a clumsy parry, but the lightning quickness of Apis's sword was too much for him. He was caught just below the place where the two sides of his rib cage came together, the sword almost to the hilt. Ketan's eyes opened wide; his mouth gaped in mute incomprehension; his weapon fell to the floor. He staggered back, and the motion jerked the sword hilt out of Apis's hand. Grasping the sword weakly, Ketan tried to pull it out. But the light of life was already leaving his eyes. He fell heavily to his knees and then slowly toppled over on his face. The motion drove the sword all the way through him, and its crimson point emerged from his back.

"Ketan!" Tuya shrieked. "You've killed him!"

By her side was an ornamental pair of iron-tipped Hittite spears that Dedmose, King Sekenenre's father, had given to Ben-Hadad. Tuya yanked one of these from the wall and, almost without thinking, ran Imiut through before he could defend himself. She pulled the spear out, not even bothering to watch him fall, and once again assumed the at-the-ready position just in time to face Tamshas, who flew at her furiously, a knife in her hand, her face a harpy's horrid mask.

Deftly Tuya swung the heavy tip of the spear, its hard head caught Tamshas on the temple and knocked her to the floor. Her face slammed into the marble floor with a sickening sound.

But when Apis advanced on her, reason and confidence deserted her at the same time. There was something of the basilisk's hypnotic glare in that evil face, in those unblinking eyes. It was like facing a cobra. She kept the spear point up, but he stayed just out of reach, feinting at her, an ice-cold smile on his reptilian face.

"You stay back," she warned. Out of the corner of her eye she could see that he was alone now in the room. Where was Meni? "The guards will be here in a moment. . . ."

"You know as well as I do that that was a bluff," he said in his deep, nasal, penetrating voice. "Do you think that drunken fool knew what he was talking about? No, my dear, it's just you and me. Just put down that spear of yours. You can't hold that heavy thing up forever. If you make me take it from you, I'll be forced to have my way with you, and then I'll drag out of you the secret of where everything is hidden. So far you've done a good job of hiding the money; I haven't found it yet. But with you to show me where it is—"

"What are you talking about?" she asked. "There's no money here. Do you think I'd be so stupid as to keep cash in my house?"

Still she retreated, one step at a time, and still he came closer. "Don't think you can talk your way out of this," he said. "I've been setting this up for days. Every day the boy would sneak out another few documents to me. I know virtually all there is to know about—"

"Are you trying to say—? Meni? No! Meni wouldn't do that to me! Tamshas, perhaps, but not—"

In her shock she lowered the point, and in a flash he was on her. His strong hands jerked the long shaft out of her hands, and in one motion he swung the handle and caught her in the face, knocking her roughly into the wall. She staggered and almost fell. As she recovered, Apis threw the spear to the ground and grabbed her by the wrists, his grip viselike and paralyzing. "Now, you little slut, I'll teach you to oppose me—"

Tuya screamed. Apis backhanded her across the face, and she almost fainted from the pain. He bunched her two wrists in one large fist and used his free hand to rip her robe off. She tried to fight him and got another blinding blow in the face that made her ears ring. Naked, defenseless, she tried to fight back, but her head reeled; the earth spun.

He grabbed her by the hair, letting her sink to the floor, and dragged her violently toward the back room. The pain gave new strength to her, and she struggled to get her feet beneath her. "N-no! Don't hurt me!"

He seemed to be talking to himself. ". . . did me a favor, when you come right down to it. Now I don't have to split the receipts even two ways. He was no damned good anyway. And if the woman and that brat of hers—"

"No!" Tuya said weakly. "You're hurting me—"

Now he noticed her again, as they passed into the back room. "Be silent!" He threw her forward onto a zebra-skin rug on the floor. "Just lie there and do what I tell you." He began to loosen his clothing—

—and suddenly he shook as if he had been struck by lightning! His eyes glazed over, and he held his hands up as if clutching at something, but they shook as if he were palsied!

Whatever the thing was, it hit him again, from behind. His head slumped forward, and there was a gout of blood from the base of his skull.

His body shook again, twisted, fell to one side, and rolled over, and he died before he knew what had hit him.

Tuya scrambled to one knee, staring. Young Meni stood over the dead body, the spear wavering in his hands, his eyes wide in horror. His young body shook as if he were a dry leaf in a windstorm. "Tuya," he cried, "I . . . I didn't mean to kill him, but I couldn't let him hurt you. . . ."

Behind the hurt eyes of the child, in the outer room, there were noises of pounding feet, the sounds of deep male voices. "Tuya!" a voice, deep, somehow familiar, called. "Where are you?" A voice from the past, almost forgotten. Baliniri's voice.

Suddenly the earth spun, faster, faster. Tuya felt sense leave her, she fell forward in a faint, the sight of the frightened, shocked boy still in her mind as she slipped away.

But when she awoke, in her own bed, a coverlet discreetly drawn up to her chin, the face hovering over her was kindly old Kedar's, worried, concerned. "Tuya," he whispered in a gentle voice. "Are you all right, my dear? No, please, just lie still. Everything will be all right."

"Oh, Kedar!" she said in a hollow voice. "It's all coming back. Tamshas, those awful men . . ." Suddenly she tried to sit up. "Ketan!" she said. "Is he. . . ?"

Kedar's hand, stronger than one might think, forced her gently back onto the pillow. "I'm afraid we were too late," he said.

"Ah," she said, miserable. "I'm so sorry. He tried, and . . ." She let the words slip away. "The others?"

"All dead. All except the boy. He was in on it. We've decided—"

"No!" she said. "He saved me! He killed that horrible man! Don't let them take him away!"

Understanding showed on Kedar's old face. "I wondered about that. Yes, I can see it. Very well. I'll go tell them to leave him with us. They'll have to question him, of course."

Tuya stared. "With 'us'?" she said. "Then you've decided. . . ."

Kedar smiled gently. "Of course, my dear," he said. "Did you think I could leave you now? After this?" He took her hand in his. "Now see if you can get some rest. I'll be here when you awake. Now, and at any time you need me."

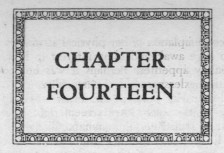

CHAPTER FOURTEEN

The Western Desert

I

They had left Sakhmak at the El-Kharga oasis, along with the rest of Riki's party. Now Seth and Riki marched westward, accompanied only by the towering, statuesque Weret and a handpicked band of a dozen of her warrior-women. Hourly the track grew harder and harsher, and the air drier and hotter. Riki and Seth had adopted desert dress and wore only their loincloths and their sandals.

As he marched along, Riki reflected admiringly upon how the warrior-women adapted to the austere world in which they had chosen to live. With only Seth and the tall, spare Weret before him, and with a critical eye uncorrupted by desire, Riki idly watched the spare and hard-muscled beauty of Weret's naked body as she strode along easily ahead of him.

For some reason, the slim back, long and slender legs, and compact buttocks of the warrior-maiden aroused little sexual interest in him. He was not quite sure why this was.

The mere contemplation of her physical attributes ought, he thought, to have awakened some interest in him, given his normal, healthy appetites. Perhaps it was her coldness toward him, the sexlessness of her personality.

Well! In this, it would appear, Weret was atypical of the women here. The night's revels seemed to have involved virtually all the women in her command, and when, at breakfast, Riki had overheard some of the men's conversations, he had chuckled at their stunned descriptions of the voraciousness of the women's appetites. Several of the men had boasted of disporting themselves simultaneously with two of the girls at a time and had spoken of them as being not quite of this earth.

Others, however, had told of conversing with the women, learning of an almost universal bisexuality among their ranks. If men were present, they would take advantage; if not, they would coolly pair off with one another. Perhaps Weret was of this breed—or perhaps she gave her favors only to women. Given her chilly attitude toward him, he found this thought lingered in his speculations.

They marched on, ever westward. After a time Seth dropped back and joined him, to his delight; he had begun to weary of his own company. "Well!" Riki said. "Have you had a nice conversation with the ice maiden?"

Seth chuckled. "Oh, she's not so bad," he answered. "I learned quite a bit about the wildlife of the area, and the mineral deposits. If you were wondering why Baliniri sent us out here—"

"I was," Riki admitted. "It's not the mineral wealth of the area, I can tell you that. This isn't the kind of country in which you find iron ore."

"True," Seth said. "You're full of surprises, Riki. I'd no idea such things interested you."

"Would a soldier not be interested in the notion of having iron weapons?" Riki asked earnestly. "But it isn't the presence of ore here. It's the presence of the secret of making it, of that I'm sure. You've noticed that sword of Weret's, I take it?"

Once again Seth brightened. "Yes indeed. While we

were getting ready to move out, I asked her if I might have a look at it. She very proudly passed it over."

Riki stepped aside for a moment to let Seth go ahead where the path narrowed and went through a narrow defile.

Seth waited until Riki had caught up, then fell into step with him again. "I told her it was nice workmanship, but the formula could use some work."

"*What?*" Riki gasped, startled, breaking step. "You told her that? What do *you* know of the formula for iron? If you've known all this time and were holding out on us, I'll skin you alive."

Seth made a moue and shrugged. "Hers is a sword made from natural ore occurring within the earth. And it doesn't bear comparison with iron made from the chunks that fall from the sky. Meteoritic iron works better. It's harder, less brittle. But there's only just so much of it, so if you want more, you have to wait until it falls from the sky—"

"Ah!"

"—or until you come up with a formula that allows you to make smelted iron that's as good as meteoritic iron."

"You're a fountain of information! How did you—"

"You forget. My granduncle knew the secret, even if he didn't live to pass it on to me. So did my great-grandfather. I've seen samples of both men's work. Kirta, my great-grandfather, learned it from a man in the Greek Isles back before the Shepherds came to Egypt. He taught it to my granduncle Shobai, but after Shobai had been blinded. Shobai dictated notes, which I've read, to this scribe and that. They don't tell the whole story, but I've some hints. I can make an educated guess." He shrugged. "To put it all together, I need to talk it over with a practical person, the kind who gets his hands dirty. In a word, I need to talk to the person who made Weret's sword."

Riki kicked a rock in the road and sent it skidding. "Somehow," he said, "I tend to forget you are a Child of the Lion too. I see now that the blood of Ahuni runs in your veins as well."

"I suppose so," Seth said. "I've inherited a bit of the talent, although I'm clumsy with my hands. I think that the ancestor I must be most like is my great-grandfather Kirta, who abandoned his wife and children to spend twenty years trying to learn about iron. I've inherited his curiosity and mental restlessness."

He was silent and pensive for a long interval, his eyes on the path before him, his face dark and brooding. When he at last spoke, it was to say, "I tell you, Riki, I begin at last to understand what drove Kirta and the others. I begin to see how a man could easily go overboard on the subject. The implications of mastery of this metal alone . . ."

Riki snorted. "I can tell you one implication. We could go approach the Shepherds and say, 'Look here, boys, the great drought has come and gone. You can go back home now. And if you don't, we'll be glad to carve you into—' "

"Drought?" Seth echoed. "That old story about the Shepherds migrating south because a great drought drove them from their homeland of Hayastan is total rot. That wasn't why they left Lake Van. No, indeed."

"What are you talking about?" Riki asked testily.

"I spent time in the stockade. I met a Hai officer there. Scholarly chap named Nushin, pressed into service by Apophis during the great mobilization. No more talent for soldiering, or inclination either, than I had. But he'd got into the court records, going back to the original Shepherd migration. Remarkable stuff." He seemed to be talking to himself, almost muttering.

"Could you speak up?" Riki said, a little annoyed.

"The Hai weren't fleeing a drought when they came here! They were fleeing a nation! A nation that, if they'd stayed where they were, could have wiped the floor up with them." He shook his head. "A nation—a very small one, as a matter of fact, much less populous than they were—very dangerous to the Hai. They called themselves the Chalybes, and they lived in the narrow area between Lake Van and the great Caucasus Mountains."

Riki blinked. "Do you mean to tell me that the Hai, millions of them, were driven away from Hayastan by a tiny nation?"

Seth nodded. "The Chalybes had the secret of iron. They discovered it. They made the finest iron swords in the

world. Better than those of Kirta. Better than those of Turios
of Tyre, who taught Kirta. Better than those of Karkara of
Sado."

Riki's face showed his disbelief. "Next you'll tell me they
made iron objects better than the Hittites do."

Seth shook his head. "No. The Hittites can't make iron.
That's why they won't teach it to other nations. They don't
know the secret themselves."

Riki sputtered. "B-but everyone *knows* the Hittites are
the masters of the iron culture. Everyone who tries to invade
them soon finds that out. The Hittites' weapons cleave through
the bronze weapons of their enemies like—"

"Everyone's wrong," Seth said firmly. He looked up
ahead. "Oh, by the way," he said airily, "I think we're
getting pretty close to where we're going. We've been watched
for some time. Did you catch that signal Weret gave? There!
She did it again!"

"Don't change the subject," Riki said.

"The Hittite guild that so rigidly controls the secret of
the smelting of iron—it's composed entirely of Chalybes.
They guard the secret jealously. It's a kind of religion with
them, a guildsman's sacred craft. Nushin told me all about it.
If the Hittites try to force them to reveal the secret, the
Chalybes commit suicide. Each one of them carries a vial of
poison and is sworn to—"

Riki put a hand on Seth's arm to stop him. They looked
at the cliffs up ahead, and the deep cleft in the earth that was
the El-Dakhla oasis. To either side of the path, rising almost
out of the ground, new women stood, their slim nude bodies
gleaming with gold ornaments, their black swords glinting
dully in their hangers. "Seth," he said, "do you mean the Hai
were—"

"Driven away by their numerical inferiors. They ran to
keep from being destroyed utterly. They've carefully guarded
that shameful secret for generations."

The column now passed between menacing lines of the
warrior-women and turned slowly downward to work its tor-
tuous way down into the great rift. Riki was still struggling to
assimilate all this. "Then you mean that with iron weapons,
we, too, could be as great a threat to them as—"

"Exactly," Seth said. "They're frightened to death of iron. They think of it, in their hearts, as the work of evil gods. If we got iron weapons, they'd think we were the Chalybes themselves, migrated to Egypt to destroy them and drive them once again into the desert to die."

Riki's face bore witness to the shock of what he had heard. And the rest of the way down the cliffside he was silent, pensive, virtually oblivious to everything around him except the path beneath his feet and the tumultuous thoughts tossing wildly in his mind.

In stark contrast to the El-Kharga oasis, the settlement at El-Dakhla was all armed camp. Tents covered the open space between the groves and orchards, and everywhere was the constant evidence of soldier-women drilling, always naked, always fully armed, always gleaming here and there with golden ornaments: anklets, bracelets, earrings, even an occasional gold chain worn around the waist.

A more refined taste was at work here: The ornaments were beautifully made by a master hand, and all followed a distinct pattern, unlike the pleasantly individualistic turn of the El-Kharga women's jewelry. The bodies were as hard and trim as before, but there was among the inner oasis's complement a distinctly feminine touch. Weret looked out of place in this desert haven.

Riki and Seth were escorted to a beautifully landscaped garden, fed by springs flowing directly out of the rocks just above their heads and trickling musically down over the stones to feed a merry little creek that wound around the stone benches. Weret dismissed her women and sent one of the local soldier-women off on an errand as yet undisclosed. "Wait here," she said. "Food and drink will be brought to you." She turned and strode away silently on hard bare soles.

Riki sat on a bench and dipped his hot feet into the little stream, then bent over the ornamental shrub that flanked the bench. "Curious," he said. "I don't know this species. It must have been brought from somewhere else. A lot of this more delicate greenery assuredly did not come from here."

"You're perceptive," a low, vibrant female voice said behind him. Both men wheeled and looked at the speaker. "They come from the Mountains of Fire."

Alone among the warrior-women, she wore no ornament at all, other than the golden band that restrained her dark hair. Her calm face, her exquisite body—at once athletic and intensely female—these burned into Riki's brain with a vividness and intensity that made this moment the most memorable of his life. She was nude like a goddess, her matchless skin tanned a beautiful bronze color, yet she seemed robed in the imperial glory of a queen. There was no flaw in her anywhere.

Riki, stunned, struggled awkwardly to his feet and made the sort of obeisance one might make to royalty. He fumbled for words but found none.

Seth, by contrast, was calm. He rose and smiled, warm and friendly. "Riki," he said in a matter-of-fact voice, "I'd like to present my cousin Teti. Sister of Ketan. Daughter of Shobai and granddaughter of Kirta of Haran. Pupil of Karkara of Sado. *And* Child of the Lion."

II

Attendants had brought wine, dates, olives, and bread. In a normal desert oasis, where the ancient amenities were observed, servants would have poured scented water over one's hands before one ate, and slaves with fans would have placed a visitor at his ease; but here, in Teti's austere domain, there were no servants. Everyone worked. The hand that served them was Teti's own.

"I can't get over this," Riki said, wiping his forehead. The day was a warm one even under the overhanging palms. "I'd heard of you, of course. The first female Child of the Lion to take up the family profession"—as she bent over Seth's wine cup and poured, he gave another glance at the red birthmark on her lower back, just above where the swell of her hips began—"but I'd heard that you'd withdrawn from life ten years or so ago. I took it for granted that you'd moved to another part of Egypt, or married, or something like that."

He pursed his lips in thought for a moment, then went on. "I can see now that there was a kind of conspiracy of silence. Everyone knew but me."

"That isn't quite true," Seth said. "I'd heard rumors. They do get in from the desert now and then. What I didn't hear, I guessed. I think everyone was just respecting Teti's privacy."

Teti put down the wine jar and sat down opposite them. Riki blinked, as he had every time she had looked into his eyes so far. He could not look away from those eyes. "There's some truth in what both of you say," she revealed. "I . . . lost someone very dear to me at the battle of El-Kab. The first person I'd ever loved. Then my mother died. In despair I resigned my position with the army and went first to Thebes, then Nubia on impulse."

"Nubia?" Seth said. "*Hmmm.* Looking for Karkara?"

"Partly that," she said. "But mainly I didn't want to see anyone I'd known, not even my twin brother, Ketan. I landed at the court of Nehsi, Akhilleus's son, and I met Ebana, Akhilleus's wife."

"You stayed there for a time?" Seth asked.

"Yes. Ebana took me under her wing. She knew what I was going through. Just about that time Baliniri came up on a state visit, to settle the details of the armistice between the Nubians and Egyptians. He heard Ebana telling me about her Black Wind, how it had become an independent unit of fighting women who didn't believe in entrusting everything in the world to the wisdom of men. They lived apart and acted as a tempering force."

"This is fascinating," Riki remarked. "What did Baliniri have to say?"

"He thought as you do. And he thought that if I were to create such a unit over here on the desert route, we could become an important if independent unit guarding our western regions from incursions from Libya—*and* keeping the Hai out of this part of Egypt. There are, you must know, hundreds of places along every desert track where a mere squad of archers can halt or even destroy a whole troop of invaders who don't know the terrain."

Riki nodded. "We were in your women's hands the

whole way," he admitted. "I found it daunting. When I post pickets, I usually do a good job of it. I don't expect a warrior from the other side to be able to penetrate our defenses as easily as your scout did—particularly with a tame cheetah at her side."

Teti smiled. Riki's heart pounded. "The cheetahs aren't tame. They're wild. We hunt with them. No member of the cat family is ever tamed."

Seth broke in, "The same thing can be said of the female of every species. Subdued, but not tamed."

"My celibate cousin, for all his wisdom and learning, sometimes wanders off course and sounds like a Bedouin claiming expertise on the ways of the Great Sea," Teti said, a mischievous glint in her dark eye. "Or have you changed your ways, Seth? Tell me, Captain, did Seth pair off with any of my women at El-Kharga?"

"I haven't any idea," Riki said. "And he won't tell. Go on, please."

"Very well. Baliniri and Ebana took me in hand. The first thing I had to do, they said, was find Karkara, if he was still alive. Then I had to take him to the desert with me and, with a small group of Ebana's women, build and fortify a place where I could study, then perfect, my mastery of ironwork. I did these things. Next I began recruiting young like-minded women to come here and train with me. You have no idea how many daughters—daughters who, with no hope of dower, have no prospects of marriage or a normal life—there are among the poor."

"I beg your pardon," Riki said, "but you grew up the daughter of a rich ironmaker, if I'm rightly informed. I grew up an orphan on the streets of Avaris, never knowing where my next meal was coming from. I do know what the prospects of a poor girl are."

"Forgive me," Teti said. "To continue, they took to the desert life as I did. Ebana's women trained them, with some help from Baliniri, who came out from time to time in secret and conferred with me." Riki, blinded by the beauty of that lovely face, tried to isolate a feature here, another there: the long and graceful neck, the delicate bone structure of the face—but when she chose to look into his eyes, he could not

tear his eyes away. "We became, a little at a time, the
guardians of the trade route—*and* of the desert road from
Hai-controlled Lower Egypt into your own domain. We enforced the caravan tax, but by Baliniri's special edict we
poured all the money into iron ore imported from Nubia and
beyond. The lands of the South," she said, turning to Seth
now, "are very rich in iron ore. We are stockpiling."

Seth's tone lost a bit of its nonchalance. Indeed, there
was a hard edge in it that Riki had never heard before. "And
have you mastered the formula? Can you make iron the way
they make it in the Hittite domains?"

She hesitated, stood, and paced about for a minute or
two before speaking. Riki's eyes went to her body. He had
never imagined the family birthmark of the Children of the
Lion could be so fetching or so adorably placed. Finally she
turned, her eyes once again on his. "Come with me, Seth.
Get your hands dirty. Have a look at my forges. Judge for
yourself." She smiled at Riki and her tone softened. "You too,
Captain."

Seth blinked. His voice had the same edge to it. "Actually, Teti, he's a general. A war hero. He won a great battle
before the walls of Lisht, broke the Hai advance. He's earned
your respect, and everyone else's. Call him by his proper
title."

Her eyes widened. "Well spoken, Seth. I apologize.
Come critique my work. I'm sure you'll have much to say
about it. And you, General——"

" 'Riki' will do." Riki stood now and underlined his con-
ciliatory words with a small bow. "I am eager to tour your
forges. The more we learn, the better. Our current position
is quite desperate. If you have something to contribute,
either in the way of manpower—"

"Womanpower," she interrupted.

"I stand corrected. That, or iron weaponry itself, we
need it. We need all the soldiers we can get. And Seth has
recently learned something that suggests that the Hai will be
unusually vulnerable to any army that comes at them with
iron weapons—"

He stopped dead. Before him something horrible was
happening to Teti! She reeled back, as if she had been struck

a death blow! Her beautiful eyes glazed over. Her hands
clawed at her middle, at the place where the ribs came
together in her chest. The beautiful face was a mask of deadly
pain. Both men stood as if stunned, then rushed to her side.
They were too late. Soundlessly she pitched forward onto her
face before they could reach her, and lay as one dead.

El-Dakhla was not the giant oasis of El-Kharga. There
was no learned chirurgeon. There was, however, a woman
who doubled as first-aid worker and midwife who took Teti to
her own tent and stretched her out, comalike, in her own
bed. She gave the men a distrustful stare. "You must go," she
said sourly.

"But—" Riki began. He looked down at the outstretched
body under the coverlet, and the sight of her tore at his
heart. He had counted on hovering over her, on being the
first person she saw when she awoke. "If she comes out of
it—"

"You'll be among the first informed. Now go."

Riki let himself be pulled out the doorway by Seth. "I
can't understand it," Riki said. "One moment she was so
vibrant and alive, and then—"

"Something's happened to her brother," Seth said flatly.
His tone was sober, concerned. "I fear the worst. The two of
them have felt each other's pain since birth, whether the hurt
was a bruise or a broken bone. I've often wondered what
would happen when one of them died, leaving the other
alive. It appears we're about to find out."

"She can't die!" Riki cried out. "Not when—"

"Come along," Seth said. "I saw some palm wine on the
table outside. A stiff drink will do you good. You've had a
shock." He took Riki's arm and virtually dragged him down
the long line of palms. When they reached the table under
the trees, Seth sat Riki down, retrieved the cups they had
drunk wine from, and replaced their contents with much
more potent palm wine.

Riki drank and shuddered. "Gods! Powerful stuff!"

"It is," Seth said. "Just what you need right now. Not

only have you just watched something shocking and frightening, you're in the grip of something bigger than yourself."

Riki went on, unhearing. "If she dies —"

"I don't think she'll die," Seth said. "If she were a weaker-minded person, perhaps . . . but no. Teti is as tough as leather inside. Look how she recovered after witnessing the death of her first lover ten years ago. She only grew stronger than ever." He drank and shrugged but did not shudder. "She has the assurance, the controlled forcefulness, of a woman seven or eight years older than she is. I suppose someone not related to her might find her attractive."

This finally had the desired effect, that of breaking Riki out of his shocked state. "Attractive!" he said. " 'Someone *might* find her attractive'! What a statement! And here I thought you'd finally joined the human race, Seth."

Seth paused with his drink halfway to his lips and smiled. "That one got to you, didn't it? Just as I thought. Baliniri was right. He usually is in such matters."

"What are you talking about? This is serious! That unearthly creature is more dead than alive, and you—"

" 'Unearthly creature,' he says! Ah, Baliniri! Who would have suspected you knew people so well!" He drank, then put his cup down. "Actually it's rather funny. Teti 'unearthly'? You'll find out soon enough how earthly she is. Of all the younger Children of the Lion, she was always the sensible, practical, down-to-earth one. Ketan only wanted to make pretty things, not weapons of war. There was always something ineffectual about him, though I probably speak ill of the dead—"

"You've taken leave of your senses!"

"—and as for me, Teti hit me right dead center when she twitted me, just now, with not wanting to get my hands dirty. I've always been a theory man, leaving others to do the work. In a lot of ways she's the best of us, for all her bossy ways—"

"Don't you talk that way about her! She may be dy—"

"There," Seth said, pouring himself another drink. "Proves my point. The prosecution rests its case." He made an ironic half flourish. He looked at Riki, sitting there half-angry, half-hurt. "My congratulations. You'll be getting quite a prize.

And an enormous lot of trouble, too, I suspect. Although with the way she looks at you, a complete stranger—"

"What kind of nonsense—"

"I doubt she's looked at another man since Netru was killed. But she looks into your eyes, fascinated with you and sure of the spell she's casting."

"Seth!"

"Isn't it obvious? Wouldn't a blind fool have noticed by now? Love at first sight! Both of you! Helplessly, head over heels!"

III

She was one with her brother at last, and there was no distance between them. They had drifted apart years before and had only been reminded of the link between them by the fact that they shared, as always, each other's pain. But that sharing had been a huge annoyance in their existence, when each was being dragged willy-nilly into the other twin's world. There had been no union in it, certainly nothing at all of the kind of union they had known when they were devoted children and their personalities had not so far diverged.

Now the years were gone, indeed as though they had never been, and she and Ketan were a single soul, and she knew the helpless, abject fear as he slipped slowly down, drawn by a powerful force, toward the blinding pool of light below. In the vortex they spun around the sinking walls of the eddy, drawn ever downward. She thought with Ketan: *I'm losing the life I've always known! All the things I was, all the things I am, all the things I would have been.* The pain of this was much greater than the pain in her midsection had been a moment before, when she had had a separate body that moved, that felt, that yearned.

She knew his feelings as surely as if they had been hers.

Now, however, she felt the magical melding of their souls coming asunder breath by breath, though she felt herself, after that marvelous moment of blending and sharing, slowly and inexorably becoming Teti, a separate Teti, once more. The light into which they were falling at a greatly accelerating rate was no longer blinding and white-hot, a fearful thing, but had become instead a neutral white. It was the absence of the fear. It was the absence of insecurity, suspense, and apprehension. There was no need to fear the passing of time and the thing that lay ahead, because there was no time now. Nothing ahead and nothing behind. As the part of her that was now Ketan continued to sink toward the whiteness, it became evident that this moment was not a new thing, but had always occurred, and that all moments since the beginning of time had partaken of this moment and had pointed to it.

Lo! There was no life-here and death-faraway! There was a change as inevitable, as painless, as the change from worm to butterfly inside the cocoon. Ketan was slipping away from her and turning into something new—but it was something he had always been. She felt him leave her and felt the last touch of his mind: It knew no pain, no fear, no regret. There was no formal good-bye, but still somehow it was as if he spoke to her.

Not in words. Not even in pictures—but with feelings, the last he would ever know in this world. And they were feelings that, she realized even while sharing them, human beings were not meant to feel while still in this life. Through them she knew that her time to join Ketan in that world of light and painlessness, that world free once and for all of fear, had not come, but then when it did come, she would know it in advance and would not fear it.

Somehow, too, she knew that for the rest of her life a new gift would be hers: that of seeing the events that were to come, and of understanding things that no ordinary human being could understand. These moments of knowledge, of intuitive understanding, would not be with her all the time—who, after all, could live with that?—but would come upon her at times over which she would have no control. She had been, for the briefest time, in that world to which Ketan had gone, and ever afterward the memory would be with her—and ever afterward she would be given tiny glimpses of the fabric of time that Ketan could now see completed, as if it had all already happened.

She would be given a glimpse of destiny. She would be able to see a fragment of some person's future as if it were painted on a wall. But because one still in this life cannot live with the white heat of that world of light without experiencing a complete transformation, such as Ketan had undergone, she would not be able to take more than a tiny fragment of it at a time.

A single phrase flashed across her mind, and she could never afterward say in whose voice it had come to her, or how, or why: *What you can know in this fashion, you will not understand: What you can understand, you will not see clearly. . . .*

One thing she did know, though: When the time came for her to go as finally as Ketan had gone and become at last what Ketan had become, this she would see clearly; this she would understand. The rest would be a vision seen blurred, through eyes half-blinded by that one glimpse of the light.

"If only we could do something!" Riki said. "She's been out a long time. If only there were a healer here!"

Seth sat at the water's edge beside the little creek and extended his legs into the water. "There are times, my friend, when nobody can do anything—and when nothing is the best thing one could possibly do. This may well be one of those times. How I wish, though, that I could see into her mind! I can guess, from the outside, what's happening: She's sharing Ketan's death."

"She's not dying! Tell me she's not dying!"

Seth smiled tolerantly. "I don't think she is. Riki, there was a time when I studied medicine. I was . . . oh, thirteen or so. I hung around the chirurgeons, the *sunus*, the magi. I watched them, pestered them with questions, and made a nuisance of myself. I don't know how they put up with me, or why. Perhaps they saw in me something of themselves. I watched births and deaths. I watched men, women, and children saved by nostrums, and I watched them die under the knife."

Riki looked at him, his eyes dull with apprehension. He said nothing.

"More to the point," Seth continued, "I watched people go into the land of death—and come back. It happens, you know."

"I . . . yes. I've spoken with soldiers who said they or their friends have had it happen."

"Then you know what I learned. They said they had found themselves drifting toward an unearthly light, but at the last moment before joining it, before becoming it, they had been called back into this life. They almost all said they greeted this quite differently than with the jubilation one might envision. They were, to a man, regretful about having been dragged—several of them used that word, dragged— back to this life. Because they said this life hurts, and the other one doesn't. . . ."

"And you think that Teti—"

"I don't know. If I'm right, she'll come out of this in a moment or two. When she does, it will be important to have someone close to her when she awakens—someone truly important to her, truly close to her."

"You mean . . ."

"Go to her. Shove the midwife aside. Make sure it's your hand that she feels holding hers when she comes out of it. Make sure your eyes are the first ones she looks into. This is a very important moment, I believe."

Riki rose in great haste. "Yes!" he said decisively, and he set off toward the tents at a trot that quickly became a dead run.

Seth became aware yet again of the person standing behind him, but he did not turn. "Approach," he said. "I'd guess it is Weret. Am I right?"

The warrior-woman moved into view now and stood glaring at him. "What sort of spell have you put on her?" she demanded in a tight voice. "I went to see her. She's as a dead person. If harm comes to her through you—"

Seth benignly looked up at her, feet still in the water. "Whatever happens, she'll have come to no harm through us.

She had a date with destiny, and she met it. How I wish I could have shared it with her!"

"If she dies, be assured that you will indeed join her in the Netherworld," Weret warned. "I'll see to that myself."

Seth looked at her. There was not a single feature in her face or form that was not worthy of a goddess; but the goddess would have been, most likely, one of those sexless wood spirits like the one the Greeks called Artemis—a huntress, virginal and severe of spirit. There was, despite the exquisitely female outward form of the naked body before him, nothing to attract the man he was. "You're very devoted to her," he said.

"I'd die for her. Many of us would. She took us, outcasts, nobodies, and made us people of consequence, sisters, people who valued one another and learned to care for one another."

"Care?" Seth asked simply. "It's more than that. You personally, you're in love with her. Isn't that it?"

She flushed. "She is my leader and my sister and my friend."

"More than that," he insisted. "I see it in your eyes. You're in love with her, but she isn't in love with you. You yearn for her, but she doesn't respond. You'd be filled with joy if you could lie with her, with your arms about her—"

"Shut up! Mind your own business! Or I'll—"

"You won't harm me. Oh, I know you could. I'm no warrior. I'm as weak as a child. But I'm safe from you. You wouldn't harm her cousin. You know how she'd view that."

"Damn you."

"Oh, you don't need to be that way about it. We don't need to be enemies at all. You know very well that I'm not the one you have to fear. My friend is. He's the man she's going to go away with, not me."

"No! That's not true!"

"She's in love with him already, and there isn't a thing that you can do. Not without losing her friendship." She blanched but said nothing. He went on, gently, sympathetically. "Relax, Weret. In her own way she loves and trusts you. I can tell. I've known her a lot longer than you have.

She can't help the fact that she simply isn't interested in women's bodies, as you're not interested in men's bodies."

"You see too much," Weret observed with grudging respect. "You've many qualities of the woman in you."

"Probably," Seth said. "I think all men do. And all women have much of the man in them. Otherwise how could we understand each other at all, being as different as we are?"

"Most men don't talk this way."

Seth smiled. "Oh, don't mind me. Everyone knows I'm crazy. I go around muttering to myself. I ask crazy questions and don't have any small talk. I'm interested in things nobody cares a hang about, and the things others find fascinating bore me."

"I don't really know what you are, but you're not crazy."

"Who cares what I am? Who cares what you are? I'll say one thing—I don't bore you, and you don't bore me. Maybe we have something to learn from each other. We could be friends."

"I've never been friends with a man. I don't like men." But there was something in her tone, a weakening of her hostility. . . .

"Think of me as something else, then. A friendly desert demon, maybe. Or a cheetah who walks upright. Cheetahs are curious like me. Come, show me Teti's forges. I've been wanting a peek at them."

"No outsider has ever—"

"Now, now. I'm a Child of the Lion." He turned to show her the birthmark, smudged but unmistakable. "Surely you've noticed it by now. Come on. Show me." He stood, smiled noncommittally, comrade to comrade. It was that smile that won her over. "There's something about the formula she's using that I don't understand. I could wait for her to show me, but there's not much time. Things are getting desperate in Thebes. The faster I know—"

"Come with me," Weret said, her voice gruff but accepting.

*   *   *

Suddenly the stiff face relaxed, and it was as if life and warmth and animation abruptly flowed back into the chill hand he held in his own. The lovely eyes opened but did not see him clearly for a moment. Then she got him in focus, and her hand closed on his. "You're here," she said. "Why does that make me so happy? I hardly know you."

"You're back. That makes *me* happy."

"Something wonderful happened. I must tell you."

"There's plenty of time." Indeed, he had never felt so miraculously free of strain or tension. It was as if time had stopped. He held her hand up to his lips. It was the strong hand of a warrior, of an armorer—and yet it was soft and yielding to his touch. "I'll always be here."

She looked at him, and his heart beat fast. He had never had a woman look at him *that* way before. "Riki," she whispered. "That's a boy's name. You have another name. It isn't clear just what it is. I'll know soon. There's something about your parents—"

He smiled. "I'm an orphan. I'm trying to find out who I am."

"You'll know. Soon. Oh, it'll be something wonderful. That's all I know now." Her voice was soft and sweet. "Oh, Riki. Of all the people to find waiting for me when I came back from—"

"I know. What's happening to us? It's as if we've been steered together by destiny." He looked into her eyes and almost bent over to kiss her; but then the thought hit him. "Baliniri! *He's* been steering us together!"

She stared, smiled, laughed. She rose to a sitting position beside him on the bed and put her arms lightly around him. Her breasts brushed his naked chest. "The old fox," she said. "If so, he's an even better friend than I'd thought him all these years. Oh, Riki, I've been off among the stars, on a journey I can't describe. But I'm back in this world. And I'm so happy. I can't begin to tell you how happy I am."

"I know," he said in a hoarse voice, deeply moved. "I *know*. If this is happiness, then I've never been happy before. Nothing like this has ever happened to me."

They locked eyes. Something indefinable passed between them, something to which neither of them could have put a name. Embracing was like putting the two halves of a broken heart back together again.

IV

"I really ought to go have a look at her," Weret said. But there was an undecided quality to her words, as if her feelings were deeply divided. What was duty? Watching over her stricken leader? Or giving the young savant from Thebes the tour of the forges, as she had been asked to do?

Seth, whose mind had been totally involved with questions concerning the smelting process at work here, turned to look at her. "She's all right," he said calmly. "I'm sure of it." When she did not respond, he added, "Look, you don't know me very well yet. Perhaps if you did, you'd know that people who listen to me seldom get into trouble. Oh, true, I sometimes get in trouble myself, but it's always through inattention to the world around me while I'm thinking about something else. But when I am paying proper attention to something, I usually have a very good grasp of it."

"Huh," Weret said skeptically. But her manner softened a bit a moment afterward. "Your friend, uh, Riki, he'd be with her now, eh?"

"Yes. I'm almost sure something's happened to her brother. You know about their shared feelings."

"Yes. I've seen it work from time to time."

"Then you know that serious injury to him would mean constant pain for her. In this case she showed no sign of being still in pain after she collapsed. She went into a sort of coma or trance afterward, as if she were dead."

"Yes," she said grudgingly. "But what—"

"I think he's died. This could be a rare opportunity for all of us. We might get a glimpse through her eyes of the world beyond—if she remembers it when she awakes. But her awakening should be gentle, without you hovering over her anxiously. Or me asking questions. She should have someone who loves her and accepts her completely, and who won't make any demands—"

"B-but *I* love her! I accept her! I—"

"Do you?" Seth asked quietly. "Completely? That means accepting that she'll never share the physical love you want with her. Good friends though you are, that's something you don't share, making you feel lonely, rejected, and frustrated. And you don't accept that about her, do you? Ah, you *do* see, don't you?"

Weret stared at him with eyes misted over with unshed tears. "Come on," she said hoarsely. "You've seen the forges. Now I'll show you—"

"Oh, I don't care about the rest," Seth said. "All I wanted was a peek at the forges. Now I need to talk with Teti about them, her formula, and the process. I can't quite put my finger on the problem. It's driving me crazy."

"Problem? What problem? The formula is perfect."

Seth shook his head sadly, looking down the long line of furnaces set against the side of the hill. "She understands design very well. The furnaces themselves are worthy of Shobai."

"What's the matter with the formula?" Weret asked, forgetting herself and grabbing him by the arm. Ordinarily she did not like to touch men or be touched by them. "What would you know of formulae? She was instructed by Karkara of Sado himself, and—"

"I don't care if she was instructed by one of the gods come down to earth in a golden chariot. There are things she's going to have to do with iron that don't have to be done to copper and bronze."

"You've seen my sword, haven't you? Well, she made that. She made it herself. And—"

Seth shook his head patiently. "Yes, I know. And that's exactly what I'm talking about. Have you ever used it in a real battle?"

She stared blankly. "Well . . . no. The last fight I was in was before she made it for me. We were still using bronze weapons at the time. Karkara was still alive."

"You'd probably have done well against most bronze weapons, the kind inferior armorers make. But the Hai don't have inferior armorers. Their arms are made by men whose grandfathers learned from Shobai, back before the fall of Carchemish, while he still had his sight and when he was working under contract for Karakin the Mighty. Shobai made *hard* bronze."

"Iron is harder than bronze!"

"Yes, it is." He explained slowly, patiently, as if to a child. "But the process for making it is very delicately balanced, and if only one small thing goes wrong, the whole thing goes wrong. And if a good bronze sword hit yours, forte to forte, there's no predicting whether his weapon or yours would shatter—"

"Shatter! You don't know what you're talking about!"

"Bear with me, please. Quenching the iron makes it hard—*and* brittle. There's where things went wrong. There, or some place during the carburizing process."

"But—"

"Tell me: Soldiers of your units test these weapons, right? I mean, weapons less ornate than a beautiful presentation sword like yours?"

"Yes."

"And sometimes they find that after every stroke they'll have to straighten their swords with their foot against the ground, and—"

He saw the sudden, stunned look of comprehension in her eyes. "H-how did you know that? You who never worked at a forge in your life—"

"I've got it in the blood, just as Teti does. The problem is getting it to be both hard *and* rigid. The usual carburizing process gives you a sword that has a thin hard shell around a relatively soft interior, right? And even to accomplish that, you have to get exactly the right proportion of carbon absorbed by the ore, get the temperature just right, and keep the ore, in that spongy state, in contact with the charcoal while keeping it out of direct contact with the open air. . . ."

He looked down at the row of forges again and sighed. "I could probably list the stages you had to go through to get this far. At first everyone was looking for a process that would start producing pure iron, which would separate from the slag and produce the spongy stage. Then they wanted a hotter forge so the spongy stuff would absorb carbon from the charcoal."

"G-go on."

"The trouble is, at that temperature it tends to take on too high a percentage of carbon. It's obvious that Teti solved the first problem, only to run into the second. She's got the temperature way, way up, by digging the furnaces into the side of the hill. There's a natural draft here, particularly when the hot wind blows off the desert. How Karkara must have enjoyed having this sort of situation to work with for a change! My guess is that your best work in this little valley was at sundown, right? I can just imagine the laborers working feverishly just as the last rays of the sun faded, their bodies illuminated only by the light of the forges themselves. Am I right? Yes? Of course the wind changes direction at sundown in a valley like this. You'd have a natural breeze to sweep through the furnaces and blow the hot coals, and raise the temperature. . . ."

"Are you sure you've never worked in a forge?" Weret asked.

"Look at my hands. I've never worked at anything physical. You'll find a bit of callus there from the work details they put me on in the army, but otherwise I was a rich kid. No matter that I mixed with the poor because there's more to be learned from them than from my peers. I ran around in rags to mix with them more easily, but I could always retreat to my mother's house if I got too hungry, and my neighbors in the market couldn't. We were all in the same water, but I was swimming and they were drowning." He thought about that for a moment. "I can see now that was reprehensible. I could have alleviated a lot of suffering."

"Get to the point."

"Eventually the ideal furnace for this will be a tall structure with walls of stone, surmounted by a stone shaft about so high"—he held up his hand waist-high—"that you can use to charge the materials through, and with a tapping hole at the base for removing slag."

"You've just described a cross section of the forges we've built into the hillside here. Only we dug it into the stone instead of making it with bricks. Otherwise there's no dif—"

"And a very sound thing too. The natural breezes fan your fire." His brow knitted, and he seemed to be agonizing over something. "Confound it, there's something missing here. You've gone and got the stuff *too* hot, and that gives you iron that's hard but brittle. There has to be another stage." He sighed. "Or—what about the earlier stages? Look, what do you use for flux, to take away the slag and purify the iron?"

"Why . . . why, limestone. Limestone, good pure stuff from Abydos and Gebelein."

He frowned. "Nothing wrong with that. I'm told the Hittites, up along the shores, sometimes use crushed seashells. But that wouldn't be significantly better. You're doing nothing wrong there. What could it be? *Hmmmm.* If the ore contained a certain percentage of manganese and was free of impurities such as sulfur, arsenic, and phosphorus . . ."

He thought about it for such a long time that Weret, standing there looking at him, hands on hips, grew impatient. "What are you muttering about?" she demanded. "Manganese? What about manganese? What has that got to do with iron?"

He shook his head and frowned. "Oh, don't mind me. I was just speculating on a different process altogether. More charcoal, less ore. *Horribly* high temperatures. I haven't any idea how to get the temperature that high. If I could solve that problem . . . but no. Irrelevant. Pardon me. I go off on these wild-goose chases sometimes. I have this fantasy that I can solve all the problems of the world in my head, without experimentation. Sometimes I can, but it's unreliable in the long run. I'm going to have to get practical about this."

"You? Get practical? Look, you're a decent enough sort, and I have no wish to offend you, but—"

Seth held up his soft rich-man's hands and looked at them. "I think I'm going to have to get strong. I'm going to have to get my hands hard. Apparently this is what's necessary at this stage. Once we've won this war—"

"Won? You mean beat the Hai? Now I *know* you're mad."

"Oh, we'll win . . . sooner or later. We've found our leader, a chap named Kamose. We can rally around him. But a hero has to have a hero's sword, and that's why Baliniri sent Riki and me here. He knew that only one thing in the world would woo my cousin away from the nice safe world she's made for herself out here in the desert. Baliniri knew Netru, Teti's lover who died. He knew that Riki looks a bit like him. And—well, he's the same kind of person, really. Honest and loyal and true, the kind of straightforward fellow my cousin can trust. He knew she'd fall for him, and—"

"You! Shut up!" Weret put her hands over her ears. Her face was a mask of pain.

But as she turned away from him, she could look down the hillside path toward the oasis below and see Riki and Teti coming, holding hands. And what was that new element in Teti's manner? Was the stiffness, the pseudomasculine rough-and-ready air, gone? Was there a softness, a femininity, in her manner?

Weret stifled a cry of anguished rage and turned away, her hands balled into rock-hard fists, her whole body quaking with emotions she could not control, no matter how she tried.

V

Worse and worse: After a few moments Teti, yielding to the seriousness of the two men's mission to El-Dakhla, bustled Riki off in Weret's care while she herself talked with Seth. Weret bristled but said nothing: Teti was her leader, of course, not to be questioned or disobeyed. Weret stiffly led Riki away to show him the elaborate system of defenses that protected the oasis's last line of protection.

It could be worse, she was thinking. With specific orders to fulfill, she had been given a structure to follow and could thus avoid anything personal. It would take quite some time to explain the system of defenses that Teti had set up under the tutelage of both Ebana and Baliniri, and by the time she had explained and answered his questions, she hoped there would be little time for awkward, half-hostile attempts at small talk.

In practice, however, Riki proved a keen-eyed, quick-witted, and thoroughly professional soldier, a man who had evidently earned his general's baton despite his youth. The material she had hoped would take a couple of hours to pass along came and went in well under one hour, and to her intense annoyance, there was time to talk. She stalled as long as she could, telling of the network of outlying pickets who kept the inner circle informed of travelers and caravans via a system of signal fires. "By the time a caravan is within a day of us, we have them surrounded, outflanked, ready to kill or capture, as their intentions dictate. When they approach—"

"I understand," Riki said. "I was also trained by Baliniri and set up the defenses in the eastern desert too, just the way you're talking about, all along the routes to the Red Sea and the copper and tin mines. But thank you for explaining."

"Mines?" she said. Something took her fancy just then and she pursued it. "Copper? Tin? What else? I don't know the eastern desert at all."

"Lead and galena near the seacoast and, thank the gods, plenty of gold to pay for it all. Most of it's technically in Nubian lands, but—"

"Any manganese, perhaps?" she inquired a bit too innocently.

He missed the change of tone. "Not that I know of. Mostly precious and semiprecious stones and minerals. Amethysts. Malachite. Jasper and feldspar. Down the coast, small but important deposits of beryl and emerald. The best pottery clay in the world. Otherwise, building materials for the most part. Why?"

"Oh, nothing. But as I was saying—"

"Come, sit," Riki said, choosing a large stone under a spreading palm and sitting down. "I seem to have gotten off on the wrong foot with you. We share a number of concerns. We ought to be friends. How have I offended you?"

The question, far from putting her at ease, caused her to stiffen once more. He took note of the tension in her lean body. "There is no question of offense," she said. "I have my orders to—"

"Orders be damned. What's the matter? You lead a good life here. Do you think I'm here to take you away from it? I'm here to buy iron swords for our army. I have letters of credit from Thebes and can pay promptly. More specifically, I'm here to get Teti to make one specific sword. Something special. When I get it, I'll leave."

And she'll go with you, Weret thought bitterly. "For yourself, General?" she asked coldly. "Something to show off with?"

"You're out of line," he said quickly. "I'll forget you said that, but you'd best remember that this unit is still under Baliniri's command. I don't want to sound like a garrison-minded old martinet." He snorted. "The sword's for a chap named Kamose, who may wind up king of Egypt one of these days. He's the natural son of Apophis. Sekenenre has no proper male heir, having married a woman at the end of her childbearing years. Kamose can rally the Egyptians first to defeat the Hai, drive them back into the delta, and eventually out of Egypt altogether."

"So?"

"So he needs a sword. Something special. You know how the stories go—the hero has to be a mysterious fellow who appears from nowhere and turns out to have royal blood. He has to find a special weapon, one blessed by the gods. By following folk rules like these, we gain the confidence of the common people. We rally them around us."

"It all sounds so hypocritical."

"Perhaps, but it's also good thinking. You command troops. What lengths would *you* go to to motivate them if something really important were riding on it?"

Weret did not say anything for a long, long moment; then she looked at him with new respect and understanding. "I'd do whatever it took," she admitted. There was a sudden twinkle in her eye, although her face lost none of its hardness. "You wouldn't be working on this Kamose fellow the same way, would you? I mean, this 'special' sword. What does he care what sword he uses?"

"Other than its being made of iron, it doesn't matter to him. But it could mean something to his father and the Hai in general. Seth's learned something about them that they don't put out for public consumption. Something having to do with their fear of iron."

"Tell me about it," she said soberly. "I want to hear everything you've got."

By now both Seth and Teti were smeared with black virtually from head to foot. He had stripped to his loincloth and was covered with sweat, which turned to a mucky grease from the charcoal dust. "I don't understand how you knew," she marveled. "You've never worked iron, or any other metal. How could you have worked it out in your mind?"

"You know better than to ask me that. I've always had this gift to see into the middle of things. I can anticipate problems and often can find a way around them." He put down the tongs he had been holding, wiped his forehead (leaving yet another black smear across his face), and looked at her. "What was it like, Teti? I mean, out *there*."

"With Ketan? I've been trying to describe it to Riki. You know what it's like standing behind a big loom, the kind they use to make a rug or a wall hanging? You can only see the threads hanging, all knotted, all chaos, making no sense."

"Yes," he answered patiently. "And that's the way *this* life is, eh?" He smiled, and she smiled lovingly in return.

"Well, in *that* world you can walk out front and see the pattern, the pattern of *all* of it, from all the ages past and all ages to come. And, Seth, it's blinding! It's too beautiful and too fearful for words! It burned my mind . . . but I could feel no such fear or pain in Ketan's mind—just in mine. He was ready for it. I wasn't. Me, it hurt and frightened and excited. I think I used up all the emotions in that one moment of it. All but hatred."

"You saw all of it? The whole pattern?"

"Just a glimpse. It's as if it were still in my head, but

seen in a blur. Some of it I can't remember, or perhaps I don't want to remember it. I'm afraid to. But . . ."

"Yes?" His voice was low, and his eyes were intent on her face.

"Perhaps fear isn't the right word. Seth, what would *you* think if you knew how it was going to come out? Would *you* be afraid? Would you feel regret? Would you live in apprehension and terror, the way we do here in this world?"

Seth stood pensive for a long moment. "I don't think so. I think I would try to enjoy each moment as if it were my last. I think I would—" His eyes brightened. "I think, Teti, that I would try to go about my business just as before, because that would be what I was supposed to be doing. Because that would be part of the pattern. But I wouldn't feel frightened or sad about it, I don't think."

Teti's face was transfigured by a new light from within. Seth could almost feel it, her gratitude for his understanding. "That's the way it is with me, Seth," she said simply. "I . . . I know when I'm going to die, and how. But it doesn't bother me. And I know that the time has come, right now, for me to end my sheltered life out here in the desert. It's time for me to get back into the world, to get involved and take chances. Only you see, they're not chances anymore. They're the way things are. I have to accept them. And it doesn't bother me."

"Amazing!" he said softly. "This is why . . . you *have* decided on Riki, then? Just like that?"

"It's what the pattern shows me doing. That far I could see, and very clearly. And I can't tell you how happy I am about it. It's a very calm kind of happy. Seth, I know this person Riki. Not because I know anything about his past, but because I know something about his future. The pattern shows me being happy with him, until—" She smiled. "How I wish I could have seen a bit of your pattern, so that I could tell you about it. Perhaps I did, but could only focus on my part. Perhaps I'll get visions from time to time that will tell me a bit here, a bit there, about you, about other people whose lives touch mine."

Seth made a wry face. "And I'm sure you can't tell me anything about the solution to our problem here. I mean, how to make this 'perfect sword' for Kamose."

Teti put a kinswoman's friendly hand on his shoulder. Her smile was beatific, even under the layers of sweat and grease. "We don't need a perfect sword just yet. I think you and Riki have figured that out already. We just need to have one that will pass as one for now. The mere fact that it's of iron in the first place—even if the formula isn't perfect—will have some special magic connected with it. Mark my words, my dear cousin, that insight you got from the prisoner, back in the stockade, is *very* important. I can't fix the details in my mind exactly. Maybe I will if I think about it a lot."

"Do you know anything about what to do?"

"I . . . I don't know. There's something about a journey. A very great journey for you, one in which you—"

"Yes? Yes?"

Teti's face darkened just a bit. "I see. I see."

"What do you mean? Why can't you tell me?"

"You're not to know. Not through me. Not through anything but your own experience. To tell you would be to cheat you. You wouldn't believe me anyway. That's the way of things. The pattern doesn't show your knowing in advance. You have to live through it."

For the first time Seth showed his frustration openly. "Damn!" he said, pounding the forge's stone wall with his fist. "I understand what you're saying, but . . ." He shook his head. "All right. The question's off limits. Meanwhile, what do we do for a weapon for Kamose? We have to create something for when we leave tomorrow for Thebes. And before we do, we have to send a message to him in Nubia, through one of the Black Wind women in El-Kharga."

"I know. I'm coming with you."

He stared. "You are? But I thought—" He swallowed. "Of course. You said this life is over. It's time to move on."

"It is. The pattern shows it very clearly. I'll have to dress more modestly," she said with a slight giggle. "The desert favors getting back to basics, reducing everything to essentials. I got the idea for this life from Ebana and her warrior-women, and I've liked it very much." She sighed. "You know, I thought I was doing it because I was sick at heart from Netru's death. I didn't want another man, another attachment. I didn't want to take chances. I was afraid. The truth is, this interlude was part of the pattern. And it doesn't seem to matter, you know . . . whether I chose to live this way, or whether it was all preordained."

"Are you sure?"

"No. I keep thinking I did have choices, and I made them freely. But when I caught that one tantalizing glimpse of the pattern, I saw myself having done the things I did as if they'd been carved in stone a thousand years before I was born."

"Will you be leaving your women out here?"

"A token force. In order to police the desert routes, we don't need as many as we have now. But there is the chance that Apophis could move some units over the desert track from the Fayum and see if he could outflank us."

"But they won't get through?"

"No. I'll leave twenty women here. You know how vulnerable you were to us in the desert."

"Yes. The rest will come with you? Thebes will need every able-bodied soldier it can get."

"Of course. They're very good fighters, in or out of the desert. They were trained by the best. Baliniri used to sneak away out here when he took a holiday. People thought he was getting away by himself, I suppose. He was like a second father to me. I think . . ."

She stopped. Her eyes grew misty for a moment, and when she spoke again, there was a great gentleness in her voice. "I think he was in love with me, in a way, but daren't show it. Foolish girl that I was, I must have let him know I thought he was too old, a man of another generation. I hope I didn't hurt his feelings."

"He's a tough old bird."

"Not as tough as you think. But never mind. What do we do for a sword for your friend Kamose?"

Seth looked up and down the line of just-completed weapons gleaming in the afternoon sun. "The magic sword. The one that will win the battle at Thebes and perhaps kill Apophis. But no. That will happen later, in the delta, if The Prophecy's to be trusted." He turned to look at her. "Is it?"

She shook her head lightly. "I can't say. You know the rules."

"*Huh!*" There was the faintest hint of impatience in his voice. "Magic sword. One, two, three . . . damn it. I can't remember my counting rhymes anymore. I wasn't a child for very long, really. I never wanted to be one. I wanted to be grown up. I wonder if I ever will be. You couldn't tell me that either, could you?"

She laughed. She seemed to have lost ten years of her life and to stand before him young and fresh and proud again. And happy. Truly happy. She pointed at the swords on the ground. "Just pick one. Any old one."

"All right, confound it. *That* one." Totally arbitrarily.

"That one it is," she said in a voice with music in it. "Pick it up. We leave tomorrow at dawn."

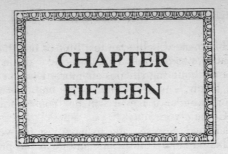

CHAPTER FIFTEEN

Avaris

I

The giant Buchis, after entering the alley circumspectly and slipping as unobtrusively down the passage as was possible for a man his size, finally rapped on the door. It opened a crack. He was instantly recognized and shown inside. But the moment the door was safely bolted behind him, a voice rang out, low but cutting: "All right, stop right there! Move a muscle, and you're a dead man!"

Buchis looked around him. All around the doorway men of the Brotherhood of Shai stood, their long compound bows drawn, their bronze-tipped arrows pointing at him. He blinked. One of the archer's forearms quivered with the effort required not to release the deadly bolt and let it drive into Buchis's heart.

The giant mimed incomprehension. Isesi stepped out of the shadows behind the archers. "If you want consideration from us," he said, "you'll have to ask for it. Aloud, Buchis, aloud."

352

Buchis pointed helplessly at his open mouth.

"That's no good anymore," Isesi said. "We know you can talk. Search him!" Rough hands probed his garments. He kept his hands high and his eyes on Isesi's face—but able every moment to see peripherally the drawn bows, the deadly shafts. "Come clean, Buchis. We know everything. I'm sure you have a lot to tell us."

Buchis sighed. "Tell them to put the arrows down. They make me nervous," he said in a great gentle voice. "I'm not going to do anything."

"Keep your weapons trained on him until he's in the inner room," Isesi ordered. "Then chain his arms and legs to the floor. Take no chances. Through here, Buchis, and don't make any hasty moves. Your size and strength aren't proof against six arrows in the heart."

Buchis went along with them and patiently let himself be chained to metal rings in the stone floor. The fifth chain connected to a neck manacle, which turned out to be too small to contain him, so this was left off. Sadly, Buchis looked at Isesi all the while. "How did you find me out? I thought I'd been so careful."

"You can't hide anything from Tchabu for long," Isesi explained. "He picks up emotions. Any that seem out of line, I ask him to concentrate upon."

Buchis nodded at the little cripple at Isesi's side. "My compliments," he said. "I suppose you're going to kill me."

"We'll see," Isesi replied. "I'm waiting to hear how much you tell us." He made a face. "And, I suppose, how much you've hurt us so far."

Buchis made a wry smile. "Hardly at all," he said. "I've been reporting to Joseph. And whether you know it or not, he's on your side. I've kept your secret from everyone in the world but him—and he hasn't told anybody, not even his brothers—not even his wife, for all I know."

"A likely story. If you expect—"

"You've got him wrong, all of you. You think he's just another foreigner intent upon wronging the Egyptians. Nothing could be further from the truth. He—"

"—is a foreigner whose huge family comes here and lives off the fat of the land while Egyptians starve," Isesi said harshly. "When we get rid of Apophis and restore the Egyptian monarchy, we'll know what to do with the likes of them."

"No! They bought their land! Paid the full price for it! Their dealings with the locals have been scrupulously honest and fair! Ask anyone who's dealt with them!"

"You're stalling. Tell us what you've told him so far."

Buchis's huge sigh seemed to fill the room. "I wish I could get you to believe me." Then he thought of something. "Look, Isesi! There's an important message I have to get to him! He's in great danger!"

"You're quite right he is," Isesi said. "Sooner or later. When our revolution is finally successful—"

"No! No! Right now! It's very important! I have to tell him—"

"You'll tell him nothing. What? Let you go now? Let you go report to him on our activities?"

"This doesn't concern you at all. If I could get the information to him in time, he'd be out of your way once and for all. Look, if you won't let me deliver the message, at least send one of your own men. But it's extremely urgent that he get the message, and immediately. I shouldn't even have stopped by here on the way. But—"

"Indeed you shouldn't," Isesi said with a chuckle. "But you did. And now we have you—the traitor in our midst."

"Traitor? You fool! I've been acting to protect you! Joseph told me to! He's on your side!"

Isesi let out a disgusted little snarl. "Sem, have one of the men interrogate him, and you come with me." He watched as Sem barked out an order, then turned his back on the big man chained to the floor. As he went out the door, he could hear Buchis still pleading for a chance to deliver his message.

In the well-guarded office in the rear of the building, Isesi reached up onto a shelf and pulled down a scroll from the tall stack. He unrolled it and studied it. As Sem came through the door Isesi said, "I know what you're going to say. It was I who trusted him. I'm to blame. You're quite right."

Sem's brow knitted. "He *could* be telling the truth. Joseph could very well be—"

"Bah! *All* foreigners out of Egypt, I say. Regardless of whether their manners are genteel or not. Do you know how

many years Egypt has suffered under the reign of foreign
princes and their foreign lackeys?"

"Everyone knows that, but—"

"The question's closed. Is that clear?"

"There was a time when you'd have been a bit more civil
about it," Sem said resentfully.

"Let's change the subject, eh? What do you hear about
Apophis?"

"Part of Buchis's message was that the king suddenly
decided to move early. Plans had been for him originally to
wait another three days. But last night he changed his mind.
The boats left at dawn."

Isesi frowned. "Let me think about that. What would
have made the king change his plans?"

"The arrival of the flotilla of mercenaries from Crete and
mainland Greece, I think. That'd put confidence into the
great coward, if anything would. But, Isesi—"

"Yes?"

"I wasn't supposed to tell you, but . . . Mara's hidden
herself to be with the flotilla. She's cut her hair off and is
disguised as a subpriest of Amon, come along to bless the
endeavor. She's bribed the priest she's supposedly serving."

Isesi stared. "A *priest*?"

"Yes. The priesthood are the only overdressed people in
the fleet. Under those long robes she can conceal her figure.
In virtually any other guise—"

"Yes, yes. I understand. Dressed any other way she'd be
raped a hundred times and tossed into the river to drown.
But—confound it! What a chance to take!"

"She wants to be at the kill with Kamose."

"Kill? There's a good chance Apophis could *win* this
time. I saw the manifest on that Hellenic flotilla. And this
new general Rasmik is no slouch. He's put new heart into
those troops who came straggling back here with their tails
between their legs after the battle of Lisht."

"And if he wins?"

Isesi looked at him. The anger was gone from his eyes
now, replaced by a combination of resigned apprehension
and stubborn determination. "A good question. We'll have
our hands full when he comes back downriver. All the more

reason to step up our present campaign." His eyes burned with a sudden and unreadable light. "I wonder how thin the city guard here will be a day or two from now. Apophis has raided them for more and more troops. If we were to strike now—"

"Strike?"

"Yes. What if, when Apophis came back downriver, there was nothing to come back to? What if we pushed back the deadline for our revolution? What if instead of doing it two years from now, as we'd planned . . ."

He let the question hang intently and studied the changing expression on Sem's face.

The brothers, mindful of Reuben's newly friendly relationship with his younger brother, had taken to sending him as go-between to Joseph. Now, as Joseph opened the front door of his villa to see Reuben standing there, he could see little trace in the rugged, weather-beaten old man of the rash youth who had made Jacob's life so difficult so many years ago. "Come in," Joseph said. "Is everything in readiness?"

"Yes. The advance tip on Apophis's early departure helped immeasurably. We're leaving from several different places at the same time to avoid drawing undue attention to ourselves."

"An hour from now, right?"

"Yes. I've distributed all the signed permissions to travel that you gave us. I hope this works. If it does, with any luck we could be across the border and well out into Sinai by—"

"But if it doesn't? I don't mean to alarm you, but this has been wearing away at me. I haven't slept a wink since we finally packed everything and made ready to go. With Petephres dead, I won't have his support at court to fall back on. If the smallest thing goes wrong—"

"Now don't get timid on us. Not at a time like this. Why, you've been a tower of strength—"

"Reuben," Joseph said. Reuben looked at his younger brother's face; suddenly it was an old man's, tired, fearful. "I've been trying to be stronger than I was all these years I've been in Egypt. I mean, before you came, before I became vizier. Going back to when I was still a slave, with my

master's love-starved wife always following me around wherever I went. I'm exhausted. I feel like a man who's been
drawing on the same dwindling account all these years and
has suddenly found out the reserves are gone, once and for
all."

"Don't be that way! We are all counting on you—"

"I know you are. But there's no disguising from myself
that—"

There was a knock on the door, bold, masculine, pe-
remptory.

The brothers stared at one another.

"I . . . I'd better answer it," Joseph said.

As he walked the long distance across the big room, the
sinking feeling was there again, the one that had kept him
awake all night. And suddenly he thought: *Am I having
another premonition, after all this time in which, despite all
my prayers, God has remained silent to me?*

He opened the door—and saw the soldiers. A dozen of
them, led by a Hai officer he did not know, a man armed to
the teeth.

"You're under arrest, sir," the officer said in a flat voice.
"By orders of the lord of Two Lands."

"That's absurd!" Joseph said, knowing somehow in his
heart of hearts that it was not, it was not at all. "If this is a
joke, it could cost you your position. I'd advise you to think
very carefully before—"

"That's all as may be," the officer said matter-of-factly.
"But my orders come directly from His Majesty. He called
me and the others together this morning before the boats
took off. He told each of us captains—"

"Each of you? What do you mean? Speak up, man!
You're speaking to the vizier of Egypt!"

"I may be, and then again I may not be. Yesterday you
were the vizier, and nobody but the king could say that you
weren't. Today you're just another foreigner under detention
for possible crimes against the country."

"Foreigner!" Joseph said in a large and terrible voice.
"You dare to use such a term!"

The soldier shrugged. "I'm to treat you with courtesy,
sir, unless you offer resistance. Those are my orders. So if

I've said anything to offend you, I'm sorry, sir. But the rest of the orders remain. I'm to detain you and your entire family and wait upon the pleasure of the king."

"My entire—?" Joseph exchanged glances with Reuben and saw the stunned look on his brother's face. "You mean—my wife, my sons, my—"

"Your brothers and their families and in-laws. And their entourages. There's a military detachment like this at the home of every one of them. And while I'm at it, sir, this place gives sign of a rather unusual sort of activity, sir. Pack animals all loaded as if going on a journey."

"That's none of your affair," Joseph said.

"Oh, yes it is, sir. I mean no disrespect, sir, but until I'm told differently by the king himself, everything about you and your family is very much my business. Now, sir, begging your pardon, I'll have the men inspect those pack animals and the rest of the house."

The word got back to Isesi almost immediately. He had his own spies, many of them in the army. "Sem!" he said, calling his friend in from the outer room to hear the news from the runner. "They've arrested Joseph! And his whole family!"

Sem did not show the shock he might have. "That could actually be a good sign. That's a big family. It'll further thin out the number of troops left here in the area. It'll weaken the local garrison—"

"You don't understand! He knows everything about us! What if Joseph decides to buy his freedom by turning us in?"

CHAPTER SIXTEEN

Upper Egypt

I

Six pickets belonging to Baliniri's army, stationed on both sides of the river below Lisht, went on duty at midnight two days after Apophis's great flotilla left the docks nearest Avaris. Their reliefs came on an hour after dawn and found all six lying dead, their throats cut. They had been attacked from behind by Hai assassins who came by land. And in the night the flotilla passed undetected.

Three miles below Lisht, still in darkness, the flotilla had joined with the left half of the two-pronged advance of the Hai's Fayum garrison, which had been brought up in great stealth. The right half of the pincer movement had, also under cover of darkness, moved into place just above Lisht. Without knowing it, the city garrison had been surrounded on two sides by a hostile and immeasurably superior force.

In the first clear and gentle light after dawn the two halves of the pincer movement came together and converged on the city. The surprise attack was as effective as the predawn tactics of the lone assassins had been. Outmanned, outweaponed, outmaneuvered, the Lisht garrison fought bravely for four hours. But without Baba of El-Kab, or Riki, or any other noteworthy leader to rally them, they were overrun and battered into submission. Surrender came at noon.

Apophis, in full war equipment, strode through the ranks of the prisoners, glaring at them with contempt. "There aren't very many of them," he observed to General Rasmik. "Surely Riki and Baliniri sent more than this number up against us?"

"These are the ones left alive," Rasmik said with some pride. "The smoke you see downstream is the pyre for the dead. We're burning the bodies downwind. The civilian population seems to have been evacuated earlier. The city has been systematically picked clean. They left nothing for us here but shelter. These defeated soldiers are all that's left." Magnanimously he added, "They fought honorably and well. I think that the best thing to do with them, Sire, might be to—"

"Impale them!" Apophis cried out. "All of them! Leave not a one of them alive! Leave the bodies on the stakes for the vultures to pick at. Make sure they can be seen from the river, every last one of them. I want the end result of opposing us to be visible to every fisherman who passes by."

"But, Sire, the rules of war—"

"Damn the rules! Do as I say! Every last man!"

The Hai army waited to leave until the next morning. Brought over from the Fayum were provisions ample enough to fuel the army through a long siege if one were necessary. But of course no one thought that Thebes would present much resistance. Not to *this* army, which had just destroyed the Lisht garrison and completed the job of securing the important food-raising lands south of Memphis for the Hai—and broken the back of the Upper Egyptians. With the Fayum in the hands of their enemies, the Upper Egyptians could be starved out quickly, even if they opted to defend Thebes, and even if they showed mettle in this.

In the morning the ships sailed again, this time manned by a force twice the size of the one that had just sailed upriver from Avaris. The line of sharpened stakes, each decorated with its grisly burden, was clearly visible from quite a distance upstream, and the vultures were already beginning to gather hungrily on the shore. Lisht itself had been set on fire just as the boats cast off, and the morning breezes were beginning to fan the flames to a terrible heat.

The smoke from Lisht's burning was visible to the next line of pickets upriver. They quickly and correctly guessed what had happened and lit signal fires to inform the others upriver, even before the sails of the victorious fleet came in sight.

Thus the news was in Thebes by day's end. It caused panic in the city. No one had expected the Hai to get past Lisht, not after the terrible beating they had taken only a short time before. Fear set neighbor against panic-stricken neighbor. There were fights, riots, and incidents of looting. The guardsmen were called into the city to restore order, and several civilians were killed before some semblance of calm was achieved.

The night was worst of all, with outlaw gangs roaming the streets, out of control. Details of guardsmen prowled in search of them, but there were half a dozen rapes, a murder, and many robberies. The bad element simply had to be cut out of the city. Baliniri visited the central headquarters of the guardsmen and laid down the law: Anyone caught violating the curfew would be nailed to the outside of the city wall, spread-eagled, spikes through his hands and feet, and left to the tender mercies of his fellow criminals. By morning order had been restored, but the carnage around the city wall was horrible to behold. The jackals and hyenas had left little for the birds to devour.

And with the dawn, Baliniri's captains had secured their posts and called out every available man for help, including the sick, the lame, and the elderly. Shuttle boats had begun crossing the river in a continuous stream, carrying the women and the children to the supposedly safer haven of Deir el-

Bahari. But no one in his right mind believed that he would find safety just by crossing the river. Most were content with the notion that, on the western bank, at least, they would not be underfoot and hamper the army's efforts.

Even when the panic had passed, there seemed to be a dark cloud of doom over Thebes, a cloud betokening impending defeat and death, or enslavement. With Lisht fallen, no one seriously believed that Thebes could be defended. Or that the Hai could be driven away as they had been before. And in a hundred shrines large and small on both sides of the river, not only Amon but all the gods of the Egyptian pantheon were being invoked and asked for succor all over the area. *Save us, O mighty one! Rain fire on the head of the heathen! Make his arm weak and his body weary! Spread confusion in his mind, fear in his heart, and weakness in his belly!*

From her curtained compound on the roof, through the latticed wall that separated the harem from the rest of the palace, Queen Ah-Hotep, both wife and cousin to the great king, Sekenenre, watched as her young husband, fifteen years her junior, purified himself at the shrine, preparatory to going to war to defend the country his father, Dedmose, had reigned over so long and well.

It was curious, she was thinking. She had known Sekenenre all his life. She distinctly remembered the day of his birth: It had been the same day she had been betrothed to Shishak, who should have become king but had died in the same year as his father. She had known Sekenenre so long, she had thought she had known everything there was to know about him.

But what a surprise to find that the sheltered young man, even now seemingly hardly out of his boyhood, had in him the soul of a fighter! He had been so withdrawn and retiring all his life. But on the day he had seen the fall of the border garrison, witnessed the deaths of Mekim and Baka, and had rallied the soldiers at Lisht, he had really come into his manhood and had spent a good part of every day in ardent practice with the weapons he had disdained so long, grunting and sweating like a raw recruit in his own army. And from what Daliniri had said, the king was actually making rapid progress with the sword and battle-ax. Who would have believed it?

She looked, however, at his thin, reedlike body as she thought of this, and a sudden wave of apprehension swept through her. *He's still not strong enough! He won't have a chance against those brutes! Against the likes of that horrid usurper Apophis, half again his size.*

Her eyes widened. She remembered the absurd personal challenge Apophis had sent her husband a while back, ordering him to silence the crocodiles in his private pond and let him, Apophis, get some sleep. Sekenenre, taking the thing for what it was worth—the bluster of a Hai parvenu— had sent back some sort of sarcastic response full of mock weeping and false contrition. "Crocodile tears," some had called the message.

But now it appeared that the challenge had been made in deadly earnest, and that Sekenenre was accepting it that way. He was preparing for war. He was preparing for death.

She shuddered, remembering those thin, weak arms of his from last night's embrace and then, by contrast, remembering the rock-hard, thick, powerful arms of the burly soldier she had taken as her secret love in her long-gone youth. Now, Baba—*he* could have handled Apophis with ease! With that mocking grin on his face all the while!

Ah, Baba of El-Kab! What a memory to take into your old age! Ever since circumstances had forced them to part, she had hardly gone a day without thinking of him, of his stout, hard-muscled body, his bowed legs and round, humorous, likable face—and the vigorous virility he had brought to their dangerous liaison.

How she had loved him! And how devotedly, how passionately he had responded in kind! To be sure, it had not been *he* who had seduced *her*. She smiled secretly, remembering. She had contrived every way she could to show herself naked before him and had finally stepped out of her bath as bare as an egg and walked into his embrace, feeling the press of his hard body under its soldier's tunic against her damp nudity.

She sighed long and deep. But of course it could not have lasted for long—not with him a commoner and her the daughter of a king's brother, herself promised to a king's son. And when he had requested a transfer far away—the both of them heartbroken at this, but aware of the dangers if he had stayed—and she had turned up pregnant, it had taken some very agile maneuvering on her part to get her sent to the family manor at the El-Kharga oasis, ostensibly for a change of air to fight the lung disease she had had as a child—but actually to have her baby in absolute secrecy and give it to another woman to raise as her own.

She bit her lip, thinking, as she had done so many times before, about that lost son. What had happened to him? Had he lived to adulthood? What kind of man was he now? Would he, grown, look like her or like Baba?

And would he have learned by now that the woman Net was not really his mother? Would Net, or perhaps the servant Maryet, who had been paid to stay with her and help raise the child, have told the boy who he was?

But no. They were sworn to silence. They would not dare. And so the lad would have grown to adulthood thinking he was of common blood, thinking that his father was—who? On whom would Net have blamed his advent?

Oh, how cruel it was to have the son of your flesh, the son fathered by the only man you had ever loved, raised away from you, so that you could never know him and he could never know you. To have him, a child with royal blood in his veins—yes, and the blood of a hero too, one of the greatest heroes of all—growing up thinking himself the bastard son of a nobody!

How old would he be, now? Why, he would be one year younger than her husband! What a strange juxtaposition that made!

Fate, she thought. *How cruel! How heartless and merciless!*

Baliniri was waiting outside the king's chamber when the purification ceremony was over. "Sire," he said, "the city is secure—at least as secure as I can get it at the present juncture. It's time to get the royal family across the river to safety." He frowned. "I wish you'd let me send them upriver to some *real* safety."

"We mustn't have the people thinking that the royal family isn't sharing their dangers and woes," the king responded. "No, my friend. If Thebes stands or if Thebes falls, the house of Dedmose will share its fate. And I with it."

"If only you would reconsider."

"I won't and that's that. Now let me hear about the disposition of troops, the—what's the term?"

"Order of battle, Sire."

"Yes. I keep forgetting." His smile was warm, confident, totally endearing. Baliniri had never liked Sekenenre more. "I wonder sometimes what it would have been like, Baliniri, if I'd been born poor, as you were, and you instead of me had been born to royal things, to a future like mine. You'd have made a fine king, I think: You're an able administrator and a good judge of men. But would I have made any kind of soldier at all, I wonder?"

Baliniri did not allow himself even the ghost of a smile. It would have been an insult to a valued and respected friend. "You might well have made a good officer, Sire."

Sekenenre's smile showed that he knew what was going through his vizier's mind. "But not a real soldier, eh? A staff man, not a fighting soldier? Well, so much for my attempts at self-delusion. This is no time for fooling myself. It's time for relentless, hard, ice-cold realism. All the better, my friend." He clapped Baliniri familiarly on the arm, and Baliniri winced at the thought: How weak that hand was! How ill-equipped to hold a sword, an ax, a spear! And how brave the heart that knew this, but refused to walk away from the challenge!

"Come, Sire," he said with respect and affection. "I'll take you to the staff offices. The maps are there. And I'll fill you in as we go. We're going to give them a fight they'll never forget, however it comes out!"

II

They stood to one side, away from the long line of people waiting to take one of the boats across the river to Deir el-Bahari: Tuya, Meni, Cheta, and Kedar. Their meager belongings—each person was allowed to bring out only as much as he or she could carry—were piled beside them neatly.

Tuya looked impatiently up at the sun. "It's getting late," she said. "I wonder where she is? Oh, what a fool I was, Kedar, not sending someone after her! With things the way they are in the city streets—"

"Oh, I'm sure there's no danger of that kind," Kedar said in that calm, understated voice of his. "The guardsmen are on every block. Baliniri's not letting anyone get away with—"

His voice continued, but she could no longer hear it, for she had noticed on the quay, trailing a retinue of tough-looking guardsmen armed to the teeth, the vizier himself. He was heading her way, and he had seen her. She suddenly wished she had the power to disappear altogether, to melt away like the dew; and as much as she wished to look away and feign not having seen him, she found she could not.

"Ah! My lord!" Kedar said, bowing. "I'm afraid I was just speaking of you. We are honored—"

Baliniri gave Kedar no more than a friendly nod and a half smile. "Tuya," he said. "I've been going around, checking on my friends. I'm glad to see you're on your way. Is everything all right?"

Tuya tried to speak, but it came out a hoarse croak. She tried again. "Oh, yes," she said in a not very convincing voice. "Thank you, Baliniri. We're due to go over as soon as the nurse arrives with Ketan's child. They were supposed to be here by now. . . ."

He caught the note of apprehension in her voice and without further ado beckoned to one of the burly guardsmen behind him. "Captain!" he said. "I need an escort for someone, immediately. A woman carrying an infant." He quickly gave Ketan's address from memory, and the officer set off toward the city without another word. Baliniri turned to Tuya again. "I heard about your—problems. The next time you have any trouble with anything, please be quicker to call for me."

"I didn't want to bother—"

"Nonsense. I still consider myself your friend—whether you think that way or not—and I'm still the representative of your king. The safety and well-being of each one of his subjects is my concern." They locked eyes for a moment, and he started to say something else again, but his voice, soft and low, was drowned out by the sound of rough voices nearby: a platoon of soldiers being called to assist in the loading of the boats.

Baliniri let it pass. He looked at Meni. "So this is the lad," he said. "My soldiers told me a lot about you, son. You're brave. Very brave. You struck a good blow."

"Thank you, sir," Meni replied. "I was very frightened, but there was no time to think about that. With someone trying to hurt Tuya—"

"I know. But a real man rises above his fear." Over the boy's head Baliniri's eyes engaged Tuya's. "Particularly when a woman's safety is concerned." He looked back at the boy again, smiling. "I understand Tuya is going to adopt you. I'm glad." He looked at Tuya again. "And you've announced intentions to marry. My best wishes."

"Thank you," she said. Embarrassed, she turned and indicated Kedar. "This is my husband-to-be, Kedar the scholar. Kedar, you have, I think, met the lord Baliniri?"

"Yes, my dear," Kedar said. "My pleasure, sir."

Now Baliniri's eyes caught hers again and much, very much, passed between them in the way of complete understanding. Mirrored in Baliniri's mildly shocked eyes, she saw herself as she was: a middle-aged woman marrying an old man in a passionless union. A woman settling for less. She knew that Baliniri saw this and could not help thinking the less of her for it. *Ah, Baliniri! If only . . . if we had just . . .*

"Oh, look, Tuya!" Kedar's voice broke in, as dry as dust as always. "Here they come! The child and the nurse and . . . there seems to be someone with them."

Baliniri turned. "Ah! Captain! You found them."

"Yes, sir. And this lady was helping them. The nurse had

taken a spill in the street. This lady was helping her when I arrived. I thought it best to give her an escort to the boats while I was at it. She doesn't seem to have anyone."

But it appeared Baliniri recognized the girl. "Aset! This is a pleasant surprise! I thought you'd have been across the river by now."

Tuya, sharp-eyed, looked the girl over. Was there something going on between— But no, the girl just appeared to be someone Baliniri knew. The wife of a friend, perhaps. "Maybe she'd like to come with us? Anyone who helps Ketan's child is a friend of ours. Baliniri, introduce us, would you, please?"

"Certainly. Tuya, this is Aset. She was instrumental in bringing Kamose to Upper Egypt. She was one of the liberators of the Children's Refuge in Avaris. Aset, meet Tuya, widow of the late court armorer Ben-Hadad. And this is Kedar the scholar."

"My pleasure," the girl said. Tuya decided she liked Aset's clear-eyed smile. An honest person, and a gentle soul, it would appear—sensitive, but as brave as a lioness.

"I'm so pleased to meet you," Tuya said, thinking that Aset looked as if she had been hurt by someone or something recently. "Come with us, won't you? You don't want to have to stay at one of the shelters on the other side. I've a whole villa to myself, and we'd be delighted to have you. Where's Kamose?"

"I wish *I* knew the answer to that," Baliniri said with a tense sigh. "Him, or Riki. We need both of them right now, with or without the reinforcements I sent them after. I sent Kamose to Nubia to ask Nehsi to join us here. I sent Riki after Teti."

"Teti! I'd thought perhaps she'd married and moved away. Where is she?"

Baliniri laughed, but as he did, his eyes scanned the river. Far away, a tall plume of smoke rose above the northern hills where the Nile wound its way through the red rocks. "No, no," he said. "She's making iron in the desert, surrounded by a band of warrior-women. She's my secret weapon. But if she doesn't get here in time . . . well, I was counting on Riki to get her here. I was counting on that wonderful charm of his. I hope he doesn't let me down." He glanced downriver again nervously. "Captain! That signal smoke . . . can you make it out yet?"

"No, sir. Just the first greetings so far."

"Keep an eye on it. Tell me what it says." He turned back to Tuya. "Ah, here's your boat, I think. I recognize Ben-Hadad's seal on the prow. Have a safe passage, all."

He bowed and joined the captain, searching the northern horizon. As Tuya and the rest began to load their possessions on the boat, she heard scraps of their conversation:

". . . so soon! I was hoping it'd take another half day at least. . . ."

". . . alert the king. Battle stations on all units. On the double!"

Tuya, shocked, looked downriver herself. Nothing was in sight yet, but she could see the signal very clearly now: dark puffs of smoke, emitted at differing intervals, drifting heavenward. Behind her the captains were barking orders at their men. There was a woebegone wail from one of the women on the boats. Suddenly there was activity all along the waterfront.

The war had come! The war had come to Thebes!

From the roof of the palace, Sekenenre also saw the signal. He had no idea what the exact meaning might be, but the general message was quite clear.

He sighed, then smiled sadly. "So it's come," he said very softly to himself. His thin fingers drummed on the parapet, and his eyes strained for the first signs of hostile sails on the river.

It was odd how little apprehension he felt now. Instead of fear and foreboding, he felt as if something good were coming, something to which a man might look forward with eager anticipation rather than fright and dread.

Perhaps this was bad. Perhaps it was wrong for a king to look on the matter as hardly more than a personal contest, one in which he might at least test his mettle. After all, if the Hai won this battle, Thebes would fall, and the victors and their barbaric mercenary cohorts would savage his city and his people. There would be rapes and murders and torture, and all sorts of barbarity practiced upon the poor and defenseless, and the rich as well: against his wives, against his daughters.

He shuddered. And once again he thought: *I should have sent them all to safety. Perhaps there's still time.* . . .

But no. The word had already got out that the king and his family would share the fate of Thebes, and the story had given heart to all those who had not left the city. It had also given heart to his army, and when he had spoken to them yesterday—a good, rousing speech, if he did say so himself— they had cheered him long and lustily, as they had never cheered his father. And now he could not back down from this position.

He found the darker thoughts slipping willy-nilly into his mind, thoughts of death, defeat, destruction. He closed his eyes and cursed the demons that had put the negativism into his heart.

He would probably die today.

He would probably die, not as a man of power and riches usually dies, in his bed, gently, easily, with friends and relations hovering over him and easing his way out of this life with soft and honeyed words.

He would probably die violently, at the hands of a vicious, half-insane barbarian who, having stabbed him to the heart, would cut his head off and display the ghastly relic atop a pike to cheer his men and throw fear and dread into the hearts of the Egyptians.

His violent passage to the Netherworld and the violation by Apophis's sword of his broken body would send his spirit to the dark lands, unable to rest in peace.

Stop it! he told himself angrily. He must not give way like this. He must not let the unknown fears get to him. It would weaken his men's ability to function under the deadly assault. He must be brave. Brave for the army, brave for his people, brave for himself. He must summon from somewhere the strength and the courage to face this—

"Husband?" ventured a soft voice behind him.

He wheeled. Ah-Hotep, his wife of wives despite her barrenness, stood watching him, her hands folded before her breasts. There was a look on her face he could not read accurately. Then she smiled. "I wanted to speak to you before they came. Do I intrude?"

A wave of sudden affection rushed through him. "Intrude? Of course not," he said, and came forward to embrace her. Standing with his arms around her, he drew new strength from her warmth. "Of all the people in the world I might wish to join me just now," he said fervently, "none could come before you. Thank you for coming to me."

She stepped back, holding his hands. He could see the signs of the years on her, the wrinkles here and there, the coarsening of her skin, but they were no more than welcome reminders of the happy years they had had together. She had been married to him when he had been hardly more than a child—and he had grown up with her. She was, and had remained, all women to him: wife, mother, concubine, and lover. When her barrenness had forced him to take other wives in search of the son he never had, he had serviced them dutifully, but it had been her bed that he had always come back to for his pleasure.

"I had this premonition—" he began.

"Don't think about it," she said. "Think about coming home to me, victorious."

He looked at her. And somehow, some inner voice inside him told him that somewhere, at some time in her remote past, she had said those same words to another man. Perhaps not while she was married to him, but there had definitely been another man. A strong man, perhaps: a burly and powerful soldier, the sort of person you would say such things to. He wondered if she sometimes compared him with this earlier lover, compared the strong arms of the soldier with his own weak ones.

"I wanted you to know," she confided, "that although we were mated at another's command, although you did not pick me out, and I did not pick you, fortune favored me. How could I have known how happy you would have made me? How could I possibly have divined, so many years ago, the richness and the variety and the pleasure I've derived from our time together?"

"My dear," he began, hoarse voiced, "I—"

She put two soft fingers over his mouth. "I just wanted

you to know. Once and for all. If fortune parts us, I want that
to be the thought you carry with you when we are torn apart.
If you return to me, I want you to know that the woman to
whom you return is grateful and loves you."

She kissed him, embraced him warmly, and went away.

And when he turned back toward the parapet, the Nile
was full of warships with broad sails, warships that bore the
Hai colors.

War! War had come to Thebes!

III

From his vantage point atop the Temple of Amon, Baliniri
could see the ships maneuvering toward the shore. He looked
down at the next to the lowest level, where his archers stood
poised, arrows nocked but their bows undrawn. He shook his
head no. *Let the bastards get closer,* he thought. But his
hands flexed, and tension tightened his broad shoulders. Idly
he rehearsed once more in his mind the system of hand
signals through which he would relay orders to his subordinates. And, not idly at all, he wondered for the fiftieth time
where Kamose was and why the blazes Riki had not joined
him by now. Damn it, this was no time for procrastination!
This was—

"Sir," the officer below called up to him, a note of
urgency in his voice. "Now? They're almost to shore."

"All right," Baliniri said. And his hand went up, palm
facing forward. He watched the enemy boats steering to
shore. *"Now!"* he roared, his arm sweeping down. The bows,
bent at his first command, released their arrows. The shafts
arched high in the air and fell silently, gracefully, onto the
men in the first boats.

Simultaneously with the falling of the arrows, Baliniri's
drums began, and as they picked up the pace of their pounding, the men in the rear let out the high-pitched wail of the
Nubian soldiers, the war cry old Musuri, Akhilleus's long-

term second in command, had learned far up the Nile and brought back to teach to the soldiers of Upper Egypt.

The effect was striking—the more so because the archers' arrows had found their marks. The decks of the first boats now bore many fallen bodies, and even from his lofty perch atop the temple Baliniri could see the blood spreading beneath the dead and wounded.

Baliniri's hand went up, this time with his fingers balled into a fist. As the first boats touched the quay, his hand swept down. And now, from the massed ranks of the infantrymen who formed the first line of defense, spears flew through the air. As Baliniri watched, one of them caught a young Hai subaltern and ran him through. The force of the blow threw him violently back against his mates, and he was dead before the strong hands that caught him could lower him to the ground.

Baliniri's left arm went up, fingers splayed. Then the right went up beside it. He moved each arm in a rough circle, then let both fall together.

Now the flankers attacked from two sides. As the first Hai troops swarmed onto the shore, they were struck from the right and left. The wailing rose to a fevered pitch as the drums pounded!

Now other ships were steered to land. Baliniri counted them, and his heart sank as he made a quick estimate of their superior strength. And more were coming from farther downstream.

Below, on the quays, the flanking attack had driven the invaders back a trifle, but other ships were now landing, coming to the rescue of their compatriots. Baliniri looked down at the bowmen again, making the sign to draw bows. His arms flashed down, the arrows sped to their marks, and on the ships yet to land, men clutched their breasts and fell. . . .

Well out on the river, one ship anchored just out of the main current. Anchors fell fore and aft to stabilize it at one position, opposite the fighting. Atop the high poop of this command ship Apophis shaded his eyes and scowled at the scene before him. "Fight, you cowards!" he screamed at the men of the front ranks. "Press on! Damn you! Take the quay!"

Beside him Rasmik stood silently, watching the scene. As Apophis paused to catch his breath, the general said, "Sire, they're doing quite well. A little patience—"

Apophis's fist pounded on the railing. "Patience! When I see them faltering like a bunch of unfledged striplings—"

"In fact, they're performing a bit better than I had expected. I had allowed for the total loss of the first five ships. Now it looks as though we'll lose one, perhaps two. And look, Sire, our left flank is advancing while their right wing is falling back. If the other flank can do as well, we'll have the quay totally cleared in a matter of moments!"

Apophis stared . . . and smiled. "You're right! They're pressing forward! They're taking the quay!"

"Yes, Sire," Rasmik said mildly. "It'll be ours quite soon, if they've no other tricks up their sleeves over there." He stopped, paused a moment thinking, then swore softly under his breath. "Confound it! The old fox!"

"Eh?" Apophis said.

"I see what he's up to. He wants deliberately to fall back one level at a time, drawing us toward him. Then as we follow him into the abandoned city, we'll find it's not so abandoned after all. It'll be full of experienced street fighters who have the advantage of knowing the city plan. There'll be a hundred ambushes, one at every street corner. Exactly what I'd have done myself if I were the one under siege." He pounded one balled fist against the other palm. "He learned that one at the siege of Mari, when he was on the receiving end of the ambushes."

The corners of Apophis's mouth drew downward. "Do you mean he's drawing us into a trap?"

Rasmik smiled sourly, grudgingly. "Yes, Sire." He pointed to the group atop the great Temple of Amon. "There he is, giving them orders. See?"

"Yes, yes. I see him. But where's Sekenenre? He's the one I want. Unless he's turned tail like a coward and gone slinking out of the city."

"I don't see him, Sire. But look. Our men are advancing

too quickly. I don't like that. Sire, I think I'd better get to shore and take charge. Orderly!"

An aide appeared at his elbow. "Yes, sir?"

"Sound the horn to fall back!" The aide blinked, stared. "Damn you, did you hear me? The horn to fall back! Now!"

The king joined Baliniri atop the parapet, wearing the uniform of an officer of Upper Egypt. "What are they doing?" he asked. "I don't understand. They were winning. They were beating us. Why would—"

"We were letting them advance," Baliniri said. "I wanted to suck them into the city, where our cutthroats could deal with them one squad at a time. But it seems this Rasmik fellow's no fool. He won't take our bait."

"Bait? But—"

"I've got to figure out something to lure them in. Men!" he spoke to the aides and staff officers standing beside them. "Have you any ideas?"

There were no solutions offered.

"Luring them into the city is one way of handling it. But there's another, I believe, and maybe it's time I intervened," Sekenenre said. "Even a king has to pull his own weight in a fight like this."

"Sire, I don't understand."

"Look! Apophis's boat! It's drawing anchor! It's coming to land! That's he atop the poop, isn't it?"

"Yes, Sire, but—"

"Messenger! Get me a messenger!"

A runner stepped forward and stood stiffly at attention. "Yes, Sire!" he said.

"Memorize this message to Apophis: Tell him your master greets him with scorn, hatred, and small regard. Tell him that if he delivers his own person into the hands of our guards for public execution before the shadow of the temple disappears, the rightful lord of Two Lands will consider the possibility of sparing his men and allowing them to return to their homes untouched."

"But, Sire—" Baliniri began.

"Don't interrupt me." He spoke to the runner again.

"Tell him your master does these things to allow him to save face and to spare him the necessity of running away from the fight in abject fear, as he did at Lisht. Have you got that?"

"I think so, Sire."

"Tell him that things might have worked out differently if he had been a man, and not the diseased offspring of a one-*outnou* Hai slut who mated with a three-legged donkey in a sexual exhibition staged for a convention of Nubian dealers in hog manure."

"Sire—"

"Don't stop me, Baliniri, I'm just getting wound up. I'm just beginning to have some fun." To the runner he said, "Have you got that, my friend?"

"Yes, Sire. Dealers in hog manure."

"*Nubian* dealers in hog manure. You know what the Hai think of the blacks."

"Yes, Sire. Nubians."

"Very well," Sekenenre said. He looked Baliniri in the eye.

"Sire," Baliniri said softly, "I know what you're up to, and I absolutely forbid it."

"You can't forbid it. I can countermand any order you give. Who's the king here? All I have to do is say the word, and these officers will kill you. Don't make me do anything rash, Baliniri."

Baliniri stared silently at his king, a look of great concern on his face.

Sekenenre went on. "Very well. Tell the Shepherd impostor—be sure to use that word, unless you can think of something worse—that if he were a man with the full count of arms, legs, and sexual appurtenances, rather than the hunch-backed spawn of beast and whore, he would meet me man to man, weapon for weapon, before the walls of Thebes. And fight until one of us was dead."

"Sire!" Baliniri objected. "I can't—"

The king ignored his general. "Now, runner, have you got that?"

"Yes, Sire."

"Then deliver it. And when you've finished, spit at his feet, and tell him that I told you to do so."

"Yes, Sire."

Baliniri and the young king locked eyes. There was a strange look on Baliniri's face. If it had been anyone else but the battle-hardened conqueror of Mari, one would have thought he was no more than the blink of an eye away from weeping.

From atop the bluff, a league downriver, Riki and Teti stood looking down at the boats on the river. "Gods!" Riki gasped. "We're too late! They're here already! Now how are we going to get across the river with them blocking the quay like that? We can't just sail right through them."

Teti smiled. "Weret!" she said in the voice of command.

"Yes, mistress?"

"You and Seth take one detachment and sail behind them. Fire their ships with flaming arrows."

"Yes, mistress!"

"If you can fire the whole fleet, so much the better."

"Yes, mistress."

"Riki and I and the rest will swim the river. You do swim, Riki?"

"I'm kin to the fish."

"Very well. Do you have your sword? Good. Sling it around your neck."

He grinned. "I'm supposed to be in charge here. But you seem to know what you're doing."

She winked at him, smiling. "A wise commander who finds such a subordinate always knows when to let her have her head. And of course you're the wisest of commanders, my love." She leaned forward and spoke in a whisper, for his ears only. "Don't forget. I know how this will come out. I know what to do, my darling. This much I remember very vividly." She turned to Seth. "Here! Take Kamose his sword! Tell him what he needs to know!"

Burly, heavy-shouldered, weighing in at perhaps twice the young king's fighting weight, Apophis lumbered to shore. He wore the heavy helmet of the Hai, and forearms and shins were protected by greaves of bronze. But what caused the

murmur of chagrin from Sekenenre's camp was the body
armor on which the sun shone brightly. "Sire!" Baliniri said.
"Your sword won't have any effect on his armor!"

Sekenenre smiled. "That's all right. The armor will also
slow him down. It'll play to my strength." At the word
"strength" Baliniri, despite himself, found his eyes instinctively going to the king's skinny biceps, bared by the brief
fighting costume of an Egyptian officer. "I'm very quick. The
more he's weighted down, the easier it will be to dance
beyond his reach."

"But he has the choice of weapons, Sire. The Hai sword
is longer than ours. He'll be able to reach you when you're
beyond reaching him."

But now, fifteen paces away, Apophis's hand went to his
side and slowly withdrew the weapon of his choice from its
hanger.

Sunlight glinted on its bronze length.

The ax! The dreaded Hai battle-ax!

IV

Baliniri felt a new respect for his king but also felt it
incumbent upon him to try to talk Sekenenre out of this
suicidal challenge. "Sire," he pleaded, "you can't—"

"The battle-ax isn't my weapon," the king admitted affa-
bly. "To be sure, it's the one with which I am least profi-
cient. Nevertheless, he does have the choice under the rules.
And above all men, kings must obey rules or lose honor." He
smiled at his second in command, and the fear left even his
eyes now. "I'm afraid I didn't bring an ax to the battle," he
said. "Could I perhaps borrow yours, old friend?"

"Of course, Sire. Is this necessary? You don't have to—"

"Ah, but I do. Ah, yes, a fine weapon." He hefted the
heavy ax; Baliniri looked at the slender arms with foreboding.
"Now, a buckler, I'd say. Captain? Could you be so kind as
to—"

The officer indicated handed over his shield. Baliniri gauged the weight of weapon and shield together. The king's forearms would tire quickly, carrying loads like these into battle. "Sire," he said, "if you must do it, a word of advice: Watch his eyes. And remember the trick of feinting with the buckler. You can sometimes knock a man off balance—"

"Too late for advice, old friend," said the king. He looked out at the towering Apophis now, at the great barrel chest encased in the distinctive Hai body armor. "However I fare, Baliniri, sell the city dearly. Take as many of their lives as you can."

"The walls will be awash with foreign blood," Baliniri vowed fervently. "Sire, I . . ." His voice broke, and he balled his fists so tightly for a moment that his arms shook. Eyes closed, he mastered himself, then reached to clasp the king's hand. "Sire . . ." he began again, but fared no better in this attempt.

"I understand," Sekenenre said kindly. "Look after my wife. I have no son. See that a suitable—" He bit off the words and forced his features into a smile.

"Farewell, Sire," Baliniri said, blinking away tears.

The drumming and the shrill yells had stopped. In a strange and unearthly silence, the two rulers emerged from the ranks of the opposing armies and walked slowly, easily, to the appointed place—a great semicircle before the great gates of Thebes.

"Well, well," Apophis said, a black sneer on his face. "I hear no boasts. I hear no taunts. Does the popinjay grow silent when faced with a real, live, flesh-and-blood enemy? Has the cat perhaps got his tongue? Or is his mouth frozen with fear?"

After the boom of Apophis's great bass voice, the light tenor of Sekenenre sounded more boyish than ever. "I talk when it is time to talk," he said. "I fight when it is time to fight. Perhaps the customs are different where the Hai come from. Or do we mistake one another? Did the herald perhaps garble my message? Or should we throw away these our weapons and argue one another to death?"

There was a murmur from both armies.

"Very well, my little bird," Apophis growled. "If it's fight you want, let's fight!"

And he attacked!

It was surprising how fast the big man could move. Two steps took him to within reach of Sekenenre. His vicious swing of the ax would have cut a less agile man in two; but Sekenenre danced lightly out of the way and, not even bothering to parry, reached way out over Apophis's shield and lightly knocked the Hai leader's helmet off.

Apophis's eyes blazed with rage. He did not bother to retrieve the helmet. He swung again, and once again Sekenenre was no longer there.

"I could have brained you," Sekenenre said. "I just wanted to show you I could touch you any time I wanted to. Like this!" And, feinting first high, then low, he suddenly lashed out with a sandaled foot and kicked the ax out of Apophis's grasp.

There was a roar of approval from the Egyptian side. "Now!" Baliniri bellowed. "Now! Finish him now!"

But here Sekenenre's inexperience in the art of fighting seriously and to the death betrayed him. Gallantly he let Apophis retrieve his weapon.

"You've made your first mistake," Apophis said from between clenched teeth. "It may well be your last." Taking a fresh grip on the ax, he advanced one step at a time, methodically swinging, swinging.

Sekenenre gave ground, parried with his own ax, and turned another swing aside with his buckler. So far he had not struck even the first blow.

"Sire!" Baliniri cried. "Look out! Watch his other hand!"

It was almost too late. Suddenly Apophis swung the buckler instead, slamming it into Sekenenre's own shield. The contact jarred him badly, and he almost dropped his ax. And in a blink of the eye Apophis was on him, pounding away at his upraised shield with blow after powerful blow. Sekenenre gave ground, feebly parrying yet another mighty smash and backing up one step at a time. He stumbled and almost fell.

"*Haaaaaa!*" Apophis screamed. He sprang forward, pounding, hacking. The young king's guard fell. He tried to struggle to his feet.

Then, in a desperate move, he ducked under the next blow and hacked at Apophis's legs. One blow to the thigh drew blood. Apophis staggered, off balance. He cursed loudly in the strange tongue of the Hai.

"Now, Sire!" Baliniri bellowed.

Sekenenre lunged forward, ax raised!

But Apophis recovered and, enraged and in pain, leveled a last mighty blow!

Afterward the moment lingered in Baliniri's mind as if it had been painted on a wall by an artist. Ever after he could remember, with perfect and total recall, the look of shocked surprise on the young king's earnest, unspoiled face as the ax fell. There was that one fixed second in which the mixed look of expectation and fear blended into a confused half smile.

And then the razor-sharp blade of the bronze ax smashed into the king's skull.

The powerful stroke of Apophis's burly arm drove the ax blade deep into Sekenenre's brain, killing him instantly. The legs crumpled. The weapon fell from his lifeless hands. The weight of his body and the angle of his fall dragged the ax out of Apophis's hand. Its blade was buried deep in his opponent's skull.

The body fell flat and did not move.

Thus died, in single combat, Sekenenre, king of kings, son of Dedmose, lord of Two Lands, defender of Thebes.

There was a moment of stunned silence, then a great roar rose from the ranks of the Hai. And, after the shock had sunk in, there came an answering roar of rage from the Egyptian side.

In vain Baliniri and his commanders screamed orders. In vain Apophis, drawing his unused sword, cried out to his men: "Rally to me!"

Beyond all control, the two sides rushed together in a red orgy of rage and hatred.

Behind Baliniri, from the open gates of Thebes, the reserve hordes poured in. "Back, you fools!" he screamed. But they swarmed past him and beat aside the sword with which he tried to turn them toward their proper positions. He was knocked to the ground. A glancing blow from a Hai sword caught him on the head. There was a flash of blinding light before his eyes, and suddenly he knew no more.

From the rear Rasmik looked on, unable to make up his mind. Should he intervene? From all he could see, his men seemed to be doing splendidly. All the better that the other side had dissolved into chaos, abandoning all pretense of acting under orders. Leaderless, they might well be cut to pieces. Already their reserves, disobeying the orders of their superiors, had swarmed out of the city gates, losing all advantage of the superb battle plan Baliniri had devised. Now the advantage was no longer with the besieged, but with the besiegers. The Hai army's numbers were greater, and their troops were fresh and experienced. In the open, the Hai would win. Whereas if the battle had taken place within the walls of Thebes, as per Baliniri's strategy . . .

"Should I sound the alarm, sir?" the subaltern at his side asked.

"No," Rasmik replied. "Let them go for a few minutes. We'll see how this works out before we do anything to alter it. They may have just played into our hands once and for all."

Baliniri awoke, blinking the dust out of his eyes. He got his hands under him and pushed himself to his knees. All around him the battle raged. What had happened? If he could only get to his feet and have a look around . . .

Then it came back to him. "Gods!" he said in a hoarse voice that sounded unlike his own. "They've lost it! They've thrown it away!"

He struggled to his feet and rubbed his dusty eyes. He looked down for his sword, but there was nothing. Left with an empty scabbard and nothing to fight with but his hands, he scanned the crowd around him, his heart drowning in despair.

Near him, a Greek, helmeted but otherwise naked, battled lustily with an Egyptian half his size. Baliniri, his head splitting, kicked the legs out from under the man and watched as the Egyptian killed him. He spat in the Greek's dead face and stole his sword. Where, in all this mess, was so much as a single one of his officers? One of them would have a horn at his belt—a horn that he, Baliniri, could blow to call retreat, to bring his men under a single control. But there was no one, no one that he could see. He cursed and killed a man just for being near him.

If only he could see what was going on! But he was in the wretched middle of it all, blinded by the dust, and could only see what was closest to him. If he could get above the battle, perhaps he could make sense of it and figure out what to do.

Another Greek came at him, snarling. Baliniri put his sword down the man's throat. He could see the teeth break as the Greek fell, clutching his face, his throat. Baliniri took to his heels. The wall! From atop the wall he could see!

But the Hai controlled the wall—or at least as much of it as he could see. He approached the staircase inside the gate, where two Hai soldiers were finishing off an Egyptian guard. Baliniri growled like an old lion and hacked the first one to ribbons with three strokes. The second took a bit longer and gave him a bit of a fight. He sighed and ducked under a wild swing, stabbed the man in the groin, and then, as his opponent clutched his privates, hacked open the great artery on the side of his neck. Blood gushed. Baliniri put a shod foot in the man's face, kicked him to the ground, and thought no more of him.

He bounded up the stairs, puffing, disgusted at himself for being out of shape. At the top he ran into a Hai soldier who had mounted the walls. He carried a compound Hai bow but could not nock the arrow in time to prevent Baliniri from slaughtering him. Baliniri kicked him off the wall, keeping the bow and the archer's fallen quiver.

He mounted the parapet. It took a moment or two to make out the true pattern of things. And when he finally began to make sense of it, he cursed long and bitterly. It was either that or weep.

"Gods!" he said. "We're so few! Surely there must be more! Surely our reserves didn't all come out of the city."

But just as surely, he knew they had. And when he turned and scanned the streets below him, he saw no sign of any activity at all. The curses stuck in his throat when he turned back to the battle outside the city. There was a woebegone pocket of his men far over to the left, totally surrounded by a much larger Hai force. Directly to the left a vast, sweating, naked mob of those damned Hellenes was meeting stiff resistance from an Egyptian unit, which fought valiantly despite heavy odds. In the exact center of the line his men battled Bedouin and Shairetana and some others he could not identify: Phrygians? Pamphilians? Here the numbers, at least, were fairly even. But the Shairetana and the strangers fought viciously, and their arms did not seem ever to tire. Was there a ray of hope?

He looked out over the river for the first time and was struck dumb by what he saw.

The boats! The Shepherd boats were on fire!

Quickly he scanned the Nile. How had this happened? Who could have— But there! There were the small vessels, twisting in the tide, turning slowly in the current, heading downriver now that their mission had been completed. The people who had come up behind the Hai fleet and shot flaming arrows into their sails had then apparently abandoned the boats and somehow found their way to shore. But where? Where were they?

He could not see. As he moved down the wall to get a better view, he stumbled over something at his feet. He looked down, found a dead Egyptian subaltern lying there, an arrow through his chest. He stopped and retrieved the ram's horn at the man's waist. Now! Now he could signal them, call them together, plan a new maneuver, and—

He looked out over the Nile again. To the south, a fleet of ships appeared, its sails as black as the pitch on its decks!

And on the shore, on the quays, a line of slim, naked female figures, facing the backs of the Hai! They were armed fearfully with black swords and long bows, their wrists and ankles gleaming with golden ornaments!

I'eti had come, with her women!

Teti and Riki—and, on the river, Kamose with the Nubians!

V

The second unit of Teti's warrior-women came out of the water, with Teti at its head. Riki, winded, brought up the rear and had to catch his breath on the quay for a moment. *Gods!* he thought. *I thought I was in good shape!* But these women were extraordinary. They had not at all been fatigued by the long swim against the strong current of the Nile. They were ready to fight, and right now! He shook his head, wiped the water out of his eyes, and let out a low whistle.

Teti turned back to him. "Come on, Riki! You're going to miss all the fun!"

He gritted his teeth and trotted after her. Up ahead the rear ranks of the Hai force had turned to face them, and already several of Teti's women were battling lustily with the foreign invaders. There had been a first rain of arrows, but now it was time for the hand-to-hand work. He drew his sword and dived into the fray, hacking mightily right and left.

In a moment he had cleared a space before him and left three dead men at his feet. He took a second to look around: To his right one of the slim women dueled with a towering Hai warrior; as he watched, the Shepherd disarmed her with a clever flip of the wrist and drew back for the great lunge forward. He saw the woman's face. It was Weret.

With a mighty leap Riki sprang forth. His iron sword— product of Teti's forges—deflected the lunge, and withdrawing, he swung the heavy weapon to one side and smashed the flat of the blade into the Hai soldier's face. He could feel the bones give.

"Weret!" he called. "Retrieve your sword! This fellow's mine!"

He saw her dive for it and scurry out of his way. The Shepherd soldier, his face bleeding, let out a savage growl and attacked. Riki caught the powerful swing on his sword and watched his opponent wince as bronze met iron. Riki quickly thanked the gods that Teti's imperfect iron weapon proved the better of the Hai's excellent bronze sword. The Hai fighter stepped back, changing numbed hands on the sword, and faced him left-handed.

Riki obligingly changed hands himself and saluted ironically. "Well, if you're going to be that way . . ." he said. When the Hai feinted, then leveled a terrible wild swing at his head, Riki once again caught the bronze sword on his own heavier, more solid one. This time the Hai sword gave, cracked in two, and fell from the warrior's hands. Riki laughed joyously and ran him through.

There was something to this iron business after all! To be sure, the heavier instrument in his hand would cause him to tire more quickly—at least until he had retrained for the feel of a heavier sword. But in the meantime, it felt splendid. Chuckling with eager anticipation, he bore forward, cutting a swath through the Hai line, hewing right and left.

Seth stood on the quay, glancing nervously from time to time at the battle going on behind him and then turning back to the scene of the black-sailed ships coming to shore. At first he had wondered whether it was right of him to avoid the battle and let the women do the fighting for him. Then his old powers of analysis had taken over. "What earthly good would I be in a fight?" he had said. "Meanwhile, someone has to be here when Kamose arrives, and there's no use wasting an able warrior on the job, whether male or female. . . ."

He looked up as the tall black sailors yanked powerfully on the lines to shorten sail and the first of the boats glided smoothly to shore. Two of the tall tribesmen leapt onto the quay and quickly secured the vessel, enabling the black soldiers to disembark.

He nervously scanned their numbers for a single white face. *What if they think I'm one of the enemy?* he thought.

But now the man he was looking for appeared, in the

second rank. "Kamose!" he yelled as loudly as he could. "Kamose of Avaris! Kamose, to me!"

The dark eyes brightened and burned into his own. As the first of the black soldiers drew dangerously near to Seth, Kamose barked an order at them. "No!" he said in a powerful voice, a voice of command. "Leave him to me!"

The blacks shrugged and let Seth be. The white warrior drew near and looked at him. "And you'd be—who?"

"I'm Seth. Teti's cousin. I have something for you, with her compliments." He handed over the sword belt slung around his neck. "There's something I have to tell you about this."

Kamose unsheathed the sword, turned it to and fro, and made a few practice thrusts with it. "This is magnificent! Is this . . . *the* sword, then?"

"No, it isn't," Seth admitted, "but that doesn't matter. Act as though it were. For now it'll do. But let me tell you what I learned about your father—" He stopped, embarrassed. "I . . . I didn't mean to offend you, you know."

"It's all right. I didn't choose him. With any luck I'll soon be rid of him. Go on."

"Thank you. Well, there was this Hai officer we captured back at Lisht. . . ."

Now the odds were dead even, and in some places the Hai were actually in retreat. From atop the wall Baliniri looked on, his face set in a fierce grin, pounding his fists on the parapet. "Smash them!" he yelled out. "There! There by the wall! Now cut off their retreat!"

He scanned the crowd. Where was Apophis? Ah, yes, there he was, surrounded by fierce Shairetana guards who shielded him from the worst fighting. Baliniri looked back toward the river. The boats had landed and were disgorging their load of tall, slim black warriors. Yes, there was Kamose, stocky, intense, talking with—who was it? Seth!

"He's got the sword!" Baliniri said with a fierce laugh. "He's got it! Now if we can only steer him and his father together!"

Just then, though, a sudden strategic retreat by the

Greeks bared a circular area just to one side of the great gate
of Thebes, and for the first time he could see the frail, fallen
figure of the dead king. The thin limbs were splayed and
thrown awry; his body had been trampled upon, kicked aside,
desecrated many times as the battle raged above his body.
Even the battle-ax Apophis had left in his skull had been
knocked loose and was now nowhere to be found. The slim
body lay like a discarded doll, bereft of pomp or pretense or
even the smallest sign of dignity.

Baliniri was suddenly overcome with emotion. The little
fellow had died like a hero! Who would be so base as to assert
that the heroes were only winners? Sekenenre, by his own
choice, had faced the enemy and fallen honorably in battle,
trying to interpose his own frail body, unskilled in the arts of
war, between his people and the foreign invader. Not even
the harshest interpretation of war protocol would have demanded what the young king had sacrificed so freely and
ungrudgingly.

Well, there was no king now—not for the time being, at
any rate. For all practical purposes, he, Baliniri, ruled as
vizier in place of a king. And if Thebes got through this
safely, he would see that Sekenenre was remembered properly. He would see the plans drawn for a great temple in his
honor and a feast in his name would—

The thought suddenly cut through his meditations like a
red-hot knife.

No king now? No royal male issue? Not even an under-
age son whom he, as regent, could replace until . . . What
if . . .

As soon as the thought had invaded his mind, he drove it
away. No! He, Baliniri, was no king. A kingmaker, perhaps,
but not a king. A man who ruled behind the throne, not atop
it. He was sure he would not accept the role, even if it were
offered him.

But perhaps a change of status . . . He remembered
promising Sekenenre, just before the battle, to look after his
widow. Ah-Hotep had been too old for her young husband,
but in many ways she would prove just right for a man his,
Baliniri's, age. He had seen her, spoken to her, many times,
and always he had seen the look in her eye. She was a woman

in whom the passions had not cooled, that was quite evident. And there was that rumor that continued to circulate, the one about her having had a fling in her youth with some young soldier assigned to guard her apartment.

She was still a beautiful woman. And the man who married her would gain status and riches as well as the incomparable gift of her still comely person.

"Bah!" he said. Time enough to think of such things later. What kind of vulture was he, to be thinking of a friend's widow when the friend's blood, spilled in the cause of freedom, was hardly dry on the sands of Thebes?

Just then he saw Kamose looking up at him atop the wall. The young man waved, then made a sign signifying puzzlement. "What's he saying?" Baliniri muttered to himself. Then he knew! He looked down and found Apophis, still surrounded by the Shairetana fighters. He gestured wildly, pointed, using both hands, the better to specify the location.

Kamose signaled understanding. Baliniri smiled and made a sign of approval. And held up one fist in the universally recognized sign that urged a man on and wished him luck.

At the head of a squad of Nubians, Kamose fought his way forward, aiming toward the area Baliniri had indicated. As he pressed forward, though, a towering Phrygian warrior attacked him from one side with a long, curved sword. He did not see the man until it was almost too late. The sword swept down toward his neck in a deadly curve, and quite unexpectedly fell on the wrong man! Kamose turned to see two robed, hooded Amon priests standing near the Phrygian troop. As the soldier had lunged, the second of the two priests quite deliberately pushed the first into the way of the blow! The sword cut into the priest's neck, and he fell to the ground!

Kamose blinked. The second priest pushed the hood away from the face it hid. It was a comely face, topped with close-cropped hair. "Mara!" he gasped. "What are you doing here?"

She smiled and ducked as a Hai soldier lunged at her. "Getting into trouble," she answered.

"Get to safety!" he ordered. He handed her over to one of the Nubians. "Take her to the rear!" he said. But as she passed, his free hand touched her shoulder and squeezed affectionately. "I love you," he whispered, then watched her eyes widen, startled. He had never used the word before. "Wait for me!" he said as the Nubian bore her away.

Again he fought his way forward. Now he could see the hated face, surrounded by bearded warriors. "Apophis!" he bellowed in his loudest voice. "Father! Come to me, Father!"

The word was loaded with emotion. It fairly rang with hatred. Apophis blinked, looked at him, and recognized him. And for a second a look of fear and loathing contorted the older man's features, but then it was replaced by something else.

"That's right!" Kamose said. "It *is* time, isn't it? Time for you and me to meet and settle our score once and for all."

His words, ringing with passion, carried. Miraculously, the battle around them cooled. Men who had, a moment before, stood eye-to-eye and hacked away at each other like maniacs now stepped apart and lowered their weapons cautiously. The two lines, spiked, irregular, drew apart.

Into the space thus created stepped Kamose. The sword at his side was sheathed. He bled from half a dozen small cuts, but he still looked fierce, unfatigued, fresh, and deadly.

Across from him Apophis moved slowly into the open area, the sword still in his hand, its bronze blade still stained with the blood of Sekenenre and several others.

"Father!" said Kamose, his voice dripping with hatred. "You've acquired a trifling dignity since I saw you last, trussed up like an ox ready for the spit. Let's see how many strokes of my blade it takes for you to lose it."

Apophis smiled sourly. "Soldiers! Behold a lesson to be learned. When the street-corner whore bears you a bastard, drown it. Otherwise, when it grows a beard, it may grow some pretensions with it. And he'll have to be dealt with, and it may cost you a whole quarter of an hour of your valuable time someday." He spoke to Kamose now. "You, boy. I assume you've some surprise for me? You've taken swordsmanship lessons from some dolt of Thebes, perhaps? You've fortified your courage with *shepenn* and palm wine and now think to fight a grown man?"

"Surprise?" Kamose asked menacingly. "Try this."

He slowly drew the sword at his side and held it high so that everyone could see that the sun did not gleam on its dark, dull blade.

Apophis blanched but held firm.

"Iron," said Kamose. "And not just any iron, Father of mine. Iron from the land north of Hayastan!"

Apophis stared. "*N-north?*" he said.

Kamose grinned angrily and pressed on with the lie. "Iron of Chalybia! Iron from the forges that drove the Hai from their homeland generations ago! It's come to get you, Father! It's finally come home! The iron that the Hai can never face, can never defeat! And as it drove the Shepherd Kings from the shores of Lake Van, it will drive them from the banks of the Nile! Your ancient nemesis, Father! A curse lies upon you, and just as its magic drove you from the land of your fathers, so will it drive you into the desert to die!"

There was no answer from Apophis. His face was a mask of fear. His lips moved, but no sound came.

Kamose's voice was a lion's roar. "Fight, damn you!"

VI

Still Apophis hesitated, mesmerized by the sight of that black sword in the hand of his natural son, like a desert rat rooted in its place by fear while looking into the cold eyes of a viper. This close, Kamose could see the chill drops of sweat on the older man's face and could see the shaking of his hand.

"All of you!" Kamose called out, pressing on. "Hear me! You of the Hai! Sons and grandsons and great-grandsons of the Shepherd Kings, who came here across Syria and Canaan! Did your fathers and elders tell you that our people fled the drought, before which the mightiest warrior is as

weak as a child? Is this what they told you? Don't believe it!
It's not true!" He paused to let his words sink in.

As he did, one of the Hai commanders nearest the two
men in the circle shouted, "Don't listen to him!"

But several voices chimed up from the rear: "Let him
talk! Let the king's son talk!"

"You acknowledge who I am, my countrymen. I have a
right to be heard, and by all of you. I'm half-Egyptian,
half-Hai, the son of a king; whether or not my father's claim
to the throne of Lower Egypt is any more legitimate than the
circumstances surrounding my birth is another matter." He
shot Apophis a sharp glance as he said this, but his father's
eyes were still locked on the black sword in his hand.

He went on: "I tell you that your elders lied! They
wished you to think that your nation—and mine—is invincible, fearless, supreme among nations. That is false! Our forefathers were driven from our homeland by a nation a tenth
our size! A nation before whose iron weapons they could not
stand! A nation whose wizards and magi put a spell on them,
a spell that said that iron would always be their undoing! That
the black metal would never serve the Hai, but would ever
be their nemesis!"

He could hear the gasp of shock from many a throat now.
He pressed on once more. "Now, see!" he bellowed. "See for
yourselves! See how my father, the son of two noble Hai
families, blanches when I show him the sword that will kill
him! Indeed, the Hai half of me fears it—but the Egyptian
half of me feels no dread. Do I speak truth? Does he go white
with fear? Does he sweat? Does his hand shake?"

The murmurs rose a bit at a time. "More!" came a voice
from the back of the Hai ranks. "We would hear more!"

"You have heard. Now you will see," Kamose said. "Father! Put up your guard! Put up your guard, or I will kill you
with your sword down! Do you hear? I count to three.
One! Two!" He hesitated a beat, then said, "Thr—"

A convulsion shook Apophis's heavyset body. He gritted
his teeth, let out a low growl, and attacked!

His powerful thrust would have skewered Kamose like
an ox on a spit if the younger man had not danced nimbly to

one side. He recovered with a vicious slash aimed at Kamose's vitals, but Kamose was no longer there.

"Ah!" Kamose said, grinning viciously. "My father has mettle! He defies the curse! He ignores it! But see! It will not ignore him!" He saluted Apophis and once more held his sword at the ready. "Come, Father. You'll find I'm no un-fledged, unblooded half-child like poor Sekenenre, but a man as good as you with the sword—perhaps your better. It doesn't matter, you know, how good I am, though, because the curse is your master. Even as I speak, it drains the hot blood from your limbs! Your strong arm becomes weak! Your legs shake under your weight! The cold sweat drains off your forehead into your eyes!"

"Die!" his father screamed suddenly and, feinting once, aimed a powerful blow at Kamose's neck.

Kamose held up the iron sword. The blades came to-gether with a loud clang. Apophis withdrew—looking with shock at the broken stump of a bronze sword in his hand!

Kamose's deadly smile was a basilisk's.

"Someone give him another sword!" he said in a voice as cold as the Great Sea in winter. "It will fare the same as this one! So will the next! Three weapons will I allow him! But the fourth will never come into his hand. Before he can take the fourth, I will run him through! I will kill him as he killed my mother!"

Silently, eyes blazing with mixed fear and hatred, Apophis accepted a new weapon from a subordinate. But now his eyes locked with those of his son, and something beyond words passed between them. He gripped the borrowed sword. His mouth worked silently. He held up his sword. With a motion too quick for the eye to follow, Kamose battered it out of his hand.

"Give him a third weapon!" Kamose commanded in a voice that dripped acid. "Quick, someone, give him a third!"

Apophis's empty hands clawed at the air. He turned to the officer at his side. "Attack!" he ordered, and fled through the crowd.

After a moment's hesitation, the two armies rushed to-gether, hacking and stabbing. There were no war cries, though;

except for the clash of weaponry and the grunts of the wounded, the fight took place in a curious and inexplainable silence.

And now, from the rear of the Hai ranks, the Nubians joined in the fray. They respected no silence at all but raised their voices in the curious falsetto wail that had for centuries struck terror into the hearts of their enemies. Half the Hai turned and fought the newcomers with cold fury. But the battle had turned into a riot beyond the command of any officer—Hai or Egyptian. There was neither method nor science in it; it was pure lust for battle.

From the parapet Baliniri looked on in wonderment. His orderly had joined him a few moments after the duel began and stood beside him now. "There, now," Baliniri said. "Wasn't that the most amazing thing you've ever seen?"

"Very impressive, sir," agreed his subordinate. "That story the young man told—do you think there's anything to it?"

"I don't know. At first I thought he was bluffing, but I could see the fear on Apophis's face all the way from here. Of course, it could just be The Prophecy that Apophis's son will kill him and drive the Shepherds out of Egypt. If he's superstitious, that might be all he'd need to frighten him. But . . ." He hesitated, thinking.

"You're right, sir. There was more to it than that, I think."

"I've also been wondering what we would do about the succession. After all, Sekenenre died without leaving a male heir, and there's no one in the royal family of the right age who has the proper combination of bloodlines and intelligence."

"And you think perhaps—"

"I think perhaps we've found our king. Whether he's the promised deliverer or not. Did you see the way he handled that crowd? The way he took charge?"

"Yes, sir. Very military, too, sir, if I do say so myself."

"Yes, and— Look! The Hai and their allies! They're turning! They're letting themselves be forced slowly back toward the Nile! They're making for the abandoned Nubian boats!"

"Yes, sir! Do you think we might drive them into the river?"

"No. No, that's the last thing I want done. Before the battle one of my spies came up via the Red Sea and then overland through the desert. He says that Isesi's revolution has already begun back in the delta. Let the Shepherds go back to their Black Lands! When they get there, they'll find themselves up to their eyes in trouble, I'll wager!" His eyes darkened for a moment. "All this is splendid news—everything but the news of Joseph's arrest. I'd counted on being able to enlist Joseph's help when we invade the delta. But Isesi's people consider Joseph one of the enemy, so he'll fare badly even if we win there. Unless . . ." He chewed his lip, thinking. "There's one ray of hope. . . ."

"What's that, sir?"

"Never mind. I'll deal with that later." He leaned forward over the parapet, bellowing down to a familiar figure standing before the great gate. "Kamose! Kamose, up here!"

"Yes, Baliniri?" the young man called up. He grinned at the two of them. His tunic was torn and he was bleeding from minor cuts here and there, but otherwise he looked unharmed, fit, even fresh.

"Signal to our men! Let the Hai escape!"

"I already did!" said Kamose with a smile. "I'm going to kill him all right, the next time I see him with a sword in his hand. But if The Prophecy's going to be fulfilled properly, it has to be done in the delta!"

Baliniri nodded. He himself was smiling now. "There's news from Isesi. The revolution has begun! When they arrive in the delta, they'll have their hands full!"

"Splendid! And Nehsi is sending a new force, twice the size of this one. It'll take some time to muster and train them. I saw the advance men. They're some of those giant Nuer and Dinka, from the Sudd. They hate each other— they're hereditary enemies—but they'll fight as allies for a son of Akhilleus!"

"How long?" Baliniri asked. A roar from the Egyptians, fighting directly on the quays as Apophis's beaten army desperately tried to hold off their pursuers and board the boats, drowned out his words, so he repeated them.

"A month. Perhaps two. I'm having trouble hearing you. I'm coming up!" And, sheathing his sword, he bounded up the stairs and joined Baliniri and his orderly on the wall. Baliniri took note of the fact that Kamose was not even winded. "Look at them! When they arrive in the delta, they'll be thoroughly demoralized. Twice they've come south, and twice they've been handed an embarrassing defeat."

"And twice Apophis has bolted and run."

"Yes," Kamose said, grinning again. "Wasn't that something? That story Seth told me—it's true!" He chuckled. "But I admit I did lie about this being one of the Chalybian swords. Look, there are nicks in it, and the blade's going to need straightening." He flexed it between his hands. "In fact, it's a no-better-than-average one of Teti's, it appears." He suddenly leaned far out and called out a name. "Mara! Up here! Atop the wall!"

Baliniri looked down at the girl. She had discarded her priestly robes and wore only a shift, which revealed her ripe femininity and gave the lie to the short haircut. "I haven't seen her for years! Since she and Riki escaped Hakoris's household all those years ago. She's grown to be a beautiful woman!"

"She is beautiful, isn't she?" She ran up the stairs and into Kamose's arms. "She saved my life down there. Well, that's the last time she'll ever have to risk her own. From now on—"

"From now on what? Do you think I'm going to stay behind and spin and cook, and—"

Kamose silenced her with a kiss. Baliniri looked on with pleasure: They were a handsome couple. They would make a good—

He blinked. "Kamose," he said. "Have the king's body borne to the Temple of Amon. We're going to call a feast in his honor. He fought with great bravery. He knew he was going to die but met the challenge anyway. My pride in him knows no bounds. I want you to make the speech over his body."

"Certainly," Kamose said. Then his face changed and showed his surprise. "But isn't such a speech commonly made—"

"By the fallen king's successor," Baliniri finished for him. "As vizier I am well aware of the proper protocol, my friend." He smiled. "You thought you were going to have to kill Apophis for a crown. I'm going to give you one anyway. You won it today. You'll bring the crown of the Two Lands with you when you invade the delta. That will have more impact on the Egyptians there. It'll just be a matter of uniting Black Lands with Red Lands under one rule once more."

Doubt entered Kamose's expression for the first time. "But I'm a bastard. A half-Hai bastard."

"Some of the best monarchs in the Egyptian king list have been bastards." He smiled at Mara. "I gather you'll be marrying a full-blooded Egyptian woman. Give us an heir who's three-quarters Egyptian, and that ought to be enough. Nobody since Amenemhet the Fourth has had a decent claim to the crown. Blood isn't as important as winning the hearts of the people. You've shown today that you can win the heads of the soldiers. If you make a good enough speech at Sekenenre's funeral—"

"I'll have them weeping like babies six sentences into the address. Never fear."

Baliniri put a big arm around each of them: Mara on his left, Kamose on his right. They looked out over the now-cleared battlefield. Several of the stolen Nubian boats were already out on the water; rearguard units were fighting over the rest. The second boat bore the familiar face of Apophis, glowering at them. Kamose held up the black sword and gestured with it; the figure on the boat shook his fists in impotent rage.

"There's just one thing," Baliniri said. "I thought it might be best to mention it now. Joseph—"

"Joseph will have to look out for himself, I'm afraid. He, and all those ragtag foreigners he brought up from Canaan with him. You've no idea how much resentment people have against him and all the other alien rabble who live well in Egypt while our own people starve."

He continued in this vein, venting long-suppressed anger and hostility. Baliniri smiled wryly, remembering how recently Kamose had been apologizing for his own alien blood. He would have to exert what influence he could on Kamose, a bit at a time. Joseph had his uses. He would be of great help in stabilizing the new government once it was installed in the delta; Joseph, after all, had more experience in statecraft to draw upon by now than anyone else.

Meanwhile, the last of the boats stolen by the Hai turned slowly out into the channel, and the men on the shore celebrated the enemy's departure with jeers and catcalls. And when the last boat disappeared around the bend, there arose from the throats of the assembled Egyptian soldiers a great and lusty cheer.

Baliniri drove doubt from his mind and hugged Mara and Kamose to his huge chest. Thebes was saved! And the first leg of the long journey to freedom had begun!

VII

Wearily, gratefully, Ah-Hotep dismissed her maids and closed the door behind her. At last she was alone in the room that, technically at least, was still hers. She had not been alone for what seemed like days. She shrugged, stepped out of her beautiful leather sandals, and walked over to the dressing table, taking great pleasure in the delicious feel of the cool tiles against her bare soles. She carefully took off her golden headdress, with its projecting golden cobra's head inlaid with amethysts, carnelians, and turquoise. Then she removed her black wig and shook out her short hair.

The mirrored face looked back at her, looking tired, alienated, drained of emotion. She sighed and dug her fingers into the jar of cleansing cream and slowly began taking off her makeup.

With one eye clean, she looked at herself. The bared eye had crow's feet, yet somehow it looked younger than the one outlined in black kohl and green shadow.

She sighed again, more deeply this time. *You're growing old*, she told herself. But that was inaccurate. Actually she had been oldish for some time. Now, with the day's events

behind her—her husband's lavish funeral, the coronation of
the new king Kamose and his bride Queen Mara—it seemed
that not only her youth but her middle age were suddenly
behind her forever. A part of her life had ended.

What lay ahead? What surprises, what delights, could
lie ahead for an ex-queen who was leaving the palace in
which she had lived out her youth and middle years? She,
who had not children or grandchildren to comfort her in the
years that remained?

She smiled ruefully at the mirror. Kamose's eulogy of
Sekenenre had used all the usual imagery: "He, like the
sun-god, has set below the horizon, and all the customs of
Osiris have been fulfilled for him; he has passed over the
river in the royal bark and gone to rest in his eternal home to
the west of Thebes." That was all very high flown; but her
own exodus from the world she had known was going to be a
much less gaudy and pompous affair; nobody would make
speeches or write poems for her. That was fine; that was the
way she wanted it. The less attention, the better. With
Sekenenre gone . . .

No! She had promised herself not to think of him today,
not to feel sorry for herself. Only then could she maintain her
composure and dignity. Thus, when Kamose's ceremonies of
investiture had taken place, she had forced herself to think
only of the lovely pageantry, the gorgeous costumes, and the
surpassingly beautiful song the court harper had written for
the occasion, a hymn to Ra, "richest of beings and king of
beauty." Forget the emotion; concentrate on the pure aes-
thetics of the event. All other roads led to madness and
despair.

With a sad smile she dipped her hand in the cream jar
and quickly finished taking off her makeup. She straightened
her hair, then changed into a white dress, presentable but
plain. Only then did she look about the room. Soon she
would have to supervise the packing for her move to her new
home.

There was a knock on the door.

Startled, she called out, "Who's there?"

"Baliniri, ma'am," a deep voice answered. "I'm sorry to

bother you, but there are documents that require your royal seal."

She shrugged and let him in. "Pardon my informal dress," she said, not apologetically at all. "I'm getting used to a new way of life, and that includes a farewell to needless formalities."

"It's I who should beg your pardon for intruding," he said with a graceful bow. "I came, among other things, to assure you of the permanent and loyal support and protection of the court. And to express my own regret at seeing you leave."

There was something unusually warm and sincere in his tone, and she turned to look him in the eye. "I accept your assurances with thanks," she said. "I heard through channels that you tried to stop my husband from doing—what he did. I want you to know I appreciate that."

Baliniri accepted her thanks with an incline of his head. "It is my job to obey the king. It is not my job to love him. Yet I had come to love him very much. I thought him twice the man his father was, but he never believed that. He always considered himself a step down from his father's generation of men."

Something in her warmed to him. "I'm glad someone besides myself knew better." She started to speak, hesitated, started again. "Baliniri, I know your assurances of support are partly for the sake of protocol, but . . . could I perhaps ask a favor of you?"

"Anything, my lady," he said fervently.

"Very well. There were stories about me. About my youth. The young princess who gave herself to a brave soldier and had then to be parted from him." She took a deep breath before continuing. "And of her having a child by him. A child who was taken away and raised by others."

"Yes, ma'am," he said forthrightly.

"Good. I'm glad you don't deny it." She sighed. "It was all true, of course. Mind you, it happened long before my marriage. Any stories about such affairs after I married Sekenenre—"

"There are no such stories," he said with a tiny bow. "If there had been, I would have suppressed them."

"Very well. But you do know about me and—and Baba of El-Kab."

"Yes, ma'am."

"And the child? And the woman Net, who raised it?"

He did not speak for a moment. Slowly his face broke into a benign, warm, infinitely friendly smile. "Yes, ma'am. Would you like to meet him?"

She stared, thunderstruck. "You *know* him? He *lives?*"

Baliniri folded his great hands before him. "Ma'am, *you* know him. Well, you've seen him, anyway. He's been around the court as long as I have. And, ma'am, he's someone you'll be proud to know is of your blood. I virtually raised him. I brought him here from Avaris, where Net had died. He grew up an orphan in the streets, living by his wits—"

"Oh, no!"

"Don't upset yourself needlessly. It was the making of him. It made him strong and brave and decent. He's seen the worst life can offer, and yet he's never lost a certain innocence of spirit. There's a great and wonderful goodness in him, which no amount of hardship can spoil. He's always been that way. The new queen tells me that in his heart of hearts he hasn't changed a bit since *she* first met him. He was always brave and true. I wouldn't trade him for a kingdom on the Indus."

She stared. "D-does he know?"

"No. But he wants to very badly. I want to tell him . . . but telling him would mean revealing your secret. I had to clear it first with you, ma'am. Do you want him to know?"

For a moment she thought she was going to faint. She gripped the back of the heavy chair near her and regained her equilibrium. "Let me digest this," she said. "I don't know what to think. Who is he, Baliniri?"

"His real name—although *he* doesn't know it—is Ahmes pen-Nekhbet. He bears, for the time being, the street name they gave him as a child."

"You say I've seen him? I know of him?"

"Yes, ma'am, and he's just outside. He doesn't have any idea why I've brought him here. He doesn't know whose part of the palace this is. May I show him in?"

Her heart was beating fast—too fast. She sat down in the

heavy chair, hand pressed to her chest. She could not speak. Silent, eyes blinking rapidly, she nodded.

"Very well." He went to the door, held it wide for the young man to come in. Yes, she had seen him before and knew him by reputation. The hero of Lisht. The single universally loved and respected officer in Baliniri's army. Of all the young men known mainly to her by repute, this was the one she would have been proudest to know was her son. She smiled through joyful tears but found that she could say nothing, nothing, at all. She shook her head back and forth, scarcely able to believe it.

Riki stared, then bowed deeply. "My lady!" he said. "I intrude! A thousand pardons. I—"

Baliniri, smiling, put a hand on the young man's shoulder. "Riki," he said. "Or Ahmes pen-Nekhbet. You always wanted to know who you are."

"Yes," Riki replied, a confused expression twisting his features. "Did I tell you? I found Maryet just in time to bury her. Now I'll never—"

"Riki," Baliniri said quietly, "Meet your mother." His voice broke as he said it. He bowed low to both of them in respect and deep affection and without another word went back out into the hall and closed the door. But not without a last lingering look at both faces. He smiled, blinked damp eyes, and closed the door behind him.

Seth sat in his mother's house, looking curiously down at the tiny bundle in his arms. "He does have Ketan's eyes," he noted. "At least I think so. I'm not used to babies. What's his name?"

"We haven't named him yet," Tuya said. "Ketan was too distraught to do so. I rather thought you could help us."

"Very well," Seth said with a smile. "Call him Sinuhe. Sinuhe, the hero of the story we all hear on our nanny's knee. The mighty wanderer who, after many adventures, comes home at last to live in peace and with great riches. If you're going to name him after someone, let it be someone whose story has a happy ending."

Kedar and Tuya exchanged delighted glances. "Sinuhe it

is," Tuya said. "Seth, I can't tell you how delighted we both are at the change in you. Every day I see a new side of you."

He shook his head. "Today I wandered down to the Market of the Four Winds. Nobody recognized me. And do you know, Mother, while I stood there, it all seemed so unfamiliar, as though that whole part of my life had happened to someone else. I looked around me—looking for some sign of a ghost, some sign of the raggedy young man who used to hang around the market thinking and answering people's questions—that is, when they could ever succeed in getting his attention—and generally acting like an idiot or a clown. He's gone, Mother. I'll never find him now."

Tuya's hand closed on his. "I know. There was a little ragamuffin girl in Avaris . . . I went looking for *her* once, too. These things pass, Seth. We all change. It's part of growing up."

"I know, Mother. At least, my mind knows. My emotions remain confused by it."

"Welcome to the human race, my son," Kedar said slowly. "But what are you going to do now? Have you made plans?"

"Well, there is one thing I have to do—something very important, if we're to drive the Shepherds away forever. You see, we lied about the sword with which Kamose faced his father, and sooner or later they'll learn that." He sighed. "I think it may just fall to me to rectify the situation. I have to go to Chalybia."

"Why you?" Tuya asked.

"Mother, I'm a Child of the Lion. I've learned about every other vocation and discipline—well, virtually every other one—and now I have to learn about making arms. I'm working with Teti out at the forges now, learning the family trade." He held out his hands. "They're by no means the calluses of an old master at the trade, but they're getting harder a bit at a time. Also, I'm exercising with Teti's women, and Weret is teaching me how to defend myself with a sword. I'm going to have to be good at all of it." He frowned. "Weret won't teach me the bow. She says I'd never be any good. I'm going to prove her wrong—if I could find someone to teach me. Do you know of anyone who could show me about the bow?"

A new voice came from the door that led to the patio. "I could, I think. My brother taught me. I'm very good."

Seth stared.

"Oh!" said Tuya. "Seth, meet our friend Aset. She was the heroine of the big raid on the Children's Refuge in Avaris. She's come to live with us, and to help take care of the ba—of little Sinuhe."

"Aset?" Seth said. "I've heard a lot about you from Riki and from—"

He almost said "from Kamose and Mara," but he caught himself in time. They had, indeed, told him—about Aset's unrequited love for Kamose and how crushed she had been when Kamose and Mara had married. He decided from first glance that he liked her. Her face had an honesty, decency, and certain human vulnerability about it that made her quite attractive. There was the light of hope in her eyes. The eyes . . . Something about the moment touched his heart.

He smiled. "I'm as clumsy as an ox. Do you really think you can do anything with me?"

Her eyes were very large and warm and wide. "I can try," she said in a soft voice. "When do you want to start?"

To the disgust of Weret and her women, Teti had adopted the dress and customs of Thebes. Now, wearing a dress and sandals, she sat on a stone bench before Ketan's simple grave and looked down at the fresh flowers she had just placed there. She glanced around making certain no one else was nearby before speaking aloud.

"I'm very happy," she said. "Do you remember, Ketan? I said I'd never let another man in my life after Netru was killed. I think I was afraid of ever letting myself be this happy again."

A light wind from the river stirred her hair. She looked out over the Nile and smiled. "You know, if anyone had ever told me that it would be my fate to be happy in love twice in my life, happy with a great intensity but with neither relationship lasting for a long time, Ketan, I think it'd have made me terribly sad to hear it, even heartbroken and bitter. But I don't feel that way at all."

A little smile played on the corners of her lips. "Instead, Ketan, I feel at peace. I know how it's all going to come out, and I'm quite content. But of course *you* know how it comes out, too, don't you, my dear. And when I was in your mind, I knew how happy you were. I think some of that carried over into me, along with this gift of divination. I think that whatever happens to me in the little time I have left, Ketan, it'll never manage to make me unhappy for long because I'll have that memory, and the knowledge, and—"

A gaily painted butterfly flew past, turned, and hovered. Teti held out a finger. To her extreme surprise and delight, the tiny creature lit on her fingertip for a moment, hardly fluttering its lovely wings at all.

"Life is so brief, Ketan," she whispered. "We live hardly longer than this butterfly. And the afterlife is so long, you'd think we'd barely even notice the little time we have here. But it's so beautiful. So beautiful! And we rarely ever really pay attention to it while we're here. We're always so caught up in the passing pains and pleasures of the moment, we don't see how lovely it all is. We try to grasp it! We try to hold it! We try to control it! And we're so unhappy when we can't do so. If I tried to catch the butterfly, it'd fly away and I'd have nothing. But look: I let the butterfly do as it pleases, so it trusts me. Just because I haven't tried to force anything, I've had this lovely moment that will never come again." The little wings moved, and the butterfly flew merrily away.

Teti sighed sadly, feeling sorry for those who could not see, could not know the pattern of life she had been chosen to understand. "We're all so blind here, Ketan. The lovely moments pass us by, and we wind up with our hands and heart equally empty."

She shook her head. "I love Riki so much, Ketan. I wish I could spare him the pain and the grief. But I can try to help him see, while not letting him know that that's what I'm doing. It'll have to be by example, I think. Men are so proud, so easily hurt and easily offended. I'll have to be very careful." She smiled and stood.

"Well, good-bye, Ketan," she said. "He'll have met his mother by now, if Baliniri's had his way. And he'll be as confused by the new happiness in his heart as by any pain.

And I'll have to be there and help him handle it. Oh, he's so strong, and yet at the same time so vulnerable, Ketan. Part of him is still as sweet and innocent as a little child. That's why I fell in love with him." She smiled, and winked at nothing, nothing at all. "I'm going to have to keep a great deal to myself. I can bear knowing what I know, but I don't think he could bear knowing in advance how it's all going to come out. Or when."

For just a moment, there was the tiniest, tenderest touch of sadness in her heart. *So brief!* she thought.

She rose and looked around her at the high-walled and graceful city, at the tranquil Nile, at the untroubled sky above.

And yet . . . while it lasts . . . so beautiful! So very beautiful!

Suddenly she felt a fresh powerful wave of love and sympathy for Riki. He would need her now. Smiling, she turned her steps back to the city, feeling strong and serene. There was so little time left, and she wanted above all to use it well.

Epilogue

The coals should have been dark and dead by now, but the stubborn breeze that had struck up earlier fanned the embers to a glow that was quickly fading. The face of the Teller of Tales was barely visible, but one could still make out the intense expression on his face and the fire in his eye.

"So now Thebes was saved," he said, "and the first stirrings of the great rebellion had begun. There was a new king in the Red Lands, one who gave promise of taking the delta lands from the hated invader. As the Egyptians prepared to sail downriver to renew the war with their ancestral enemy, open revolution had erupted in Avaris and throughout the rest of the Black Lands.

"But now new trouble lay on the horizon. The very people in whose hands lay the salvation of Egypt had become the oppressors of the children of Israel, and Joseph's power in Egypt was no more. As a new dynasty began, the sons of Jacob, who had hoped to return to Canaan, found all roads *blocked to them. And little by little, they, the lords of their own lands to the north, fell deeper and deeper into bondage in a foreign land."*

There was a low murmur of sadness from the gathering on the far side of the fire from him. He peered out at them through the darkness and went on: "As the war grew more and more bitter in the delta, the fortunes of the Children of the Lion changed. Seth sought out a strange and unfathomable destiny in a foreign land, in search of a secret that had eluded his forefathers. Teti and Aset prepared to bear new Children of the Lion, and Ketan's child, Sinuhe, grew older, unaware of the destiny that would sunder him from his kin and give him a life his father could never have foreseen."

There was a brief pause before he continued. "Strange are the twists of fate, my children. Victory bears the seeds of defeat. Happiness grows in the field of sorrow. Tomorrow you shall hear how blew the winds of change. In the heart of the enemy of Israel grew a canker that would mean disaster for Egypt. From the camp of the oppressor came the seed of the emancipator. As the bonds of slavery tightened daily around the necks of Jacob's children, as the oppressor's edict forbade their women to bear sons and raise them to manhood, there was a woman of the tribe of Levi who bore a son. And to save the child from the wrath of the king, she placed it in a papyrus boat and gave it to the Nile. And there came a princess of the royal house, who found the child in the bullrushes and took it as her own. . . ."

From the invisible gathering out there in the darkness there came a vast collective sigh. A voice cried out: "Moses! He speaks of Moses!"

But as the last light died, the old man placed his bony old hands together before him and bowed his head, and backed off slowly into the darkness, as sure of his footing as if it were noon. "Tomorrow," he said. "Tomorrow . . ."